"One of Williamson's all-t[...] characters, fascinating scen[...] der,' it's hard to beat."
—[...]

"A suspenseful adventure st[...] [aro]und a gradually revealed alien mystery, from one of the most respected writers in the field."
—*Science Fiction Chronicle*

"*The Black Sun* is fresh and contemporary."
—*The Washington Post*

"What's important here is that essential SF attribute, the sense of wonder, which Williamson once again generates in spades by skillfully evoking an unknown, alien planet and the inhuman intelligences who once populated it."
—*Publishers Weekly*

"Master craftsman Williamson evokes terror and uncertainty on the frozen planet in this highly recommended adventure."
—*Library Journal*

"Williamson offers a compelling tour of a world locked in ice at near-zero Kelvin, with the remains of a sophisticated civilization still visible.

"A haunting evocation of the abyss of time and space, of being lost in a universe of frigid and uncaring beauty and mystery, of isolation and the presence of death."
—*Locus*

"In Mr. Williamson's always lively prose, the working out of this mystery comes to symbolize the triumph of human decency and ingenuity over the forces of human depravity."
—*The New York Times Book Review*

BOOKS BY JACK WILLIAMSON

The Legion of Space
Darker Than You Think
The Green Girl
The Cometeers
One against the Legion
Seetee Shock
Seetee Ship
Dragon's Island
The Legion of Time
Undersea Quest
   (with Frederik Pohl)
Dome around America
Star Bridge
   (with James Gunn)
Undersea Fleet
   (with Frederik Pohl)
Undersea City
   (with Frederik Pohl)
The Trial of Terra
Golden Blood
The Reefs of Space
   (with Frederik Pohl)
Starchild (with Frederik Pohl)
The Reign of Wizardry
Bright New Universe
Trapped in Space
The Pandora Effect
Rogue Star
   (with Frederik Pohl)
People Machines

The Moon Children
H. G. Wells: Critic of Progress
The Farthest Star
   (with Frederik Pohl)
The Early Williamson
The Power of Blackness
The Best of Jack Williamson
Brother to Demons, Brother to
   Gods
The Alien Intelligence
The Humanoid Touch
The Birth of a New Republic
   (with Miles J. Breuer)
Manseed
Wall around a Star
   (with Frederik Pohl)
The Queen of the Legion
Wonder's Child: My Life in
   Science Fiction (memoir)
Lifeburst
*Firechild
*Land's End
   (with Frederik Pohl)
Mazeway
The Singers of Time
   (with Frederik Pohl)
*Beachhead
*The Humanoids
*Demon Moon

*available from Tor Books

THE BLACK SUN

Jack Williamson

THE BLACK SUN

A TOM DOHERTY ASSOCIATES BOOK/NEW YORK

THE BLACK SUN

Copyright © 1997 by Jack Williamson

Map by Ellisa H. Mitchell

Edited by James Frenkel

A Tor Book
Published by Tom Doherty Associates, Inc.
175 Fifth Avenue
New York, NY 10010

Tor Books on the World Wide Web:
http://www.tor.com

Tor® is a registered trademark of Tom Doherty Associates, Inc.

ISBN: 0-812-55362-4
Library of Congress Catalog Card Number: 96-31889

First edition: March 1997
First mass market edition: May 1998

Printed in the United States of America

0 9 8 7 6 5 4 3 2 1

To Patrice Caldwell

Starside

Shadow Line

Skyhold

ICE CONTINENT

Quarry

UNEXPLORED LANDS

Frozen Ocean

UNEXPLORED

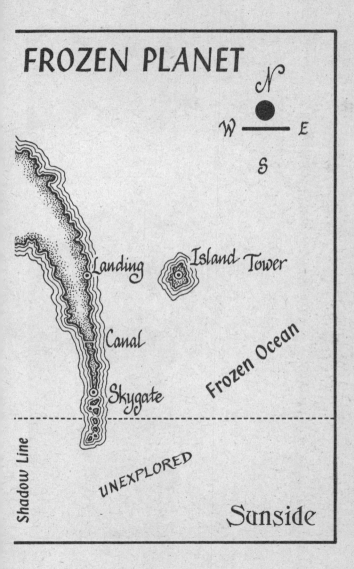

FROZEN PLANET

N
W ━━ E
S

Landing

Island Tower

Canal

Frozen Ocean

Skygate

Shadow Line

UNEXPLORED

Sunside

THE BLACK SUN

One

His mother christened him Carlos Corales Carbajal Santiago Mondragon.

"A large name, Carlito," his father told him when he was old enough to echo it all, "for a very small niñito. You must grow to fit it."

They lived in a poor pueblito called Cuerno del Oro in the Chihuahua mountains a few hundred kilometers southwest of the smoggy sprawl of Juárez. Cuerno del Oro meant horn of gold, but any gold the barren hills ever hid was dug and gone two hundred years ago. The thin soil now gave more rocks than wealth.

Longing for some right to that great name, he saw no way to earn it till he began to hear Don Ignacio Morelos speak of the stars. The don had gone north and found employment at the nest of the starbirds called White Sands. He came home on holidays with rich gifts for his gente and exciting tales of the roaring birds that carried men off Earth.

One year there was even a gift for Carlos, a postcard picture of a clumsy metal monster that climbed over bright rocks under a dead black sky on long lever-legs with fat-tired wheels for feet. "La araña de la luna," he called it. The spider of the Moon.

"Muchas gracias, don Ignacio." He bowed in awed appreciation. "When I become a man, I will learn to guide the starbirds and ride the iron spiders over the rocks of the Moon."

"Aie, muchachito. Qué tonto!" Don Ignacio tossed his scrawny shoulders and spat the brown juice of tobacco into the dusty street. "No es posible."

The Moon had no room for los pobres peónes. The vaqueros of space were men of courage and learning, chosen for vast machismo. The don himself had been allowed to touch the monstrous spiders only when he searched them for insects in the computers that were their brains. Listening humbly, Carlos resolved to master the skills of those daring gringo vaqueros and become himself a man of great machismo.

He worked hard at his lessons in the village school, even harder after Don Ignacio came home again to speak of swifter starbirds that could vanish faster than a lightning flash and alight in an instant somewhere far off among the stars. The don told of the great Mission StarSeed, which was to build a hundred such phenomenal machines. They would carry colonists farther than telescopes could see, to inhabit new worlds too strange to be imagined.

Pájaros maravillosos, the don called them. Birds of wonder, they were already flying, lifting the fortunate few from the sin-pits of Earth to dwell forever in the sky. Dreadful chariots of paradise, they rose with deafening thunder and lightning that blinded those who dared to watch.

What, Carlos dared to ask, was known of those islands of paradise?

Nada. The don shook his lean-boned head. Nothing at all, because no ships came back. Return was forbidden by some mysterious law of space. Yet new crews of fearless starmen were always waiting to go when they could, and the clever evangelistas of Mission StarSeed always found more dollars to continue the building of those miraculous ships.

Truly, could the stars have people of their own? Carlos's duty was to herd his father's goats. When winter nights found him shivering on the hills with them, and fearful of howling coyotes, he used to watch the sky and wonder. Would such beings be angels? Or devils, perhaps, waiting to capture men for the flames of hell?

He used to tremble when Father Francisco spoke of souls screaming in the pits of never-ending eternal pain. Yet, kneeling with his mother at mass, he always begged los santos to aid his escape from the dust and mud and want of Cuerno del Oro and open his way to the stars.

Mission StarSeed became as holy to him as los milagros of Jesus and the promise of paraiso were to his mother and Father Francisco. He was saddened when the don told of the Fairshare fanáticos. Their deeds of sabotage became sins beyond belief.

"Por qué?" He saw the don waiting for him to say the English word. "Why?"

"Están locos!" The don drowned an unfortunate fly with a jet of tobacco juice. "They imagine the stars to be the abodes of actual angels in danger from invading starmen, whom they denounce as los demonios del espacio. They plot to kill the birds of space, creating severe difficulties for the Mission."

Troubled, he waited in the confession stall to speak of his longings for those unknown worlds.

"Would El Dios Grandioso allow such lands to exist?" he asked Father Francisco. Would He allow a simple man to reach the heavens without the pain of death? Perhaps to make new gardens to grow the fruits of Earth and live among los santos as his mother longed to, beyond the earthly burdens of ignorance and evil?

"Think more of your catechism, my child," el padre advised him, "and less of riddles that only El Dios Himself could ever answer."

When he asked his mother, she begged him to forget the birds of space and all such devices of Satanás. His unholy dreams had become a hazard to his soul. Born a simple campesino, he must content himself to die a simple campesino.

His father was gone by then, wading the river to find employment in el norte. Preparing to follow when he had grown to fit his name, he led his classes at la escuela. He studied inglés when he found a friend who knew it. He learned from the dusty books the don had used, texts of science and math. When the don gave him a dead computer, he studied its documents and learned to revive it.

The computer became his buen amigo, a friend who spoke a language he came to love for its purity and beauty. A simple language, whose words were only one and zero, yet a tongue of truth, allowing neither doubt nor duplicity. The computer put him on the path that lead toward the stars, and showed him the vast distance he had to go. When dollars came back from his father, his mother promised to let him go on to the university.

Sadly, however, the money stopped.

"Qué lástima!" his mother moaned. "I fear for him. And for your own great plans, hijo mío."

When Don Ignacio returned for the next fiesta, they asked him for news. He spat a quick jet at an ant and observed that those too greedy for money sometimes became the victims of evil men or gringo law. A warning that Father Francisco advised him to heed. He got no comfort from el padre, however, when his mother was stricken with a malady of the heart which la curandera couldn't cure.

It was his mother's younger sister who came home from Hermosillo to care for her, and it was Don Ignacio himself who restored his hope to know the stars. Instead of returning to el norte, the don opened a computer shop in Chihuahua City and gave him a job there, with time to study computer science at the university. The first year he did little except sweep the floors, unpack new computers, and greet customers when the don was busy. By the second year, however, he had learned to diagnose the common ills of computers and relieve them of defective chips and disabling viruses.

●

He was near graduation when el padre called him home. His aunt had fallen ill and returned to Hermosillo, leaving his mother confined to her bed. All her prayers and tears had never brought his father back. Carlos made the little food she could eat, lifted her when she had to be lifted, and kept a candle burning for her in the church.

She blessed him before the saints received her, and told him where to find the American dollars his father had sent, dollars she had buried in a glass jar under the floor because she was afraid to spend them. Trusting los santos, he left Cuerno del Oro to search out his way to the stars.

New electronic devices were punishing those who tried to wade the river, and half his dollars had to go for papers to let him cross the bridge from Juárez. Beyond the mountains, a Las Cruces contractor picked him up and took him on to a tall fence of woven steel that was hung with yellow signs of danger. The wide arch above the gate was lettered,

We Seed the Stars

Clumps of dead, black stubble scattered the desert beyond, which the Spanish explorers had named Jornado del Muerto, the Journey of Death. Takeoff flashes, the contractor said, had killed the brush. When Carlos asked about the starbirds, he pointed to a thin silver bullet shape aimed into the dusty sky a dozen kilometers beyond the gate.

"Number Ninety-nine," the contractor said. "Taking off tonight."

He had no badge to show the guard at the gate. The contractor left him with a little group of people standing outside under a drooping Fairshare banner. Most of them young, they looked as road-worn as he was, sunburnt and grimed with sweat-caked dust. They carried battered signs:

> ALIEN RIGHTS!
> SAVE THE STARS!
> EARTH'S ENOUGH!

A van from a wrecking yard followed the contractor through the gate, and then a taxi with a woman and two small children in the backseat. He saw her from the edge of the road when the taxi stopped. Una rubia, young and very fair, with a beauty that took his breath. He smiled at the little girl, but she never looked toward him.

Wondering who they were, he envied those of wealth and learning and power who might hope to earn la rubia's friendship. The don had warned him of those proud masters of the birds of space. They were often clever and sometimes kind, but they scorned mojados like himself, said to come wet from swimming the river. La rubia's world was not for him, but he let his eyes follow the cab through the gate.

When the road was empty again, the Fairshare people dropped their signs and invited him to the ragged tents where they had camped. Sharing their lunch of stale fast food and melting candy bars, they spoke of their long war to stop or delay the StarSeed flights. He thanked them for the food and asked them why the starbirds should not fly.

"Look back, my friend." The speaker scowled through a dirty wisp of beard. "Look back at all we've done to the forests and rivers and native cultures of our own Earth. What right have we to foul the stars?"

Carefully polite, he said that he wished only to visit the stars for himself.

"You're a little late for that." Laughing at him, a sun-blistered girl turned to gesture toward that far silver tower. "The Mission's finished. We've killed their crazy dream of another hundred ships. Even killed one of their first. Number Ninety-nine will be the last. It's taking off tonight."

He felt sick.

"Es posible?" His inglés came slowly, because he still thought in Spanish. "Could one get aboard?"

"Stow away?"

"Is that possible?"

She laughed again, but a man in blue coveralls turned to study him.

"Why not?" Eyes narrowed, the man looked at the girl. "A man might try. With guts enough and luck enough. And a little money."

He could pray for el machismo y la suerte, the guts and the luck. He emptied his pockets to show the dollars he had left. The man counted them, nodded for the girl to follow him out of the tent, and came back to say that perhaps his dollars were enough.

"I've been inside, looking for one last chance to hit the Mission." He glanced toward the gate and dropped his voice. "Unloading trucks with supplies for Ninety-nine. Pushing dollies and stowing cargo till they laid me off. If you want my badge, we might strike a deal."

He wanted the badge. The girl wanted his dollars. Generous, the man gave him the blue coveralls as well as the badge, made him a rough map of the ship, and even marked a spot where perhaps he could hide.

"If you have to talk, say you're on the clean-up crew," the man told him. "They wear the coveralls. The foreman's named O'Hara. Better duck him. Ride the elevator up to the gym deck. Get under cover as soon as you can. You'll hear the countdown. What becomes of the ships after takeoff is anybody's guess. If your weight goes to nothing, you'll know you've been lucky."

"We'll get you on a salvage truck." The girl made a face at the ship. "But if you're really looking for luck, you'd better hope they throw you off before the ship ever lifts."

Two

Jonas Roak was born in a small South Texas town, the son of a hell-breathing fundamentalist preacher. They never got along, though his mother did her best to keep the peace. His sixteenth birthday had begun well. His mother baked him a chocolate cake. He got his driver's license and spent the check his grandmother sent for a wide-brimmed cowboy hat. When he wore the hat to the dinner table, the preacher spoiled it all.

"Take it off." The preacher preferred coconut cake. "Beg your mother's pardon. And thank her for the cake."

He cut himself another piece of the chocolate.

"Get it off!"

The hat was black, with the crown peaked high like he thought Billy the Kid would have worn it, and Billy was his hero. He pulled it low on his forehead and took a big bite of cake.

"Listen to me!" The preacher stood up, red in the face

and breathing hard. "You ain't grown up, not by a damn sight. Better cast out the evil rotting your soul, or you'll wind up in hell."

"I ain't afraid of hell."

"Down on your knees!" The preacher unbuckled his belt. "And beg the Lord's forgiveness—"

"I don't need to pray." He shook his head, grinning. "I know a better way. When I get ready for heaven, I'll go to New Mexico and ride up to it on one of them quantum ships."

"Godless—" The preacher stripped off the belt. "You godless whelp!"

"Joseph!" His mother caught the preacher's arm. "For Jesus' sake, not today!"

"For your mother's sake," the preacher muttered, and sat down, but in a moment he was shouting again. "You hell-bent kid, you ain't to touch my new pickup. Not till you can kneel with your mother and me and make your peace with God."

He never knelt. Before daylight next morning he took the preacher's wallet and the keys to the red Chevy pickup and drove west to try his luck in Las Vegas. Near Flagstaff, he ran off a curve and totaled the pickup. When the police brought him home, the preacher told them to take him on to the lockup where he belonged, but his mother begged till they agreed to drop the charges and send him to a military school.

He got by for a few years there, till an angry instructor accused him of cheating. The commandant ordered him expelled, but he struck first. Writing checks on the preacher's account, he disappeared with the commandant's daughter in the commandant's brand-new Cadillac. The car was found a few days later, abandoned and out of gas, the girl sprawled in the backseat, dead drunk.

Missing for months, he was arrested again on narcotics charges and spent three years in a Texas prison. His parents had separated before he got out. The preacher wanted no more of him. Living on Social Security, his mother prayed for him and promised to do anything she could. He forged a check to clean out her savings and called Johnny Vega, a one-time cellmate who was now back in El Paso.

"Juanito? Remember me?"

"Who?"

"Jonas Roak. They used to call me Whale-Bait."

"Back then?" Vega didn't want to think about it. He was driving a taxi, making a new life for himself and his new wife with two new kids. He had no money to spare.

"Hold it, amigo," Jonas begged before he could hang up. "Un minuto. Remember how we used to talk about the quantum ships? You told me how you'd seen them taking off. A sure getaway from all the cops and pens, remember?"

"I still see 'em," Vega said. "Lightning and thunder in the north a couple of times a year."

"Remember how we used to plan our final getaway?"

"You in trouble?"

"Not just now, but I've had too much of this whole damn world. If them ships do go out to find new planets—"

"You're loco!" Vega laughed. "Crazy as you ever were. Better beg Huntsville to let you back inside."

●

Crazy or not, he bought a ticket to El Paso and rang Vega's number again. The new wife picked up the phone and told him to get lost. He hitchhiked to Las Cruces and found StarSeed headquarters. A busy woman in the front office asked what he wanted, and told him the Mission couldn't use him. He'd never get to space, not without high-tech skills or high-up contacts.

Yet he stayed to talk to the Fairshare pickets outside. They were protesting a takeoff due that night. He waited with them to see it from the motel parking lot. Sirens howling, the police stopped traffic on the streets and warned people to cover their eyes. Watching through dark glasses, they counted the minutes and seconds.

He found the takeoff itself a little disappointing. The site was still fifty miles away. Mountains blocked most of the flash, though the lifting ship did burn a hot bright line to the top of the sky. The sonic boom was only a muffled rumble, a long time coming, yet the wonder of it woke something he had never felt. If the ships really went out where men had never been . . .

"Sucker bait!" A Fairshare organizer laughed when he tried to ask how he might get aboard another ship. "Thousands take the hook. God knows how or where they end up. Dead or alive, or nowhere at all. A man's a damn fool to think about it."

But he was tired of trouble. He did think about it. A contractor was recruiting a crew to clear a new launch site. Asking no questions, the man looked him over, gave him a pass, and put him on a bus. The job kept him sweating all day in the desert, clearing rocks and charred stumps off the new site, but he could watch the trucks and cranes around a new ship on its launch pad, tall and shining in the sun.

Could StarSeed give him the second chance the prison chaplain used to promise? If he really straightened up, if he learned enough and worked hard enough, like his mother used to say?

He resolved to try.

With the Tex-Mex Spanish he had learned in prison, he got along with the foreman and his fellow workers. The quantum engineers were another challenge. They spoke a language of their own and worked at tasks he never entirely understood. His dream dimmed till he got help from Mort Nunin, the Fairshare organizer who brought his volunteers to march against the Mission.

Nunin was a shrewd, bald, thickset cynic who smoked vile cigars but always had money for beers and time to relay rumors of Mission affairs, most of them ugly. StarSeed was a scam, promoted by crooks who skimmed off the top of the take. Maybe the engineers were crazy enough to think they were sending explorers to the frontiers of paradise; maybe they were just plain crazy.

Aaron Zeeland didn't care. Maybe crazier than the engineers, Nunin said, but he was president of Fairshare and the chief financier of the war against the Mission, with money to pay for anything Roak could learn inside the fence. Reports of problems in the Mission. Anything to help him kill it.

Roak refused at first. He felt awed by the towering splendor of the quantum craft. He lost heart, however, as he saw ship after ship taking off without him. The girls at the motel reserved themselves for richer men. Drinking Nunin's beer, he began taking money for the gossip he heard.

Only a few dollars now and then, tips for small facts that never seemed to matter. He'd do better, Nunin said, with a job that would give him better contacts and better information. He let Nunin sign him up for night classes in remedial math and science, let Nunin invent a prettier picture of his past and teach him to speak better English. Sweating less and earning more, he had just been named a launch inspector when the preacher wrote that his mother was dead. The news hardly troubled him.

●

"Perfect for us!" Enthusiastic about the new job, Nunin drove him to Juárez for fajitas and an evening in the bars. "You'll be boarding every departing craft to certify the fusion engines and quantum converters. You'll be meeting officers and engineers, hearing all they know."

Doubtfully, he shook his head. "They'll wonder how I got the job."

"Not if you play it right." Nunin ordered another round of margaritas. "I'll drill you on the basics and the patter."

"I'm afraid—"

"No great risk." Nunin shrugged. "Don't talk when you don't have to. Just ask questions and act like you understand. The takeoffs are all you have to care about. What happens later is no skin off your tail."

He felt jittery at first, crouching in the bunker time after time to watch ships blazing into oblivion. When none blew up on the pad, he began to enjoy himself. Nunin was generous with the bonuses. He dreaded the takeoff of Ninety-nine and the end of everything.

"Maybe your best luck yet." Nunin grinned. "Zeeland wants to see you in Albuquerque to talk about a special assignment."

●

Nunin took him to Albuquerque in a driverless electric Cadillac. In the Fairshare offices, a leggy blond called Zeeland out to meet them. The financier was a big, soft, fair man with round blue eyes in a round hairless head. He stood a moment blinking as if the light were too bright before he gave them a wide baby smile.

"Mr. Roak, you've done good work for us." His voice was as soft as his warm, pink hand. "Come on in."

Nunin waited outside, drinking coffee with the blond. Roak followed Zeeland into a huge corner room with a wide view of thunderclouds billowing above the rugged Sandia crest a few miles east. Zeeland waited for him to take in the antique Navajo blanket that hung above the Taxco silver and rare Pueblo pottery arrayed on the mantel above a massive fieldstone fireplace. The wall behind a wide marble-topped desk was covered with photos of crumbling glaciers, flooded cities, and dust-drifted farms.

"The cost of the Mission." Zeeland scowled at the photos. "The idiots are trashing the planet before they take off."

"Whatever they did is already done." He stood wondering what Zeeland wanted. "Ninety-nine's the final ship."

"But I want to make certain."

"Aren't we certain already? One Hundred's junked for lack of funds to finish it. Salvage crews are already trucking the wreckage away. The Mission's over."

"Are you sure?"

"I'm there." He peered into the smooth baby face, wondering what it hid. "I listen. Top people say it's dead. Thanks to Mission mismanagement. Funds always short. Paychecks delayed. Bills unpaid. Ugly rumors about Herman Stecker."

"Let's talk about it." Zeeland gestured at a bar in the end of the room. "Over a drink."

Moving with a shambling, bearlike grace, he brought two glasses of ice, a silver carafe of water, and a bottle of scotch. Waiting, Roak studied the Mexican silver, the Zuni pottery, the Navajo blankets. He thought of the unpaid volunteers he had seen marching under the desert sun. Zeeland had done better for himself.

"My question." He poured himself a generous drink and pushed the bottle across the desk. "What's so ugly about Herman Stecker?"

"All I know is what I hear."

"Let's have it."

"Stecker's run the Mission like his own empire. Flies a luxury jet. Lives in luxury hotels. Entertains like a prince. Charges it all to the Mission."

"He's gone too far?"

"Milked the Mission dry. Ninety-nine will be the last takeoff. Old hands used to dream of another hundred ships, but that will never happen."

"Not if I can stop it!" Zeeland stiffened, that soft, pink jaw set in the scowl of a baby about to lose its bottle. "That's your new assignment, Mr. Roak. To make damn sure."

"Really, sir." Roak shrank back, alarmed by the violence boiling in the financier. "I'm already sure."

Ignoring him, Zeeland bent to pull a desk drawer open. He reached into it, hesitated, and pushed it shut again. He drained his glass, set it back, and leaned to fix that baby glare on Roak.

"I trust Mort Nunin," he muttered at last. "He knows your record, and he says you're our man for a very delicate errand."

"Yes?"

He waited till Zeeland asked, "You know why Fairshare exists?"

"I've read Dr. Zeeland's book—was he your father?"

"My uncle."

"I know his theory that the takeoff trails increase global warming—"

"Theory?" The child voice grew shrill. "Look at the facts! The takeoff flashes disturb the upper atmosphere. Disturb world climates." He gestured at the photo murals. "Glaciers melting. Sea levels rising. Deserts spreading. Hurricanes, famines, floods—"

Checking himself, he reached for the bottle, set it back, and intently bent closer.

"Mr. Roak, the Mission orphaned me!" His voice had turned bitter. "Let me tell you how. My father had a twin. Classmates at MIT, they were a genius team. They invented the quantum wave drive and got obsessed with the damfool notion that they could sow the human seed across the galaxies.

"The actual founders of StarSeed Mission, they lost control to operators slick enough to peddle the lunatic dream. When the first ship was ready, the promoters granted them passage for only two. Both married by then, they wouldn't leave their wives. They flipped a coin. My parents went out, and left me with Uncle Harry.

"I'd begged to go, and I felt like I was dead. My uncle felt cheated and soon grew bitter against the Mission. Used his science to model the climatic effects of the takeoff flashes. Tried to warn the Mission leaders, a crazy mix of star-mad dreamers and money-mad promoters. They laughed at him. He set up Fairshare to stop their suicidal project."

Zeeland was speaking faster, his fat face reddening. He stopped to mop it with a white silk handkerchief.

"Sorry if I seem emotional, but it still gets to me. I came to love my uncle. When he had to give up the management of Fairshare, I promised to take it over. And here we are."

Zeeland caught a wheezy breath and wiped his face again. "That's my story, Mr. Roak. The reason for this last assignment. Your final job for us."

Zeeland sat breathing hard till he seemed a little calmer, and went back to the bar for more ice. He filled his glass and pushed the scotch across the desk.

"Let's drink to it."

"Not yet." Roak pushed the bottle aside. "Frankly, sir, I don't quite get you. I think your victory is already won. The Mission's dead—"

The round baby face reddened again, and the baby voice exploded. "We've tried hard enough to kill it. You can make StarSeed dead to stay."

"So what do you want me to do?"

"You're there on the spot. You blow up Ninety-nine as it lifts out of the launch pit. A final public signal that the Mission's really done for."

Roak sat shaking his head.

"Fifty thousand." He felt dazed at the madness behind the baby grin. "Fifty thousand clear. Ten here and now. Mr. Nunin will hold the other forty till he sees the ship explode."

"Sir . . ." He held up his hand. "I don't know. . . ."

Zeeland was again bent over the drawer. Gingerly lifting a heavy little device cased in dull gray plastic, he laid it before him on the desk.

"Two kilos of plastic explosive, already wired to the timer and igniter. You will have it in your briefcase when you make your last inspection. Set the timer for ignition at the moment of the scheduled takeoff. Plant it where it's safe and get off the ship."

Three

The cab stopped at the foot of the passenger ramp. She slid out, a trim quick woman in a green Mission jump-suit, and turned to help the little girl, who held a huge panda doll hugged close against her. The boy was already out.

"Dr. Virili?" The guard read her badge and smiled. "You're coming with us?"

"Rima Virili. Chief of the bioservice team."

He looked at his monitor and turned to the children. "Kipler Virili?"

"Kip," the boy said. "Just Kip."

"Day Virili?"

"And Me Me." The girl held up the panda. "Don't forget Me Me."

He frowned at the doll and looked at Rima.

"I'm sorry, dear." She bent to hug Day and the panda. "I told you the ship won't have room for Me Me."

"But it's so big. . . ."

Day choked up and squeezed the doll tighter. The driver was lifting three small bags out of the cab. The guard set them on his scales.

"Too bad." He tried to warm his voice. "The ship does look big, but we have to load another ninety people. For kids the limit on personal effects is only five kilos. Your bag's already four point nine. That means your panda friend will have to wait."

She turned to her mother, blinking hard. Rima gulped and said nothing.

"Please, sir." She kissed the panda's nose and handed it back to the driver. "Please won't you take care of Me Me? Till we get back?"

"Don't you know—" The driver caught himself and set the doll beside him in the cab. "Sure, sis. I have a little girl named Velda. She'll take good care of Me Me."

The guard set the bags on a conveyor. Rima wiped her eyes and paid the driver. Catching the children's hands, she led them up the ramp and stopped at the edge of the concrete pad, turning with them to gaze out across the fire-scarred landscape.

"Look around us," she urged them. "All around!"

"Why?" Kip muttered. "It's all so black and ugly."

"The ground is burnt here, but look at the hills. Try to remember how white and bright they are, under the new snow beyond the flash-burnt plain. Snow! The sky so blue and clean! Our own good Earth! Take a long look."

Kip shrugged. Day stood waving after the departing cab. Rima was turning to lead them aboard when Captain Alt came off the ship. A seasoned veteran of space, graying at the temples but still hard and straight in his Mission green-and-gold, Alt had returned from Farside Moon Base to take this last command.

"Rima!" He caught her in his arms and held her away from him to search her face. "Are you sure?"

"I'm sure."

"I do want you with us, but the children—" He looked down at them and sharply back at her. "You're really sure?"

"It's cost a lot of sleep." She made a wry mouth. "But you know my situation. The Mission's gone and my job with it. I've got the kids to care for, and this looks better than anything we're leaving. I talked to Kip about it. He takes it as a great adventure."

"The greatest."

He caught her hand for a moment and went on down the ramp to a temporary platform set up for the waiting media.

●

"Fairshare, sir?" The first question was shouted from the back row. "What do you think of them?"

"I've met them." He tipped his head toward the distant gate. "They're sincere about environmental harm to Earth. I think they're wrong, but I agree that we're flying into danger. Our basic difference is assumption and philosophy. They imagine the galaxies are full of Earth-like planets inhabited by innocent primitives we might mistreat the way Cortés and Pizarro misused the Aztecs and the Incas.

"We're not conquistadores. We are pledged to respect the rights of any life we find. Frankly, however, we have found no evidence of the friendly universe they assume. We're launching a hundred wavecraft instead of four or five because we can't be sure of reaching any world where humankind might survive. An ugly risk, but we're playing for the ultimate survival of mankind.

"Primitive life-forms may be common, most of them perhaps hard to identify as life at all. All the evidence, however, indicates that intelligence is rare. Ours may be unique. We can be pretty certain nobody else has developed quantum wave technology. Otherwise they'd have been here. If we find a universe empty of sentience, it's surely ours to claim."

"Captain?" A lanky man in the front row raised a hesitant voice. "A more personal question, if you don't mind. With odds like that, what brings you yourself to the Mission?"

"I accept the risks." He nodded soberly. "Because of our goal. Escape from our gravity trap. Before wavecraft, we were prisoners here, doomed to suffer all the vicissitudes of our small planet and finally perish like the trilobites and dinosaurs. The Mission exists to scatter our seed wherever we happen to land, every ship another pod. When you look at that—the final survival of our kind—odds hardly matter."

"Have you no regrets?" the reporter persisted. "For your own family? For all the friends you must be leaving? For the world you'll never see again?"

"It hurts." He nodded, with a lingering glance at the white dust of snow on the distant mountains. "But I'm ready. My wife's gone. We had no children. My estate is helping fund this final flight.

"And look at Ninety-nine!"

His weathered face warmed with a sudden smile, he turned to gesture at the wavecraft, a thin silver projectile poised over the launch pit behind him.

"My Farside tour was over. I'd planned to travel, maybe write a history of lunar exploration, play a bit of golf. Nothing that really mattered to me. This command is a new life. It excites me. If you want to know how I feel, think of Magellan. Think of the Apollo astronauts."

●

"Jane Blake, Global Vues." Two rows back, a stocky, rust roan woman slung a holocam to her shoulder and came to her feet, announcing herself in the voice of a hoarse bullfrog. "You've been launching these so-called seed ships for nearly twenty years. They've cost a lot of money and carried a lot of good people off Earth. Off to nowhere. You're admitting now that most of them have died. Right?"

Sober-faced, he nodded.

"Your Mission StarSeed?" she challenged him. "It looks to me, to a lot of us, like a very crazy game. Can you explain the game, the risks and the rules? In words that we can understand?"

"I can try." Alt shrugged rather wryly and paused for a moment to find the words. "Though there is no way to estimate the risks. And we don't make the rules. They come out of physics. Relativity. Fractals. Chaos theory. Quantum science."

She swung her holocam to scan the shimmering hull, and he waited for the lens to return.

"Thanks." An ironic snort. "Go on."

"Taking off, the ships flash and vanish because they have become virtual waves, moving at the speed of light—"

"What's a virtual wave?"

"I'll try." He shrugged again. "Though the science gets abstract. Briefly, quantum mechanics gives every particle certain aspects of a wave. Taking off, the ship may be regarded as a virtual quantum particle converted into a virtual quantum wave. As a wave packet, it has no definable parameters. No measurable mass or velocity or position. Reconverted to a virtual particle at the point of destination, it recovers the aspects of momentum and location.

"If you get that."

"I don't." She swung her holocam to sweep the faces around her, most of them frowning. "Who does?"

"The paradoxes can seem confusing." He nodded sympathetically, trying to restrain a grin. "We do prove the theory, however, with every takeoff. Though they may seem contrary to common sense, the relativistic paradoxes make wave flight feasible. Time slows as speed increases. It stops at the velocity of light. A flight may last a thousand years, as we on Earth perceive the time. Perhaps a million years. Only an instant, however, on the ship itself."

"How do you know?" Her voice sharpened. "If they never get back?"

"They can't return." His grin turned quizzical. "Because the reconversion has to happen somewhere in the future. Probably in the very distant future. Perhaps a billion years from now. Maybe ten billion, when you think of the odds. We'll never know, because time runs only one way."

"Thank you, Captain." Her tone ironic, she swept her lens from him to the ship. "That suggests another question. If time stands still and they're frozen on the ship, how do they steer it?"

"They can't," he said. "Or stop it either. If you recall the paradox, they can't even know where they are. Literally they're nowhere. The ship is a waveform that moves on until it encounters a gravity field strong enough to reverse the launch conversion."

"A planet?"

"More likely a star. Nothing else has the concentrated mass."

"So they land on a star? Like our sun?"

"I hope not." He shrugged at her mocking tone. "We have auxiliary nuclear rockets. Once out of quantum mode, we can move under rocket thrust within a planetary system. With luck, we have a chance to reach some Earth-like planet where we can land and live."

"Suppose you don't hit a star?" Eyes narrowed, she lowered the holocam. "Or anything big enough?"

"That probably happens. Often, I imagine. One strong reason we're launching a hundred ships."

"What becomes of those that don't get stopped?"

"Nothing nice." He made a wry grimace. "Ultimately, I suppose, interference from cosmic dust and debris would de-

grade the waveform. Scatter it, finally, into a burst of gamma
radiation."

"You're welcome to your flight." Lips tight, she lowered
the lens and shook her head. "I'll stay home."

●

A jet had come down on the nearby airstrip. Now a Jeep came
roaring to the ramp in a cloud of yellow dust, horn howling.
Holocams swung to pick up Mission Director Herman
Stecker as he tumbled out of it and came striding to the platform, another Mission man trotting behind him. Alt turned
to greet them.

Younger than the captain, Stecker made a dapper figure
in stylish crimson mods, his golden hair waved and long. His
companion was more rumpled than modish. Wearing a black
beret and black sunglasses, he prowled around the edge of the
group till he found a vacant chair. Sliding into it, he sat watching Stecker with a sardonic grin.

Stecker sprang to the platform. Ignoring Alt's extended
hand, he stepped forward and posed like a model for the
lenses before he turned to the lectern. With a gesture for silence, he let his well-practiced voice roll out into the flash-
blackened desert.

"Fellow citizens of the universe . . ." He shook a gold-
nailed finger to reprove a reporter's grin. "That's who we are,
we in StarSeed. More than just Americans or Asians, Latins
or Russians, we have become the champions of our species,
striving against ultimate extinction."

He paused for effect, and shrugged in comic dismay when
Captain Alt lost his balance and nearly fell on the steps in his
retreat from the platform. With a murmur of assumed regret,
he turned to lift his voice again, now above the rumble of a
passing truck.

"Here on the launch site, we kneel at the altar of a magnificent dream, our grand plan to sow the human species
across the virgin worlds of other suns, even those in distant

galaxies. If we succeed, our race may live forever. Ultimately, we may rule the universe! Our sacrifice has been enormous, in resources depleted, in herculean effort, in precious human lives. Through twenty years of devotion to that noble cause, we have offered almost a hundred of these splendid wavecraft and ten thousand daring volunteers.

"If we fail . . ."

●

His words were drowned by the roar of trucks lumbering off the site, loaded with salvaged steel from dismantled cranes and gantries. With a shrug of exasperation, he stood waiting for them to pass.

"Alt just told us that," Jane Blake murmured to the man beside her. "In plainer English."

Perhaps he heard her. Flushing, he concluded the briefing and climbed the ramp to follow Alt aboard Ninety-nine. The jet waited for him on the airstrip. The driver sat sweating in the Jeep, but Director Stecker never came off the ship.

It was Captain Alt who finally emerged, tight-lipped and looking dazed. His shaking hand clutched a crumpled envelope. Without another word to anybody else, he had the driver take him to the jet.

The media departed. Security closed the gates, cleared the area, and broadcast warnings of the takeoff flash. The Fairshare protesters piled their tents and sleeping bags into their ancient vans and drove away. Launch crews reported to their work stations in the underground bunkers. Sirens hooted, diesels droned, and the ship sank smoothly into the launch pit.

●

Mort Nunin had called the launch complex a few hours before the scheduled takeoff, asking for Captain Alt. He gave no name; the matter was confidential. The operator told him that Alt was no longer available, and put him through to First Officer Glengarth.

"I'm calling as a friend of the Mission," he said. "I have information that a Fairshare agent is aboard Ninety-nine, planning mischief."

"Can you identify the agent?"

"He's employed by Aaron Zeeland. I didn't learn the name. I'm informed, however, that Zeeland is planning a coup, something dramatic enough to finish the Mission forever."

Nunin hung up. Glengarth called the captain's cabin and had to wait half a minute before he heard the rusty growl of Jake Hinch, the man who had come aboard with Stecker. Hinch listened, made him wait again, and finally snarled, "So what?"

"A question for Captain Stecker," he said. "You can tell him we've always had crank threats. There have been a few efforts at actual sabotage. We should not discount the danger, but we have several hours to search and secure the ship before our scheduled takeoff. We can postpone the takeoff until that's complete. Or we can ignore the threat and continue the countdown. I'm waiting for a decision."

Waiting, he heard heated voices.

"Stecker says it's up to you," Hinch rasped at last. "He doesn't give a damn."

Four

Aboard Ninety-nine, they found themselves in a room shaped like a generous slice of pie. Kip couldn't help staring at the big black woman sitting at the desk. She wore Mission gold-and-green, and her head was shaved bare.

"Welcome aboard, Dr. Virili."

She stood up to open their bags and took Kip's Game Box.

"Why?" he protested. "It's in my mass allowance. And it's mine."

"But on the prohibited list." She turned, explaining to Rima. "Electronic devices are possible hazards. They could create anomalous eddies in the conversion field."

She promised to return it after the flight and told them how to find their cabin.

"Be there when we take off." Her voice was deep for a woman, and she spoke louder to impress the command on Kip. "Get into your berths when you hear the countdown beginning. Secure your restraints. Watch the screen for information. You'll probably hear a loud sound at takeoff, and see a bright flash. Afterward, you should feel a sudden loss of weight."

Uneasily, Day looked up at her mother. "Are we going far?"

"Far." The woman nodded when Rima appealed to her. "Very far."

"I had to leave Me Me." Day's chin trembled. "Can I come back for her?"

"You won't—" The woman caught herself. "You need these."

She gave them each a black blindfold, a paper bag, a tiny envelope.

"Ear plugs," she said. "Insert them after the countdown begins. Cover your eyes. Keep the sick bags ready, just in case." She asked Kip, "Understand?"

"I won't be sick," he told her. "But I've got a question. If nobody ever came back, how do you know about the boom and the flash?"

"We don't. Not exactly." She turned again to Rima. "What we do know is what we observe at every launch. Wave conversion does happen. We expect reconversion to occur when we enter an adequate gravity field."

Kip asked, "What's a gravity field?"

"The pull of some massive object. A sun like ours, if we're lucky. We hope to be stopped a safe distance out, with a friendly planet in rocket range."

"Lucky?" He blinked at her. "You don't know?"

"Not for sure. That's the thrill of it." He wasn't sure about the thrill. "We'll probably come out in free fall, but of course we don't really know how wave flight feels. Or even if there's time in flight to feel anything."

"I see." He nodded. "A risk we take."

"True." She turned to Rima. "If you like, Dr. Virili, you can ask the medics for sedatives—"

"No sedative," Kip said. "Whatever happens, I want to be awake."

●

Wave conversion and reconversion were hard to understand, but he forgot them as they explored the ship. It was like a round tower with a fast elevator that ran up the center. The landings were small round rooms with many doors. One door on Deck G let them into Cabin G-9, which was theirs.

It was shaped like a very stingy slice of pie. Berths and seats and a little table folded out of the walls. There was a bathroom across the wider end. The big holoscreen on the wall was like a window that kept moving to let them see the snow on the mountains and the trucks and cranes driving off the site and even the ship itself as it looked to a holocam in a bunker where the launch crew was waiting.

"Hear this!" Something chimed and a sudden loud voice boomed from nowhere. "Now hear this!"

The screen lit to show a round control room walled with gray-cased consoles and flickering monitors. A stern-faced man in a uniform cap looked out of the screen.

"First Officer Glengarth speaking, to report a change of command. Captain Alt has been replaced by Captain Herman Stecker, who will address you now."

He stiffened to salute and vanished from the screen.

"A most regrettable event." Stecker had changed out of his crimson mods into official green-and-gold, and Kip heard no regret in his voice. "Captain Alt has been disabled by a sudden unexpected illness. He was rushed back to a Las Cruces hospital for examination."

"Gerald wasn't sick at all," Rima whispered. "Not when we saw him."

"No diagnosis has been reported, but our takeoff will not be delayed." Stecker's brisk voice lifted. "I've assumed command. Final preflight inspection is now complete. We're entering takeoff mode. Wave conversion will take place as scheduled."

His image vanished.

"Gerald Alt was my father's best friend." Rima sat staring at the empty screen. "He used to stay with us when he was home from the Moon." Kip saw her face go hard. "I can't believe he's sick."

●

She said they should stay in the cabin, but takeoff was still hours away. Kip felt bored, longing to be with his friends beyond the Game Gate, Captain Cometeer and the Legion of the Lost, who fought alien enemies on the hostile worlds of the Purple Sun. When he begged, she said he might go out to look the ship over if he kept out of everybody's way.

He stayed in the elevator on the lower decks, where busy men were shouting orders or rushing to obey, strange machines were drumming, freight dollies rolling out of the service shaft, a drill whining somewhere, somebody hammering metal. The higher decks were almost silent. He looked into the galley and the dining room. Vacant now, they were all bright white porcelain and shining metal, no food in sight.

The gym on the deck above stank faintly of cleaning chemicals and stale sweat. It was a huge dim space where treadmills and squirrel cages loomed like the monsters of the worlds beyond the Gate. About to leave, he heard a crash and a jangle of falling glass, and saw a man opening a door under a red-glowing sign that said Escape.

"Hola." The man had seen him. "Qué tal?"

He wondered if he should run, but the man wore a workman's blue coveralls instead of a uniform, and he seemed more anxious than angry.

"Bien." He decided to try his Spanish. "Cóm' está?"

"My name is Carlos." The man came halfway back across the room. His voice was quick and hushed. "I conceal myself because I wish to ride the ship. I do no harm. Except to break the glass."

"I'm Kip."

"Por favor!" The man spread his hands, and Kip saw that one was dripping blood. "Please! If you will not report me." The man needed to shave and wash his face. The coveralls were soiled with grease and paint. Perhaps he ought to be reported. Yet he had nice eyes, and the wounded hand needed a bandage.

"Okay," Kip decided. "They say the flight is risky. If you don't care, I won't talk."

"Amigo mío!" The man put out his hand, saw the blood, and drew it back. "If you speak to nobody, gracias!"

"Good luck!" Kip told him. "Buena suerte!"

With a quick look around the gym, the man stooped to gather up the biggest pieces of glass and stepped back through the door. The space beyond was tiny, nearly filled with tanks marked oxygen and a yellow space suit. The door shut with a hollow *thunk*.

●

Wondering about Carlos and hoping now that nobody found him, Kip went back to the elevator. It stopped outside a door marked COMPUTER AND COMMUNICATION. The door didn't open. He went up to another deck and found an impatient man in Mission uniform scowling at him from a screen under a lens he hadn't seen. The man advised him sharply to get back where he belonged. In their own cabin, he found Day asleep in her berth. His mother sat watching the holoscreen. She turned the volume down to ask if he was okay.

"I guess." He hesitated. "But if you think Mr. Stecker lied about Captain Alt—"

He stopped when he saw the tightness on her face.

"I don't know." Her voice dropped. "No matter how it happened, he's the captain now. We have to respect him. But we don't have to like him."

He wanted to talk about Carlos, but he had his promise to keep.

"I don't understand why we came." He knew the words might hurt her, but he couldn't stop wondering. "If we don't know where the ship will go, or anything except that we can't ever come back, the whole business seems—well, pretty risky."

"It is." He saw her bite her lip. "But really, Kip, the way things were, I didn't see much choice."

He waited, feeling sorry he had spoken, till she turned the holo off.

"Your father." She looked down to pat Day and sat for a moment staring at nothing before she went on. "I've never told you much about him. Maybe I can say more, now that we're leaving Earth and all the past behind. If you want to know."

"Please." The moment was suddenly important. "You did say he went out on Seventy-nine. I've always wondered why."

"For a long time I couldn't bear to talk about him. Or even think about him." Her voice was slow, and her face looked older than she was. "I loved him once. I never wanted you and Day to hate him. And I guess he did try to treat us right, at least almost till the end."

Day had made a little whimper in her sleep. Rima stopped to pull the sheet higher over her and then sat frowning at the blank holoscreen as if she had forgotten him.

"My father?"

"I'm sorry." She shrugged to shake her sadness off. "We were both very young. New to the Mission. Planting mankind in far-off galaxies seemed a very noble thing. We planned to go out together, but I'd trained as a terraformer and bioengineer. He became chief of a launch crew. For a long time we were needed here. I worked with the engineers designing special gear that might be needed on different planets. Later, when those projects were finished and slots did open, you were four and Day was on the way. The medics said I should wait for her. Your father went out alone."

Still unhappy about it, she said no more till he asked, "Why?"

She reached to smooth Day's hair.

"Another woman." Her face went harder for a moment, but then she shrugged and looked past him, seeing the woman in her mind. "Holly Horn. Blond and very bright. A quantum technician. I'd roomed with her at Tech. We were friends. Or had been." Her lip twisted and quivered. "Of course she said she was sorry. Your father said he felt terrible. Maybe he really did. They left what money they had in a trust fund to help with your support. I always tried to forgive them, but—"

Her voice went sharp and stopped, but in a moment she went on more quietly.

"That's the bare bones of it. The reason we're here. We'd used up the trust fund, which was never very much. I was never able to save anything. The Mission's dead. My job's gone. I had no skills for anything else, there's no future in sight for us here on Earth, and Ninety-nine . . ."

She smiled again at the dead gray screen as if she saw something beautiful there.

"Who knows? We're on the last seed ship. Beginning the most exciting voyage I can imagine. I can't wait to see where it ends." Her voice slowed. "Maybe I wasn't quite fair to you and Day, but we have a chance—an exciting chance! I hope you'll try to understand."

"It's okay, Mom." He stood up to put his arm around her. "I'm glad we came."

●

Still they had to wait. When she turned the holoscreen on again, it was repeating a program about ship discipline and ship security. A woman in a white cap came on to call them down for a quick meal of soya soup and sandwiches. When Kip got sleepy, his mother helped fix his berth. She woke him when the countdown began and buckled the web over him. Still half asleep, Day whimpered for Me Me and crawled into the berth with her.

"Five minutes to launch." He pushed the soft plastic plugs into his ears, but still he heard the count. "Four . . . three . . . two . . . one minute . . ." His mother called to remind him about the blindfold. He put it on and lay waiting for something maybe like a lightning strike. "Thirty seconds . . . twenty . . . ten . . . five . . ." He shivered and tried to breathe. "Four . . . three . . . two . . . one . . ."

He heard a brittle *tock*, not very loud. The room was very dark when he slipped the blindfold off, but in a moment the screen lit again with a pale green glow. Day was begging again for Me Me, and he felt himself floating off the berth.

Five

Boarding Ninety-nine early on the takeoff day, Roak found his chance to leave the device in a supply locker on the gym deck. Down on the engine decks, he listened to the engineers as if he understood all their crisp status reports on the fuel reserve, the fusion reactors, and the quantum propulsion system. Anxious for Andersen's initials on his clearance certificate, he felt vexed when the big engineer wanted to talk.

"A funny feeling, saying good-bye." Seeming to forget the certificate, Andersen offered a muscular hand. "I've worked three years here, waiting for my chance to go, but now . . ." He grinned and scratched his initials when Roak pushed a pen at him. "Sorry to hold you up. It's just that actually leaving seems so damn final."

"Good luck." Roak gripped his hand. "God be with you."

They were his father's words, and he hadn't meant to say them. The sound of them gave him an uneasy twinge, but he hurried back to the elevator. With the captain's signature, he could be off the ship in half an hour, on his way to the Mission office in Las Cruces to file his final report and pick up his final salary check. Nunin was to meet him for dinner and give him the rest of the money when they got news of the blast.

Fifty thousand, all told. He might look for a clean little motel somewhere on the Gulf coast that would bring in enough to make the payments and give him a living with no hard work. Time for a little fishing and a chance to meet interesting women.

The control room was a dome-shaped space at the top of the ship, arched with holoscreens that looked out across dust green desert and treeless mountains. The duty officer was Tony Cruzet, a small dark man with a faint foreign accent. Sitting at a silenced intercom, he frowned and shook his head. Roak stood looking out at the snow-dusted hills, trying not to fidget, till Cruzet finally hung up.

"You're all clear to take off." He handed Cruzet the certificate. "If you'll just sign this for Las Cruces."

"No problems?" Cruzet glanced at it, and peered at him too sharply. "Are you sure?"

"None, sir. Mr. Andersen seems very competent with the quantum system."

"He certainly is."

"If you'll sign—"

"The Mission requires the captain's signature. I'll send it down to him."

Cruzet rolled the sheet, slid it into a bright metal capsule, dropped it into the com tube beside the elevator, and turned back to his intercom. Roak bit his lip and turned to survey the earth-banked bunker just below and the abandoned construction pads scattered across the desert. The certificate never came back. Still on the muffled intercom, Cruzet ignored him till finally he raised his voice.

"Sir! Excuse me, but I've got to have that certificate."

"I know." Cruzet shrugged. "But Captain Stecker came aboard just this morning. He has ropes to learn. Give him time."

"Okay."

He muttered the word and scanned the burnt landscape till he had to try again.

"Mr. Cruzet, please! Can't you rush it up? I've got things to do."

"So has the captain." Cruzet turned briefly from the intercom. "He knows you're waiting, but he has priorities."

He could only stand there, staring down at the workmen demolishing the platform where Alt and Stecker had spoken, till he found a black-capped security officer at his elbow and shuddered at the first chill of dismay.

"Mr. Roak," the officer said "Please come with me."

●

Down on the comcom deck, he followed the officer into the ship security office. The woman at the desk looked too big for the room. She was very black and heavily muscular, her head shaved to the scalp. Zeeland's device lay before him on the desk.

"Jonas Roak," the officer said. "Lieutenant Reba Washburn."

After his first startled glance at the device, he looked up into Washburn's expressionless face and stood as straight as he could, trying for an expression of mild inquiry.

"We're still strangers." Washburn spoke at last, her booming organ voice as bland as her broad face. "But you'll get to know me. I was born in Ghana. My parents were pioneer Pentecostal missionaries there. Later they were in Brazil and Peru. I saw the results of climatic change. Flood and drought. Famine. Genocide.

"My father read the Zeeland book and blamed the Mission for everything. If I wouldn't fight the devil, he wanted me to fight quantum waves in the upper atmosphere. What saved me was not the Holy Spirit, but a bioscience scholarship to Georgia Tech. If you wonder where I come from, Mr. Roak, I've been with the Mission since I graduated. I'm on the ship because I came to see how we've wasted the planet with the greenhouse gases we've been spewing into the atmosphere for the last hundred years."

She paused a moment, her dark eyes probing him.

"As for Fairshare, Mr. Roak, we've looked for signs of actual environmental harm from our takeoff flashes. We found none at all." Her voice sharpened. "Fairshare is a criminal scam."

Eyes still averted from the device on the desk, Roak shook his head and allowed himself a puzzled frown. Washburn's voice fell solemnly.

"I love StarSeed Mission the way my parents loved God. As for you, Mr. Roak, I'm surprised to see you here. Do you recall the oath you took when you became a launch inspector?"

"Of course!" He let indignation edge his voice. "If you'll look at my record—"

"We've had occasion to question your official record, Mr. Roak. We have reason now for a harder look. A few hours ago we had a telephone call from a man we have identified as Mortimer Nunin. He is known to have Fairshare contacts. He warned us of a Fairshare plot."

"I've met Nunin," he muttered. "But what are you getting at?"

"We searched the ship with chemical sniffers, and discovered this."

Washburn nodded at the device.

"Are you accusing me?"

"I don't accuse you, Mr. Roak. Not just yet." Washburn shrugged, muscles rippling under her snug blue jumpsuit. "We've found no fingerprints, but the evidence certainly suggests that you were trying to kill us. Tried in fact to murder mankind."

"Evidence?" His anger was real enough. "What evidence?"

"You are the last outsider still aboard." She spoke in a tone of soft reproof. "Mr. Cruzet says you were greatly agitated when he delayed you."

Roak was shaking.

"I've got rights," he shouted. "If I'm suspected, I want a lawyer."

"No rights are brought aboard any StarSeed craft. We all sign the covenant that governs us. Rights here must be earned."

"I want to see the captain—"

"Captain Stecker has more urgent duties now. He's aware of you, but any action must wait till after takeoff."

Stunned, he swayed on his feet.

"You can't—" he gasped. "You've got to let me off."

"Too late for that. The locks are already secured." Washburn nodded at the waiting officer. "Mr. Kellick, take him to the brig."

●

Roak had blacked out once when a gang of black prisoners was working him over in the Huntsville yard. He was swaying giddily now, till Kellick caught his arm very firmly and escorted him back to the elevator. The brig was on the bottom deck, below the engine levels. Kellick took his briefcase, wrote his name in a book, and left him in a narrow steel cell.

Nine by five, it was furnished with a toilet, a padded steel bunk and nothing else. He sat down on the bunk and mopped his face. Damn Nunin! The greasy thief had sold him out, just to keep his forty thousand.

He mopped his sweaty face again and sat there waiting for anything to happen. Nothing did. He heard the shuffle of space boots and distant voices he couldn't understand. At last he lay down on the bunk and tried to sleep, but raw terror kept eating at him. In spite of himself he got up and walked the cell, three steps each way.

A gong rang at last.

"All clear!" a speaker brayed. "All clear for scheduled liftoff."

He waited at the door, but nobody let him out. He rattled the grill till Kellick came.

"You've got to stop it!" he gasped. "Stop the takeoff, and I'll tell you where I hid the other bomb."

"Washburn would never fall for that." Kellick laughed. "If you'd had another bomb, you'd have offered the deal right away."

"I want to see the captain."

"We've reported your detention, but I don't know when he can get to you."

Stecker never got to him. Roak paced his narrow scrap of deck, cursing the Mission and Nunin under his breath, till Kellick came back with a cup of water and a bowl of lukewarm chicken-flavored tofasoya stew. He left it on the narrow shelf inside the grill until it turned to a clammy mass that he was eating when Kellick came back for the cup and the bowl.

"Takeoff alert, Mr. Roak." He left ear plugs and a blindfold. "The countdown is running."

Kellick took his unfinished stew and left him alone in the cell. He walked his bit of deck and lay on the berth and walked again, while the chicken-flavored stuff turned sour in his stomach. He tried to remember what he knew about quantum flight.

Nothing, really. Nobody knew anything, because nobody had ever come back to talk about it. The blindfold and ear plugs might shield him from a flash and a crash that might or might not happen. The flight might end anywhere, or nowhere at all. Nunin would keep his forty thousand; that was all he really knew.

Six

Colin Glengarth was a big, rawboned Scot whose angular bones came down from one Angus Glengarth who had left his native highlands five generations ago to manage a cattle ranch in the Texas panhandle. He'd been happy to go out with Alt on this final flight, and a bitter resentment festered in him now. He kept silent as they took their places at the controls, lying side by side in the pilot seats.

"Brief me." Stecker rolled his eyes at the maze of lighted instruments winking red and green all around and over their heads. "It's ten long years since I went into Mission management. I need a quick review of takeoff and flight control procedures."

"Too late for that, sir." Glengarth was securing his low-gravity restraints. "Launch configurations were all completed and reviewed before the countdown began. We're now under computer control. Nothing more to do, sir. Not till we're out of quantum mode."

"You mean we just lie here?"

"Lie there." The ship now at the mercy of this blundering dunce! Gerald Alt had been his friend since college, a great companion for this ultimate adventure. "Use your ear plugs." His voice was sharper than he intended. "Cover your eyes. Keep still through the countdown."

"I've heard Fairshare talk about risks, but our people in promotion always played them down." A hint of panic sharpened Stecker's voice. "What are our odds?"

"Who knows?"

"All this uncertainty—" Stecker caught himself and muttered, "Not that I'm chicken."

You're a coward, Glengarth thought. Worse than a coward, a thief on the run. A pirate, really, stealing the ship with trumped-up charges against Captain Alt. Stecker and Jake Hinch had robbed and ruined the Mission, and now they were on the run.

He had been Alt's pilot on *Moon Magellan*. Driver of the first Moon Ranger. Surveyor of the Farside site and safety officer there till the Mission called him back to help design the quantum craft. On Alt's vacations since, they'd got together for wilderness hikes as long as they could find unspoiled wilderness fit for hiking. Memories of those good times ached in him now.

"Here's to the Moon!" He remembered Alt lifting a glass of bourbon and water to it one night when they sat watching it over a campfire. "Because its desolation teaches you to love the hills and skies and seas of Earth as it used to be. The Mission will be lucky if we find another planet half its equal."

"We can hope," he had answered.

Ninety-nine might have reached that goal. Planning the flight, they'd dreamed again of the virgin worlds they hoped to find, perhaps in some undiscovered galaxy, an instant and a billion light-years from Earth.

Now Stecker and Jake Hinch. Robber barons, Zeeland's Fairshare newsletters had called them, playing the con game

of the century. He and Alt had been slow to believe, even
when they saw StarSeed sliding toward bankruptcy and the
wrecking crews arriving to break up the unfinished skeleton
of what should have been Flight One Hundred.

●

"What can I expect?" Stecker nagged again. "When the
countdown ends? What then?"

"Then?" Unintended mockery edged his answer. "We'll
take a look around us. Try to see where we are. Guess, if we
can, how far we've left our good Earth behind. Look for
some possible planet. Go into rocket mode, if we do find any
likely object within rocket range."

A computer chimed. He called Andersen to begin the
oral count. Muttering something Glengarth didn't try to
hear, Stecker adjusted the blindfold and fell silent. The moment came. His breath stopped. His own eyes covered, headphones and safety goggles on, he waited.

And waited.

A brittle crack, like a dry twig snapping. Had it happened?
No light had flashed through the goggles. Had the takeoff
gone wrong? Were they still in the pit?

He realized that his weight was gone and pulled out his
earplugs.

"Are we—" Stecker's yelp stabbed through his headphones. "Where are we?"

He'd tried to imagine the moment. Instant extinction?
The deadly blaze of some giant star. A black hole's invisible
drag. Or perhaps their first glimpse of that pristine planet just
ahead, lush green continents and clean seas beckoning? He
drew a long breath. At least it hadn't been extinction.

Hopeful, he pushed the heavy goggles off. Though no actual windows broke the titanium hull, the curved holoscreens
created the illusion that the deck was open to the sky. Dead
black now, they told him nothing at all.

Yet the ship seemed intact. Floating against the restraints, he searched the dark till his adjusting vision let stars burn through the darkness. A scattered few at first, soon lost in fields of diamond frost and clouds of glowing gas and swarms of steady suns. He touched the keys to sweep them across the dome as if the ship were turning.

Orion?

Blazing Betelgeuse, the jeweled belt, the hazy fire of the Great Nebula, all twisted out of shape? He touched the keys to stop it overhead, but it couldn't be Orion. There were too many stars when the cameras swept them, crowded too densely. Earth and its small sun could be nowhere near. They must have come many thousand light-years. His world, his friends, all he had ever known had gone to forgotten dust. No surprise, yet he shivered with a pang of loneliness and loss.

●

"What the bleedin' hell?"

He heard Jake Hinch's hoarse bellow from the elevator. Hinch had been the Mission auditor. Stecker's accomplice, so Zeeland had claimed, and now his fellow fugitive. Outlined against the elevator lights, Hinch was a withered human rat, long-nosed and long-chinned, tilting his bearded head beneath a shapeless black beret as if to peer through his black-lensed sunglasses. Not worth hating, Glengarth thought, but surely not the type for pioneering undiscovered worlds.

"Where the ruttin' devil?" he was demanding. "Where've we got to?"

Glengarth had known him since they met in Mission training and still despised him for the lies that had got him there. Despised him for his bald attempts to cheat on tests he couldn't pass. Despised him utterly for his arrogance since Stecker made him Mission auditor and for his habit of disputing legitimate Mission debts.

"What the hell stopped us here?"

Stecker, roving the world to solicit funds for the Mission,

had cultivated an easy-seeming if sometimes oily charm. Hinch, the hatchet man, had never needed charm. He preferred raw power. Clinging now to a handhold at the elevator door, he glared through his wide black lenses with the wary hostility of some frightened predator.

"What next?" he yelled again. "What now?"

"Take a look." Glengarth unsnapped the restraints and swung to his feet, fixing his clingfast space boots on the clingfast carpet. He faced Hinch with a small tight grin. "Like what you see?"

"You say it took a star to stop us?" Clutching with one hand, Hinch snatched the dark glasses off and pointed at the star that wasn't Betelgeuse. "That's the star?"

"Probably not." Glengarth shrugged. "We've had no time for observation, but it looks too far off for its gravity to matter."

"A giant star?" Weakly, Stecker mopped at his sweat-bright face. "Wouldn't a giant be massive enough?"

"Of course, but I take that for a spectral type G2. A twin of our own sun. But not our sun, not in that blazing swarm."

"So what?" Hinch shuffled away from the elevator, the glasses in his hand, his black eyes stabbing at the screens, at Stecker, at Glengarth. His words were a shrill demand. "We ain't no cryin' babies. I want to know."

"So do I." Glengarth took a moment to control his temper. "Evidently we did enter the gravity well of something massive enough to get us out of quantum mode, but I haven't found it."

"A black hole?" Stecker cringed from the midnight sky. "Do you think . . ."

His hoarse whisper died.

"Possibly." Glengarth nodded. "Though I see no accretion disk. That's the luminous plasma that many black holes gather. If it is a black hole with no disk around it, we'll never see it. We do have a possible clue in its effect on our motion.

That, however, is something that will be difficult or maybe impossible to measure, since we have no nearby reference points."

"Then get us out of danger!" Trembling, Stecker seized Glengarth's arm. "Move!"

With more force than he intended, Glengarth twisted free.

"Sir, how would you do that?"

"Bleedin' idiot!" Hinch shrieked. "Shoot us out. The same way you shot us here."

"Get at it!" Stecker rapped. "Now!"

"No way, sir."

"No way?" Hinch echoed. "Why the hell no way?"

Running the Mission, he and Stecker had learned to work in tandem. "Surely, Mr. Glengarth." Stecker's tone was smoother. "You're said to be a competent quantum engineer. Get us back into quantum mode and find a likely planet."

"Sir." Glengarth raised his hand. "If you understood—"

"We understand the bleedin' shit you got us into." Hinch shook a scrawny fist. "If you want to keep your bleedin' job, get us out. I mean now!"

"Cool it, Jake." Stecker pulled him back and spoke more quietly to Glengarth. "Sir, we do respect your spacemanship. I know we can't afford to quarrel, but the ship's loaded with emergency survival equipment. You've got teams of expert technicians." His tone grew sharper. "So take us back into quantum wave propulsion, or tell me why you can't."

"If you really don't know, here's why." Bleakly, Glengarth grinned. "Remember the takeoff, how we sat waiting in the pit till the bunker crew fired us out. Very much like a bullet out of a gun. We couldn't bring the gun, and the laws of motion still apply."

"Huh?" Stecker's jaw sagged.

"Remember Newton's laws. Action equals reaction. We can't get back into quantum mode without an external launch facility embedded in some object massive enough to absorb the takeoff reaction. A planet or at least a large asteroid. Something I don't see."

"If we can't get out—" Stecker gulped. "What then?"

"Hard to say." Glengarth turned to scan the green-and-amber–winking consoles. "We can't plan anything till we know where we are."

"When—" Stecker mopped his face and peered into the starlit darkness. "When will that be?"

"We want action," Jake Hinch growled. "Action now!"

"Listen, Mr. Hinch." Glengarth swung to him, speaking bluntly. "We're competent. We know space navigation. We have trained astronomers aboard, and expert computer software. Give us time to do what we can."

"If a bleedin' black hole stopped us—" Shrill with panic, Hinch grabbed Stecker's shoulder. "I've heard the Fairshare line about black holes. The gravity will grab us. Tear us into dust and gas. Suck us into nowhere."

"It could." Glengarth nodded. "If it is a black hole."

"Better hope it is!" Hinch snarled through his ragged beard like a hungry wolf. "That ought to be quick and painless. Anything else, and we're left to drift in this black hell till the food's all gone and hungry men are prowlin' the wreck for human game."

"Please!" Glengarth spread his hands. "Gentlemen, please!"

Gentlemen, he thought, wasn't quite the word.

"Jake, you'd better leave us." Stecker waved Hinch into the elevator. "You're no pilot. I hope Mr. Glengarth can fly us somewhere. I want to let him try."

Seven

Securing the ship for takeoff, the search crew had come upon the blood and broken glass on the gym floor and opened the escape hatch. Mondragon staggered out, dazzled by the lights and stiff from huddling so long inside.

"Una bomba?" He shook his head at their questions. "Nunca!"

In his awkward English, he tried to explain himself. He knew nothing of bombs. He had hidden himself only to ride the great bird of space to reach some new world in the sky. Why would he wish to kill the machine that carried them?

They took him down to the brig and told him Captain Stecker would see him. Stecker never did. The jailer brought him water and tufasoya stew. A loud computer voice announced that the ship was entering takeoff mode. The jailer came again with a blindfold and something in a tiny plastic packet.

"Es adiós?" he asked. "Adios al mundo?"

Seeming not to understand, the jailer left before he could find the English. Examining the packet, he found the use of the tiny rubber plugs. Lying on the berth with them in his ears and the blindfold over his eyes, he listened to the countdown with his heart throbbing fast. Was his old dream coming true? They had not thrown him off the ship. The time for that had passed. He was on the shining starbird, on his way to the magic worlds among the stars!

He lay there a long time, listening to the muffled sounds of the ship. At last he heard sirens screaming. He felt the ship quiver and sink. Something clicked. He floated off the bunk, suddenly weighing nothing at all.

●

"Fun!" Day sailed off her berth. "Real fun!"

She stopped herself against the ceiling and floated slowly back.

"Careful, dear." Rima caught her ankle to pull her down. "Till you're more used to it."

Kip soon felt a little weight returning, enough that he didn't need the handholds. They sat watching the holoscreen. It stayed empty for a long time, but at last the speaker chimed. First Officer Glengarth was on the holoscreen.

"Ship status report." His voice was tight, and Kip thought he had a worried look. "We have emerged from wave propulsion with no reported harm. We have now shifted from free fall to rocket mode, moving at point zero four gee while we survey our new surroundings. Further information will follow when possible. That is all."

His image flickered out.

"That's all?" Kip looked at his mother. "What about the star that stopped us? Will there be a new planet where we can land?"

"Try not to fret," she urged him. "Mr. Glengarth will tell us more when he can." She sighed and spoke again, more softly. "They were old friends, Colin and Gerald. Mr. Glengarth and Captain Alt. And friends of my father. The three of them loved to be together when they could. I'm sure Mr. Glengarth will keep us safe."

He wondered how sure she really was.

He tried not to sleep, waiting for something to happen. Nothing did. Mr. Glengarth never came back to the holoscreen with more information. Day slept and woke up and asked if they could go back for Me Me. He got hungry.

"Patience, dear," his mother said. "People need time to get used to low gee."

He wanted his Game Box. He got hungrier. Finally the woman in the white cap called them down for brunch in the dining room. It was slabs of something that the man at the counter called starchow on novakelp toast, with syncafe or soya milk.

Day made a face at the milk, but finally gulped it down. She pushed her tray back and begged again for Me Me.

"It's not that bad." Kip ate his hard dry toast and sipped his milk. Not much like real milk, it left a faintly bitter taste in his mouth. "It's okay," he told his mother. "Not all that bad."

"Good for us," she insisted. "Everything had to be concentrated, to let the ship carry food enough to last us till we can grow our own crops."

Kip wondered when that would be.

Carlos was in the line of people waiting when they left the room, a stranger with him. They both wore yellow coveralls. A black-capped security man stood close behind them. Carlos's hurt hand was bandaged. The stranger was grimly silent, but Carlos smiled at Kip and then at Rima, and called, "Qué tal, amigo?"

"Who's that?" Rima asked when they had gone on. "The prisoner? How could he know you?"

"Carlos," Kip told her. "He came from Mexico to ride the ship."

He told her how he had found Carlos in the gym.

"You never reported him?"

"He wasn't hurting anybody. All he wanted was to come on the ship. He'd cut his hand on the glass, and he was afraid. I felt sorry for him. He has nice eyes."

"Nice eyes!" Her voice sharpened. "He could have hurt you. He could have been a Fairshare agent, aboard to sabotage the ship. You should have told the officers and told me."

"I'd promised not to tell."

"Kip!" she scolded. "You must learn to be careful with strangers."

He said nothing else, yet he felt glad Carlos was with them on the ship.

●

Back in the cabin, they waited again for Mr. Glengarth to come on the holoscreen with further information. It never happened. Missing Captain Cometeer and his friends in the Legion of the Lost, Kip thought perhaps ship security would return his Game Box. Rima let him go down to ask for it. Gone three hours, he finally brought it back.

"I had a good visit with Carlos," he told her. "I like him."

"That stowaway?" She frowned.

"He's okay," he tried to persuade her. "Still a prisoner, but not locked up. In spite of his hurt hand, he's working in the supply room. My Game Box was dead when they found it for me. Carlos fixed it."

"Fixed it? How?"

"He knows about computers. He said the wave conversion caused a static surge that had garbled the access command. He rewrote the command. Now it works just fine. And he asked about you."

"Me?"

"Remember those Fairshare pickets outside the gate? Carlos says he doesn't belong to Fairshare and never understood it. He was standing with them there because he had no

badge to let him inside. He saw you when we came through
and he wanted to know how you were. When I told him you
were my mother, he said I was very lucky."

"Kip, please!" She glanced at Day and dropped her voice.
"Mr. Glengarth called while you were out. I asked about the
prisoners in yellow coveralls. He says a bomb was found on
the ship. It could have killed us all. He doesn't know who
brought it, but those two prisoners are the suspects."

"It wasn't Carlos!" Kip felt distressed. "He told me he's
in trouble because one of the pickets helped him get aboard.
But he's nice. He certainly wouldn't want to bring a bomb and
kill himself. Or anybody else. You saw that other prisoner. I
don't like his eyes. I think he did it."

"Not likely." Firmly, she shook her head. "He's Jonas
Roak, the clearance inspector. He's had the job for years. He
has a good record. They found some Fairshare document on
the Mexican. Security thinks he was a Fairshare agent hired
to plant the bomb."

"So why was he hiding, still on the ship."

"He seems not to know much English. They think he got
lost aboard. Panicked and hid. You know he's an illegal alien.
Already a criminal when he came on the ship."

"Mom! Maybe Carlos was an alien back on Earth, but
we'll all be aliens now. I know he was poor, but he's a brave
man. All he wants is to explore the stars like Captain Cometeer. That's why he stowed away—"

"You don't know him and don't want to know him." Impatience lifted her voice. "He could be dangerous. I want you
to avoid him."

He was glad when the holoscreen chimed.

●

Glengarth came on the screen, smiling bleakly.

"Status update." The stubble on his face had grown
darker, and he forgot to hold the smile. "Thanks to the astro

team, we've discovered the massive object that pulled us out of quantum mode."

His image vanished, and a field of stars filled the screen. A dark point in the middle of it swelled slowly into a circular blot. At first it looked utterly black, but dull red pockmarks began to appear as it grew, and then faint narrow cracks the color of fire.

"There you see it," his tired voice ran on. "A black dwarf star. If you're wondering what a black dwarf is, stars are born when gravity collapses clouds of gas and dust. If a new star is big enough, the heat of collapse sets off a nuclear reaction—the fusion of hydrogen into helium—that will make it shine.

"This star was too small to keep the hydrogen burning, but it's still hot under the crust. It must have come close. Dr. Andersen thinks that its hydrogen did burn once, ignited by the gravitational collapse and the fission of unstable elements. It may even have warmed its planets before it died. If it had planets. We're searching now, but they're lost in the dark, even if they're here. Maybe impossible to find."

The black star vanished, but he came back on the screen to say that more news would follow when there was any news.

"Suppose they do find a planet." Anxiously, Kip looked at his mother. "That star won't warm it. What good would it be?"

"Wait." She shrugged, looking as tired as Glengarth. "Let's wait and see."

They waited.

She wanted to forget Carlos Mondragon, but Kip was curious. When a man came on the screen to talk about a training class for low-gravity activity, she let him go down to inquire about it. He went by the security desk to ask about Carlos.

"The Mex stowaway?" The black woman shrugged. "Gone."

He asked where.

"The computer lab," she said. "He understands computers."

"I know," Kip said. "He fixed my Game Box."

"He got a bug out of our own computer system." Her smile seemed friendly. "The takeoff had played tricks with computers all over the ship. When the astro team learned what he'd done for us, they got Mr. Glengarth to release him to them."

His mother would like Carlos better, Kip thought, if she ever got to know him.

●

Day was asleep when he got back from the training class. When she woke still pining for Me Me, Rima took her down to the rec room. Kip went back through the Game Gate to rejoin the Legion in a daring raid to rescue a captured comrade from the evil queen of the Diamond Planet.

Rima and Day came back, and they watched the holoscreen. It was still a flat gray blank when the dining-room manager called them down for another meal of the concentrates they must learn to like. She introduced two men who joined them at the table and lifted their cups of syncafe to greet her.

Andy Andersen was a red-headed, pink-skinned giant who was going to lead the landing team if they ever found anywhere to land. Tony Cruzet was a tiny, owlish man with a lean brown face and gold-rimmed glasses. The Mission astronomer, he had picked the target galaxies for many Mission flights. They both looked hollow-eyed and haggard, and they sat in moody silence till Kip and Day went to stand in line for soyasweet snowfoam.

"Bitch of a thing," Cruzet muttered to Rima then. "Stecker's drunk or in a total funk or likely both. Locked up in his cabin with that Jake Hinch. They've got empty bottles and broken dishes scattered over the deck. Hinch finally looked out when I knocked. Asked if I knew a willing woman."

He made a dismal shrug.

"A tough time for Mr. Glengarth." Andersen scowled, shaking tufacream into his syncafe. "Sixty hours in the dome with no sleep except what he's got dozing in his seat. Doing what he can to keep a lid on panic while he looks for anywhere to go."

"A landing site?" Rima asked. "A planet?"

"We've all been on the search team, but we don't know if there is a planet. Hell of a job, here in the dark. If we don't find something . . ."

Stirring his syncafe, Andersen splashed it on the table, then mopped at the spill and forgot to go on.

"So?" she prompted him. "The outlook?"

"Not good," he muttered. "If you want the truth, it's a no-win game. Planets would be invisible, if the star has planets. We know for sure there's nothing in radar range. The star's rotation might have been a clue to the orbital plane where planets ought to be, but the dwarf doesn't rotate. Not fast enough to tell us anything."

He shook his head and mopped again at the brown splash on the table.

"And what if we find 'em?" Cruzet blinked at her unhappily. "Even if we do stumble onto some dirty snowball, what can you do with it?"

Day and Kip came back with their snowfoam before she had to answer.

The message gong woke her late that night.

"Dr. Virili?" the second officer called from the control dome. "A new situation. Mr. Glengarth wants all team leaders here in twenty minutes."

Eight

Glengarth, feeling punch-drunk with fatigue, had left Sternberg, the second officer, to carry on the planet search while he took a break in his cabin. He came to the door when Andersen knocked, rubbing his eyes and asking a hopeful question.

"Found anything?"

"Maybe." Andersen shrugged. "Nothing we can see, not that we have light to see anything. But we do have a computer readout that seems to show the gravity pull of some planetary massive object. Not yet identified, but I thought you'd want to know."

"I'll be right up."

"Coffee?" Andersen grinned at the aroma filling the room. "Real coffee?"

"A peace offering from Stecker." Glengarth poured it from the syncafe machine on the end of his desk. "His man

Hinch had smuggled a truckload of gourmet goodies aboard even before they turned up."

"A double whammy!" Andersen muttered. "Stecker and Roak."

"Or triple, if you want to count Hinch."

"Maybe we should." Andersen frowned. "I don't know him, but Roak's still in the brig. I've known him, or thought I did, since he came to the site to make his first inspection. We've played chess. He's sharp enough to best me more often than not. He's supposed to be an engineering jack-of-all-trades. I thought we might use him on the search team, but when I went by . . ."

He shrugged.

"A mental wreck, useless to himself or anybody else."

"You can imagine the jolt, if he's as innocent as he says he is. Expecting to spend his days back on Earth." Glengarth scowled. "The hard fact is that some bastard did try to kill us."

"Maybe the Mexican." Andersen shook his head. "Though now I hate to think so."

"Mondragon?" Glengarth's eyebrows lifted. "He's been working with you?"

"A better man than Roak. Two dogs of very different colors." Wryly, Andersen grinned. "In spite of what he says about his origins, Carlos is a very remarkable man. You wouldn't guess it from his English, but I believe he has a better native brain than Roak. Along with a natural affinity for computers—almost as if he thinks in binary digits."

"How'd he get on your search team?"

"Thanks to Kellick and Washburn. They booked both prisoners into the brig, watched Roak go to pieces and Mondragon happy to be on his way to the stars. They've got no actual evidence that Mondragon's a Fairshare agent, or anything but what he says he is. He begged to help with any sort of work. They let him inventory the electronic devices she was holding. A lot of them had been disabled by launch effects. He fixed them. Recovered lost files in her computer. When Washburn heard of our own problems with the search computers, she sent him up to see me. He's made himself useful."

"A man that smart could tell a good lie."

"He says he likes computers because they never lie."

Thoughtfully, Glengarth rubbed the dark stubble on his chin. "So you think Roak's the culprit."

"No proof." Andersen shrugged. "Carlos did sneak aboard. He admits he did it with help from the Fairshare pickets. He had a Fairshare newsletter in his pocket. He says it was in the coveralls they gave him. Washburn likes him. I like him. I'd rather think he's just the victim of his own mala suerte.

"As for Roak . . ." Frowning, he was silent for a moment. "Washburn says he came unglued when he found himself trapped on the ship. He admits nothing. Does nothing except walk the deck or sprawl on his berth. Wouldn't eat the first day out. Washburn doesn't trust him."

●

The call for Rima woke Kip. He agreed to stay in the cabin with Day. Rima took the elevator to the control deck and came out into blinding midnight.

"Rima!" Glengarth called warmly out of the darkness. "You know Cruzet and Andersen? This is Carlos Mondragon."

In a moment she was able to make out the little group standing in silhouette against the blaze of stars across the arching holoscreens.

"Señora Virili!" She recognized the stowaway's accent. "I know your son. A child of great promise."

Kip's sudden friendship with him was a festering splinter, but she had to murmur, "Hello."

"I called the other team leaders." Glengarth turned soberly from the dimly glowing instruments. "Lieutenant

Washburn's stuck at the security desk. Dr. Senn's still on his radar search. Mr. Hinch says Captain Stecker is sleeping, not to be disturbed."

"Just as well," Andersen murmured.

"The search?" she asked. "Is there anywhere to land?"

"We were groping in the dark." Andersen's voice rang as if amplified by the dome. She thought he would sing bass. "But we have located a planet. Tony'll tell you how."

"We deployed a reference satellite." Cruzet's high, precise tones reflected no emotion except perhaps an iron control. "Tracking it, we were able to detect a gravitational anomaly. The same effect that enabled Adams and Leverrier to discover Neptune. Thanks are due, I might say, to Carlos at the computer."

With a nod for Mondragon, he pointed at a dull red disk against the field of stars.

"A radar image. The color's false, of course. The face toward us is apparently ice. Actual color probably white or gray, if we had light to see it. We came out of quantum mode already in motion almost directly toward it—and the dwarf it orbits—at seven kilometers a second."

She asked Glengarth, "Can we land?"

"Perhaps." Hesitant, he looked at Cruzet and Andersen. "That's what we must consider. At once."

"Nothing I like." Andersen made a mock shiver. "It would be cold. Close to absolute zero."

"Certainly not promising." Cruzet nodded. "Though I think it may once have been rather like Earth. Just slightly more massive, it has mountain chains that seem to show early tectonic activity. The orbit's almost circular, only nine million kilometers out from the dwarf. It rotates in tidal lock. Same face always toward the star. That's the face away from us."

He gestured at the disk.

"I take the ice as evidence that it once had seas. And, of course, an atmosphere. All lost or frozen out since the star died ages ago."

"The other hemisphere?" she asked. "Would it be warmer?"

"Once, maybe. Not today."

"When we get a better look—"

"By whose authority?" Hinch's raucous squawk startled her. He had come out of the elevator and stopped close behind her, a gaunt gray ghost blinking blindly into the dimness though thick-lensed glasses. "Captain Stecker must be consulted."

"You said he was sleeping." Glengarth shrugged and turned back to the others. "We have to act at once, because we came out of quantum mode with such a high velocity. Braking into an approach orbit will take a lot of fuel. I believe we can get down safe, though with too little left for take-off if we don't like the place. I want you to realize that we'd be there to stay—"

"Not so fast!" Hinch snarled. "Hold everything till the captain awakes."

Seeming not to hear him, Glengarth gestured at Cruzet.

"Before we decide, there's something else."

"Nothing we expected." Cruzet's thin sharp voice reflected none of the anxious tension that had seized her. "The planet was certainly warmer once. Life may have been possible, but that was long ago. A star takes time to cool. It must have stopped emitting any significant radiation a billion years ago. We'd assumed that it was dead.

"Till Andy got this."

Andersen touched the console behind him. She watched that dim red globe swell to fill its window in the simulated sky. A faint green dot appeared on the center of the great ice cap and grew to outline a wide green blot that spread across the ice from a mountain ridge.

"He'd been with Mark Senn on the search telescope. He can tell you—"

"What the bleedin' hell?" Standing close beside her, Hinch yelped in dismay. "What's that?"

"You tell us." Andersen shrugged and turned again to the others. "What you see is our digital record of something the radar sweep picked up. False color again, now to show elevation differences. A cluster of objects that stand two or three kilometers tall above the level of the ice. They look as massive as mountain peaks. Some of them have sharply defined geometric shapes. Senn thinks they have to be artificial."

Rima's breath had stopped. She heard a fan whirring faintly, and a muttered obscenity from Hinch.

"Constructed by intelligence. That's what he believes." Andersen had paused to stare at that green-glowing enigma, and she felt his awe. "There's something on the ice, maybe made of ice, larger than anything artificial ought to be. A city? A fortress? What else can you imagine?"

"Or can it be natural?" She tried to shake off her dread. "We don't know the geology, or how the planet froze. Glaciers do form hummocks and split into crevasses. Icebergs can be enormous."

"Rima, there's something else." Glengarth was still craning at the outlined images. "Evidence of something, I don't know what. Listen to Andy."

"I was on the light telescope while Senn ran the radar scan," Andersen said. "Not that I could actually see the planet, only its shadow on the stars it occluded. I wasn't really expecting to make out anything more. Not till I saw a flashing light almost at the center of that radar pattern."

She heard Hinch gasp as if from a blow.

"Only a flicker, really. Off and on. And nearly too faint to see—the planet's still half a million kilometers away. I called Tony."

"Only lightning, I tried to imagine." Cruzet's narrow shoulders twitched as if in apology for all he couldn't explain. "But lightning shouldn't happen on an airless planet so close to zero Kelvin. The colors were another riddle. Red at first, shimmering into violet before it went out. A moment of darkness, and then it came again. It repeated every time the search beam passed, as if something had taken it for a signal and tried to answer."

"Something?" she echoed. "What?"

"Ice gods?" Andersen seemed to mock her amazement, or perhaps his own uncertainty. "Ice giants? What sort of creatures would you expect to find there on the ice? What could possibly survive there, where only the stars have shone for geologic ages?"

"Are you— Are you sure?"

Her whisper died. They all stared in silence at that enigma on the simulated stars. Hinch moved abruptly, retreating toward the elevator.

"I wouldn't trust my own senses." She heard Cruzet's quiet comment. "Neither would Andy or Senn. Mr. Mondragon also had a look. We all agree on what we seemed to see. Something none of us is prepared to explain."

"If a landing can be made, I wish to volunteer." The stowaway's voice was so soft she barely heard him. "I think we must discover what signals us from the ice."

"We ought to know more than we do," Andersen added, "before we think of any landing."

"A hard option." Glengarth turned to scan their faces. "If we don't put down, our high velocity will take us past the planet and close around the dwarf. The gravity assist will sling us away at twice our present velocity. Sling us out of the gravity well."

"With no second chance," Cruzet added. "We land now or never."

"If we don't . . ." Rima shivered, staring into the empty midnight sky. "What then?"

"We've found no hint of any other planetary object. I suppose we'd drift—"

"Drift?" A harsh snort from Hinch. "Drift till our food's used up? Till we're eating each other? Till the last man's gone?"

"I hope not," Glengarth murmured. "We're surely too civilized for that."

"Think again." Hinch glared from the elevator door. "I'm going down to wake the captain."

"If you can," Glengarth called. "And let him read the Mission Convenant, a document he should have signed before he came aboard. He'll find he had a change of status when we left quantum mode. Our old laws and rules are gone forever. We're now a new democracy, governing ourselves. I doubt that he ever took the oath, but that's the situation."

Hinch stood gaping, shaking a gnarly fist.

"Idiots!" he gasped. "A ship of howling idiots if they think the captain gives a bleedin' damn for a scrap of paper he never saw!"

The elevator swallowed him.

●

"We are civilized," Glengarth murmured when he was gone. "Most of us. I hope."

"And lucky, really," Andersen said. "Lucky to get out of wave mode alive, with the ship intact and a planet to explore. Even that one."

Wryly, he nodded at the radar image.

"It doesn't look friendly." Silent for a moment, Rima shrugged and forced a fleeting smile. "But we are equipped to terraform any world we find. We can hope to find soil under the ice, or at least rock we can grind into soil. More than just water, the ice will give us hydrogen for fusion power. After all, we were never promised paradise."

"Seguro que sí!" Carlos grinned more widely. "I saw los topos de hierro in the hold. The great machines that dig."

She couldn't help casting a thoughtful glance at him.

Hinch didn't return to the dome. When a steward brought a breakfast tray to Stecker's cabin, he found the two shouting at each other over a table littered with empty glasses and dirty dishes. They sat silently glowering while he swept up broken dishes and the fragments of a shattered whisky bottle. Leaving the cabin, he heard Hinch cursing the captain for dragging him off Earth to die in a frozen hellhole.

●

Kip was awake when Rima returned to their cabin. He listened very quietly to what she said about the meeting in the dome, and asked what ice gods would be like.

"Not gods, really," she said. "Dr. Andersen was only using a Norse myth to imply that he had no idea what could be flashing a signal from the ice—if that could really be a signal. There never were any actual ice gods."

"Yet they did see something real," he insisted. "Something big, if the towers in the city are two kilometers tall. What built them, if the ice gods didn't?"

"We don't know what it is." She frowned and looked past him, speaking half to herself. "I never imagined we'd wind up anywhere like this. We've no idea what to expect."

"Won't we meet the giants?" Kip was very serious. "If they made that rainbow flash to answer our search beam, it must have been some kind of signal. What did they mean to tell us?"

"Nobody knows."

"Mom, are you afraid?"

"We're worried." She nodded, her voice grave and slow. "Mr. Glengarth and all of us. I think we have to land, but it should be on the other face of the planet, as far as we can get from that flash on the ice. If something really saw us, it might be better if they never know we've landed. Or not, at least, till we can find out what they are. Anyhow, you'd better forget Andy's ice gods and go back to sleep."

He lay silent for a time.

"Mom?" his voice came suddenly. "Are you sorry? Sorry we came?"

She thought she had to be honest.

"I suppose I should be," she said. "Because of you and Day."

"Don't," he told her. "I'm glad we're here. We're like the Legion and Captain Cometeer. I want to find out what the ice gods are."

Soon she heard his regular breathing, but she lay awake a long time, trying to imagine the future for him and Day. On a world of dead ice and naked stone, under a sky where no sun had shone for endless ages. To be here forever. To build a home for them. To plant the human seed. Could that happen? Longing for some small grain of Kip's reckless confidence, she finally slept.

The children's voices woke her. Day was molding a tiny Me Me with clay they had brought from the rec room. Kip was busy with his Game Box.

"Mom," he called to her brightly, "I had a dream that ought to cheer you up. I was on a great adventure with my Legion crew beyond the Gate. We landed the *Starhawk* on the ice cap and met the ice gods. Only like you said they weren't gods at all, but monsters with the shape of thunderclouds. They fought us with ice lightning and hail.

"But we beat them! Because heat kills them. Their hailstones all melted before they could hurt us. One of them tried to strike me with ice lightning, but my warm breath shriveled it to nothing. The hot blast of our engines drove them off the ice. We'll be okay on the planet.

"We'll be the real ice gods!"

"I hope," she whispered. "At least we can hope."

Nine

Roak asked to see Lieutenant Washburn. Kellick took him to her office on the deck above. In spite of her size and chocolate complexion, she reminded him of his mother. The same alert brown eyes in a very similar wide and patient face. A different, deeper voice, but just as quietly reasonable. He thought the same appeals should work with her.

"Mr. Roak?" She looked inquiringly at Kellick, who stood with him at her desk. "Still a suspect?"

"We have evidence to implicate him. His briefcase contains a cashmere sweater. We found fibers from the sweater on the device. The timer shows when it was set. That was after he came aboard."

"Device?" he protested hotly. "I know nothing about any device."

She turned silently to look him over. The jailer had brought him a razor and a comb, as well as the yellow coveralls that he wore now like a brand of suspicion. He saw no warmth in her searching stare.

"Imagine the shock to me." He let his voice sharpen. "I'd finished the inspection and cleared the ship for takeoff. I was planning to go down and watch it from the bunker. With no warning at all, I was shanghaied—"

"Imagine the shock to us," she broke in. "We'd be dead if we hadn't been warned. Luckily, we did discover and disarm the device. But the guards at the entry hatch kept a traffic log. It shows that nobody went off the ship after the timer was set." Her voice fell. "The perpetrator is still aboard."

"The wetback—"

"Mr. Mondragon?" Sharply, she cut him off again. "A man of remarkable ability. He fixed a glitch in our computer. He's working with the search team now. Mr. Glengarth says we're lucky to have him aboard.

"As for you . . ."

She shook her head, looking hard at him.

"Just give me a chance." Begging, he recalled long-ago scenes with his mother. "As for the cashmere fibers, ask your people if they stowed the device and my briefcase on the same shelf. You won't find any evidence to hang me, because I didn't bring any bomb aboard.

"My bad luck!" Watching her face, he managed a rueful laugh. "Frankly, I'm stunned. I don't know what to say, except that now I've got to make the best of things as they are. Don't I deserve as much of a chance as the Mex?"

"Okay." She turned abruptly to Kellick. "Get him some work clothes and take him to Jesus. That's Jesus Rivera," she told Roak. "The chief cook. He wants help in the galley."

"Thank you!" He tried to sound happy about it. "I really thank you."

The words were hard to say when he remembered the heat of prison kitchens where he had worked, the harsh commands, the stink of burnt grease, the haste and sweat and thankless toil. Spic work, nigger work. He could take the heat for a week if he had to, maybe two weeks, but a licensed and certified launch inspector was certainly qualified for a white man's job.

"Give him his chance," she told Kellick. "But tell Jesus to watch him."

●

They spiraled in toward the planet, searching out a spot for a new human home. Rima wanted to name it Hope, but Glengarth shrugged the notion off, with a small sad grin.

"Stecker and his gang are in charge, in spite of the covenant. They did give me permission to set down when I'd convinced Captain Stecker we had no choice, but Hinch wants to name the place Hellfrost."

She winced.

"We've got to hope. It's all we have."

"Hope or not, we're setting down." He turned to Cruzet. "Keep the radar off the ice cap. Stecker agrees that we must land on the sunward face, as far as we can from the source of that signal—if it was a signal. No use tipping off the natives to where we are."

He glanced at the holoscreen, where the planet was still only a small blot, hardly larger than the dead sun.

"If there are natives," he muttered. "A notion I'm not ready to swallow."

She joined the team at the telescope monitors as the orbits narrowed, scanning the ice for any possible living space, for any promise of soil and minerals and usable water.

"If it really is water ice," Cruzet muttered doubtfully. "Not frozen nitrogen or methane. If it was never contaminated with something deadly to us. If soil and useful ores were ever formed."

"I'm sure they were." Andersen had studied geology before he turned to engineering. "From all we've seen, I think the planet may have been rather like our own Earth until the sun went dark."

The ice cap, now an ice continent that covered the whole outward face, was rimmed with lofty mountain chains. Glaciers had flowed around them into a vast ocean on the sunward hemisphere. That was frozen now, a featureless plain broken only by a few chains of rocky hills that had been island groups.

Using radar now as well as telescopes, they searched a long peninsula that thrust like a narrow dagger into the frozen sea. Kilometers of ice covered half its rocky backbone but thinned toward the tip. Eroded ridges and narrow beaches looked nearly free of ice. Leaving Sternberg at the controls, Glengarth came down to study the monitors.

"Our best chance." Andersen pointed. "Open spots there on the east coast where I think we might land. There's a chance for soil down under the cliffs, water from glacier ice, maybe useful minerals we can mine or extract from the ocean brine."

"We'll touch down there," Glengarth agreed. "If Hinch and Stecker make no trouble."

●

Mondragon and Andersen took turns with Rima and Mark Senn, searching the cap again and again as their landing orbit brought it closer. Mountain peaks jutting through the ice, flow lines of old glaciers, crags and crevasses where the ice had splintered on its way to the sea. At the wide field telescope on their final pass above the cap, Mondragon caught his breath and whistled in awe.

"Un castillo!" he whispered. "La fortaleza de los gigantes!"

"Sir, we're over the source of the flash," Andersen called to Glengarth in the control dome above. "Even without radar, we can make out some detail by starlight. There is something with the look of a fortress city. A cluster of mountain-sized objects with very peculiar shapes. Rectangular, round, one oddly starlike, all too neatly cut out to be natural formations. And really gigantic. There's a wall around them that must be two or three kilometers tall."

He paused to study the monitors again.

"We're crossing overhead now, at three hundred kilometers, and I think the whole complex stands in a hole in the cap. Tall ice cliffs all around it, a dozen kilometers out. It makes you wonder. Did they have technology to fight the cold?"

"Any activity now?" Glengarth asked. "Any sign we've been seen?"

"Nothing visible, sir. Thank God, nothing flashing at us."

●

They glided over the peninsula. Using the radar again, Cruzet called altitude readings to the dome. Mondragon, still at the telescope, searched old beaches and the flat white waste of the frozen sea.

"Un otro destello!" He yelled the Spanish in sudden excitement. "Destello de todos colores!"

The colors flashed somewhere out on the desert of ice, far beyond the tip of the peninsula. A hot scarlet point burned against the dark, turned yellow, turned green and then blue, vanished in an instant. Cruzet and Andersen rushed to look and watched it blaze again, and yet again.

"Are you certain?" Glengarth was listening on the interphone. "Really certain?"

They were certain.

"Kill the radar."

"Done. And I wonder—" Andersen hesitated. "Should we abort the landing? There's fuel if we stretch it to carry us on to some ocean island. Even the far coast, with a bit of luck. We're moving fast. Only three or four minutes to decide."

Glengarth frowned, but only for a moment.

"I'll consult the other leaders," he said. "You inform the captain."

He called Stecker's cabin. The instrument purred a long time before he heard Jake Hinch's impatient snarl.

"The captain's sick. Leave us alone."

"Tell him we've seen another display of spectral colors. From somewhere out on the ice, hundreds of kilometers ahead. Mr. Glengarth is considering whether to abort—"

"Captain Stecker don't give a bleedin' damn!" Hinch yelled, and hoarsely muttered, "We're dead already."

"Not yet," Andersen told him. "This world may look grim, but with luck enough it may give us a chance—"

"What bleedin' chance! Come back in a ruttin' billion years, and you'll find our bones in the ship and the ice littered with the mummies of the cowards that ran from the hunters—"

●

"Proceed as planned." With half a minute to go, Glengarth announced his decision. "With no good survey of ocean islands ahead or the other shore, and no fuel margin for the unexpected, we've no alternative."

They came down on a rocky headland. When the rockets were quenched and the ship secure, he called the leaders to the control dome. The holoscreens showed dark cliffs climbing toward the ice in the north and west. The dead black sky fell like a curtain to the dimly starlit waste of ancient frost that spread south and east forever.

"All unknown." Glengarth spoke absently, staring at the black east horizon. "We've no such science as planetary cryonics, but I can't imagine any sort of life here. I'd rather think the flash was some harmless natural phenomenon."

"Maybe," Cruzet muttered. "But don't ask me what."

"It happened in response to our radar search." Andersen stood blinking into that dim and featureless flatness. "I take that as evidence of some native intelligence, aware of us. We can't relax till we know what it is."

"Perhaps," Glengarth muttered. "But any approach might invite hostility. If there is any native intelligence, let it make the first move."

"Agreed." Rima turned to study the westward cliffs. "I think we're here to stay. Our first concern is sheer survival. I want to search for possible resources and a site where we can build or dig a habitat."

●

Jim Cheng, who had degrees in fusion and planetary engineering, had joined them in the dome. Glengarth turned to him.

"A council. Call it a council of war." His tone was wryly grim. "With Captain Stecker indisposed, we're in a hard spot. I want to consider options, and I hope we can agree on a common front."

"I took a course in terraforming." Cheng gestured at the ancient beaches that sloped down to the ice from the ridge where they had landed. "I think we're down in a promising location."

"Promising?" Cruzet stared. "How?"

"Considering the planet." He shrugged. "Of course we'll have to begin underground. There's water enough. Hydrogen for fusion. Sand and gravel washed down from the cliffs. Silt to make soil when we add organics. The beach looks like stuff we can excavate."

"Frozen hard as bedrock now." Rima frowned. "Digging won't be easy."

Mondragon stood near them, trying to keep his eyes away from her but still captured by her bright hair and her good shape, by the warm tones of her voice, the faint scent he caught when she was near.

The perfume was Sea Rose, which she had never been able to afford. Not until their last hectic days on Earth. Saving only enough for the taxi and a tip, she'd emptied her purse to buy new adventure cards for Kip's Game Box, a cute red jumpsuit for Day, and the tiny vial for herself.

"We'll have to drill a few test holes," she was telling Cheng, "to locate a site for the habitat."

Mondragon wanted to speak of terraforming. Andersen had showed him the laser drills in the cargo hold, powerful fusion-driven machines that could explode permafrost into steam and powdered rock. Yet he kept silent. She never seemed to see him. He longed desperately to make her know him as something more than the mojado stowaway, the worthless wetback, perhaps even the criminal saboteador.

Pero cómo? How?

"You're getting ahead of the game," he heard Andersen saying. "Our number one priority ought to be discovering what's out there." He gestured. "Why that apparent signal."

"I'd like to know." She turned to frown at the black eastward sky and the black sun-disk that hung low among the unfamiliar stars. "But if the planet froze and died a billion or ten billion years ago, I doubt there's anything still alive and dangerous."

"About those flashes?" Andersen frowned. "The colors appeared in their spectral order, red to violet. I can't think of any natural cause. They seem to have been directed at us. I think they must have been produced by some sophisticated technology."

"Maybe," she said. "But those are the colors in a natural rainbow."

"Could be." He shrugged, rather grimly. "But there are no raindrops here. No sunlight to be refracted. I can't help suspecting that we're meeting something interested in us."

"A beacon lit to welcome visitors?"

"Or to lure us into a trap?"

"In either case," she said, "I think we should begin digging in. I see no better option." She turned to Glengarth. "Sir, do you?"

"Others do." She saw his jaws tighten. "Fujiwara and Krasov, in planning and logistics. They want us to get off the planet."

"By our bootstraps?" She frowned at him, eyebrows lifted. "With the fuel tanks dry, I think we're here to stay."

"They're optimists." Wryly, he grinned. "Or idiots. Trying to convince Cheng that we can dig a new launch pit. Build a new phase converter. Take the ship back into quantum flight."

"Ask Jim." Glancing at the other groups, she dropped her voice. "He'll tell you we've no equipment for that. We'd be crazy to try it."

"I guess we're all a little crazy, but a lot of our people are desperate enough to risk anything."

"You're in charge." And she urged him sharply, "Don't let them!"

"Stecker's still the captain." His face set harder. "If he ever decides to sober up." He turned to Andersen. "While we're waiting, I'll let you and Cruzet go out to find what made that flash. If you're really game for that."

"We're game!" Andersen said, and Cruzet grinned with more emotion than he often showed. "Sir, we really are!"

●

They had brought two scout vehicles, designed for the exploration of hostile environments. Andersen inflated a plastic shelter dome outside the main air lock and began assembling an eight-wheeled spider. Mondragon heard about it, and found him in the workshop.

"Señor, I wish to come with you."

"Carlos, I'm sorry." Andersen shook his head. "I like you. You've proved that you do know computers. But I'm afraid—"

"Por favor, Señor!" His plea tumbled out. "Soy Mexicano. They call me mojado, wetback, because I am illegal. But I can learn. I am strong. I wish very much to aid la Doctora Virili and her plan to transform the planet."

"Siento." Frowning, Andersen paused to study him. "I'm sorry, Carlos, but we have no notion what we'll run into. I want men with the right skills and experience. A driver for the spider. A trained mechanic. Somebody, if I can find anybody, who has experience in the Arctic. You just don't fit."

He turned away, lips quivering.

"Señor—" He looked around the shop and came back, arms spread in appeal. "Let me help you here. I can carry tools. Clean the floor. Anything."

After a moment, Andersen grinned.

"Bien, compadre. Get to work. Pick up those metal scraps and throw them in the bin."

Ten

Day woke, shivering, and crawled into the berth with Rima.

"Hold me, Mommy!" she whimpered. "Hold me tight. I'm freezing."

"What's wrong, dear?" Rima cuddled her close. "You don't feel cold."

"I am too cold! I went to find Me Me, and something chased me."

"You're okay now." Rima stroked her hair. "You must have dreamed, but you're safe here with me."

"But Me Me's freezing, out there in the dark. The black things are after her."

"Darling, please don't fret. You know we left Me Me safe, back at home with the nice man in the taxi. He said his own little girl would take care of her for you."

"But Mommy, Me Me knew we couldn't come back. She

came to look for me. She's dying on the ice and the black things are hunting her."

"It's just a dream, dear. An ugly dream you must forget."

"I can't forget. Me Me needs me."

She went back to sleep at last, but it was a troubled sleep. She huddled close to Rima. Once she started and cried out sharply.

"Me Me! Me Me! If you can hear me, try to hide. Hide till I get there."

●

The spider was a huge, ungainly metal insect that carried its bright steel shell high on eight long legs with big-tired wheels for feet. A heat lamp on a tall mast shone to shield it from metal-shattering cold. They assembled it in the pressure balloon and took it out for test runs on the old beach. When Andersen declared it ready, Glengarth named Sternberg to command it.

Joseph Sternberg was the second officer. He was past fifty, five or six kilos overweight, with short-cut hair that had gone gray, but he was still erect and fit. He called them into the spider's cabin, a narrow space between the pilot bay and the tiny private alcove at the rear. They sat on berths that folded out of the hull.

"An iffy thing," he told them. "A planet that ought to be dead. We may meet something hostile. I hope we don't. In any case, the effort is critical, and I'm happy to be here. I think we ought to know one another.

"Starting with myself, I had a career in the military. A test pilot for the spaceplanes till Congress axed the program. When my father's health failed, I retired to take over our family business. We were general contractors for StarSeed, building special equipment. Designing this vehicle was one of our projects till the Mission ran up unpaid debts for machines on order and finally put us out of business before we ever got it

built. Captain Alt was an old friend. He let me join the crew."
He shook his head, jaw set hard. "I miss him."

Los Doctores Cruzet and Andersen introduced themselves. Mondragon had found Cruzet hard to know, often
away among the stars, but Andersen had made himself muy
simpático. A red-haired Tejano engineer, he understood
Chihuahua Spanish and laughed at the dangers of quantum
flight.

"Now, Mr. Mondragon?" Sternberg nodded at them and
paused to study him. "Mr. Glengarth wants to limit any
losses. The three of us are enough to run the vehicle, but
Andy says you've made yourself useful here. If you really
want to come along, will you tell us something about yourself?"

"Gracias, Señor! Con much gusto."

Cruzet and Andersen had never seemed to care that he
was only a small brown man from a poor Chihuahua pueblito.
Sternberg, however, was still un gringo extranjero who must
be persuaded to let him come on this great mechanical spider, to earn his place among them and perhaps a smile from
la rubia.

Eagerly, mixing Spanish words with his unaccustomed
English, he spoke of Cuerno del Oro and his small computer
skills, and of Don Ignacio, who had told him of the quantum
craft that outran time, flying to the end of the universe in less
than an instant.

"You understand the risk?" Sternberg asked him. "We
don't know where we're going. We may not get back."

"I understand." He shrugged. "No le hace."

Sternberg turned inquiringly to Andersen. "I believe he
was a suspect—"

"I was accused," Mondragon said. "But por los santos I
brought no bomb."

Sternberg frowned. "I think his case went to the captain?"

Captain Stecker had come down with el Señor Hinch to

see the completed machine. Handsome as un torero, he had the grand manner of Don Alfonso Madera, who had sometimes come with Don Ignacio to the fiestas. Don Alfonso was a clever picaro, fond of women and mescal. He had stolen an ancient registro from the church and made its faded pages into maps of the lost Cuerno mine. He sold the maps to turistas, bragging in la cantina that he could persuade los gringos that baby shit was gold.

The captain, unfortunately, had never found time to consider the matter of Mondragon.

"He admits that the Fairshare pickets did help him get aboard," Andersen said. "But there are no fingerprints. No actual evidence to connect him with the bomb. He knows computers. He has made himself useful." Cruzet nodded. "We want him."

"Good enough," Sternberg nodded. "You're with us."

"Mil gracias, señor! We must reach el faro."

"The beacon?" Andersen turned to frown at Sternberg. "It's true we won't feel safe here till we know what caused that flash. But still I'm not ready to think it was any sort of signal."

●

High in the control dome, where the holoscreens let them look down across the frost-rimmed rocks on the frozen beaches and the endless waste of starlit ice that lay flat to the black horizon, Glengarth cleared them for the expedition.

"Keep in constant touch," he said. "All we want is information about what's out there. Take no avoidable risk. Get what data you can. And get back alive."

"Okay, sir," Sternberg said. "We're on our way."

They turned to shake hands with la rubia, who had come to speak of their plans. Mondragon flinched from a stab of jealousy of these fortunate Anglos, men whom los santos had favored with the culture and learning that made them her equals. One of them, perhaps, fortunate enough to win her love?

He dared not think of all he longed for.

●

Jake Hinch was waiting in the work balloon when they went down to board the spider. A hawk-faced angry man with a ragged beard and a black beret, he was Stecker's close companion but still a stranger to everybody else.

"Orders from the captain." He showed Sternberg a scrawled note on a stained and crumpled sheet of StarSeed stationery, with Stecker's signature. "I'm taking command."

"Replacing me?" Sternberg blinked at the note. "Can you tell me why?"

"Ask Stecker."

The captain was not in the control room. He didn't answer his cabin phone. Sternberg sent a security man to knock on his cabin door. At last he did call back. Listening, Sternberg made a bitter face.

"Yes sir," he said. "Very well, sir." He hung up and turned ruefully to Andersen. "Our good captain. He's tipsy and not entirely coherent, but he says he's putting Mr. Hinch in charge because he wants the truth about whatever we find. Yet I gather that he doesn't fully trust him or anybody else."

Cruzet and Andersen straightened to salute as Sternberg turned abruptly to leave the balloon. He came back to shake their hands, shrugged at Mondragon, and walked back through the lock. Hinch stood with his bag beside the spider, impatiently waiting.

"Sir," Andersen told him, "Captain Stecker does confirm that you are in command. What are your orders?"

"As you were," he muttered. "Carry on as planned."

Carrying his bag into the vehicle, Cruzet heard the clink of bottles, shrugged at Andersen, and showed him to the curtained cubicle at the rear of the cabin. He went inside and closed the curtain.

●

The vehicle was new to all of them, but they had trained on the beach and it was easy enough to drive. Andersen let Mondragon take the wheel to pull them through the lock and down the rocky slope to the frozen ocean.

"Steer by the sun. Just to the right of it. Claro?"

"Claro, señor." Elation hushed his voice. "Just to the right."

Alone in the nose bubble, he caught a faint ozone bite from the air cycler, which Andersen was still adjusting. Listening, he heard the whisper of the turbine, the muffled murmur when the others spoke, the rustle of his clothing when he moved. Nothing else, because this dead world had no air to carry sound.

Lighting the ice for only a few hundred meters, the head lamps blinded him to everything beyond. He turned them off and let his eyes adjust to the starlight. He saw a dim gray world with all color lost, except in the dull red glow of the heat lamp that was their shield against the killing cold.

Leaning over the wheel, he scanned the flat infinity of bone white frost ahead. A film of frozen argon and nitrogen, Cruzet said, the last trace of the vanished atmosphere. He scanned the splendid sky above it, steady stars burning brighter than those he had known in his boyhood in Chihuahua, set in constellations he had never seen. Ice and stars and dead black sun, nothing else.

The cold dwarf sun was a round black spot on the stars. Never rising, never setting, it drifted very slowly higher and very slowly back again with the motion Cruzet called libration. Live stars blazed close around it, never dimming or even twinkling; no air or clouds had veiled them for geologic ages. The level whiteness showed no break ahead, no mark behind except the faint dark scar their tires made.

What of la luz? The alien light?

He recalled the riddle of it when they were coming down to land. A bright sudden light, burning through every color of the spectrum from deepest red to darkest violet, but gone before anybody could be sure of anything. It had seemed to come from far out on the frozen ocean, nearly due east.

Five hundred kilometers out, Andersen said. Closer to a thousand, Cruzet thought. The ice around it had looked bright on the radar image, as if rough enough to make a strong reflection. Perhaps an island mountain? Cruzet, who had seen it at a higher resolution, said it had looked too tall and thin to be any natural mountain.

A fortress of the ice gods?

Those gods of ice had been only a joke from Andersen, but nobody had thought of anything more plausible. The flash had come when the radar search beam swept the spot. Had it been an actual warning, from anything alive?

Would it come again?

●

Cruzet came at last to take the wheel, and Mondragon climbed into the quartz-domed lookout bubble and kept on watching till he dozed and shook himself awake to watch again. Ice and stars and dead sun-disk, nada más.

Andersen came to drive. At the kitchen shelf in the cabin, Cruzet stirred dry powder into hot water to make the bitter stuff they called syncafe and opened a pack of omninute wafers. Mondragon sliced a cold slab of soyamax, wishing for the goat enchiladas his mother used to make. They called Hinch to ask if he was hungry.

"Garbage!" he shouted through the curtain, voice thick from whatever he had brought in his bottles. "I've got stuff of my own."

Andersen stopped the vehicle and came back to eat. Mondragon slept a few hours, took the wheel again, and looked out. Frost and stars and dead black sun. Still half asleep, he yawned and worked his stiff hands, stretched and stood behind the wheel, slapped his face and sat again, gripped the wheel and blinked at the level dark horizon.

Something there?

No spectral flash. Only a small black dot on the flat black horizon, but maybe something far away. He rubbed his eyes and veered a little toward it. A mountain? Another dwelling of the ice giants, like those on the ice cap? If actual giants could live here, flashing signs to visitors. His breath came faster. Should he radio the ship?

"There is something out there," Glengarth had told them. "Likely harmless, but I agree that we'd better find out. If you come upon anything unusual, anything at all, call back at once. If you approach, do it with all the care you can."

He reached for the radiophone, but stopped his hand when he saw that the object ahead looked suddenly closer, too small for any kind of mountain. When at last it crept into the heat lamp's glow, he saw that it was no monolithic obelisk, but only a solitary boulder.

Yet that itself was a puzzle to him. What had tossed it here, so far from any land? He steered closer for a better look. It was ice, a dark mass the size of a car, jaggedly broken. Searching his small pool of dim red light, he found nothing else except smaller fragments shattered off when it fell. An ice meteorite, fallen a million years ago? Perhaps a billion?

Level frost, black sun, endless midnight, scars of ancient cosmic cataclysm, nada más. He shrugged and drove on again, just to the right of the dead black disk. Frost that had never thawed and never would. Stars that never changed. He blinked his aching eyes, his mind drifting back to Cuerno del Oro.

To the flat-roofed adobes around the plaza, to the mud on the rutted streets when the rains came, the dust when they failed, the old stone church where his mother had taken him to mass. He remembered the ragged child he had been, bare feet numb and aching on frosty winter mornings when he herded his father's goats over the rocky hills above the village and wondered if the stars could be diamonds on the doors of heaven.

He thought of Don Ignacio Morelos, who sometimes returned for the fiestas and spoke of the starbirds that flew from the white sands in el norte to scatter brave men and women to find new lives on the richer worlds that might exist out beyond those shining doors.

"I'll learn to ride the starships," he used to promise the don. "When I have years enough."

"Nunca." The lean old don always shook his head. "The stars want no stupid campesinos."

Remembering, he felt glad la rubia need never know Cuerno del Oro, never feel the pain of life there, never smell the sewer ditch or swat the flies or hear the hungry niños crying. She would blame los pobres for all they could not help, scorn the ignorant mojado—

Or was the thought unfair to her?

He thought of her joven hijo Kip, who had found him hiding on the ship, seen his dripping blood and loyally kept his secret. Kip had become un buen amigo, but she was still the Anglo stranger who hardly knew he was alive. Yet she might learn to see him as a man, if he could prove his worth here among these pioneers of the stars.

If he could. Con suerte.

●

A sharp jolt bought him back to the frost and the boulders. Fragments of broken ice scattered the pale ruby glow all around him. He rubbed his eyes and found more fragments emerging from the starlight ahead, looking always larger until they became a barrier along the starlit horizon.

A sharper jolt. The spider rocked and dropped.

"Carlos?" Cruzet shouted from the cabin. "What hit us?"

He braked the spider to search his small red-lit island.
The vehicle had dropped off a ledge half a meter high, hidden under the frost.

"We fell." He pointed at the ledge. "A drop I never saw."

"A fracture." Andersen was peering over his shoulder.
"The old sea is frozen to the bottom. Old quakes here could
fracture it like any rock." He turned to scan the boulder wall
ahead. "Ejecta, I think, from a meteor crater. We'll get
around it. But then—"

He stopped himself and stood silent, gazing out across the
frost, his craggy face lit.

"An adventure I never expected." He swung to grin at
Cruzet. "You know I began in geology. Switched to astrophysics because our old Earth was known too well. Now this
whole planet's ours. A new geology for us to read!"

"Ours?" Cruzet stood with him, staring off into the east,
where they thought the flash had been. "Are you sure?"

●

Andersen went down to keep the fusion engine running.

"My turn to drive." Cruzet beckoned Mondragon away
from the wheel. "Get some sleep."

He crawled into his berth in the main cabin. Hinch was
snoring behind the curtain, but he couldn't sleep. Cuerno del
Oro was too far away, the world of the ice gods too cold and
dark and strange. He climbed again into the lookout bubble.
Cruzet had steered north to find a way around the crater. The
frost beyond lay flat again, white and flat to the black horizon. Ice and midnight, the dead ghosts of ages long forgotten, nada más.

He sat at the instrument board, staring out across that
dead starlit infinity, till the chime of the watch clock roused
him to read the temperature of the surface radiation and
enter it in the log. He used the sextant, as Andersen had
taught him, to get a position that let him add one more black

ink dot to the line of black dots on the blank page that was to be their map. And he called the ship.

"Rima Virili here." La rubia's voice startled him. A voice like a song, musical with her beauty. "Acting aide to Mr. Glengarth."

"Buenas—" He stopped himself. He should not let the Spanish remind her what he was. "Carlos Mondragon, reporting."

"Yes?" Her words were courteous and quick, but empty of the feeling that ached in him. "Anything unusual?"

"No problems." He tried to speak with the same empty briskness. "Position four hundred seventy-one kilometers east of the ship. Eighteen kilometers north. We swung north to get around a crater where Mr. Andersen says a meteor struck the ice. Ice temperature nine degrees Kelvin. The way ahead looks clear. Nothing unusual. No island, no mountain, no signal light."

"Thank you, Mr. Mondragon. I'll inform Mr. Glengarth. Have you anything more?"

He wanted to ask of el joven Kip. And of Day, the younger niñita, who had la rubia's bright hair and grieved for Me Me, the panda doll she had to leave on Earth. He wanted to tell her that even an untaught campesino might have the emotions of a man.

"Mr. Mondragon?" He had not spoken. "Anything else?"

She was still the gringo extranjera. He heard no warmth in her crisp, inquiring tone.

"Nada," he said. "Nothing more."

"Keep in touch," she said. "Mr. Glengarth is concerned. He wants full reports."

The telephone clicked.

He was nadie. Nobody to her. Nor to any Anglo, except perhaps her fine muchachito Kip. Yet he sat there searching the frost, wondering if her art of terraforming could truly be the magic that might turn this dead and desolate planet into the home she wished to make for los niñitos. How could anything survive at nine degrees Kelvin? Who except the ice gods, which were perhaps only Andersen's little joke.

Or perhaps the actual masters of the planet?

●

The endless day dragged into another endless day, and still the ancient frost stretched ahead forever. The black sun crept slowly higher. Radio contact became a matter of chance.

"We're out of direct signal range," Andersen said. "Anything we get has to be reflected back from space by, I think, a broken ring of orbital dust, which sometimes is above us and sometimes isn't."

They were six hundred kilometers out. Eight hundred. A thousand. Cruzet was ready to turn back. They had eaten their ration of soyamax and omninute, washed down with bitter syncafe, and they were in the bubble, frowning at the tiny crosses that marked their path behind and gazing out across the starlit waste ahead.

"No sign of anything hostile. What we are chasing may be just a mirage."

"Radar doesn't make mirages," Andersen reminded him. "I've spoken to Mr. Hinch. He seems happy with his bottles, and he says he ain't going back. Not to Stecker's bleedin' deathtrap."

●

"Carlos, are you awake?"

Mondragon was alone in the bubble when Cruzet's sharp voice jarred him out of sleep.

"Qué?" Groggily, he sat up in the chair. "Now I am."

"Look out ahead and call the ship. If you can."

Stiff from sitting too long, he turned to look. Cruzet had slowed the machine. A few hundred meters ahead, a cliff had risen between the frost and the midnight sky, a sheer wall of starlit ice a dozen meters high. It ran straight to the right and the left for as far as he could see.

"Madre de Dios!" he breathed. "Qué es?"

"Another geologic fault. Tony says this was once a zone of quakes."

"Can we climb it?"

"Look just above it. We may not want to climb it."

He looked and saw nothing till a hot red point exploded like a nova deep inside the ice. It swelled into a burning disk. Bright orange burst into the crimson center and swelled again, turning green at the center. Hot blue exploded in it, making a target pattern as tall as the cliff. He saw no more change for another half minute. Then darkness spread from the middle till all the color was gone.

"A word from the locals." Cruzet's sharp ironic voice crackled out of the interphone. "Welcome, stranger? Or is the message Scram? Scram while you can?"

Eleven

Rima had called people with terraforming know-how to meet for a brainstorming session. A little group in neat blue duty jumpsuits stood with her in the control room, staring after the departing spider, which had faded into the infinity of dim gray starlight under the blaze of the midnight sky and the black sun's disk. Half had invented excuses not to come, and those here were grumbling.

"If you'll excuse me, Dr. Virili—" Fujiwara was a hydroponics engineer, a slim little Asian who spoke everyday American English without accent in a thin high voice. Pausing, he turned to smile and bow deferentially. "We're still waiting for Captain Stecker. Aren't you trying to jump the gun?"

"I don't think so. We came prepared to adapt ourselves to whatever planet we happened to reach. We ought to begin—"

They all fell silent when Jonas Roak came out of the el-

evator. Wearing grease-spattered coveralls, he smelled of
stale sweat and burnt soyamax.

"Sorry I'm late, Dr. Virili. A problem with Jesus." He
made a comic grimace. "Mr. Rivera kept me overtime in the
galley."

"No matter," she told him. "We're just beginning."

"Roak?" Roy Eisen bristled at him. A fusion engineer,
Eisen was a gruff-voiced thickset man with the manners of a
pugilist. "I thought you were in the brig."

"I was." Roak nodded, with a conciliatory smile. "My in-
fernal luck. I was just clearing the ship for takeoff when the
captain received the tip about the bomb. Security detained
everybody aboard while they searched the ship. We were already in the launch pit before they found the device and the
Mexican—he must have panicked and lost himself after he
set it.

"So I'm with you." He squared his shoulders, with a brave
smile for Rima. She was the best-looking woman aboard,
which made her now the loveliest woman in the world. He
had to drag his eyes away from the tempting contours of her
jumpsuit. "It isn't something I'd planned on, but I want to
make the best of it."

"I hope you do." A neutral tone; he must learn to warm
her.

"So you accuse Mondragon?" Eisen stared at him. "What
do you know about terraforming?"

"Of course I'm no engineer." He shrugged, happy that his
forged credentials were a trillion miles behind. "Only a certified launch inspector, but I guess you could call me a systems specialist." He smiled again at Rima. "Any terraforming project will require a diverse team of experts. I think I
have expertise to coordinate the effort."

"If you do—" Eisen nodded reluctantly. "We'll certainly
have to meld all our resources."

"I never expected this." Indra Singh raised her voice, a
sharp-edged nasal drone. She was a tall, willowy woman

wearing heavy gold rings and bracelets, her thick black hair piled into an untidy bun. She had come from anthropology to earn degrees in soil chemistry and bioengineering. "We can't hope to survive on the surface. We'll have to burrow into the permafrost."

She made a dismal face at the rocky beaches below.

"I suppose we can thaw it and bury ourselves in mud. Or will we strike native granite the machines can't touch? We can't plan anything till we can drill test holes and run seismic surveys."

"Which we're already planning," Rima said.

"Not much for me to plan." Nels Norgin was the Norwegian meteorologist, an expert in atmospheric circulations and climate control. "With no air and no weather and all the water frozen close to zero Kelvin . . ."

He shrugged and spread his hands.

"Stuck or not, I think we're here to stay." Mark Senn, the astrophysicist from the search team, spoke with quiet authority. "Krasov and Fujiwara spoke of getting back into quantum drive, but that's not possible."

"Are you certain?" Roak asked. "Captain Stecker was hoping—"

"I'm certain!" Eisen cut him off. "We terraform or die. I prefer not to die."

"Which is why we're here," Rima said. "We do have problems. Let's invent solutions."

"I stand with Dr. Virili." Ignoring Eisen's cold-eyed hostility, Roak smiled at her and turned to the others. "I hope you'll let me help with those solutions."

●

Calling the ship, Mondragon waited for la rubia's voice. For a long time all he heard was the faint rush and murmur of the galaxy's distant heart. When at last he caught a voice, it wasn't hers.

". . . garbled . . . signal garbled . . . please repeat . . ."

"Alpha calling." He tried again. "Reporting a wall of ice—"

"Carlos?" Glengarth's voice, suddenly stronger, edged with sharp concern. "What's happening?"

"A wall of ice across our path, Señor. Muy alto. El Doctor Cruzet is backing the spider away."

"Take no chances—"

"Something else, Señor. Más extraño. A bright light burning in the ice . . ."

"Can you describe it?"

"Circulos, señor. Circles of light that grow from the center like ripples on water till they show every color del arco iris. Though I think they cease now as we move away."

"Strange." Glengarth paused, perhaps not wanting to believe. "Can you determine any likely cause?"

"No, Señor, except that it appeared as we came near. El Doctor Cruzet thinks perhaps it is intended as a signal."

"From whom?"

"Yo no sé. Perhaps the beings of the mountain."

"Have you seen any mountain?"

"Not yet, Señor. All we see is the white frost that covers the ice all the way to the sky."

"I hope you find no mountain. Are you in danger now?"

"Creo que no. Now we are stopping again, a kilometer from the wall. The circles of color do not return."

"Let me speak to your commander."

"Mr. Hinch is below, sir. Sleeping. Or I think borracho."

"Get me Mr. Andersen."

"Andy here, sir." He spoke at once from the nose. "On the interphone."

"This wall?" Glengarth's tone had an anxious edge. "What about it?"

"It looks natural enough, sir. A natural geologic upthrust. The fault line runs north and south as far as we can see. Nothing to tell us when it happened. Could have been yesterday or more likely a billion years ago. But still I wonder. . . ."

Doubt slowed his voice.

"A riddle, sir. It stands in our way like a barrier. That beacon was burning in it like a warning to stop us."

"What's this about Mr. Hinch?"

"He's down in his berth. Probably drunk."

"I see." Glengarth paused. "He's an odd one. A surprise to me that Stecker sent him out, unless they'd had some kind of dustup. Any trouble to you?"

"None, sir. He just told us to carry on."

"Do that. Keep in touch. Any more you can say about this light in the ice?"

"It's nothing I can explain, sir. A target shape of expanding rings. The same colors we saw in that flash from the ice cap. Maybe meant to tell us we've come close enough."

"I think you have. Wake Mr. Hinch if you can. Inform him that his orders are to turn back at once. Hold the line open. I want constant contact."

"Okay, sir."

●

Mondragon kept the headphones on, but the contact was broken. He heard Andersen calling Hinch and then the whisper of the turbine as they pulled farther back from the barrier.

"Hold it!" Hinch's hoarse sardonic bark came close behind him. "If Mr. Glengarth's still on the line, tell him I've been informed. Awake and not too drunk to run this bleedin' circus. We ain't going back."

Twisting, Carlos found Hinch behind him at the top of the cabin steps, gaunt face flushed behind the straggle of beard, a pistol in his hand.

"Qué?" he whispered. "Qué quiere?"

"Escuche!" A slurred command. "Get this! All three of you. To hell with Stecker and his ruttin' ship. We're going on to that bleedin' mountain. If it is a bleedin' mountain. Or if it's the mouth of hell."

"Señor—" He had to catch his breath. "Señor Hinch, have you looked outside?"

"I see the cliff." Hinch was breathing hard. The pistol shook in his hand. "I heard about the bleedin' flash. Maybe meant to scare us off, but Jake Hinch don't scare. We'll climb the ruttin' ice—"

"Señor!" he begged. "Cuidado con la pistola!"

"Cuidado yourself!" Hinch waved the gun. "I ain't borracho, and we ain't turning back."

"I think we are in danger, sir," Andersen called, "if we ignore that signal—"

"Afraid to die?" Hinch laughed, a brief, harsh snort. "So what the bleedin' devil! We're already done for, murdered when this crazy ship took off. We can die slow, starvin' and freezin' here on the ice. Or faster, if that bleedin' scumbag Stecker gets us back on his death-trap ship and shoots it off to God knows what. I'll take the ice gods, if you want to call 'em gods. No worse than old Rip Stecker."

"Señor . . ." Mondragon watched the pistol and searched for words. "La Doctora Virili says we need not die. She says we came to make the planet a new home for humanidad. She says we know the science to stay alive, on the ice or under it."

"Turned to bleedin' cannibals!"

"Creo que no, señor. I think we need not die." He shrank from a sweep of the gun. "Please, Señor, I think we must continue our search for the masters of the planet. Perhaps they burn the signal light to make us welcome."

"Not very bleedin' likely!"

"We don't know." Andersen's quiet voice again. "Mr. Hinch, may I ask why you're with us? Are you here for Captain Stecker? Or have you had some difference with him?"

"If you give a bleedin' damn . . ." Hinch stepped back and lowered the pistol, but his eyes were wild with desperation. "Let me tell you what a slimy bastard Rip Stecker is."

"No friend of mine." Cruzet spoke somewhere below. "A dirty trick he played, throwing Captain Alt off the ship."

Startled, Hinch jumped and tipped his haggard head.

"A filthier trick on me! Kidnapped me off the bleedin' Earth. Got me drunk and kept me aboard when I never meant to come. Just to shut me up. To stop my testimony back at home about how he'd robbed the Mission."

Livid now, his gaunt face twitched.

"But I ain't dead. Not quite yet."

"I see, Mr. Hinch." Andersen nodded soberly. "Anything you want to add?"

"No secrets here. Not among the dead." Hinch grinned, his hollowed eyes glaring past Mondragon at the ice wall and the stars. "If you care, I know enough to hang the thievin' skunk. He's a slick one. Top con man of the bleedin' century, if you ain't already guessed it. He'd embezzled millions. Jumped on the ship two minutes ahead of the law. If you wonder how I know, he used me for his bleedin' cat's-paw."

"Huh?"

"StarSeed Mission used to be big business. Real big business!" His ragged voice had slowed, and his arm seemed to relax with the gun. "Every bleedin' ship cost a lot of millions, and they launched a lot of ships. Rip Stecker's job was raising the millions. Conning it out of the bleedin' true believers. He knew how to diddle the senseless nuts into trading all they had for their chance to shape human destiny—that's what he called his one-way tickets to hell.

"Did it in his own high style." Hinch laughed again, raucously. "Mark him up for that. Ritzy apartments in New York and Geneva. Women to fit. But he had a fatal fault. Loved to gamble in top casinos all over the world, drunk half the time. Always a loser, drunk or sober. Went crazy toward the end, squandering ten times his pay. That's when he got his hooks into me."

He waved the gun, and grinned when Mondragon ducked.

"I'd made my own mistakes. Dipped into the wrong till and did eight years for it. Branded with that, I'd changed my

name and tried to make a better start. He found me out when
I asked for a Mission job. He took me on to do the worst of
his dirty work. He went so far I got sick of his tricks and set
the law on him. That's why he's done me in."

He twisted to glare belligerently at Cruzet.

"And why I ain't afraid of him, or you, or any bleedin' ice
gods. I ain't going back to end my days on Rip Stecker's death
ship and let the cannibals gnaw my bones. Got it?"

"Sí, señor." Mondragon nodded hastily. "Seguro que sí."

"Thank you, Mr. Hinch." Andersen spoke very quietly
through the interphone. "I think we've got it. I'm glad to
know where you stand, but I wonder how you hope to get past
this fault in the ice."

"Your problem." Hinch grinned ferociously. "You're the
engineer."

Muttering, he went back to his berth. Mondragon heard a
bottle clink. Another kilometer back from the ice wall, Andersen stopped the spider to inspect the reactor and the turbine. Cruzet put on his airskin and went down through the
lock to check the tires and steering gear.

"Vehicle temperature still in safe service range," he reported. "Ice fog forming around us since we stopped. Frozen
air sublimes under the lamp and freezes again as it spreads."

"Write it in your bleedin' log." Hinch was pushing into
the lookout bubble. "If you think any bleedin' idiot will ever
get here to read it."

Yet, in spite of such sarcasm, he turned suddenly amiable,
offering to share his whisky. Mondragon made fresh syncafe
and toasted omninute wafers in the microwave. They gathered in the cabin for a meal before Cruzet took the controls
to drive them along the ice wall. It sank a little, but ten kilometers north it was still four meters high.

"Let's take a look," Andersen called. "I think we can climb
it here."

"If you can . . ." Hinch twisted to squint at him doubtfully. "Do it."

They stopped near the fault. Andersen climbed down through the lock with a box of tools. In the bubble, Mondragon watched him drilling holes with a laser that exploded the ice into steam that made a thin red fog around them. Loading explosives into the holes, he gestured Cruzet to back them away.

The silent blast brought a great eruption of steam and ice fragments and a flash that dazzled Mondragon. When he could see again, the starlight showed a sloping gap in the barrier. Andersen came back aboard, and Cruzet jolted the spider through it.

"Call the ship," Andersen told Mondragon. "If Mr. Hinch doesn't mind."

Hinch didn't mind.

"What the bleedin' hell," he muttered. "The bleedin' bastard can't touch us now."

Calling, Mondragon heard only the hiss and whisper of the cosmos.

"We've dropped below line of sight," Andersen told him. "Which means that any signals have to be reflected down to reach us. No reflector above us now."

Staring from the bubble as they rolled on toward the black sun's round blot on the stars, all he saw was the same flat waste of ash white frost, the same black horizon, the same eternal midnight. Hinch roved the machine for a time, peering ahead from the nose and climbing to peer out of the bubble. He finally vanished again into his curtained cubicle.

Andersen stowed his tools, yawned, and went down to take a nap. When the watch clock chimed, Mondragon read the sextant and the surface temperature, made another black dot on the route map, and got no answer when he called the ship again. He was dozing when he heard Cruzet's excited yelp.

"Look ahead! Another light!"

He blinked his sticky eyes and found a point of changing color low above the eastern horizon. Red that changed to orange, yellow to green, blue to violet, and then faded into indigo. After long seconds of darkness, it began again.

"One more warning." Andersen looked at Hinch, who had followed him into the bubble. "Sir, I think we've come far enough."

"Drive on." Hinch's eyes were red and hollow, the whisky slowing his gritty voice. "Ice gods or bleedin' devils, I'll see how they take human heat."

Andersen turned to Mondragon. "Try the ship."

Again all he heard was the rush of energies too vast for him to understand. Andersen went down to take a spell at the wheel. Alone in the bubble, cut off from all humankind, he felt that they were utterly alone in their tiny shell, trapped under the uncaring silence of the ice and the weight of endless time. Almost, he thought, as if they were already dead.

The telephone startled him.

"Calling . . . Calling Alpha . . ."

La rubia! Her voice was a thread of life, drawn too thin, stretched too far from warmth and life and hope. In a moment like a dream, he seemed to see her as if she stood somehow on the stony hill behind Cuerno del Oro, facing a wind that blew her bright hair back and shaped a thin red dress to her fine body, holding la niñita and the panda doll in her arms.

"Ship calling spider." Her voice was suddenly stronger. "Can you hear?"

"Sí!" He gasped the words in Spanish. "Lo oigo."

"Carlos?" He was sorry for the Spanish, but at least she knew his voice. "Where are you now?"

"We blasted a way through the ice wall. We are driving on."

"You were ordered to return." A crisp reprimand. "Mr. Glengarth thinks you're in danger."

"Perhaps. Mr. Hinch doesn't care."

"Let me speak to him."

"He's below. Probably sleeping."

"Get him on the phone." Her voice grew sharper. "Captain Stecker wants a word with him."

"He won't want to talk, but I have something else to report. We see something like a new star low in the east, changing through the rainbow colors we saw from space."

"I think you are in danger. Let me speak . . ."

That thread of life had broken. Her voice was gone.

●

He called Andersen to the bubble, to be there if she got through again. At the wheel himself, he drove on toward the light. No star at all, it burned always brighter, swelled into a rippling target shape, climbed higher till he found the mountain under it. Not a mountain, either, but a thin black monolith so tall he could not believe it. He stopped the spider, and they all gathered in the bubble, hushed with puzzlement.

"What the devil!" Hinch exploded. "What the ruttin' devil!"

"Nothing natural," Andersen murmured. "Something built it. Don't ask me who. It's got to be a building, but tall as a mountain. Perhaps they *were* gods."

They drove on, stopped to study it, drove on again across an ancient beach and up an easy slope toward where it stood, on a low hill smoothed with time and silvered with frost. Higher, higher, the tower climbed to hide half the stars. The flow of color across its face cast a rainbow shimmer over them, brighter than their lamp.

"Enough." They were still two hundred meters away, but Andersen raised his hand. "Close enough."

"Qué es?" Mondragon breathed. "What is it?"

They craned their necks and kept on looking. The work of giants, Mondragon thought, if not actual gods. Shading his eyes against the unsteady light, he could trace darker seams between the enormous blocks that formed the wall, blocks twenty meters tall, maybe thirty on a side. One must have fallen from far above, shattering into a great pile of rubble.

"A door?" Cruzet frowned and pointed. "Is that a door?"

A rectangular patch of deeper darkness half hidden by the rubble, at first it looked too small to be an entrance, not half the height of the titanic blocks around it, but when he let his eyes measure it again, he thought it must be wide enough to let them drive on in. Squinting through the glow from overhead, he found only darkness there.

"Near enough," Andersen said again. "I think we've learned enough—"

"Enough?" Hinch's hoarse rasp stopped him. "Not for me. I'm going in to face the bleedin' monsters in their den and ask 'em what their bleedin' signal means."

Twelve

Kip felt worried for Carlos and the others, lost somewhere out on the ice beyond the reach of the radio. Yet he was happy when Roy Eisen let him hang out in the work balloon. A team of mechanics were busy there, putting together another spider, the Beta. At first he was a little afraid of Dr. Eisen, who was loud and sometimes sharp with people who made mistakes. He had a warm grin, though, and usually time to answer simple questions.

"You were a contractor, Dr. Roy?"

He stood gazing up at the fat-tired wheels, twice as tall as a man. They were feet for the eight tall legs that carried the cabin, a long cylinder that would hold the fusion engine and the crew. Polished like silver to cut heat loss, it reflected strange images of everybody working around it.

"You really built it?"

"Yup. When we finally got the contract."

Once, Eisen had chewed tobacco. Now instead he

munched little white pills he called joy jolts. His mass quota had limited what he could bring, and he sometimes wondered what he would do when they were gone. He paused now to pour one of them out of a little tin box and crunch it with his false teeth.

"I had a little company. A partner and I, back in Idaho." Kip thought he wished he were back there now. "We bought the Sternberg patent. The spiders cost a lot to build, and we never sold all that many. A few went to companies working in the Arctic. We shipped a couple to the Moon, but the Mission was our best customer. Bought them for the last dozen flights. Bought more than they ever paid for."

"Could we use it to rescue, Carlos?" He watched a workman with a toolbox climbing the long ramp into the spider's steel belly. "Carlos and the others? If they're having trouble?"

"Don't count on it." Eisen frowned and shook his head. "The things are so big we could only bring two. We can't risk them both, because we'd be so helpless here without them. Shut up on the ship. Our friends in the Alpha know they can't afford trouble."

"Oh." He looked down at the floor, trying not to show how he felt. "I guess we just have to hope they're okay."

"They ought to be." Eisen reached up to pat a huge black tire. "The spiders are good machines. They don't break down."

"Thank you, Dr. Roy. I hope the Alpha gets back safe."

●

When the Beta was finished and tested, Eisen took surveyors up the beach to decide where to dig caves and tunnels for habitats. Kip's mother never let him go along, even when Eisen said he wouldn't be in the way, but she let him come with her when she went to look over the site they had selected.

"The sonic probes found a lot of big granite boulders in

the permafrost under us," she told him. "Boulders the glaciers brought down before the planet froze. They'd be hard to excavate, and Dr. Cheng thinks we can do better, tunneling into the cliffs."

Eisen drove, and she let Kip climb with her into the transparent bubble over the cabin. They went fast, high above the frost, and the swaying motion felt a little like the elephant he had ridden at a zoo, when his mother had taken him to see all the Earth creatures they would never see again.

Jim Cheng came up the steel steps to join them. He was a slim, quick, quiet man with a friendly smile. His father had been a Singapore banker. He had become a cosmologist and joined the Mission because banking bored him.

Eisen stopped them a couple of kilometers north, at the mouth of a high-walled gorge a glacier had cut. The heat lamp, brighter than the starlight, cast a dim red glow over the frost around them, and the searchlight roved over gray-white cliffs that towered over the level beach. They were rust red a dozen meters up, climbing up toward a high white line of ice.

"Limestone." Eisen nodded at the cliffs. "Laid down on the bottom of a shallow sea when the climate was warm, so Dr. Singh tells me. Sandstone above, left by floods that came down off the continent when water still flowed. There's iron in it that colors it red."

He turned to Rima. "A good sign," he told her. "You'll be looking for iron you can mine."

"Our habitat?" She frowned, staring at the cliffs. "Where?"

"In the sandstone." He gestured. "It's stable. Drained dry and soft enough for laser drills. We'll have to build a scaffold to get at it now, but we'll soon have enough rubble out of the tunnels to make an access ramp."

She had Eisen drive them up the canyon as far as the floor was smooth, stopping now and then to record holo-images.

"Look at it," she urged Kip. "Our new home!"

Kip looked down at the frost white floor of the canyon, and up at the naked cliffs and the midnight sky. All he saw was ice and rock and darkness. He shivered.

"I know it looks pretty grim." She made a hopeful smile. "But we'll carve our new city into the rock, back where the cold can't reach us. We'll have fusion light and power. Hydroponic gardens for fresh vegetables. Wheat and corn and soy. They make tastier foods than soyamax."

He looked out again, at hard rock and old ice and everlasting night.

"If you like your ham and eggs, your hamburgers and steaks," Dr. Cheng was saying, "we have frozen embryos. We can breed our own livestock when we have space and grain enough."

"We'll learn to live here." Rima's arm came around him. "The valley will soon look different. We can make it bright as daylight used to be. We'll have roads and mines and shops. Interesting work to do. We can be happy here. Really, Kip, it's a great adventure."

She was too anxious for him to believe it, and he felt a little sorry for her.

"I hope." He caught her hand. "Mom, I really hope."

●

He stayed in the cabin with Day, once when Rima had a watch to stand in the control room. He was eager for news when she came back to them.

"Carlos—"

He stopped when saw her face tighten. She still didn't trust Carlos.

"The expedition?" He changed his question. "Is there anything from Dr. Andersen and the expedition?"

"Nothing, really." She looked worried. "You know they're so far out that the signal has to be reflected from the dust out in space. Sometimes it doesn't reflect. They did try to call.

Something about a wall of ice and a light shining in it, but
the signal was garbled. It made no sense."

●

She let him come with her again when they went back up the
canyon to where men had begun digging for the habitat. An
arched tunnel mouth had been cut into the reddish cliff, twenty
meters up. A man in a yellow airskin was driving a bulldozer,
moving the great pile of broken rock under the tunnel to make
a ramp that machines could climb. Dr. Singh was in the tunnel, waiting to ride with them back to the ship. She left her
airskin down in the entry lock and came up into the bubble.

"Fossils!" Her voice was quick and her dark eyes shone.
"Fossil bones that may help explain what we saw on the ice
cap. Something I hoped for, and never expected to find."

"Really?" Rima stared at her. "Tell us!"

"Calcareous bones." She was eager to tell. "In the allu-
vial sandstone stratum above the old seabed." She saw Kip's
puzzled look. "That means the bones were buried in sand that
floods washed down, when water ran here." She turned back
to Rima. "I'm using a thin-beamed laser drill to cut them out.
Delicate work, but I learned the technique when I used to
spend vacations on archaeological digs."

She had studied the biology of Earth before she joined the
Mission.

"I think we have a nearly complete skeleton. Interpreta-
tion is a riddle, of course, because we have no context, nothing whatever about the history of life here. But this is actual
evidence that high life-forms did evolve, perhaps as complex
as our own. Altogether a fascinating find. The creature must
have been a bit smaller than a man. A vertebrate, around one
and a half meters tall. I'll report when I have more to say."

●

Kip saw the skeleton when Dr. Singh brought it to the ship,
still half embedded in a heavy block of red sandstone. A gray-

white skull, oddly narrow, with two staring holes where its eyes had been. Rust-colored stumps of broken bones sticking out of the rock. He shrank back from the dead grin, wondering what the live thing had been.

"It looks almost human," Rima said.

"It was bipedal, but I think it flew." Dr. Singh stooped to look down at it. "The bones were light and hollow. Many of them are crushed, perhaps from a fall that killed it. The arm bones are elongated, perhaps for flight, though any actual wing structure was too fragile to be preserved. I found small bones that may have come from a functional three-fingered hand. The legs were short, ending in something more fin than foot. I'd guess the thing evolved in the sea and later took to the air."

"Remarkable!" Rima bent with her over it and then looked up to smile. "We're lucky to have you with us."

"Thanks." Dr. Singh nodded soberly. "There was a time when I longed to know everything about the life on Earth, but I joined the Mission to look for something new." She paused to open a little plastic bag. "Here it is."

She poured the contents of the bag into her palm.

Kip saw half a dozen short black stones that caught the light like polished gems. They were all alike, as thick as pencils. They were six-sided. When she stirred them with her finger, they stuck together to make a tiny honeycomb. He leaned down to study them and looked up at her.

"Carlos had one."

"What's that?" She stared at him. "Are you sure?"

"Where did he get it?" Rima asked.

"He picked it up on the beach. Up in the canyon where they're digging the habitat, when he went out with Andy in the airskins. They were scraping off the frost to get soil samples." He frowned at Dr. Singh. "What were they for?"

"Ornaments, maybe?" She stirred them again, shaking her head. "Maybe money? They were scattered around the bones. The creature must have worn or carried them. I can't guess what they are."

"That's odd." Rima's voice had quickened, and she reached to pick up the little honeycomb. "The way they adhere. Are they magnets?"

"Not the sort we know," Dr. Singh said. "They do attract one another, but they're not iron."

●

Rima woke that night, sensing trouble. Day had crawled into the berth with her earlier, whimpering again that Me Me was lost on the ice. She cuddled her, and they had slept again. Now, however, she was alone in the berth. She sat up, listening. Kip's slow and even breathing. Nothing else. No sound from Day. Trembling, she rolled out of the berth.

Day's berth was empty. She wasn't in the room, wasn't in the bathroom.

"Day!" She was suddenly hoarse. "Day, where are you?"

Silence.

She turned on the light.

"Mom?" Kip woke. "Anything wrong?"

"Day's gone."

She grabbed a robe and ran out of the room. Kip straggled after her, rubbing his eyes. The circular passage around the elevator shaft was empty. Calling Day's name, all she heard was silence. The ship was asleep. She pushed the button for the elevator.

"Service suspended till oh four hundred," a computer voice told her. "In emergency, use the stair or call security."

The stairway stood open. She ran up the spiral steps, Kip stumbling behind her. Another empty hall, all the doors closed. She ran panting around it, climbed again and still again until she came out into the hushed dimness of the control dome. Some instrument clucked softly. The strange constellations burned across the holoscreens above her. Second

Officer Sternberg sat at a semicircle of green-glowing monitors, headphones on.

"Sir, have you seen Day?" she gasped. "My little girl?"

Sternberg started, blinked, and put a finger to his lips. She stood trembling, getting her breath, until he shrugged and pushed the phones aside.

"Hinch and his crew are in trouble," he said. "I can't contact them. Have you a problem?"

"My little girl. She's disappeared."

"I haven't seen her. Try security." He pushed the phones back over his ears.

"Sorry, sir."

Barefoot, robe flapping, she ran back down the endless spiral, calling Day's name into every corridor ring. Emptiness, silence, fear. Her lungs ached.

"Mom, wait up!" Kip lagged behind, calling after her. "No use to panic. She can't get off the ship. She's got to be somewhere. Nobody would hurt her."

Remembering Day's dreams, she was close to panic. The planet was too old, too cold, too long dead. She had come to tame it, but suddenly it was monstrous, a world of black nightmare, full of ugly riddles. Its age-old evil had somehow entered the ship to capture her child.

Her chest hurt. She stumbled, fell on the steps, staggered to her feet, and blundered on. Round and round the endless spiral, still gasping Day's name into every empty corridor. Kip's breathless protests fell far behind. The ship seemed empty, dead as the ice and night around them, until at last she came out onto the main deck.

A black-capped security officer sat at a monitor in the watch desk near the elevator. He muttered and tapped the key, and she heard a sudden blare of recorded sound.

"Sí, señor." The stowaway's voice, distorted till it seemed as strange as the rest of the planet. "En el hielo. Todos los colores del arco iris. Una señal? Yo no sé."

He tapped a key and it boomed again.

"Una tapia muy alta— A very high wall—"

It became a scratchy roar, and the officer turned it down.

"Sir?" She raised her voice. "Have you seen my little girl?"

"Dr. Virili?" The officer shut off the sound and blinked as if he hadn't heard her. "That was the Alpha. They've come to some kind of barrier and another colored beacon." He squinted at the monitor and hunched his shoulders as if from a chill. "Another damned display of God-knows-what. Makes me wish I was still a cop, back on my beat in Salt Lake City."

"My little girl? Have you seen my little girl?"

"Sorry." An apologetic shrug. "Haven't seen any little girl." He reached for a notepad. "Give me her descrip—"

"Mom!" Kip shouted. "I see her. Out at the lock."

Wearing only her nightie, Day stood on a toolbox she had dragged to the entry air lock. She was reaching up with a screwdriver to work at the control board. Rima rushed to her.

"Wake up, darling! What are you trying to do?"

Her tiny body jerked as if an electric shock had hit it. She raised the screwdriver like some kind of weapon and turned to peer at them with no sign of recognition, her dilated eyes so wild and strange that Rima shuddered.

"Dear, don't you know me?"

Kip ran to grab her arm. She mouthed a thin mewing cry and jabbed the screwdriver at him. Rima snatched her up. She resisted stiffly for a moment and then shivered and cried out weakly in her own voice.

"Mommy, let me go! Me Me's calling me. She's out on the ice, lost and freezing, with bad things after her."

"Wake up, dear! Please wake up. It was only a terrible dream."

"It is Me Me! Really Me Me, freezing and afraid."

Yet suddenly she was shivering and sobbing in Rima's arms. The security officer said he was sorry he'd failed to see her pass the desk. He'd been taping the Alpha's reports and trying to find some sense in them. The damned planet wasn't fit for human life. Not for any sort of life a decent man would want to meet. He hoped the engineers could get them back into quantum drive and off the crazy place.

"The kid's lucky she couldn't cycle through the lock. With no suit, she'd have been dead in a second. Frozen hard as iron in twenty minutes."

He found a key to start the elevator and went with them back to their cabin.

Thirteen

Mondragon had stopped them at the edge of the rainbow rippling over the frost around the tower. Jaws sagging, they gazed up at the dark titanic blocks and the disks of rainbow color that washed across it till Hinch's nasal snarl sawed through their wonderment.

"We've found their bleedin' hive." He goggled at Andersen, his eyes bloodshot and wild. "I'm going in."

"Not our mission, sir." Andersen shook his head. "Our orders were just to look and report, avoiding needless risk. I think we've learned all we need to know. At least enough to frighten me. If you'll excuse me, sir, our duty now is to rush a quick report back to the ship. By radio or any way we can."

"Report what?" Hinch rasped at him. "What the blazin' hell would you tell 'em?"

"Altogether, sir, I take it to be convincing evidence of intelligent life somehow still surviving here. A sophisticated technological culture probably older than the ice. Likely not very friendly to us—"

"Ice gods!" Hinch mocked his measured tones. "Can you tell 'em what the bleedin' ice gods are?"

"I've no idea," Andersen said. "But sir, if I may speak, I think we've found a potential danger to the ship and any colony we might try to plant. I think we ought to get back while we can, at least into radio range."

"If you're such bleedin' cowards . . ." Hinch glared at Andersen and then at Cruzet. "I ain't! Get me into my airskin."

Andersen stared back for a moment.

"You shouldn't, sir." He shrugged reluctantly. "Really you shouldn't, but you are in charge."

"Señor—" Mondragon had to gulp and catch his breath. "Señor, you risk your life. You should not go alone."

"Want to come along?"

"Bueno. Okay, Señor."

His own words surprised him. He saw Cruzet and Andersen raising their eyebrows at each other as if to say he was a fool, but he followed Hinch down to the lock.

●

Ship supply had fitted the airskin and let him wear it on a few practice walks on the old beach. The tight-fitting fabric was filled with channels that breathed recycled air over all his body to dry the sweat and cool or warm it. The recycler module made a hump on his back. A crystal shell covered his head. Andersen sealed him inside and made him check the controls.

"Watch your cycler," he said. "The air cartridge should do you ten to twelve hours."

He scrambled after Hinch down to the frost and stood peering up at the tower. Blacker than the sky, it covered half the constellations. He shuddered as if the planet's bitter cold had already bitten into the airskin. De verdad, if ice gods by any name existed here, their power must be enormous.

Brighter than the starlight, the glow from that target shape of changing color on the topless tower fringed their shadows with shifting shades of red and blue and green. The vastness of the tower and the strangeness of the place seized him like the hand of death, turning this frozen world into the hell that Father Francisco used to warn him of, where los demonios were waiting to receive him when he died.

Hinch himself was suddenly another demon. Lean as a spider in his own tight yellow airskin, he still wore the black beret, even in the helmet. His gaunt, gray-bearded head seemed too big for it, and his haggard eyes behind the thick-lensed glasses looked blind and hardly human. With the pistol and a long-bladed knife buckled to his belt, he had become un diablo verdadero.

Mondragon shrank from him, feeling a sudden pang of homesickness for his own native pueblito, the flat-roofed adobe where he was born, the rocky hills where he used to herd his father's goats, the old church where his mother prayed. The time since he left it seemed suddenly a long nightmare of events stranger that he used to think death could be.

Un infierno de pesadilla.

A nightmare world. The ship that reached, in no time at all, this planet of fearful cold, this black sun, these strange stars that never dimmed, this monstrous work of unknown things. Ciertamente this was not the rich new Earth el Señor Stecker and the evangelistas of Mission StarSeed had promised their believers.

Yet la rubia was here, with el joven Kip. And little Day, una muchachita qué bonita. Terraforming was a magic science he did not understand, but the engineers who built quantum craft had to be respected. As for himself, with the favor of los santos, he would do whatever he could to keep them alive—

"Chicken?" Hinch's jeering voice rang in his helmet. "Or have the ice gods frozen you?"

Anger clenched his fists and faded slowly into shame. He

had done nothing for la rubia, found nothing he could even hope to do. He felt helpless in the thin airskin, naked to the cruel cold and el gringo's crueler scorn. Hinch had become un loco verdadero, urging them on till this demon winter killed them.

Yet he himself was no pollo, no chicken.

"Hijo de cabrón!" he muttered, and tramped after Hinch toward the tower. The area was level, as if an ancient pavement lay beneath the frost, but that rubble mountain had fallen half across their path, the fallen stone shattered into fragments larger than houses.

Beyond it, Hinch glanced back at him and pushed ahead into a square tunnel ten meters high. Dim starlight followed them a few dozen meters, then faded into blackness. He stopped to search it with a pale flashlight that soon found the end of the passage, a blank plate that looked like some dull gray metal, scarred with ages of corrosion.

"La puerta?"

A door? Flickering unsteadily over it, the little spot of light found no knob or handle or lock, not even any visible seam to outline any kind of door. Door or not, they had no key.

"No hay problema!" Hinch muttered. "Mr. Andersen has a very useful key."

●

Breathing deeper, relieved to be out of the tower, even here in this never-ending night, he hurried after Hinch back to the spider. Cruzet was on watch in the bubble, but Andersen came down from the nose to meet them at the lock.

"A bleedin' wall across the tunnel!" Hinch was still in the airskin, his rusty voice booming loud from the interphone speakers. "The devil-bitten monsters trying to shut us out of their stinkin' nest. I want you to get us through the way you got us past that ice uplift."

"High explosives?" Andersen shook his head. "Inviting them to hit us back?"

"If the blinkin' devils can." Hinch tilted his head to squint through the heavy lenses as if the cabin lights had blinded him. "But if you want my guess, I'd guess they're dead. Died ten billion years ago. Anything alive would have cleaned up that mess of rocks outside."

"Something is alive," Cruzet protested. "Alive enough to see us coming."

Hinch glared at him.

"Think about it, sir," Andersen begged him. "They don't want us here."

"Maybe they'll kill us." Hinch shrugged. "Maybe they can't. Maybe they've got something we could use." His gaunt head jerked toward the tower. "I'll soon see."

"Are you crazy?"

"Aren't we all?" His voice went shrill. "And dead already, don't forget. Nothing left for us to lose. No chance too bad for us to take. God knows what they've got in there that we might grab."

"You *are* crazy," Andersen told him. "You really are."

"Whatever you say, Mr. Andersen." Hinch's yellow-gloved claw gripped his gun. "Just let me into their hell-blazin' tower."

Andersen frowned, shifting on his feet.

"I'll set the charge." He shrugged at last. "With a timer to let us get back to where I hope we're safe."

Mondragon went back to the tunnel with them, carrying a pack filled with blocks of something wrapped in bright red foil. The laser drill failed to scar the gray metal plate, but it bit slowly into the stone around it, a jet of silent steam blowing plumes of black dust from the holes.

"Watch everything," Andersen muttered to Mondragon. "Warn me if you see anything move."

Uneasily watching, all he saw was the soundless dark. Andersen drilled three deep holes at the edge of the barrier, packed them with explosive, and set the timer. Gathering his tools, he led them out of the tunnel.

Just behind the rubble hill, Hinch stopped to wait.

"Far enough," he muttered. "I want to rush the devil-bitten bastards with their pants still down."

"If they wear pants." Andersen grinned and hurried on. "I don't want to know."

Cruzet drove them back down to the old beach, two kilometers below. They waited in the bubble, watching with binoculars. Hinch had crouched out of sight behind the mound. Counting under his breath, Andersen finally whispered, "Now!"

Mondragon felt the machine shiver. Hinch straightened, stood a moment peering around him, and darted into the tunnel. They waited again, taking turns with the binoculars. Hinch didn't come out. Neither did anything else.

Time passed. The stars blazed overhead, as they had blazed forever. The signal light—if it was a signal light—kept its rainbow glow flowing over the frost. Andersen updated the log. Cruzet heated water for syncafe.

"Coffee it ain't." Andersen drained his bitter cup, made a face, and set it down. "Want to go inside to look for Mr. Hinch?"

"I don't think so." Cruzet scowled. "We aren't idiots."

"Creo que no." Mondragon shook his head. "I think we must return to tell what we have seen."

"But not quite yet." Andersen looked at his watch. "We'll give him eight more hours. About the limit of his cycler cartridge. Just in case he's still alive."

On watch in the bubble three hours later, Mondragon felt a jolt that left him breathless. The sky seemed to dim. Clutching at his seat, he looked up to see that great disk of flowing fire dim and flicker and die. The tower was left a stark black shadow that spread to the zenith.

"What was that?" Andersen came muttering up the steps into the bubble. "I was asleep."

"Un terremoto? The tower light was extinguished."

They stood peering back at the tower and out across the flat whiteness of the frozen sea. Andersen typed a note into the log and shook his head. "I don't get it. The planet ought to be cold to the core, with no energy left for any kind of quakes—"

"Alli!" Mondragon caught his breath and pointed. "El senor Hinch."

Hinch had come out of the tunnel and dropped flat behind the rubble mound, though nothing seemed to pursue him. He had lost the pistol and the knife. In a moment he was on his feet again, running hard, empty hands beating wildly around his head as if fighting some invisible attacker.

"Salio!" Mondragon shouted to Cruzet. "Open the lock for him!"

"Will do."

He heard the motors whir and the muffled clang of the opening valve. Hinch came up beside them, beating desperately at nothing. The black beret was gone. The glasses had slid aside in his helmet, hanging on one ear. He ran with his head twisted to look back, darting from side to side as if he hadn't seen the spider.

"Señor!" Mondragon gasped into the microphone. "This way! Aquí!"

Deaf to him, Hinch veered around them and ran on across the ice until they lost him in the starlight.

"Follow him," Andersen told Cruzet. "He'll have to stop when he's exhausted. We'll try to pick him up."

They traced his footprints, sometimes visible where his boots had crushed the film of frost, more often too dim to see. He had run fast and far. They had come nearly six kilometers out across the frozen sea before Mondragon saw a dark scar ahead, with no tracks beyond it.

"Alto!" he shouted. "Stop!"

Cruzet stopped the machine a few meters from a sharp-edged crevasse two meters wide.

"Opened by that quake." Andersen stared into it, blankly nodding. "Since we came."

It ran almost straight in both directions as far as they could see. Still in their airskins, he and Mondragon went out to look over the edge. The rim was pink in the heat lamp's glow, but the sheer ice walls looked black a few meters down. Farther down was only darkness. They saw no bottom.

"The gods of ice were angered by el Señor Hinch," Mondragon said. "I think they opened the ice to swallow him."

Fourteen

Sweating in the galley, Roak hated the toil, and the heat, and the stink of the garbage digester. Most of all, he hated Jesus Rivera, the foul-mouthed slave driver who stood over him every minute, yelping shrill commands and cursing him for a brain-dead goof-off if he ever let a drop of spilt grease reach the deck. He had to escape. When he heard that Jake Hinch had been lost on the ice, he thought he saw his chance.

Hinch had carried meals to Captain Stecker, who seldom left his cabin. When Rivera sent a steward in his place, Stecker scowled at the tray, called it filthy garbage, and threw a bowl of hot soya chowder in the steward's face. When the man refused to go back, Roak asked for the task.

"Why not?" Rivera wiped a fat hand on his apron and surveyed him with a cross-eyed squint. "I'd better warn you that Stecker's a crazy drunk half the time and nasty when he isn't, but take the job if you want it."

"I'll take it."

Rivera shrugged. "Your funeral."

The tray held no soya or syncafe when Roak took it back to Stecker's cabin. He had filled it himself after Rivera unlocked Stecker's private stock. Baked ham, fresh asparagus in cheese sauce, hot French rolls, an apple dumpling with cream, genuine coffee with a fragrance that took his breath.

"Stecker looked ahead," Rivera muttered. "Shipped a truckload of goodies to the site a week ahead of the launch. Not that he's happy with where we landed. Don't be surprised if he spits in your eye."

He knocked twice and waited a long time for Stecker's door to open. Hollow-eyed and unshaven, naked to the waist and reeking of gin, the captain glared at him.

"Who the hell are you?"

"The launch inspector, sir. Caught aboard when they got the tip-off about the bomb and sealed the ship. My damned luck. We'd dropped into the launch pit before they ever found the device."

"Tough break." Stecker's tone warmed a little when he caught the coffee scent, but still it had a bitter edge. "If you ain't happy here, I see why. We're caught like rats in the same death trap. And no way out."

"I'm afraid we are, sir."

He cleared dirty cups and glasses off a table and uncovered the tray. Greedily, Stecker fell upon the thick-sliced ham. Roak stood a moment, shaking his head at the clutter on the deck. Soiled clothing, an empty gin bottle, spilt food drying on broken dishes.

"Excuse me, sir. May I straighten up your cabin?"

"Huh?" Stecker grunted past a slug of ham. "What the hell do I care?"

"If I may, sir. You'll be more comfortable."

Sucking down the asparagus spears, Stecker ignored him.

He gathered up the soiled laundry, found a broom for the broken dishes, mopped up the food stains, found clean sheets and made up the berth.

"Anything else, sir?"

Stecker gulped the last of the coffee and blinked suspiciously.

"Glengarth sent you?"

"No sir. My own idea. I'd heard you speak at StarSeed meetings. I always respected you."

"Glad to hear it." Muttering, Stecker pushed the tray at him. "I never trusted the bastards. Not even when they bribed me to push their scam. Peddling pie in the sky! Looking for marks stupid enough to swallow their tomfool tales of the high-tech utopias they were going to build in some future universe. I never believed a word of it. Never thought I'd be trapped in this frozen hellhole."

He belched and wiped his greasy mouth.

"I understand you, sir." Roak nodded sympathetically. "I'm in the same box, but we've got a way out. Glengarth and the engineers. They know their quantum science. They got us here. They could damn sure take us on to some decent planet if they weren't hell-bent on this lunatic terraforming dream."

"Damn Glengarth!" Stecker's voice grew violent. "Nursing a crazy grudge against me for getting rid of Alt, his old drinking buddy. Jake warned me he's got some dirty double-dealing scheme to throw me in the brig, or maybe off the ship, and grab command himself."

"Hand in glove with ship security." Roak nodded companionably. "Washburn, that black bitch, tried to pin that Fairshare bomb on me. Tossed me in the brig without a trial and finally set me to slaving like a dog in Rivera's galley."

"Sneaking rats," Stecker muttered darkly. "All against me."

"You can trust me, sir." Roak thrust out his hand, but

Stecker belched again and looked away. "I'll be back with your dinner," he promised. "Just ask for anything you want."

"All I want is a way off this snowball."

"Me too. Trust me, captain. Just remember I'm your man."

"You?" Stecker snorted. "What the hell can you do?"

I'll show you, he thought, but Stecker wasn't listening.

●

Mondragon felt a chill of fear, and a sadness for el Señor Hinch. Un loco, perhaps more unlucky than evil. Not so bad as Captain Stecker, who had made Hinch a greater thief than he had ever been, and then brought him on the ship to conceal their crimes.

De nada. Nothing mattered to the ice gods, neither human good nor human evil. They had simply moved with their terrible power to defend themselves from the intruders who violated their ancient dwelling. Por la gracia de Dios, they had not harmed the vehicle.

Aboard again, he and Andersen found Cruzet in the bubble.

"Are we trapped?" He nodded anxiously at the fissure in the ice. "Or can we get across?"

"We must." Andersen stood a moment staring grimly back at the tower. "We've got to get word of this to Glengarth. We may never get another radio contact, and he needs to know. As quick as we can."

"I'll take the wheel." Andersen studied the crevasse. "It's hardly two meters wide. With the legs extended to full span, I think I can drive us—"

The ice had rocked again.

Andersen stopped, with a hoarse croak. His body jerked and stiffened. Eyes strangely glazed, he stood rigid for half a minute, then toppled sidewise. They caught him, held him upright. Cruzet felt for a pulse.

"Stiff as rigor mortis," he whispered. "But there's still a faint heartbeat. Let's get him down to the cabin."

He was heavy and as hard to move as a stone man, but they dragged him down the narrow stair and laid him on his berth. Cruzet worried over him with the first-aid kit they found in the emergency locker.

"Blood pressure falling." Dismally, he shook his head. "Down to forty over twenty. Pulse irregular and faint. But at least he's alive."

They watched him two hours. His temperature sank, but slowly rose again. His pulse rate recovered. The rigor crept out of him. At last he breathed again, wheezing noisily. Moving convulsively, he tried to sit up and fell feebly back. Mondragon raised his head and offered him water, but he knocked the cup away and lay snoring heavily.

"Qué lástima!"

Mondragon shrank away from him, sick with pity and dread. A brave and able man of science, a new friend who had never seemed to care that he was an illegal polizón aboard the ship without rights or place.

"What maldad struck him?" Shivering, he stared at Cruzet. "What madness killed el Señor Hinch?"

Silently, Cruzet shrugged and shook his head.

Something from the black tower, something silent and unseen, some monstrous fantasma of night and ice and killing cold that had lived a billion or ten billion years ago here beneath this dead black sun—if it had ever lived at all.

He asked again, "What do you think?"

Cruzet should know. A man of science, one who preferred the signs of mathematics to the speech of words, he had seemed to feel at home in the vast cosmos where worlds were only atoms. Where humankind was only one more animal species struggling against extinction. Yet he stood still, blankly frowning at nothing, till Andersen made a hoarse gasping sound. That startled him into motion. He bent to take Andersen's pulse again and turned back to Mondragon, blinking against the wetness in his eyes.

"God—God knows," he whispered uncertainly. "If He can see this far."

●

Andersen groaned and began shaking violently. They spread a blanket over him. Cruzet took his temperature.

"Still down," he said, "but rising."

Mondragon brought a mug of hot syncafe and helped Andersen sit up to sip it.

"The ice got into me." He shivered again, his eyes still wide and strange. "And something—something else."

His hand shook and spilled the syncafe. Mondragon found a towel to wipe it off his blue jumpsuit.

"If you can tell us . . ." Cruzet urged him. "What was that something?"

"Nothing I ever imagined." He reached for the mug again, and gulped what was left. "Not hostile." Speaking hoarsely and slowly, he stared blankly at Cruzet. "Nor friendly, either. Just curious, inspecting me like a bug under a lens. If that makes sense."

"Alarming sense." Cruzet nodded. "Can you say what it wanted?"

"Not really. I think it was doing a sort of autopsy, as if I were already dead—if it knows the difference between life and death. I felt it reaching into me. Studying me like you would a plastic model in an anatomy lab. Looking at the organs and the way they work together. It did my body. And then—then my mind."

He waited for Mondragon to refill the mug.

"Thank you, Carlos." He drank it eagerly. "I got cold. I need the heat."

"Your mind?" Cruzet urged him again. "What was it doing to your mind?"

"I don't know what." He stared away, as if to search the

empty air. "Or how. I was a rat in the lab. That's how I felt, jerking at first to jolts of pain. That was physical, just for starters. It shook me with waves of emotion that had no cause I understood. Terror, too, that I did understand."

Jaw clenched, he made a bitter little grin.

"Because I was so helpless. I couldn't move a muscle." He convulsed again. "Sorry!" he muttered. "A dozen kinds of hell. Nothing I want to remember. Thank God it's already fading."

"Tell us," Cruzet urged him. "While you can. Anything you do remember."

"Memories. Memories." He grimaced at Mondragon, seeing nothing. "That's what they wanted. Everything about me, everything I ever felt or was. A blur of things I forgot long ago. A little steam engine I built when I was a kid. My elation when I discovered Euclid. A rocket I made that exploded in the air and brought the cops. On and on. Down to quantum engineering and wavecraft and StarSeed and how we got here."

"It was measuring your mind." Cruzet seemed relieved. "Deciding, I hope, that you weren't another Jake Hinch."

"Maybe." He nodded uncertainly. "But I don't think it ever really understood what I am. It made me repeat some of the recollections again and again. It wanted more than it ever got. More than I ever knew. I don't think it was ever satisfied. Finally it just stopped and left me."

He shivered, holding the mug toward Mondragon for yet another refill.

"Pure nightmare!" He gulped the syncafe and grinned at Mondragon. "Un sueño malo."

More soberly, he turned to mutter at Cruzet.

"No comfort for us. They just inspected me. The way we might have inspected a green-skinned corpse off a saucer ship. Found me as strange to them, I think, as they are to us. Yet I got no sense that they care or really want to know what we are or why we're here, except to make sure we can do no harm to them. I think that's why they left me alive. Anxious to be rid of us."

He shuddered again.

"I hope they've had enough."

Mondragon whispered a prayer.

"We'll wait and see," Cruzet murmured. "Nothing else to do."

Andersen shut his eyes and lay back on the berth, breathing as if he were asleep. Half an hour later he sat up and said he felt okay. Still chilled, but okay. Yet for a time they stayed together in the cabin, grateful for one another and the shelter of the steel-shelled titanium hull.

Stirring reluctantly at last, Cruzet climbed into the bubble to try the ship again. He stayed so long that Mondragon went to look for him and found him silent at the radio, so intent that he made no answer when Mondragon spoke.

"No ship," he told them when he came down. "We're too far out, even for that chance reflection."

"Podemos—," Mondragon began. "Can we . . ."

Looking into their tight faces, he swallowed the question and turned to heat water for syncafe. Cruzet joined him at the counter to make a soya stew and toast slugs of novakelp. They ate in silence, with little appetite. Mondragon cleaned their bowls and spoons. Andersen rose heavily, went to the toilet, came out to shrug at Cruzet.

"Let's try." His voice was hoarse and slow, but at least he was himself again. "They stopped Hinch, but that was after he dynamited the tower. Let's see what happens if we just start the engine."

"Why not?" Cruzet nodded. "No good just sitting here."

He went forward to the controls. Mondragon climbed with Andersen into the bubble and shivered when he looked out. Nothing was different. The frozen ocean still lay flat to the straight black horizon; the strange constellations blazed as they had blazed forever; the dead black sun hung among them as it had always hung, only slightly higher here; the black stone tower stood where the ice gods had built it before Earth was born. A world of night and ice and death, without life or time or motion . . .

Except for that deep black crack in the ice, which the ice gods had made to swallow el Señor Hinch. Blacker than midnight, blacker than the tower or the sun, its bottomless depth chilled him to the bone. The ice gods ruled here, angry that they had been disturbed.

He heard the turbine hum. Cruzet backed them away from the fissure and drove a kilometer north along it in search of a better crossing.

"No difference," Andersen called. "Let's try here."

Cautiously, Cruzet pulled them close to the brink and stopped. Mondragon got into his airskin, climbed down to the ice, and stood near the crack, where they could see his signals. Front and rear wheels extended, the machine inched forward. He watched and signaled Cruzet to stop when the front wheels touched the other side. He climbed back aboard. Cruzet drove on across.

Out of the airskin, he climbed back to the bubble.

"The ice gods must love us," Andersen greeted him. "Why else?"

Cruzet came to join them, passing a flask of Hinch's cognac. Sipping it, they stood there a few minutes looking back across the chasm at the black tower and the black sun and the sky's starshot black infinity.

"So now?" Cruzet was still shaken. "Are they playing with us?"

"We'll see." Andersen shrugged. "They didn't like Hinch and his dynamite, but they have let us go. At least this far. Drive on and we'll see what happens."

"Quiero—" He spoke on impulse. "I wish—I almost wish we could go farther. I know the great ice cap is too far, but I would like to climb it to see that city of the ice gods.

"If we could—"

They turned with him to look past the tower across the featureless black horizon.

"It's halfway around the planet." Cruzet shook his head, speaking half to himself. "Twenty-five thousand kilometers. Ten or twelve thousand across this frozen stuff, till we come to another ten or twelve thousand kilometers of the cap itself, old glaciers, ice cliffs and crevasses, and who knows what."

●

They found the marks their wide-set wheels had left on the frost and followed them west. The tower dwindled into the timeless night. Slowly, slowly, the black sun sank behind them. Mondragon took his turns at the wheel, made syncafe and starchow stew, dozed in his berth, called the ship when he was in the bubble. Two hundred kilometers out from the tower, he got an answer.

"Mr. Mondragon?"

La rubia! His heart beat faster. Her voice seemed relieved and pleased. Concerned for the Alpha, of course. For Andersen and Cruzet. For him? Would she see him now as something more than the mojado stowaway?

"Sí, señora." Not thinking, he used the Spanish words. "We are returning."

"Your report?" He had been too slow to speak. "Good news, or bad?"

"Yo no sé."

She would wish to know if they had found dangers that might stop the terraforming of the planet, but he found no words to tell of the tower's sealed door or the light in the ice or how the gods of the planet had split it to make a trap for el Señor Hinch. Or el demonio that had seized Dr. Andersen.

"Good or bad, I do not know." He tried to speak in English, though he had never mastered the correct Anglo accent. "We encountered phenomena I did not understand. We lost el Señor Hinch, but we have been allowed to return."

"Phenomena?" He wondered for a moment if his language had confused her. "What do you mean?"

"Strange things, Señora. Muy extranjero."

Perhaps the Spanish would not matter now. He wanted to tell her all he'd seen and felt. The vastness of the tower, the weight of the ages it had stood, the miraculous opening of the ice, the alien power that had taken and released Dr. Andersen. Yet he knew he could never make her understand.

"Siento. I have no words to say."

"Mr. Hinch?" She seemed sharply impatient. "You mean to say he's dead? Let me speak to somebody else."

"Un momento."

Cruzet was in his berth. Mondragon called Andersen and went down to take the wheel. Driving on, following the wheel marks on the frost, marks that might be here forever, he thought of her and Kip and la niñita. Kip would be glad of his return and eager to listen when he spoke of the ice gods. Day cared only for her mother and the panda doll.

La rubia herself? Her concern was los niñitos. If he could help her find or make a good home for them, she might be grateful. He wished to have her close, to hear her actual voice again, to share her Anglo world and share his own with her. Or was the gulf too great? The gulf between the quantum engineers and el pobrecito who had herded goats on the bare Chihuahua hills, a gulf as deep as the rift the ice gods had opened to defend their fortress tower.

●

Cruzet woke and took the wheel. Mondragon made syncafe and heated one more chicken-flavored novakelp stew. They stopped to gather in the cabin for a last quick meal. Andersen drove on while Mondragon slept. When he woke to take the wheel again the ice white crest of the peninsula was rising against the stars ahead.

Andersen was above him in the bubble, humming some quick-paced melody, when at last they crossed the old beach and jolted up the rocky slopes to the ship. The air lock of the work balloon stood open to welcome them. They rolled inside. Air roared in around them. The inner gates opened. The wide floor was nearly empty, but in a moment people came streaming in through the safety gate. Among them were the engineers who had helped assemble the spider, and the security officers in their stiff black caps.

Mondragon saw Glengarth and Senn, and even Jesus Rivera in a greasy apron, a cabin steward, an assistant cook who was also a hydroponics engineer with knowledge of terraforming. All were smiling and expectant, anxious for news.

He looked for la rubia and found her at last, coming through the safety gate, Day clinging to her hand and Kip running ahead. A man walked beside her, a tall stranger in blue seamed with the black security stripe. He caught a quick breath and looked again. The stranger was Jonas Roak, walking very close to her.

Fifteen

Kip was sitting with Rima and Day in a booth at the side of the dining room when he saw Mondragon coming down the line of serving machines.

"Mom! There's Carlos. I'll ask him to sit with us."

She saw Andersen and Cruzet at another table, grinning at Mondragon and waving him toward them.

"Kip!" she called. "Don't you see . . ."

He was already running to meet Mondragon, eager to carry his tray. Mondragon followed him back to the table, smiling hesitantly at Rima.

"Señora, perdoname por favor—"

"Won't you join us?" Graciously, she waved him to sit. "But let's speak English. Your own English is really excellent."

"Gracias—" He caught himself. "Thank you, Dr. Virili, but I left Chihuahua so recently. I do not have the good accent."

"No le hace." She smiled. "I like your accent."

Happy with her kindness, he wanted to explain himself. "Everything has been so strange to me."

"To all of us, since we took off." He liked her smile. "I hope we can relax a little now."

He wasn't sure of that, but he didn't want to spoil her smile. He thanked Kip, who was setting the dishes out of his tray and urging him to sit. He slid into the booth beside him, glad to be back from the encounter with the demons of the ice, glad to be sitting here with la rubia—with Rima, if he dared to think her name. He felt a little awkward, uncertain of what he could say that would not break the moment, but she was already speaking.

"We all appreciate what you have done for us, Mr. Mondragon. You and your companions." She paused to nod at Cruzet and Andersen, who were walking on to another table. "I've heard their reports. I think we can be pretty safe in the habitat now, but I want to hear your own story."

"If you have talked to Mr. Andersen," he said, "you know more than I do. They—the beings of the tower—examined him. They could have killed us all, the way they killed Mr. Hinch. But they let us go. I don't know why."

"I don't expect to ask them." She grew serious. "Now, perhaps, Captain Stecker will let us go on digging for the habitat."

"Mr. Carlos?" Day looked up from her bowl of cereal and soya milk. "Did you see Me Me?"

"I didn't." He shook his head. "I'm sorry."

"She's my panda. She's lost on the ice."

Blue eyes wide and bright with tears, she looked so tiny and pathetic that he wanted to pick her up and comfort her. "Don't worry," he told her. "We saw many kilometers of ice, all of them empty. I don't think Me Me is out there. If she had been, we'd have found her."

"I know she's there, Mr. Carlos. She—" Day swallowed hard, trying not to cry. "She keeps begging for help."

"Dear, you mustn't fret so much." Rima put her arm

around the child. "You know we left your panda back on Earth, with a friend to take care of her."

Day looked stubbornly unconvinced.

"She's got this silly idea," Kip tried to explain. "I don't know how."

"There's a lot we don't know." Mondragon stirred soya-sweet and tufacream into his syncafe. It tasted almost good. He turned hopefully to Rima. "You're already digging for the habitat?"

"The work's going well," she said. "We're already finished cutting out a chamber for the entry air lock. Tomorrow we can begin spraying sealant on the walls to make them airtight."

"Exciting!" Kip added brightly. "We went with Mr. Glengarth to see the cliff where they're digging. The place still looks cold and dark as anywhere, but the habitat will let us move off the ship. We'll have our own apartment. Mr. Glengarth says there will be a school with big playrooms, and hydroponic farms where we can grow our own garden."

"One more question, Mr. Mondragon." Rima spoke when he had run down. "This tower you found? How old is it?"

Quién sabe? But he must speak English.

"Very old," he said. "Maybe older than the ice."

"Are you sure?"

"It's made of black stone, or something like stone." Wanting her to think him something more than the ignorant mojado, he spoke slowly, careful with the accent. "Great blocks like brick, larger than houses. So tough it's hard to drill, even with a laser. Change must be slow here, yet stones have fallen from the top and shattered on the ground, so long ago that ice has covered half of them. We saw nothing that seemed alive. Nothing except things I do not understand. The rings of color on the tower wall and the ice quake that trapped Mr. Hinch."

"Who does understand?" She shrugged and pulled little Day closer before she looked back at him. "I asked because of a fossil skeleton we dug out of the cliff. Dr. Singh thinks the creature was able to fly. Probably intelligent. She found puzzling objects with it. Perhaps beads or money—"

"Like that black pebble you found on the beach," Kip said. "The one you gave me."

"Sí. I remember."

"A riddle to us." For a moment she looked hard at him. "Dr. Singh was wondering if the creatures were advanced enough to invent a high technology. If perhaps they built the tower while the planet was alive. And if some of them might still exist. I guess we have no way to know, but what do you think?"

Quién sabe? Careful to avoid Spanish, he was glad she trusted his opinion. "Something did sense our ship still out in space. Something lit the signals on the ice and on the tower—if the flashes of color were meant to be signals. Something did kill Mr. Hinch. But what the something is, I don't know."

He saw the shadow of worry on her face.

"We may be in no danger," he assured her quickly. "The beings studied,"—he stopped to find the English word—"interrogated Mr. Andersen. Searched his memory, he says, trying to learn all about us. They could have killed us, but they let us go. . . ."

His voice trailed off when he saw four men in black security caps coming down the serving line. One of them was Jonas Roak.

●

"Mr. Roak." Kip dropped his voice and spoke to his mother, his blue eyes narrowed. "I don't like him. He says Carlos brought the bomb to blow us up."

"Eat your breakfast," Rima told him.

"I brought no bomb." Rima was searching his face, perhaps not so certain as Kip was. He repeated, with an injured emphasis, "I know nothing of the bomb, except that Mr. Roak accuses me."

Kip ignored his soyamax toast and alga-egg omelet.

"It was Mr. Roak himself." Almost whispering, he frowned at the men. "Dr. Cruzet says he was furious when they got the phone call and sealed everybody on the ship. He's the bomber."

"You mustn't say that." Rima rapped the table by his plate. "I'm not all that fond of him, but he was the launch inspector. His duty was to keep the ship safe, not to kill us. There seems to be no real evidence against anybody. Earth and Fairshare are a long way behind us. The bomb didn't explode. It's no threat to us now—"

She flushed, turning suddenly in her seat.

"I'm sorry, Mr. Mondragon. Mr. Glengarth says you are no longer suspected. You've proved yourself a brave and able man. I hope you can forgive me—"

"De nada—" He caught himself. "A Fairshare activist did help me get aboard. There was a Fairshare document in the coveralls they gave me. But most certainly—" His voice caught, and he glanced into Kip's anxious face. "I swear by the saints that I am innocent."

He stopped abruptly, with a sharp catch of his breath.

"Thank you, Mr. Mondragon," she was saying. "I have to believe you."

Hardly listening, he was watching the four security men as they walked past toward another table. Roak saw them and turned to the booth with a tight smile for Rima.

"Dr. Virili." He ignored Mondragon and the children. "If I may interrupt for a moment, I should tell you that we'll have to pull most of the people and equipment out of your habitat project."

"Why . . ." She was speechless for a moment. "Why is that?"

"We're opening an excavation on the south beach."

"What for?" Anxiety edged her voice. "We surveyed the beach, as you probably know. The seismosonic probes found enormous boulders in the permafrost. The sandstone cliffs in Daybreak Canyon have proved to be a far preferable site—"

"Not for our purposes." Blandly, Roak interrupted. "Many of us never liked the notion of living like rats here under the ice. When the survey team failed to find what we wanted on the north beach, we sent them south. They've found a site with three hundred meters of clay and a soft sandstone, stuff we can excavate.

"Plenty for a launch pit."

"Impossible! We can't relaunch." After a moment she tried to smooth her voice, but Mondragon heard the tension in it. "Ask Mr. Glengarth."

"I've heard the objections." Roak shrugged. "It's true that building a launch facility will strain our resources. True that we have no assurance that any new destination would be better than this one."

"Reason enough to reject it."

"Not for everybody." He grinned as if her tone amused him. "Captain Stecker and I have been working with a group of engineers who feel very strongly that any chance whatever is better than anything here."

"That's insane!" her words burst out. "It's suicide!"

"One opinion. Not Captain Stecker's." He reached to touch her shoulder. "I'm sorry, Rima. . . ."

"He isn't!" Kip whispered hotly. "Not a bit."

Roak ignored him.

"I stopped to warn you that our plans for the pit are almost finalized. You'll get new orders from Captain Stecker. Orders to abort your excavation at once."

"Stecker!" Indignation exploded in her. "He's a drunken idiot, sulking in his cabin! He's got no right to order anything."

"He's still captain of the ship."

"Then tell him the truth!" People around them were turning to look, and she lowered her voice. "Make him listen."

"What truth?" He shrugged, blandly ironic. "Our hopeless situation has never been a secret. The question is what we do about it. Captain Stecker has had very competent advice from Krasov and Fujiwara. In fact, a whole team of able quantum engineers—"

"A team of cowards!" Her voice had flared again, and she paused to calm herself. "Men who sneer at the whole science of terraforming. If you recall, we set out from Earth pledged to establish humankind wherever the waveships happened to take us. Some of us remember that. Ask Mr. Glengarth. Ask Mr. Andersen."

She gestured at Andersen and Cruzet. They were listening intently from their own table. Andersen grinned, nodding silently.

"We've been trying to remind the captain," she drove on, quietly desperate. "To convince him that our only actual chance at long-term survival anywhere is right here. Beginning in a very modest way with the habitat and a hydroponic garden. We'll have problems, but we can learn by doing. We'll have to search for whatever resources the planet happens to offer and extend all our efforts when we have the know-how to make extensions possible—"

She stopped when Roak walked away.

"Excuse us, Mr. Mondragon." She rose, shaken and trembling, and turned to the children. "I think we've finished eating." She picked up Day, who was staring after Roak and about to cry, and left the booth.

Kip looked back to shake his head at Carlos.

●

Late that night, Day crawled into Rima's berth and clung to her, shivering.

"Help me, Mommy!" she was begging. "I'm afraid!"

"What's wrong, baby?" Rima cuddled her. "Tell me what's wrong."

"The bad thing," she sobbed. "The bad black thing out on the ice. It got Me Me. Now it's coming after me."

"It can't hurt you, darling." Rima sat up on the edge of the berth, rocking her. "You're here in the ship with me. We're all of us cozy and safe."

"But we're not safe." Day stiffened against her. "I see it coming over the ice. Coming to take me. Nobody can stop it."

"Mr. Glengarth can," Rima said. "Dr. Andersen can. Dr. Cruzet can. They went out on the ice, and they came back safe. They are braver and stronger than any bad thing."

"Not the black thing." Her voice grew slow and strange. "It's worse than anything, because it belongs in the dark and loves the ice and hates everything alive."

"Don't forget Carlos." In the old jumpsuit he wore for pajamas, Kip had come out of his own curtained berth. "You're not a baby anymore. Don't be so silly. You sound like some adventure with Captain Cometeer. Carlos has just been a thousand kilometers out across the ice. He didn't see your precious panda doll. He didn't see any black monsters either."

"You're the big silly." She shivered in Rima's arms. "You play too many silly games. The bad thing's real. I see it closer now. It's coming to take me, the way it took Me Me."

"Do you have to be so stupid?" Kip yawned, sleepily scornful. "We're sealed inside the ship. It has a thick titanium hull. We have brave men to guard us. Like Dr. Andersen and Carlos—"

"Don't call me stupe!" Day protested. "You're the stupe, or you would see the bad thing coming."

"We're all looking for it," Rima said. "I don't see anything. Can you tell us what it's like? Maybe we can help, if you try to tell us what it is."

"It looks like . . ."

Shuddering, Day whimpered and huddled closer to her.

"Hold me, Mommy! Hold me tighter! Don't let him get me!"

"I'll hold you, darling. We'll all protect you, if you can tell us what it looks like."

"A man." Her voice was hushed and faint. "A thing that used to be a man. It's Mr. Hinch!"

"Crybaby Daby!"

"Don't call her Daby!" Rima scolded him. "You know she hates it."

"She ought to know Jake Hinch is dead. Carlos saw the ice gods bury him under the ocean ice a thousand kilometers away." He made a face at Day. "How can he get here?"

Trembling in Rima's arms, her breath a slow, raspy wheeze, Day took a long time to answer.

"Poor Mr. Hinch!" A strange slow croon. "I see him better now. He's in a tight yellow suit. His cap and his glasses are gone. Ice is frozen in his beard and his hair. He's all white like the ice, with a terrible dead look frozen on his face. He walks stiff and slow because he's really dead."

"Silly!" Kip whispered. "Sil—"

He stopped when Day went on, her voice shrill with fright.

"Mommy, he's coming. Coming to take me with him down under the ice. Coming faster than anything!"

"My baby girl!" Rima swayed to rock her. "It's just an ugly dream. Can't you try to wake up? You'll be okay when you do."

She was quiet, except for the labored wheeze, till her body jerked abruptly.

"He got in! He's in the ship. He's coming up the stairs."

"He can't possibly be," Kip said. "The air lock is sealed. Nothing can get in."

"But he did. He came to take me. Mommy, don't let him—"

She screamed, a quavery shriek that rose higher and higher till something choked it off. Her body went lax. Rima rocked her a little longer, and laid her down on the berth.

"Is she dead?" Kip asked. "She looks like she's dead."

"No! No! She can't be dead." Rima bent over her to listen at her chest. "Her heart's still beating. She's still breathing."

"What happened?" Kip demanded. "Can any nightmare be like that?"

"I don't know." She shook her head. "It frightens me."

Day lay limp on the berth, but Kip saw that one little fist was clenched. He pried it open and found a bright black bead.

"The pebble." He held it up for Rima to see. "The six-sided pebble that Carlos found on the beach, up where they're digging the habitat. She thought it was pretty, and I gave it to her."

Sixteen

Glengarth in the lead, they came out of the elevator on the comcom deck and waited in the darkness of the conference room till he turned up the holoscreens to let the starlight in. Serious and silent, they took seats at the long table, which curved against the hull. Andersen, Cruzet, and Mondragon on his right. Rima, Reba Washburn, and Jim Cheng on his left.

They all turned to watch the elevator door.

"Only us." Cheng shrugged when nobody else emerged. "With a tough nut to crack."

He bent over a little pocket computer, slender fingers dancing over the keys, myopic eyes close to the tiny screen. Rima picked up the knitting she was learning to do, beginning with a red cap for Day. The skill should be useful here if they survived to use it. She glanced at Mondragon and felt a shock.

He was nervously fingering a small bright pebble. She

thought for a moment that it was the six-sided bead they had found in Day's clenched hand. Relieved, she saw that it was worn round, blue and not black. A harmless bit of stone off the ancient beach.

Earlier, when she had returned the bead to Mondragon, she had told him about Day's dreadful dreams and begged him to get rid of it.

"Maybe it caused the nightmares," she had told him. "Maybe it didn't. But it's exactly like those odd beads Dr. Singh found on the amphibian skeleton. They're still a riddle. Day cried to keep the thing, but I'm afraid for her to have it."

"I'll turn it in to Dr. Singh," he had said. "Tell little Day I'll look for her panda when I'm out on the ice again."

●

They waited in the conference room till Glengarth looked at his watch.

"Twenty minutes," he muttered. "Stecker promised to have his people here twenty minutes ago."

Another twenty had passed before the elevator door slid open. Krasov and Fujiwara came out. Silently, Fujiwara bowed. A small restless man with gold-rimmed eyeglasses and a mouth full of gold teeth, he took a seat on the inside of the table's long curve. Dropping his dark-circled eyes as if somehow abashed, he wiped his sweat-beaded forehead with a yellow silk handkerchief. Krasov followed. A big man, stolid and deliberate, he sat staring across the table at Andersen and Cruzet as if to take their measure as chess opponents. Neither man spoke.

Jonas Roak and Stecker followed five minutes later, Wyatt Kellick behind them. Stecker muttered a response to Glengarth's greeting and sat glaring across the table, saying nothing else. As the tension grew, Rima dropped her knitting to study them. Roak met her eyes with a smirk that made her flush. Krasov glanced sharply at her and frowned again at

Glengarth. Fujiwara's restless hand balled and squeezed the yellow handkerchief, spread it to mop his face, balled and squeezed it again.

Stecker wore a gold-braided uniform jacket over a white jumpsuit, both of them unpressed and dirty. He needed a shave, and Rima thought he had put on weight. He sprawled back in his chair with an air of bored impatience.

Kellick sat erect, his narrow gray eyes sweeping the starlit frost and the dead black sun behind them. Rugged and tall, his long pale hair held off his forehead with the skin of a diamondback, he might have been the Caribbean pirate in a holodrama. She thought he must have been handsome once, but his face was now a mask of scars, his nose flattened and misshapen.

She had asked Reba Washburn for his history.

"We'd all like to know." Reba frowned and shook her head. "Jake Hinch sent him to us not long before we took off, with orders from Stecker to put him on ship security. No documents. He says he's been a pugilist and a mercenary soldier. Trying to check him out, we got hints of a colorful past. At various times, he seems to have carried passports from Norway, Chile, and South Africa, under a variety of names. I think he has done prison time. He's Stecker's hired gun."

Now, staring out of the ship, he seemed indifferent to everybody.

"Okay. Here we are." Stecker looked around him, hiccuped, and hunched forward in his seat, scowling at Glengarth. His voice was thick, and he stopped to clear his throat. "What's this all about?"

"Mr. Stecker." Glengarth straightened to face him. "We have a bone to pick. We're out here on our own, Earth and its laws behind us forever. You should recall the covenant we all signed before takeoff."

"I signed nothing."

"Nor I." Roak blinked and caught his breath. "I was shanghaied, remember?"

"No matter." Glengarth paused to survey the five men lined up against him. "Mr. Stecker, the covenant governs us now whether or not you or anybody signed it. The point now is that your status changed when we landed here."

Cruzet and Cheng were nodding.

"Gerry Alt!" Andersen spoke, his voice edged with bitter emotion. "An old friend. You robbed him, Mr. Stecker. Robbed him of his ship and all he lived for. You might as well have put a bullet in his head."

Blinking blearily, Stecker turned to Roak as if for help that didn't come.

"Our feeling, sir." Cruzet spoke with the dry-voiced precision that was almost itself an accent. "But that aside, you have never appeared to be the sort of leader who might enable us to survive here. Our hard situation demands a better man."

"Huh—" Stecker's grunt became another hiccup.

"Mr. Stecker," Glengarth resumed, his tone grimly grave. "If you don't know the covenant, it provides for such situations as this. It allows the ship's company to call an election to replace the chief officer. We are calling such an election now."

Stecker shrugged and looked again at Roak.

"Watch yourselves!" Roak snarled. "If you recall, Mr. Stecker was director of StarSeed Mission. Under our international charter, he had full authority over all Mission operations. He was simply doing his duty when he replaced Alt for embezzlement of Mission funds—"

"Who?" Glengarth stared at Stecker. "Who's the embezzler?"

Stecker flushed.

"Mr. Stecker is still your captain." Roak ignored the interruption. "He is not bound by your so-called covenant, and he will certainly punish any insubordination.

"So what's your gripe?"

"Dr. Virili?" Nodding at Rima, Glengarth waited for her to speak.

"Sir, I think you know." Searchingly, she looked at Roak. "We set out from Earth to establish a colony on any habitable planet we happened to reach. This planet does seem hostile, but we have the skills and the technology to survive here. That's our duty to our children, and to the human race."

"Maybe," Roak muttered. "Or maybe that's your own crazy dream."

"We'll have problems." She shrugged and sat straighter. "But we've already made a promising start. Our gripe, if you want to call it that, is the way you've pulled men and equipment out of the habitat to excavate a launch pit. That's the real lunatic dream. Sheer suicide."

"A matter of opinion." Roak glanced at Fujiwara, who was mopping his face again with the yellow handkerchief. "Some of us believe we have a good chance to get the ship back into quantum mode. Right, Doctor?"

"Possibly." Huddled in his seat, Fujiwara looked miserably uncertain. "We have inventoried available resources, but quantum computations are always difficult. Our results leave critical factors in doubt, but I believe we do have a certain possibility—"

"Certain?" Andersen demanded. "Did you calculate the odds?"

"We did," he admitted unhappily. "I hoped for better—"

"Nyet!" Krasov burst out, almost violently. "I won't go underground!"

They all waited till he went on more quietly.

"My father was a coal miner in Siberia. The dust ruined his lungs. He died in a gas explosion while I was still a child. Soon after, a union agent took us down into the mine. I was afraid to go, but the teachers wanted us to know what the mines were like. The cage dropped us into a horrid pit, a wet little cave with water dripping.

"The power went off while we were there. Most of the group had already gone back to the top. Just a handful of us were left there in the dark. The sudden darkness was suffocating. The air had a stale stink, like something dead and rotten. The silence was terrible till somebody screamed. We waited for the cage to come back.

"It didn't come. The teacher wanted us to sing, but too many kids were crying. The stillness was terrible when she finally got them stopped. All I heard was the loud drip of water, like I thought it had dripped onto my father's face. It echoed in the dark. I thought we were all going to die the way he did, with the water dripping on us."

He laughed uneasily.

"Of course the lights finally did come on. The cage rattled back. We got out alive, but I'm not going underground again. Not even into that pit in the cliff where Singh found the dead monster." He stopped to blink at Glengarth. "If you want to know, that's why I've got to get out of this black hell. Dead for a billion years, unless those monsters are still alive under the ice.

"Or underground!"

Breathing hard, fists knotted, he turned defiantly to Rima.

"We've seen no sign of that." She nodded sympathetically. "I know you were dreadfully hurt. But you won't have to go underground. You can stay on the ship till we can set up surface buildings—"

"Nyet!" he shouted again. "Better die quick than slow."

"You will die quick," Andersen promised him. "If you attempt quantum flight. You'd have to improvise essential wave conversion equipment we didn't bring. You wouldn't have adequate power. Something would certainly fail."

"Perhaps we die in a nuclear blast." Grim-faced, Krasov nodded. "Perhaps our best way out."

"No sweat." Roak turned to Kellick. "Wyatt, tell 'em why."

"Remember the bomb? No matter who set it." Kellick grinned unpleasantly at Mondragon. "The captain and Mr. Hinch needed an expert to disarm it. I'm the expert. Trained in high explosives, military and civilian. You can call me a pro."

His eyes were a dull slate blue. One of them, with a deep scar above it, seemed slightly out of focus. He fixed the other on Reba Washburn for a moment, and then on Glengarth.

"We did disarm and examine the device. A professional high-tech job, with nothing left to identify the maker or the planter. Mr. Hinch had us lock it in the ship security safe when we were through. Lieutenant Washburn found us a brown soyasweet carton that happened to fit it."

Reba gasped.

"Your box is still there." He leered at her. "But it happens that I'm an old pro on both sides of the security racket. I made contacts on the crew that installed your safe. I've got the know-how to look inside. We've removed the device."

His seeing eye swept Glengarth and his companions.

"We've set it again, this time more professionally. Naturally I can't tell you much about the location, except to say that it's where nobody is likely to run across it by accident. And it's set to detonate if anybody touches it."

He finished with a small smug nod for Roak and Stecker.

"Thanks, Wyatt." Blandly, Roak turned back to Glengarth. "That's the reason, sir, that you'll call no election. Wyatt is a pro. You can trust his expertise. The ship is in no danger, not as long as you take your orders from me and Captain Stecker. If you balk . . ."

He shrugged.

"Your move, Glengarth," Stecker growled. "Think about it."

"Let's all think about it." Glengarth paused, urgently scanning the hostile faces across the table. "We're on our own, here forever. Under the covenant, we agreed to set up a new democracy wherever we landed. Free elections, equal rights for all—"

"Huh?" Stecker grunted. "Get back to duty, or we'll blow you to hell."

"Threats can't help anybody now," Glengarth said. "But let's be reasonable."

"We've gone past reason." Kellick squinted defiantly with his one working eye. "The bomb can blow us up. A problem at the pit can blow us up. An accident in quantum flight. A neutron star, if we happen to hit it. We'll take our chances." His hard face worked and his voice rose scratchily. "What we won't do is dig our own graves here in this black hell."

"Gentlemen—" Glengarth turned to Krasov and Fujiwara. "Can't you see—"

"We've seen the alien signals flashing at us." Fujiwara frowned uneasily at Andersen and Cruzet, his restless fingers twisting and untwisting the yellow handkerchief. "That black tower. The queer quake that killed Mr. Hinch. We aren't wanted. I don't want to sit here till they decide how to kill us."

All silent for a moment, they sat face-to-face across the table. Fujiwara's nervous fingers froze. Stecker belched. Krasov raised his head to stare at the starlit frost and the dead black sun on the holoscreens.

"You asked to talk." Stecker's puffy eyes quinted at Glengarth. "Now what?"

Glengarth turned to Rima. Her face stiff and pale, she shook her head.

"Here's what." Roak's chin thrust out. "We've heard your case. What's your answer?"

Glengarth frowned at Andersen and Cruzet. Stonily, they shrugged.

"If you're all insane—," Roak began.

Not listening, they rose to leave.

"One moment more." Roak raised his hand. "Mr. Glengarth will remain as first officer." He glanced at Stecker. "Right, Captain?"

"Right." Stecker nodded, with an uneasy smile. "Carry on."

"Thank you, Captain." Roak turned back to Glengarth, assuming a tone of brusque command. "You will continue to keep the ship and crew in order. You will support our effort to complete a new launch facility and get us back into quantum drive. Understand?"

"We do." He spoke with bitter emphasis. "We certainly understand."

"You're all a pack of cowards!" Rima burst out bitterly. "Fools, too, throwing our only real chance away."

"Sorry, my dear." Roak grinned at her. "If you're disappointed."

"We are." Bleakly, Andersen nodded. "You've sentenced us to death."

"Think so?" A sardonic inquiry. "I'd like to remind you that we all got the same sentence when we left Earth. The flight was simply our appeal for reprieve. This dead planet is no reprieve. Another takeoff will be a new appeal—"

"A new appeal?" Mocking him, Andersen looked at Fujiwara. "Let's ask Kobo."

Fujiwara dropped the yellow handkerchief, staring blankly back.

"Speak up," Roak snapped at him. "You and Nikolai said you could get us back in space."

"Not exactly." He shook his head. "We only promised to try. Promised because we see no choice. We told you it all depends. If we get the breaks. If we can really do useful work in this vacuum and darkness and cold. If we can dig an adequate pit and find bedrock under us strong enough to absorb the recoil effects. If we can rig all the gear we need . . ."

His voice trailed unhappily off.

"Nik and I—" Stammering uncertainly, he began again. "We're certified quantum engineers, but we don't know all we should." He turned, appealing to Roak. "Sir, you know we're not sure of our skills. We need help—"

"You'll get it." Roak turned dictatorial. "Dr. Andersen. Dr. Cruzet. You have the know-how we need. You will join the launch team, under Dr. Fujiwara. Understand?"

"We do," Andersen muttered. "I'm afraid we do."

"Thank you, gentlemen." Roak pushed back his chair. "That concludes our business."

Seeming relieved that it was over, Stecker led the group into the elevator. The last to go, Roak stopped to look back at Rima. She faced him defiantly for a moment before she flushed and dropped her eyes from his bold stare.

"That pretty bitch." His words came faintly back through the closing door. "She's mine. . . ."

Seventeen

Dismally, they followed Glengarth back to his cabin on the deck above.

"I heard him." Mondragon spoke to Rima in a hot undertone as they left the elevator. "If he touches you, I'll kill him."

"No!" Her voice was husky with emotion. "Not that."

"Carlos, please!" Close behind them, Glengarth caught his arm. "Don't think of killing. I wish we were rid of him, but that could turn us into a mob. Without some sort of order, we're all dead."

"My mother prayed to los santos, but we've found no saints here." He shrugged unhappily. "We must help ourselves."

"If we can." Glengarth gave him a grim little nod. "In any way we can. Any civilized way."

Rima stood looking around the cabin. It seemed small, because the ship tapered toward the bow, but Glengarth had made it a home. Its familiar comfort cheered her for a moment. The holowall glowed softly white, shutting out the frigid dark.

The sofa against the wall was also his berth. There were good chairs, a library table, shelves filled with books and tapes.

Her glance lingered wistfully on the small bits of his past on Earth. A framed photo of an elderly couple standing in a farmhouse door, a tall white silo in the background. His parents? A small Kurdistan carpet on the floor. A glass case that held a pair of Chinese ceramic vases, a worn family Bible, a toy locomotive with a broken wheel, a conch shell, a fossil trilobite, the bronze figure of a rider on a bucking horse.

Her despair came back when she turned. The others were seating themselves around the room, looking silently at Glengarth. He stood staring bleakly at a signed holoshot of Gerald Alt till Reba Washburn came out of the elevator, her mouth set in a bitter line.

Glengarth turned to her, silently inquiring.

"The soyasweet carton is still in my safe." Her heavy body sagged. "Empty. They do have the bomb."

"Kellick!" He mouthed the name like a dirty word. "Obviously, the pro he said he is."

"So." Jim Cheng nodded. "What can we do?"

"Play their game, at least for now." He shrugged in dull resignation. "They're desperate enough to kill us all."

"Do they have any chance?" Rima asked. "To get us back into quantum flight?"

In silent inquiry, Glengarth turned to Cruzet and Andersen.

Cruzet shook his head. "None I can see."

"Nor I." Andersen nodded somberly. "We aren't equipped for it. We don't know what to expect from the locals. Maybe they'll tolerate us. Maybe they won't. We don't have a clue."

●

Indra Singh came to Glengarth the next afternoon, asking to continue the dig in the cliff.

"A remarkable site," she said. "It was on the shore of an ancient lake or shallow sea, where floods buried their victims. I've protected it, and all I need is permission to keep on digging."

He called Stecker's cabin. Roak answered and listened impatiently.

"Request denied." He was sharply curt. "She'd need a vehicle. We're using both spiders at the pit."

She went to Roak himself.

"We ought to learn more about the natives," she urged him. "The amphibian skeleton is exciting evidence of advanced life that once existed here. Even if you hold up the habitat, I think we ought to explore the peninsula."

"Looking for what?"

"Fossil remains. Artifacts. Ruins. Perhaps another tower."

"Sorry, my dear." His smirk made her flush. "The pit takes all our resources."

She appealed to Cruzet and Andersen, who were working with Krasov and Fujiwara to survey and clear a site for the pit.

"I'll make a pitch," Andersen agreed. "First to Fujiwara. He lives in terror, convinced that the aliens are hiding in the dark all around us, somehow watching every move we make. He might relax and do better work after a look at the lower peninsula."

●

Singh brought Krasov and Fujiwara with her to Glengarth's cabin. Fujiwara was jittery about undertaking any search, afraid of what might be discovered. Krasov didn't care.

"What if the aliens do decide to slaughter us?" He laughed. "Likely more interesting than a blowup in the pit or a collision with a black hole a billion years from now in another universe."

They called Roak, who balked at first. Captain Stecker,

he said, would allow no delays. When Krasov assured him that Cruzet and Andersen were ready to lay out the launcher, with no more to do till the excavation was complete, he agreed to let them go.

"Take a few days," he muttered, "if that will pacify you. Run down the peninsula and get back to work."

Singh could go along to drive them, he said, so long as she didn't squander time digging for petrified bones.

●

Rima volunteered to monitor the radio. She left Day with Alma Sternberg, who was a nurse as well as a hydroponics engineer. Day was sometimes happy with the Sternberg children, but grieving more often for Me Me.

Kip came to the control room with her. The lights were dimmed to let them see the starlit world outside. He had brought his Game Box, but he laid it aside to watch the sledge loads of heavy equipment creeping south to the pit from the abandoned habitat and the ship itself. He followed the red spark of the heat lamp bobbing and weaving over the frost-dusted ice and the frozen beaches. It was visible a long time after the machine itself had sunk below the ice horizon.

"Call them," Kip urged her. "Ask what they've found."

Static crackled in the radio, until Singh's Oxford accent boomed suddenly.

"A surprise that the ice is so smooth. Nik says it's because the planet's rotation had stopped and the cooling sun gave too little energy for wind or waves. Expansion did fracture the ice in spots, but we can steer around them."

"Miss Indra?" Kip asked. "What do you see on the land?"

"Frozen rocks and gravel on the beaches," she said. "Barren cliffs beyond, getting lower as we go. No sign of anything alive, now or ever."

Her loud voice stopped, and the radio thumped.

"What are they looking for?" Kip asked his mother. "What could they possibly find that would do us any good?"

"If we knew," she said, "they wouldn't need to go. What I hope—" Pausing for a moment, she decided he was old enough for the truth. "I hope for something that might help us stay alive."

"So you think Roak's scheme will kill us?"

She had to nod. "I think it would."

Nodding quietly, he reached for his Game Box, then laid it down again.

"I want to help," he told her. "Show me how to work the telescope and the radio."

●

She showed him, and asked if he understood.

"No problem," he told her brightly. "They're simpler than the Game Box."

He sat with her, watching the lamp's red dot dim and flicker and slowly sink. Singh called again. She had left the ice for the old beaches, wider and smoother toward the tip of the peninsula. The cliffs had sunk into eroded ridges. They had seen no ruins, no beacons, no hint of active intelligence. Rima left Kip at the radio while she went down to check on Day.

He met her with an uneasy frown when she got back.

"The lamp and the radio went out," he said. "Both together. Dr. Singh was talking. She seemed excited about something they were finding, but her voice stopped before she could say what it was. I kept calling back, but nobody answers. I'm sorry, but I didn't know what to do."

"Don't fret," she said. "There's nothing we can do. Nothing except listen for a signal and hope they're okay."

They hoped and waited, until at last the red point did flicker again.

"Alpha to ship," Singh's voice came back. "Alpha to ship."

"Ship to Alpha." Just like Captain Cometeer calling the Legion, Kip thought. "Alpha come in."

"If you lost our signal, it was because we'd entered a gap in the cliffs. A remarkable feature, though hard to explore by searchlight. At first we took it for a high-walled natural fjord, though the walls were oddly straight and vertical. I don't think the glaciers ever came this far. We drove a dozen kilometers into it, till a rock slide stopped us.

"Nik has a theory. . . ."

A moment of silence, and they heard Krasov, his stolid Ukrainian tones quickened with wonder.

"It's a straight cut across the peninsula. A canal, most certainly. Which has to imply the existence of a very considerable native population here before the oceans froze. An advanced technological culture and a busy maritime commerce."

"Commerce?" Rima asked. "In what?"

"Not much basis for a guess. The sun was probably never high here, but perpetual daylight would have reached across several thousand kilometers of ocean beyond the ridge. Maybe the natives fished. Maybe they opened mines along ice-free coasts."

Singh's voice murmured something they didn't hear.

"Geology?" Krasov spoke to her and raised his voice again. "The walls of the cut do tell an interesting story. The ridge was formed by a seismic upthrust and worn down by erosion long before the ice came. No sign of any change since the rock slide closed the canal. Which means, I think, that the end came pretty suddenly, put in relative terms."

"How do you get that?"

"The sun's a dwarf. The hydrogen fusion that lit it for a time must have depended on the fission of unstable elements. When they were used up, fusion ceased. Rather abruptly—abruptly in geologic time—the dwarf went black. The planet died. I can't imagine that anything survived."

"We're pushing on," Singh's voice came in. "Looking for clues. The tip of the peninsula is still ahead. If the creatures were actually seamen, they could have had a lighthouse there. I want to see."

●

Mondragon had worked all day with Cruzet and Andersen, driving the Beta to drag their sledgeloads of equipment to the pit. Off duty, he came to relieve Rima at the radio. Kip went down with her to pick up Day and the Sternberg children for dinner. When they had eaten, he went back to the dome with two lemon rolls for Mondragon.

The rolls were made from mutant kelp, with no natural lemon in them, but they were tart and sweet. He had almost learned to like them, and Mondragon said they were poco bueno. They sat together in the dim twilight of the dome, watching the faint red point of the Alpha's faraway lamp.

"Your mother?" Mondragon asked. "Does she speak of me?"

"Only when I ask her. She knows I like you. She doesn't—" Awkwardly, he hesitated. "She doesn't say much about it, because she knows how much I like you, but she can't forget how you got aboard. I know you didn't bring the bomb, but she's still not sure."

"I'm sorry." He shrugged in the Mexican way, and slowly shook his head. "Very sorry, because I admire her greatly."

"She knows you do." Kip's tone grew solemn. "But I think she's afraid."

"How can I show her . . ."

He didn't have to answer. Mondragon turned to adjust the telescope again, and they sat searching the dark horizon where the red search lamp had been. They never found it, but Singh's voice came with a brief blast of static.

". . . near the end of the ridge. We'll soon turn back, un-less . . ."

Her signal died.

●

They listened together till Rima called on the intercom for Kip to come down to bed. She took turns with Sternberg in the dome the next day. Andersen and Cruzet took their own turns when they came off duty at the pit. They heard no signal. On the third day they begged Glengarth to authorize a rescue expedition.

"I've already spoken to the captain," he told them. "Or at least to Mr. Roak. They say forget it. I told them we'd better find out what happened to Singh and her people in the Alpha. I think they're afraid to know. Afraid we'd lose the Beta."

They got nothing on the fourth day. Rima let Kip watch the monitor on the fifth day, when she had to care for Day and the Sternberg kids. All he heard was the mutter and rattle of interstellar static. Tired of that, he set up an adventure on the Game Box.

He joined Captain Cometeer on an expedition to rescue the Silver Queen from the Steel Eaters. Guiding his para-matter craft through a magnetic storm, he had landed on the battle planet of the Iron Emperor when suddenly he was listening to the static again, wondering what had become of the Alpha. He had given up the game before the interphone rang.

"Good news, Mr. Kip!" Glengarth was calling. "You can tell your mother that Roak and the captain have agreed to a search-and-rescue expedition. They didn't like to stop work on the pit, but Andy gave them no choice."

He called his mother. She was with him in the dome a few minutes later, along with Cruzet and Andersen. Mondragon was close behind them.

"How did you do it?" Rima was asking Andersen.

"Gentle persuasion." He gave her a bleak little grin. "I re-minded them that establishing a launch complex was a major undertaking even back on Earth, with materials we could order from anywhere. Building it here on the permafrost is going to need a strong team.

"The missing engineers are key players on our team. Dr. Fujiwara is our expert in quantum math. Dr. Krasov is the systems engineer that Roak claimed to be, with know-how to pull the whole job together. I told the captain we'd never get off the ground without Krasov and Fujiwara here to do their share. I slipped in a hint that Tony and I couldn't do much at all without them."

"Roak called just now," Glengarth added. "Captain Stecker has agreed to let you go. You and Tony. Carlos has volunteered to drive you."

Kip saw his mother looking hard at Mondragon. He looked back with an anxious half-smile. They both stood frozen so long Kip wondered what they were thinking. Neither one spoke, till she caught her breath and turned suddenly back to Andersen.

"The risk?" she asked. "What about the risk?"

"Quién sabe? as Carlos puts it." He nodded amiably at Mondragon. "Who knows? We've promised to take no needless risk. So did Indra and the engineers. So far as we know, she'd had no hint of any danger."

He shrugged and turned soberly to Glengarth. "Are we cleared to go?"

"Cleared," Glengarth told him. "To leave as soon as you can service the machine and load supplies."

Kip stood beside his mother, watching wistfully as they turned to leave the dome.

"Carlos . . ." His voice quivered, but he caught his breath and stubbornly went on. "I wish I could go with you."

They all stared in surprise.

"Better stick to your Game Box," Glengarth told him. "This is a game for men."

"Ahora no." Mondragon gave him a very grave smile. "But sometime, perhaps, if your good mother is willing."

Eighteen

They left early the next morning—morning by the ship's clocks, which still ran on Earth time. Mondragon drove while Andersen looked after the fusion engine and the air recycler and Cruzet stood in the lookout bubble, sweeping the searchlight along the ice-bound coast.

The Alpha vehicle had left its tracks on the frost, but Singh and the engineers had kept to smoother ice farther out, pushing steadily south till they reached the canal. There, they drove deep into the narrow cut and Andersen radioed Glengarth to report.

"The builders were certainly competent engineers. The site itself is proof of that. The peninsula ridge, as we mapped it from space, is low and narrow here, the rock so stable that we saw no caving till we came to the rock slide that closed the canal. It's deep and clean; they must have dumped the rubble into the sea."

"And all so long ago!" Glengarth's voice was hushed with awe. "Could their descendants have survived?"

"Not as navigators." Andersen made a quizzical shrug. "Their sun took a long time dying. These oceans were probably frozen before our Earth was born. Any link between the canal and that black tower seems pretty remote."

"Too many such riddles!" Glengarth was silent for a dozen heartbeats. "We need answers now."

"We're looking."

"Keep looking. The ship's become a volcano."

"Sit on it," Andersen said. "Sit on it."

●

After a hurried meal of the decent Earth food Jake Hinch had left aboard, Andersen climbed into the lookout bubble to log his survey of the canal. Cruzet drove them on, sending Mondragon down to rest.

"Sleep," he said, "if you can."

He couldn't. Restless in the berth, he thought of Rima and her hope for a safe future for Kip and Day. He thought uneasily of Jonas Roak, who wished to claim "the pretty bitch." He thought of the missing spider and wished for something better than he expected.

After an hour he rolled out of the berth to make a fresh pot of Hinch's fragrant Kona coffee, and took it in insulated mugs to the others. Relieving Cruzet at the wheel, he watched the red glow of the ship's own heat lamp dim and finally disappear below the horizon behind. Driving under strange stars through a silence older than time, he kept them to the Alpha's wheel tracks and kept on wondering.

The canal diggers? He groped for any sane image of whatever had sailed this ocean before it froze. Had amphibians really ruled the planet? And really built the lighthouse Singh expected? Perhaps before the canal was dug? Might something still be haunting it, waiting through endless ages on guard against unwelcome strangers?

Afraid to think of what they might learn about the Alpha's fate, he wished he were back in Cuerno del Oro, even with all its cruel poverty—if Rima and los niñitos could have been there with him. The planet was too cold, too dark, too long dead. Her dream of conquering its ice and everlasting night began to seem like madness.

Fantasmas crept into his mind, the ghosts of the creatures that had left their bones in the sandstone and flashed their warnings from the ice. He almost thought he felt them now, watching through the starlight, angered by these rude strangers with their strange machines and dynamite.

●

They had lost radio contact with the ship. And no answer came when they called the Alpha. Or when they called again. Joining Cruzet in the bubble, Mondragon found him motionless at the console, staring blankly off into the midnight sky above the ridge.

"Those stars." He started when Mondragon spoke, and turned to explain. "You see them rising very slowly now, as the planet's orbit takes us around the dwarf." He pointed. "They're denser in that direction, toward what must be the galactic core." He made a wry face. "And easier to understand than anything we find down here around us."

Moodily silent when they stopped to eat, Andersen seemed deaf when Cruzet asked for butter.

"I was thinking." He grinned a little wistfully. "Thinking of a woman I once knew and liked. Liked a lot. We had a senseless quarrel. But for that, I might have been a professor of engineering back on the Colorado campus, doing a bit of research and skiing the Rockies with her."

They ate a little of Hinch's smoked salmon and radiated asparagus, finding no appetite even for his walnut torte or Grand Marnier. Mondragon dozed a few hours in his berth and drove again. The ragged shadow of the ridge had sunk till it was hard to follow, and he steered by the stars to keep on level ice a few kilometers out. He was nodding at the wheel in spite of himself when Cruzet shouted from the bubble.

"Indra's lamp, still shining! Maybe twenty kilometers ahead. I'm hailing it by radio."

He got no answer.

"Veer toward them," he called. "Just a little."

Veer was a new word to Mondragon, but he turned a little and watched the black horizon. The dull red point rose and grew a little brighter, but they had come within a kilometer before the spider's dim red-lit shape emerged from the twilight. When he called again, Cruzet heard only the murmur of the cosmos. Andersen stopped them two hundred meters off, while they put the searchlight on it and studied it with binoculars.

"No cruising light," he muttered. "Nothing except the heater. I see no damage. It just looks—" His voice fell. "Looks dead."

●

Andersen got into his airskin and climbed down through the air lock, Mondragon behind him. Leaving Cruzet at the searchlight, they tramped out across the frost. The Alpha's air lock hung open, the access ramp down. Mondragon stopped beside it, pointing.

"Huelas! Huelas digitales!" It took him a moment to find the English word. "Footprints." He stooped to study them with his own flashlight. "Indra's and the men's." Almost whispering, he stood up to stare at Andersen. "They wore no boots. Their feet were bare."

They climbed into the empty lock and cycled through. The three airskins hung in the entry chamber. Boots and jumpsuits lay tossed on the floor. Andersen picked up one of Singh's boots and stood staring at it, shaking his head in disbelief. Pushing past him, Mondragon found the berths in the cabin neatly made up, the fusion engine humming smoothly on standby, the green-lettered log still glowing on the monitor. The last entry read:

> *Location 944 kilometers south of the ship, 3 kilometers off the coast. We're near the peninsula tip, though we saw a chain of reefs and rocks running several hundred kilometers on beyond us. The searchlight has picked up something on land. Possibly the ruin of the lighthouse we half expected. We have stopped to study it further.*

Andersen leaned in to scan the log.

"Nothing useful." Dazed, he shook his head. "No clue to what drove them crazy. Or how they were able to walk away alive." He scowled at the monitor again, and turned to Mondragon. "Try the radio. If it's working, call Tony back in the Beta."

It was working.

"So?" Cruzet seemed beyond surprise. "Where'd they go?"

"God knows." Andersen's voice was hushed and brittle. "I guess we'll have to follow."

"Not on foot!" Cruzet protested. "Let me drive you."

"We have to go on foot," he said. "To follow the prints. And out of caution. The Alpha's hull failed to shield them from whatever hit them. I don't want you that close."

"Andy, wait!" Cruzet raised his voice. "Stop a minute, and think about it. Indra and the men are five days gone, we don't know how. Let's cut our losses. Take both machines and get away while we can."

"Or hope we can," Andersen mocked him. "What if we run? What could we gain? No matter what became of them, we're stuck here. Not a ghost of a chance to get off the planet. Not without Nik and Kobo. I want to know what happened."

"I doubt we ever will—"

"Stand by with the searchlight." Andersen beckoned for Mondragon to follow. "Light our way as far as you can."

●

Back down on the ice, Mondragon walked ahead, tracking Singh and the engineers the way he used to track his father's wandering goats. The searchlight swept the dark east horizon and stopped on a shadow darker than the frost.

"See it?" Cruzet's voice crackled in their helmets. "The binoculars make it bigger. But what it is . . ." His voice fell. "I hope to know."

"The lighthouse?"

"Never finished, or what is left of the ruin, if it ever was a lighthouse. But there's no tower standing. Nor the rubble of anything fallen. What I do see—" His voice stopped in a startled way. "Something odd! The land's low and narrow here. I see what looks like a road or ramp that climbs out of the sea, leading up to the building. And another like it, running down on the other side."

"Interesting," Andersen said. "We're pushing on."

Cruzet dropped the searchlight back to them, and the prints were easier to find: Singh's, small and narrow; Fujiwara's longer; Krasov's wider. They had walked side by side, straight toward the ramp that led out of the ice.

"How the hell could they keep moving?" Andersen's rapid breath was a ghostly rustle in Mondragon's helmet, his voice stifled with an unbelieving dread. "Naked, outside in this vacuum, the temperature close to zero Kelvin."

Remembering stories his grandmother used to tell, of brujas and the dead called out of their graves, Mondragon shivered and followed the prints. He expected to find bloated bodies lying stiff and frozen on the frost, but the trail led him on. Never faltering, the footsteps had been vigorous and long, leading straight toward the ramp.

Cruzet swung the light to it. They stopped in wonder,

went closer, stopped again. Nearly a hundred meters wide, it was a smooth pavement of some dark stone. A low parapet edged it, built of the same dark stone. Or was it something more permanent than stone?

"No sign of erosion." Andersen rubbed the parapet with his glove. "But built for the use of creatures climbing out of the ocean, back before it froze. But the stone—it still feels as smooth as it must have on the day it was laid."

They followed the footprints up the ramp to a square platform that was walled with the same low parapet, and stopped when Cruzet lit it for them. Three hundred meters across, surrounding a vast blot of shadow at its center. A building when the searchlight rose to show it: an immense block-shaped structure of the same dark stuff, fifty meters wide and half that high.

Mondragon wondered if the three had gone inside, but he saw no entrance. He was following the tracks around the building till he saw that Andersen had stopped, staring up at the towering wall. The roving searchlight had filled it with unexpected color. An inlay of gem-bright stone. Andersen brushed his glove across a wide blue-gray oval.

"A mosaic!" He backed abruptly away to look higher up the wall. "The creatures themselves!"

Cruzet broadened the searchlight beam to light the whole wall. What it revealed was a colorful panorama of the beach and the ramp and the building itself. The sea had not yet frozen. The creatures were wading out of the waves, climbing the ramp, crowding in front of the building.

"Bipeds!" Andersen murmured. "They were amphibious bipeds."

They stood very erect on stubby legs. A little like penguins, Mondragon thought, awkward out of the water. Their arms were short finlike flippers, spread as if for balance. Waddling up the ramp, many had stopped when they reached the platform, staring up at the towering wall with strange green eyes set in oddly crested heads as round and sleek as a seal's.

"They were born in the sea." Cruzet was moving the searchlight, and Andersen gestured. "I think this is a place where they came to change for life in the air."

Cruzet swung the light to follow the foot of the wall. It showed dozens of the creatures sprawled on the ramp, their bodies bloated. Farther along, they were bursting out of their swollen skins, opening delicate rose-colored wings. Those near the end of the wall were spreading the wings, climbing into the air.

"The climax of their lives." Cruzet was raising the beam to reveal them soaring over the building in a sky that had still been azure blue. "This must have been a holy place."

"For all?" Mondragon wondered. "Or los jefes only? The chosen leaders?"

"No telling." Andersen shrugged. "Could be we're trying to read too much out of just one picture."

He gestured at the footprints and they tramped on around the corner. The wall above them here was blank black stone, with no inlays. High up, it was set back to make a railed balcony. Oval windows behind it were blacker than the stone, but still he saw no doors. Perhaps flying things needed none.

The prints on the frost led them on around the next corner toward the farther beach and the other frozen ocean. Here, beyond the searchlight's reach, the wall was only blacker blackness, shutting out the stars. Mondragon found nothing on it till his flashlight caught a yellow flash.

Stepping closer he saw that it was an eye, a long shape of some yellow crystal, inlaid in a monstrous head cut into the ink black stone. Moving on, searching with the feeble beams, they found more unearthly eyes shining out of heads that chilled him.

"Demonios!" he whispered. "There were demons here."

"If their heaven was what we saw on the other side," Andersen said, "this was their notion of hell."

They tramped on, probing with their flashlights, till he stopped again.

"Their story," he muttered. "The devils of the amphibian hell."

Undulating lines cut deep into the base of the wall were waves on their native sea. Higher, carved in sleek outline, the swimmers were leaping out of the water in flight from sulphur-eyed, half-reptilian monsters that dived after them with sharp-hooked talons and saber-fanged jaws.

"Qué malo!" Mondragon turned to stare at Andersen. "Demonios!"

"Predators," Andersen said. "Preying on the amphibians."

"Demonios!" Mondragon murmured again.

The yellow-eyed killers had been real. Had they evolved to become the demons of the ice? The fantasmas that watched from the dark and welcomed no strangers? He shivered, even in the insulated airskin, and reached for Andersen's arm.

"We should not be here."

He felt Andersen stiffen and heard his breathless gasp.

"There! There they are. . . ."

The flashlights had picked them up. Finding no doorway, Singh and the men had tried to climb the wall. Krasov stood on the frosty pavement, broad feet planted wide apart. Fujiwara had climbed on his shoulders. Indra Singh stood on his, fingers clinging to the head of a yellow-eyed horror leaping out of the waves.

Frozen into ivory, their jaws gaped wide, their teeth grimly gleaming in the starlight. Their eyes were blindly bulging, glazed by the airless cold. Agony and terror were printed on their faces. Mondragon shrank back and swept them again with his trembling light.

"Las cuentas negras!"

Quivering across them, his light stopped on a dark glint between Singh's glassy eyes.

"Beads!" He found the English. "The black beads Indra found with the bones in the cliff. I think the beads have killed them."

Nineteen

As gently as they could, they pulled the bodies off the wall and lowered them to the frost. All three wore the six-sided beads frozen to their foreheads. Andersen snapped them off and zipped them into the breast pocket of his airskin.

"Demonios malvados!" Mondragon protested. "The evil demons of the ice inhabit them. Leave them here with los pobrecitos."

"We don't know what they are." Andersen shrugged. "Our job isn't done till we do."

Beyond the next corner, they came back into the searchlight's dazzle and heard Cruzet.

"Andy? Andy? You okay?"

"Alive," Andersen said. "Ready to get out, if you'll pick us up. Come up the ramp. We'll wait behind the building."

They waited with the bodies till Cruzet drove around the corner and stopped the spider beside them. In his airskin, he came out to stare a long time at the creatures on the wall before he found the three stiff bodies. Gone pale in the helmet, he listened in silence to what they said and beckoned them stiffly toward the spider.

Mondragon wanted to bury the bodies.

"We owe them," he said. "They died for us."

"No time for that," Andersen said. "Nor tools to dig graves in the frost."

"Spread blankets over them," Cruzet said. "They'll be covered forever."

They spread the blankets. Standing over their heads, beneath the red-lit images of those hunting predators, Mondragon bowed his head to recite words he recalled from his mother's funeral. Cruzet drove them back around that doorless block of coal black stone, back beneath those lofty oval windows and that vast panorama of the amphibians waddling out of the sea to unfold brilliant wings and climb into a bright blue sky. Looking back from the bubble, Mondragon crossed himself and whispered the prayers his mother had taught him when he was three years old.

●

He and Andersen in the Alpha, Cruzet in the Beta, they drove back north. When they were again within radio range of the ship, they called Glengarth.

"Thank God!" he greeted them. "I need you here."

Andersen told him that Singh and her crew were dead.

"I was afraid." His voice had fallen, but he was silent only a moment. "Make it back as fast as you can. Or we could all be dead."

Reba Washburn met them in the hangar balloon when they came off the ramps from the spiders.

"They're waiting for you," she said. "On the concom deck. Right now."

With no time even to wash or shave, they followed her into the elevator and found Captain Stecker seated across the long curve of the conference table, an empty glass before him.

He looked pale and puffy; gaining weight, Mondragon thought. Jonas Roak and Jesus Rivera sat at his right. Washburn took the empty chair between them, all three in black security caps.

Silently, Glengarth rose to shake their hands and beckon them to join Sternberg, Jim Cheng, and Rima, sitting on the inside curve of the table. Mondragon saw Rima's quick smile of relief when Andersen came out of the elevator; he wished her welcome might have been for him.

"Sit." With no show of pleasure, Stecker waved them into place across the table. "Give us your story."

"Make it complete," Roak muttered. "If Singh and her crew are lost, tell how."

"They are dead." Bleak-faced, Andersen nodded. "Frozen hard as rock. As for how it happened . . ." He shrugged uneasily. "I don't know."

"Let's have what you do know."

"Sir?" Like a schoolboy, Cruzet raised his hand. "We're worn out. Half dead ourselves. Can you get us some coffee?"

"Jesus." Roak scowled at Rivera. "Get it done."

"*Hay-soos.*" Rivera corrected him stiffly and disappeared into the elevator.

"Get at it." Roak turned impatiently to Andersen. "We've got no time to squander."

"Thank you." Andersen turned back to Glengarth and his companions. "It's not a pleasant story, but we did learn something about the past inhabitants. From the canal, first of all. It's evidence that a strong industrial technology and a busy maritime commerce once existed here. The canal, however, must have been abandoned long before the oceans froze. On beyond—"

"If they're dead," Roak interrupted him, "how did they die?"

"I'll get to it, but it won't make much sense till you hear the whole story."

"Okay. Get to it."

"—Out of radio contact," Andersen resumed deliberately, "we pushed on. Nothing remarkable till we came to the tip of the peninsula. We did find something there. A temple, perhaps—I don't know what else to call it. Indra thought the skeleton she found came from a flying creature that evolved in the sea. I believe the natives—or at least whatever built that structure—were her amphibians."

"Huh?" Scowling impatiently, Stecker lifted his empty glass and set it down again. "What are amphibians?"

"These could swim, and also fly. The building is convincing evidence of that, though it does raise questions we can't answer."

"Get on," Roak muttered, "with what you know. We don't want guesses."

"I'm trying to tell you what we saw," Andersen answered evenly. "I don't pretend to understand it. One strange thing, the place looks perfectly preserved. That black tower wasn't."

"Forget your black tower."

"Okay." Andersen nodded rather grimly. "A very remarkable mosaic on the face of this building shows the native amphibians climbing out of the still-liquid sea. It was long ago, yet we saw no sign of damage or erosion. Which made us wonder if something is still caring for the building."

"What has that to do with Indra?"

"A good deal," Andersen said. "We found the Alpha abandoned a few kilometers off the beach. They had left it without their airskins. They came out naked—"

"Naked?" Stecker sat up in his chair, suddenly sober. "That's crazy!"

"Sir, they certainly were." Bleakly, Andersen nodded again. "Though I don't know why they were crazed. Their bare feet had left footprints in the frost, leading away from the spider. Without airskins, totally exposed, they were somehow able to walk several kilometers to the building. They walked around it, searching for an entrance. There is no entrance. Not at ground level.

"They died, sir, trying to climb—"

"What the hell?" Stecker barked, and swung to glare at Cruzet and Mondragon. "Do you expect us to believe . . ."

He saw their solemn nods and let his voice fade away.

"Sir, it's nothing we wanted to believe." Cruzet shook his head. "But they left their airskins in the vehicle. Naked and barefoot, they walked at least three kilometers. We found their bodies frozen hard as iron."

"Nik and Kobo?" Jim Cheng bowed his head, whispering the names. "My best friends." Shivering, he stared blankly at Andersen. "What got into them?"

"One clue, which may mean something." Andersen looked back at Glengarth. "You recall those tiny six-sided prisms Singh found with her skeleton? They all wore them, frozen to their foreheads."

Rima's face went white.

"My little girl was playing with one of those beads." Mondragon flinched from her accusing glance. She turned to Andersen. "It gave her terrible dreams. Do you think . . ."

Her lips went tight, the question unfinished.

"Could be." Andersen shrugged, his red-stubbled face set hard. "I want to know. I brought them back, to run them through the lab."

"Sir." With a nervous glance into Rima's anxious face, Mondragon raised his hand. "The bead little Day had was not one of Indra's, though it did look like them. I found it on the pebble beach near Dr. Singh's dig. It seemed so harmless that I let Dr. Virili's children take it for a toy. She returned it to me. I gave it to Dr. Singh."

"It's certainly no toy!" Rima gave him another hard look and turned to Glengarth. "Day was having those dreadful nightmares. Walking in her sleep and trying to get off the ship. Her panda doll was left back on Earth. She grieves for it."

"So what?" Stecker muttered, his bleary eyes rolling uneasily toward Andersen. "A damned doll?"

"She's trying to save it," Rima said. "She's convinced herself—or something in the bead convinced her—that the doll tried to follow and got lost on the ice. One night we caught her trying to get out of the ship to search for it. With no more protection than Indra and her people had. I'm afraid of those beads. Prisms. Whatever they are."

"Get rid of them!" Stecker snapped at Andersen.

"I will. But first, sir, I want to run them through the lab. They may be dangerous, but we don't know how. They may be harmless. They're certainly puzzling. Perhaps they can tell us things we ought to know. Early on, I wanted a chance at them, but Indra kept them for herself."

Stecker turned uncertainly to Roak, who only shrugged. "Okay," he muttered.

"We'll get at it," Andersen promised. "I want to X-ray them, study that anomalous attraction, file samples for analysis, test them every way I can. We'll report what we find and destroy them when we're done."

●

Rivera came out of the elevator with a steward and a wheeled tray loaded with mugs of coffee and a platter of soyasweets. Cruzet and Mondragon reached for them gratefully. Stecker tapped his empty glass with a fingernail that had lost most of its gold enamel. The steward took the glass away. Andersen pushed his coffee aside and looked back at Glengarth.

"That's our story, sir."

The room was quiet for half a minute, people turning uncertainly to one another.

"I don't like it," Stecker muttered at last, scowling at Andersen. "What does it mean for us?"

"Sir, that's hard to tell." Andersen shrugged and paused to frown. "Most of what we learned is very ancient history. The amphibians may once have been the dominant race, but they had powerful enemies. One whole face of the building is covered with carvings that depict gigantic predators hunting them.

"God knows what has happened in all the ages since, but I think something intelligent has survived. Something able to detect us far out in space and flash that signal from the ice cap. Something in that island tower able to kill Jake Hinch. And something now . . ."

He shook his head.

"Something what?"

His shoulders hunched.

"We'll tell you what." Stecker paused to let Roak speak. When Roak sat silent, he glared across the table. "We've got to get off the planet. As quick as we can."

"Sir . . ." Jim Cheng hesitated uncertainly. "Without Nik and Kobo, I don't think we can ever launch—"

Stecker stiffened. "What's that?"

"Nik was our systems designer," Cheng said. "Leader of the team. Kobo was our top quantum engineer. You probably know that the wave conversion algorithm has to be recalculated for half a dozen factors before any takeoff. Gravity field, magnetic field, angular momentum, air pressure, mass balance, quantum vectors. A very slight error in any function could blow us up in the pit or drive us into collision with our own dwarf star."

Stecker opened his mouth to speak, but only gaped. His small eyes darted desperately around him. He looked, Mondragon thought, like a frightened animal in a trap. With a defeated shrug, he turned to beckon imperatively at Roak.

"Mr. Glengarth—" Roak stopped for a moment, but raised his voice and stiffened himself commandingly. "Captain Stecker will not abandon our launch. You're a trained officer. Dr. Cruzet and Dr. Andersen are competent quantum engineers. You will organize another team and complete the facility."

"Sir, I respect Jim's opinion that we can't launch." Glengarth turned inquiringly to Cruzet and Andersen. They looked at each other and shook their heads.

"A suicidal gamble," Andersen muttered. "The effort would take time and resources we don't have left." His voice lifted. "Sir, there's another alternative Tony and I have discussed."

"What's that?"

"We still don't know anything about our neighbors. They killed Jake Hinch when he dynamited the door to their tower, but they let the rest of us go. Maybe they felt offended when Indra tried to enter their temple. We just don't know."

"So what?"

Andersen turned to Cruzet for the answer.

"Sir, we want to find out." Cruzet nodded, without visible feeling. "That first flash from the ice cap came from a cluster of what appeared to be enormous artificial constructions. A city? A fortress? Anybody's guess, but it could logically be the center of some surviving power. We want to visit it—"

"Are you crazy?" Stecker goggled at them. "It's halfway around the planet. Twenty thousand kilometers, a good half of it across the cap. Even if you got there, what makes you think you'd do any better than Jake and Indra did?"

"We certainly wouldn't dynamite anything."

"What the hell do you hope for?"

"Anything." Andersen shrugged. "Nothing. We've no basis for any sort of guess. No clear sign of welcome. No firm sign of malice. That's why we must go. If something intelligent doesn't want us here, it might just possibly help us get away. We don't know."

He reached for his coffee. The steward had returned with a fresh drink for Stecker. He gulped half of it and turned expectantly to Roak.

"In any case . . ."

Andersen was sipping the coffee. Scowling at him across the table, Roak raised his voice.

"You've heard Captain Stecker. He's not crazy enough to think any friendly native is going to help us complete the launch installation. You two may want to go exploring, but we need you here. We've got to get back at the job, with every man we have."

He gave Rima a look that made her flush.

"And every woman."

Twenty

Earlier, when Kip wanted an airskin, Rima said he was still too young to need it, but Mondragon had persuaded Jim Cheng, who worked sometimes in ship supply, to cut one to fit him. She thought he was getting too fond of the Mexican, but she let him keep the suit.

"Let me try it," he urged her when Cheng gave it to him. "You've been driving the spiders. The Alpha's just sitting there while Andy and Tony test those black beads. Let's take it out."

"You shouldn't call them Andy and Tony." She shook her head at him. "They're officers of the ship and quantum engineers."

"They're my friends. It's okay with them. Let's go up the beach, to where you were digging the habitat."

"Not anymore." She made a face. "They killed it."

"Maybe things will change." He tried to lift her spirits. "Andy and Tony are smart. Maybe they can manage something."

"Maybe." She stopped to think and nodded soberly. "Now that we've lost Nik and Kobo, the launch facility will take a long time to build. If we ever can. We're all tired of dehydrated synthetics and the captain does like to eat. Maybe he could be persuaded to let us grow a hydroponic garden in the chamber we've already dug."

"Let's try."

She stopped to consider and suddenly decided.

"Okay. I'll ask Dr. Cheng to come with us to measure the space."

They parked beneath the mound of rubble from the excavation, and Cheng helped him into the airskin. It felt stiff and strange at first, and the breather unit gave the air in the helmet a faint sharp scent of hot plastic, but the real space suit made him feel like he was with Captain Cometeer and the Legion of the Lost, landing on an unknown planet.

That eagerness faded as they cycled through the lock and walked down the ramp. Even with his mother and Cheng so close behind him, he felt suddenly naked and alone. Standing here with no ship to shield him, no wall except the blackness and blazing stars standing far beyond the frozen ocean, he looked down at the icy beach where Mondragon had found that bright black bead. He remembered what the beads had done to Dr. Singh and the engineers. The cold and the darkness seemed to close in around him. He shivered and caught his mother's hand.

"Come along," she told him, "if you want to see the dig."

They climbed the rubble ramp into the abandoned habitat. Cheng walked ahead, his helmet light flickering over rough rock walls scarred with the teeth of the digging machines.

"Let me see the dig," Kip said. "Where Dr. Singh found the beads and the bones."

Rima led him out of the big room and into a narrow cave. Her light danced over a shelf of rock where Singh had left her small digging tools. He saw a strange seashell and the end of a yellow bone sticking out of the rock.

"It was the floor of a lake where floods came down," his mother said. "Creatures caught in the floods were buried with mud that finally turned to stone. It was a fabulous find, Indra said. She was bitter—really disappointed—when they shut down her dig."

Rima walked on with Cheng. He stood there, playing his own light over the shell and the bone, trying to imagine what sort of creatures had lived in these old seas before they froze. The planet must have been a nicer place, though Mondragon thought something evil must have died here to leave the fantasmas that haunted the dark.

He hurried after his mother.

". . . melt water from above, with heat lamps on the ice," she was saying to Cheng. "Soil from the permafrost. We'll have to spray the walls with sealant, install a power source, build an air lock. I figure three hundred square meters of usable space."

"If they let us use it." Cheng frowned. "Roak will want us all at work on their relaunch project." He eyed her speculatively. "He'll need persuading, but I've seen the way he looks at you. Maybe you could talk him into it."

Conscious of the way the airskin fitted her form, she felt a flash of anger.

"I don't deal with Roak."

●

Stecker sat with Roak and his black-capped security detail at the long table in the conference room. Waiting for Cruzet and Andersen, he was fondly nursing a tall gin and tonic from the precious store Jake Hinch had brought aboard. He scowled expectantly when at last they came out of the elevator.

"Those black beads?"

Deliberately, they took their seats with Glengarth and Rima. Cruzet's eyes were hollow, his face drawn with fatigue.

Andersen rubbed his red-stubbled chin, grinning bleakly across the table.

"Those damn beads?" Stecker demanded again. "What did you learn?"

"Not much," Andersen said.

"Forty hours in the lab." Cruzet raised a rusty voice. "I'm dead for sleep. Can you get us some coffee?"

"Forty hours wasted," Roak muttered. "Time you could have been at work in the pit."

But he sent Rivera for coffee. Stecker ordered another gin and tonic. Waiting, they turned impatiently to Andersen.

"So what have you got?"

"Artifacts." Andersen frowned. "Riddles we failed to resolve."

"Don't feed us riddles. What exactly did you find?"

He paused for a moment, choosing his words. "The black prisms are mostly carbon, though the spectrograph shows a little gold, with trace amounts of a dozen elements. They're harder and denser than diamond. And nothing nature ever made."

He turned to Glengarth, his face very sober.

"Sir, they were manufactured."

"Manufactured?" Sharply, Roak echoed the word. "How do you know?"

"Under the microscope they look like stacks of very thin diamond slices, connected with fine threads of what I take for gold or a gold alloy. I'd guess they're doped with the other elements, like silicon chips, but we've no way to tell."

"If they are chips," Roak demanded, "what's your riddle?"

"They aren't chips. Not silicon. Certainly not electronic. They adhere to each other like magnets, but they are not ferromagnetic. They seem, in fact, to be shielded from magnetic fields. A bigger riddle is their age. No artifact of ours would last a billion years. Even frozen here. You might expect time to change them, but I believe they still retain at least some trace of their original activity. Whatever that was."

"So what?"

"If I may finish—"

Andersen stopped when he saw Rivera emerging from the elevator with the steward and his cart. He and Cruzet accepted their coffee gratefully, but Stecker ignored his drink. He glanced nervously at Roak and sat scowling expectantly at Andersen.

"If I may finish," Andersen went on, "the objects appear to be insulated from heat as well as from electromagnetic energy. They have no temperature. We tried to fuse or burn them in the electric crucible. Let them freeze again. Put them on an anvil and struck them with a heavy hammer. They're never damaged. Not by anything. They never even feel hot or cold when you pick them up."

"What does that mean?"

"I don't know." Andersen looked at Cruzet, who merely twitched his narrow shoulders. "If you want a guess, I think we're dealing with creations of a science unknown to us."

"Is that all you've got?"

"All we really know. There are inferences we might make. Singh found six of the things with the skeleton. Mondragon picked up another on the beach. That suggests that they may have been common and somehow important to the native amphibians. Ornaments? Money? Religious emblems? We know too little even to guess."

He shrugged and reached for his coffee.

"Are they a danger to us, here aboard?" Roak demanded. "Did they really kill Singh and her crew?"

"It's a fair assumption, which would lead to the question why." He shrugged again. "Who knows?"

●

"Sir?" Rima asked. Stecker scowled and set his drink back on the table. "If I may bring up something else."

"Huh?" he muttered as if he didn't care to listen.

"Yes?" Roak surveyed her, his eyes too bold. "What's your problem?"

Trying not to cringe, she kept her eyes on Stecker's face.

"You know, sir, that most of us are getting tired of soya that and algae this. We're going to be here a long time. We'll get hungry. I think we can use the habitat excavation to grow half our food."

Stecker pushed his glass aside and sat glaring at her, his pasty face turning slowly red.

"It's close to eight hundred cubic meters." She tried to ignore his mounting fury. "I want to seal it, install a fusion engine and a heat lamp for meltwater. With carbon dioxide from the cyclers—"

"You went back there?" Stecker exploded. "Where Singh and the Mexican found those beads? A wonder they didn't suck you out to die on the ice."

"They didn't," she said. "We're getting rid of them." She spread her hands in appeal. "Sir, our real danger is more than those beads, whatever they are. It's starvation."

"You disobeyed me," Stecker snarled. "I won't have it." He turned to Roak. "Tell her, Jonas."

"I'm sorry, Rima." He smiled, but she heard mockery in his tone. "But we've got important people dead. We've been listening, but Captain Stecker and I are not as happy here as you are. The launch pit's our only hope to get away. It's a desperate undertaking that will require everything we have. Forget your garden."

●

Later that afternoon, Kip and Day went down to the playroom. Mrs. Sternberg was telling the younger children stories of Earth, now a fairyland they would never see again. Day had demanded one about a panda named Me Me. She shook her head when it was over, and said the end was wrong. Me Me wasn't really happy in the bamboo forest. She wasn't anywhere on Earth, or happy at all. Kip wanted to slip away to work out in the gym with Mondragon, if Mondragon was through servicing the spiders, though he didn't tell his mother.

Alone in the cabin, Rima heard a loud rap and found Roak at the door.

"Hi, doll." He gave her an ingratiating smile. "May I see you for a moment?"

She let him come in. He looked around the cabin and shook his head sympathetically. "Narrow quarters for a woman with two children. I think I can find you something better."

Uninvited, he settled himself into the folding seat beside her berth.

"We're making do." She stood by the door, waiting to know his business. "Everybody's crowded."

"Not quite everybody." He looked up at the small holo of Kip and Day over her berth. "Charming children."

"Thank you, Mr. Roak." Speaking stiffly, she swung the door wider.

"Jonas," he said. "To my friends."

She said nothing.

"About your hydroponic project." Affably, he smiled again. "I'd really like to help you. Maybe later I can, but you know Stecker. I have to deal with him. Not always easy. Those queer beads have him in a blue panic now. He's determined to get away or kill us trying.

"But that's not why I came."

He relaxed in her chair, smiling up at the holo.

"A lovely little girl in her red jumpsuit." He turned intently back to her. "But here we are, marooned forever, unless the natives wipe us out. We may as well make the best of it."

"I'm trying."

"Let me help you, Rima." He paused to scan her body, and she felt a flush of anger. "For the little girl's sake, and the boy's, if not for your own. They deserve the best you can give them."

"We're making do," she said again, but he seemed not to hear.

"The loss of the Singh group was a dreadful tragedy." She heard no regret in his tone. "A cruel loss to all of us, and a mystery we've been unable to solve. But here on the ship it has left us with a bit of open living space. Singh had been allowed two cabins, the spare for her books and equipment. I can move you into them if you like. A cabin for the kids. The other cabin . . ."

He stopped to eye her again, with a half-smile that chilled her.

"No sale, Mr. Roak." She let her voice lift. "We'll stay right where we are."

"Rima, dear, look at the facts." Scolding, he shook his finger at her. "The world we knew is gone forever. The ship's our own little kingdom, with Herman Stecker for our king. I know you don't like him. I have my own problems with him. He can be nasty. But the Glengarth gang failed to throw him out, and I'm afraid Stecker could become a threat—"

"That's enough, Mr. Roak." She cut him off. "I want nothing from you."

"Darling . . ." Grinning too widely, he stopped to shake his head at her. "We're caught in a harder situation than you seem to understand. In public I have to stand with Stecker. Privately, I agree with Andersen that we'll never get off the planet, but Stecker has the bomb. I've helped him organize ship security to hold it safe. Reba had a lesson to learn, but she's with us now."

"Too bad for her."

"On the contrary, my dear, a lesson for you. If you haven't seen the story, I'm something more than Stecker's front man. He may still think we're playing his game, but I make the rules. And you, my girl—you'd better play ball."

"I don't play ball." Anger crackled in her voice. "Just leave. Now."

"If you ask."

He rose deliberately, but stopped in front of her, so close that his male body reek enveloped her, mixed with the odors of Stecker's whisky on his breath and an evil hint of Jake Hinch's lemon-scented hygienic cigars. She backed away, gesturing him out. He came closer.

"Get out!" she gasped. "Now."

"As you ask, my dear." Tolerantly, he shrugged. "Till you learn the rules."

●

She lay awake most of that night, thinking of him and what might happen to the children. She saw no way of escape. Now and then toward morning, she dozed. The last time she woke to a silence that frightened her. Listening, she heard no breath sounds from Day or Kip. Trembling, she turned on the lights. Their berths were empty. They were not in the shower. Not in the cabin. Not anywhere.

The elevator was out of service. Calling Glengarth, she found him on watch in the dome. He roused security to power the elevator and search the ship. The children had vanished. Andersen and Cruzet were also gone from their quarters. They woke Reba Washburn, who had stood the night watch on the main deck.

"Sir, didn't you know?" She rubbed her eyes and shook her head at Glengarth. "Dr. Andersen said he'd cleared it with you."

"Cleared what?"

"The test run." She yawned and blinked again. "He said they had to get out early, because both spiders would be needed when the crews went down to the pit. They were taking the Alpha out to test a new heat lamp. He said Dr. Virili was letting the kids go along for a lark—"

"Lark?" Rima gasped. "I never heard anything about it."

"Nothing to alarm you." Reba yawned again. "They were excited, and I guess they just forgot to let you know. Dr. Andersen and Dr. Cruzet are always free to use the spiders unless they're requisitioned for the pit. They said they'd be back in time for breakfast."

"You say . . ." Her breathless whisper died. "My children were with them?"

"Happy to go," Reba said. "The little girl looked like she was up too early, but Kip was real excited. They'd been cooped up in the ship too long, he said. They were going on a mission, he said, just like his Captain Cometeer."

The watch officer opened the lock to let them out into the hangar's dimly lit balloon. Their shouts woke empty echoes in the dim half-dome. The Alpha was gone.

Twenty-one

In the control dome with Glengarth, Rima searched the holoscreens and found the frozen ocean empty out to the dark horizon. She called the Alpha again and again, with never a response. With binoculars and then with the remote-controlled telescopes, she swept the starlit frost again and yet again, but always failed to find the heat lamp's glow.

Mondragon burst out of the elevator.

"Is it true? What I heard at breakfast? That Kip and his little sister are on the missing spider?"

She nodded dismally.

"Cómo?" He stared at her in stunned dismay. "How is that possible?"

Her white face quivered.

"Where have they gone?"

"No sign," she told him. "Nothing."

"Nada?" Shaken, he whispered the Spanish word. "Who would kidnap them?"

"Kidnap?" A bewildered shrug. "Dr. Andersen is missing. And Dr. Cruzet. They told Washburn they had permission to take the Alpha out. And my permission for the kids." She bit her trembling lip. "I don't know where they went."

"They can't be far. Can't you see their heat lamp?"

"Nothing," she said again. "Perhaps they forgot to turn it on."

"Andy knows cold metal can shatter." He stared out into the eternal midnight. "He would never forget. Not—" He caught himself, remembering Singh and the engineers. "Not if he's himself."

"I'm afraid." Trembling, she shook her head. "They aren't themselves."

●

Glengarth called Roak and Stecker on the interphone, and got no answer.

"Up late last night," Jim Cheng told him. "A steward heard them quarreling. Cursing each other. Drunk, he said. They're probably sleeping it off."

He sent Washburn to rouse them. Another hour had passed before they appeared, Stecker red-eyed and wheezing for his breath, Roak grimly silent, a dark bruise around his right eye.

"What the devil?" Stecker growled at Glengarth.

"It's devils we've got to deal with," Glengarth muttered. "Diablos, as Carlos calls them."

"Carlos?" Roak sneered. "That stupid Mex?"

"He's not the problem." He turned to Stecker. "Sir, we've got a situation I don't understand. Andersen and Cruzet are gone in the Alpha spider. They took Rima's kids. I can't imagine what got into them. Unless those black beads . . ."

He looked at Rima.

"Evil things!" She was hoarse with emotion. "I'm afraid . . ."

"Sir?" Glengarth raised his voice. "Didn't Andersen get rid of them?"

"He tried." Stecker shook his head, bleary eyes blinking. "Or said he did, after he'd finished his tests."

"Actually," Roak added, "he never really finished. He wanted to keep on testing, because he said they were so exciting. We finally made him quit. Captain Stecker ordered him to destroy them."

Stecker blinked uneasily, and continued where Roak left off.

"He couldn't do it, or said he couldn't. In the end, he brought them back to us. Said he'd tried to burn them, tried to dissolve them with every acid in the lab, tried to smash them on an anvil. Said they wouldn't burn, wouldn't shatter. Said no reagent touched them. He left them with me. I gave them to Jonas. Told him to keep them where they couldn't hurt anybody."

He swung to glare at Roak.

"Ask Reba," Roak muttered uncomfortably. "I left them in her care, till we found a way to dispose of them."

Glengarth called ship security.

"Sir?" Reba Washburn was on the intercom a few minutes later, her voice hushed with shock. "I had those beads in the office safe. I thought they'd be safe—"

"But they're missing?"

"Yes, sir. Three of them."

"You didn't know?"

"No way to know, sir. I'd sealed all seven in a brown envelope. The six Dr. Singh dug up and the one the Mexican found. The envelope is still in the safe. Still sealed, with no sign of tampering. None I could see. I just tore it open. Three are gone."

"How could that happen?"

"I can't explain it, sir. I thought they were secure. I changed the combination after the bomb was missing. I gave it to nobody else. I'd written my name across the flap. I found it still there. The same envelope."

"The safe wasn't forced?"

"No sign, sir. No sign of anything. I've kept somebody in the office around the clock. No problem ever reported. This loss—I can't explain it."

They shook their heads, blankly staring at one another.

"Only three?" Rima spoke at last, a breathless hush in her voice. "We have four people missing."

"Only three, Dr. Virili."

●

Roak and Stecker drew aside, muttering to each other.

"We're going below." Roak turned abruptly back. "The captain wants his breakfast."

"A moment, sir," Glengarth called after them before they reached the elevator. "Shouldn't we send out a search party in the Beta?"

"I'll go, sir." Mondragon spoke on impulse and stopped to look at the others around him in the dome. They stood silent, frowning uncertainly. "We have to follow," he urged them quickly. "Dr. Andersen and Dr. Cruzet are our best engineers. And your children . . ." He turned to Rima. "I love the little girl. Your son is my good friend."

He saw from her face that she didn't want to think of the friendship. But Kip was el amigo querido who had found him hiding on the ship and kept his secret. Kip's disabled Game Box had let him prove his knowledge of computers. Kip always smiled to see him.

"I wish to go." He looked at Stecker, and had to gulp at the tightness in his throat. "With your permission, sir."

"And I," Jim Cheng volunteered. "Without Andy and Tony, we can't even begin the launch facility."

Stecker belched, scowling doubtfully at Roak.

"How could you trace them?" Roak demanded. "If you can't see the heat lamp?"

"The track of the wheels," Mondragon said. "Left in the frost."

"Nonsense." Roak shook his head. "The spiders have been all over the place. Wheel prints on top of wheel prints."

"I used to track my father's goats," Mondragon said. "I can find the newest trail."

Fists clenched and red in the face, Stecker glared at Mondragon and caught Roak's arm to pull him aside. They huddled together again.

"The captain says forget it." Roak swung back to Glengarth, his voice abrupt and harsh. "We don't know what happened. We can't risk the Beta. Without it, we'd be dead."

"Sir?" Glengarth looked inquiringly at Stecker. "I see no new risk in a cautious search."

"I do," Stecker snapped. "Jonas speaks for me." He belched again, hugged his belly, and swung to Cheng. "This puts us in a hell of a mess. Digging the pit, we're digging for our lives. We'll get the Beta busy, right here on the job. Push it with every man we've got."

"Okay, sir." Cheng nodded without enthusiasm. "We'll get right at it."

"Carry on, Mr. Glengarth." Nodding for Roak to follow, Stecker stalked toward the elevator. "We're leaving you in charge."

"Hah!" Glengarth grunted when they were gone. "Adiós."

●

Back at the telescope, Rima kept scouring the empty ice till Glengarth made her come down with him for breakfast. In the dining room, scattered groups sat huddled over their tables, anxious voices murmuring beneath a nervous hush. She was ordering soyamax toast with syncafe when the waiter came to Glengarth with a covered tray.

"Real ham and eggs." He uncovered it with a flourish. "Kona coffee, with real dairy cream. Stabilized for preservation. Compliments of the captain and Mr. Roak, from their private stock."

"Great friends!"

Glengarth made a sardonic face and told the waiter to give his thanks to the captain. Moodily silent, he seemed to enjoy his ham and eggs, but Rima found no appetite, not even for the coffee. She drank a little of it, begged him to excuse her, and went back to the dome. On watch there, Sternberg laid his binoculars aside.

"Still no heat lamp," he told her. "No sign of anything."

She returned to the telescope. Mounted outside the hull, it projected its field of view on the holowall. At highest power, the fallen boulders along the peninsula looked close enough to touch. Once more she followed kilometer after kilometer of starlit frost and starry midnight as they crawled across the screens, all the way from the southward coast of the peninsula to the continental ice that walled the north.

Nothing. A cold lump of dread ached in her stomach, but she kept at the search till Glengarth came back to relieve Sternberg and sent her down to rest. Her empty cabin offered no rest. In an hour, she was back again.

"The lamp!" It was late afternoon when she called Glengarth to the telescope. "That red spark, just above the horizon."

"Nearly due south." He read out the bearings. "They've gone down the peninsula the way Singh went. I hope they don't—"

He caught himself, but that was the direction of the temple at the peninsula tip, or whatever it was, where the amphibians had waded out of the sea to grow their wings and take to the sky. She shuddered, trying not to let her mind dwell on the naked bodies of Singh and her crew, frozen as they tried to climb the monstrous figures carved into the wall.

"Don't brood." Hastily, he tried to cheer her. "We don't know where they're going. It is frightening, but we have to hope they're still okay. Try the radio again."

She did, beaming the signal toward that far-off point of dull red light. Still all she heard was the surflike whisper of ceaseless cosmic energies.

"I've got to know." Baffled and desperate, she appealed to him. "Now that we've found which way they went, could you possibly get the captain to authorize a rescue party?"

"Not a prayer." He shook his head, with a small grim shrug.

"Cheng and Mondragon are eager enough to go," she told him. "And I'm learning to drive the spiders."

"I've spoken again to Roak and the captain. They won't risk the Beta."

She tried the radio again and yet again. She watched that faint red spark sinking slowly toward the flat horizon until it flickered and vanished. Still she stayed at the telescope, searching that empty line between starlit ice and star-blazing blackness, till Glengarth's watch was over.

Roak came to relieve him.

"You've done all you can," Glengarth told her. "Let's go down for dinner."

"Not yet. I want to speak to Mr. Roak."

Glengarth gave her a sharp look and stepped into the elevator.

●

"Rima?" Roak turned expectantly to her. "What did you want to say?"

Facing his ambiguous grin, she took a moment to gather her resolve.

"We need to recover the Alpha. Mr. Glengarth says we'll never get the launch facility built without Cruzet and Andersen."

"So what?" His eyes narrowed.

"Won't you—" Her voice broke. "Won't you speak to the captain? Persuade him to let Cheng and Mondragon make a search?"

"I might." Relief took her breath. "Let's talk it over."

Trembling, she listened.

"I understand your concern for your kids." His eyes narrowed shrewdly. "I've tried to tell the captain how hopeless our situation is. Perhaps I could get him to authorize a search—if you and I can make a deal?"

"Yes?"

He paused to study her.

"I'm no total fool." His half-smile chilled her. "I know you dislike me, but for better or worse we're here on the ship for the rest of our lives. We have to get along, if you follow me?"

"I'm afraid I do."

"So here's my proposition." She saw his sardonic shrug. "I can get Stecker to allow the expedition. With luck enough, it will return with the men and your kids. Most likely they'll be found naked and frozen on the wall of that amphibian temple. . . ."

He saw her shudder.

"Nothing nice to think about, but here's what I want from you."

Swaying on her feet, she waited through another tormenting pause.

"By all odds, Rima, you're the most attractive woman on the ship. I've admired you since we left Earth. I want you with me for the rest of—"

"No deal."

"Please, my dear, give me a chance." He must have learned his oily surface charm back on Earth, she thought. "I respect your sense of the proprieties. I'll get the captain to pronounce us man and wife, with whatever ceremony you like."

He paused for her response. A gold crown gleaming through an empty smile, his face looked cold and hard. She saw the thickness of his lips, the black hair in his nostrils, a thin blue scar across his forehead. Again she caught his rank body scent.

"So what do you say?"

"No!"

"Don't you love your children?"

She was quivering, her fists clenched, but fury would get her nowhere. She tried to relax, to control herself, to slow her rapid breathing.

"Of course I do." Her voice came unsteady and shrill, but she kept on. "But if I give in and we find them dead, what have I gained?"

"Don't you want to know? Don't you care?"

"You know I do." She gasped the words and stumbled toward the elevator. "And I know you don't." Huskily, she whispered at him, "You—you despicable monster!"

"Rima, please!" he called after her, hands spread in a gesture of tolerant appeal. "Reality has given us some very bitter pills. We must learn to take them. I'm trying to sweeten your pill in the best way I can."

Weak and shaking, she clung to the doorway.

"I'll kill you!" she gasped. "If you make me."

"You'll get to know me." He shrugged, laughing at her. "I won't press you now. I'll need time to bring the captain around. The Beta will have to be checked out and refueled. Cheng and Mondragon have been at the pit. They'll need rest. I see you're exhausted. I'll let you sleep on it."

"If you think I can sleep . . ."

"You must rest." He shook his head in a mockery of sympathy. "Sleep if you can. I'll give you till breakfast. Think about it. Tell me then, yes or no."

His avid grin followed her into the elevator.

⬤

In the dining room, she found Glengarth sitting with Sternberg. They beckoned, and she brought her tray to their table.

"Joe's briefing me." Glengarth dropped his voice. "On our situation."

"Which is scary." Sternberg glanced around to see that nobody was near. "Stecker and his stooges have us sitting on a powder keg."

"With the fuse lit." Glengarth nodded gloomily. "Since we lost the Alpha."

"Cheng took his work crew out to the pit." Sternberg bent closer. "They're just going through the motions, he says. There's nothing useful for them to do. The ship's ripe for mutiny. If Roak and Stecker didn't have their bomb, they wouldn't last another minute."

"I talked to Roak." Rima's bitterness burst out. "Begged him to let us send the Beta out. He promised . . ." Her voice quivered. "If I'd be his mistress."

"What a beast!" Glengarth muttered. "Don't trust him."

"Never." Sternberg looked again for listeners. "Stecker wouldn't agree to anything. He's sick with panic. Wants to keep the Beta here for escape, if things get too hot for him."

"Roak . . ."

Her voice was gone. She caught the edges of the table to support herself for a moment until she could push herself to her feet.

"Sorry," she whispered. "Sorry . . ."

"Rima?" Glengarth stood up. "Can I help you?"

"I—I'm okay." She bit her lip and shook her head. "It's just—I feel used up. I'm going up to my cabin."

Still in her jumpsuit, she fell on her berth and tried to sleep. Roak's gloating, gold-toothed grin still haunted her. She saw no escape from him, no hope for Day and Kip. She was used to listening for their sounds as they slept; the dead silence of the room ached in her mind.

The night was endless, but at last she dozed. When near gunfire crashed, she thought she was dreaming till she heard shouted curses outside in the corridor. Groggily, she sat up on the side of the berth. Another gunshot echoed. She heard a piercing scream. Breathless voices shouted orders that made no sense. Hard-heeled boots tramped away and left a maddening stillness.

Had a mutiny begun?

Was Stecker desperate enough to detonate his suicidal bomb? And now did she really have to care? She turned on the holoscreen and found it blank. Listening, she heard rapid footfalls that stopped outside. Then she heard a muffled knock.

Twenty-two

Kip had gone to the gym that afternoon, hoping to work out with Carlos. Carlos wasn't there. Probably still driving the Beta for Dr. Cheng, taking men and tools to the launch pit. Disappointed, he went back to the playroom where Day and a few other young kids sat listening to Mrs. Sternberg tell fairy tales. He didn't care for the soyasweet cookies or soya milk. Day squirmed unhappily through another silly tale about Me Me, but he waited with her till story time was over.

When they got back to the cabin, Rima sat staring at the dead holoscreen. She gave them a tired smile and asked if they'd had fun, but she didn't seem to care how silly the fairy tale had been. They went down for dinner. It was more soya stuff. His mother had always eaten it, telling them cheerfully they must learn to like it because it had all the food elements they needed, but tonight she pushed her tray away without tasting anything. He wondered if some new trouble was on her mind, but decided not to ask. Anxious about her, he slept uneasily that night till a sobbing cry from Day brought him half awake.

"Me Me?"

Had he heard someone moving beyond the curtain around his berth? Or was it just a dream? He heard her curtain rustle, and her sleepy voice again.

"Me Me? Wait for me!"

He slid out of his berth in time to see her dart out of the open door. His mother still breathed softly inside her own curtain. She needed her sleep, and he didn't want to wake her. The circular corridor around the elevator shaft was already empty. He started for the elevator door and remembered that service stopped at midnight. He ran around the shaft and caught another glimpse of Day in her red jumpsuit, vanishing down the spiral stair.

"Daby!" The name he always called her when he felt vexed with her. "Wake up! Wait for me!"

Of course she didn't, but he could surely overtake her. He ran down the spiral, deck after deck, and never caught her. Panting hard, he came out into the bright lights on the main deck and found her at last. Cruzet and Andersen stood at the security desk across the room. She was with them.

"Day!" he called across the room. "Come with me. Come back to Mom."

"Not yet." She shook her head, smiling up at Andersen. "We're going after Me Me."

"She's okay, Kip." Andersen turned to him. "We've just overhauled the Alpha. We're taking it out for a short test run, and your mother thought you kids would like to come along."

Kip peered at him doubtfully. It was awfully early in the morning. He hadn't heard about any test run, but maybe his mother had been too worried to remember. Andersen and Cruzet were quantum engineers and friends she knew and liked. This wasn't the first time Day had frightened everybody, slipping out of the cabin in her sleep to look for Me

Me. He looked hard at her. She did seem okay, hanging on
to Andersen's hand.

"Mom never told us," he said. "We don't have our coats."

"No matter." Andersen laughed. "We'll keep the spider
warm enough, and you'll be back in time for breakfast."

Reba Washburn sat behind the desk. They had asked her
to open the ship's air lock.

"Why so early?" she was asking. "Nobody's up."

"We are." Andersen gave her an easy grin. "And we do
have the captain's permission to test the Alpha, if you'll just
let us into the work balloon."

"I don't know." She frowned at the monitor on her desk.
"Dr. Cheng has both spiders reserved for the pit."

"I know." Andersen nodded. "Tony and I are on his crew.
That's why we have to make the run so early."

"Security should have been informed."

"The captain has a lot on his mind." Andersen shrugged.
"You can call him if you want a confirmation."

"He'd be asleep."

"The test is pretty urgent," he said. "We don't want the
Alpha stalling on the job."

"Okay." Still doubtful, she reached for her keys. "I guess
it's okay."

●

He followed them into the little anteroom beside the lock.
Hanging there with the others was the airskin that Jim Cheng
had cut down for him. Nodding at it, he caught the sleeve of
Andersen's yellow jumpsuit.

"Can I bring it?" he begged. "My airskin?"

"Why not?"

Andersen didn't seem to care. He was proud of the airskin,
and the test drive would be more real if he had it with him.
He pulled it off the hook and carried it with him the way Jim
Cheng had carried his, slung over his shoulder.

The lock opened with a soft thud of metal on plastic

foam. Day kept a tight grip on Andersen's fingers, and Kip followed them into the balloon. It was a great dim cave, cooler than the ship. He shivered a little in the worn jumpsuit he had worn to bed, but the spiders were always exciting.

His mother should have been told, but Andersen and Cruzet were men she trusted. With luck, he and Day would be back in their berths before she ever woke up. He followed the ramp up into the Alpha and hung his airskin with the others inside the lock.

Pulses throbbing, he listened to the hums and thumps as the ramp lifted into place against the hull and the air lock sealed. He imagined he was going out on an interstellar mission with Captain Cometeer. Andersen let Day come with him to the controls in the nose of the machine. Cruzet stayed below to check the engine and the cycler. They were already rolling out of the balloon when he climbed into the lookout bubble.

Andersen was driving fast down the beach to the frozen ocean. This was real! More exciting, he thought, than a flight in Captain Cometeer's *Conqueror Queen* could ever be. The spider moved like a ship, he thought, or maybe a camel, swaying on its long legs as they crossed a boulder bed on the beach and a patch of rough ice near the old shore.

The bubble around him was made of something clearer than glass, and the black planet seemed stranger and more wonderful than any world the Legion of the Lost had ever found. It was a world without clouds or haze or dust. Everything looked cold and clean and perfect. The sky was a great dome of many-colored stars blazing out of midnight blackness. The dead sun was a round black shadow that seemed never to move. Nothing here ever changed; nothing ever would. The planet almost frightened him, yet somehow he loved the icy splendor of it. He wanted to tell his mother how beautiful it was, if she wasn't too angry when they got back.

The heat lamp had made a pink glow on the frost when

he went with his mother up the beach to Dr. Singh's dig. He didn't see it now. He knew heat was important, meant to keep the metal and the tires from getting too cold. He called on the interphone to warn Dr. Andersen that the lamp was out.

"I know." Andersen wasn't bothered. "Probably a bad contact. That's why we're running the test, to make sure everything's okay. We'll be back in the balloon before the temperature gets to be a problem."

He drove them east, straight toward the low black sun. The ship and even the ice-capped cliffs behind it were soon lost in the starlight. Kip kept expecting them to turn back. When they never did, he called again.

"Dr. Andersen, shouldn't we go back? Mom will be anxious if we aren't there before breakfast."

When he heard an answer, it came from Day.

"Silly Willie, we're not going back. Not till we find Me Me."

"Dr. Andersen!" he shouted into the intercom. "Listen to her! Talking in her sleep. Can't you wake her up?"

Andersen didn't answer, but he heard Day again, speaking in a voice he had never heard, strange and hard, too old for her.

"Turn south now."

"South?" Andersen asked, his voice suddenly as strange as hers. "Why?"

"East is wrong way." Her new voice seemed slow and hesitant, as if she had to search for words. "Right way is west. Me Me is calling from the ice cap west."

Waiting for Andersen, Kip heard nothing. Ventilator fans were whispering and the machine had grown warmer, but he shivered again.

"Don't listen!" His own voice was suddenly shrill from something tight in his throat. "She's crazy! We left her doll back on Earth a billion years—"

His voice choked off when he felt the spider turning. The

starlit frost was always the same, flat and featureless in every
direction, but the dome of stars swung around them till the
black sun hung low on his left. They were rolling fast toward
a constellation of bright golden stars in the shape of a very
lean pyramid, or perhaps an arrowhead. He ran down the
steps to the main deck and heard Day's new voice from the
control bay.

"Farther right," she was saying. "Six degrees, to avoid
rough ice around a reef."

What could she know about a reef and broken ice?

For a moment he couldn't move, but then he caught his
breath and tiptoed into the bay. Day sat on the holomonitor,
where she was level with Andersen's head. Her eyes were
fixed on him. They had a dull, glassy look, as if she were still
asleep.

Trying to understand, he looked for the black beads that
had given her those crazy dreams of Me Me lost on the ice.
He saw nothing on her smooth baby face. His mother had
said the beads were all safely locked in Reba Washburn's safe,
where they could hurt nobody. Yet she frightened him.

"Farther," that hard voice was saying. "Slightly farther."
Andersen moved the wheel. "There! Hold us there."

He caught the sleeve of Andersen's blue jumpsuit.

"Dr. Andersen—" His voice shook. "Please—listen to
me!"

"Kip?" Andersen turned for a moment, his surprised grin
almost normal. "I'd forgotten you were here. What's your
trouble?"

"My sister."

"What's wrong with your sister?"

"Don't listen to her! Can't you tell she's walking in her
sleep, like she did before? She's got this crazy notion about
her panda doll. She thinks it's here, lost somewhere out on
the ice. It can't be here."

He turned to shout at Day.

"Wake up, Baby Daby! Don't you know we left your silly doll back on Earth?"

Day sat motionless on the monitor, as if she didn't hear him.

"Leave her be." Andersen shrugged and grinned again. "No matter what she thinks, she's showing us the way."

"What way?" His voice had shrunk to a whisper. "Where?"

"You remember when we were still out in orbit?" Andersen seemed relaxed, almost his natural self. "On our last pass around the planet, we saw a strange light from the middle of the ice cap. It seemed to flash in answer to our radar beam. Remember?"

"I heard about it."

"Tony and I always wanted to know if it was meant to be a signal to us. The captain was afraid to let us try, but your sister is giving us a chance—"

"A chance?" His teeth were chattering. "What kind of chance?"

"Your sister seems to have established a mental link with whatever flashed the beacon. Maybe the senders want to establish some kind of contact. If they do, we want to know."

"We're going to the ice cap?"

"The signal came from what looked like a complex of gigantic structures on the middle of it. We're headed there. It will be a long and terribly difficult journey. With your sister's help, we think we can make it."

"Dr. Andersen—" His voice was so husky he had to try again. "Dr. Andersen, what about our mother? She'll be terribly worried. You should have told her."

"We couldn't." Andersen hardly seemed to care. "Mr. Roak and the captain refused to let us undertake the expedition. We had to make a secret departure."

"Don't we have a radio?" Andersen didn't answer, but he saw the microphone on the console. "Won't you let me call?"

"I'm sorry." Andersen shook his head. "But we can't risk any interference."

"Please!" His voice quivered again. "She'll be worried sick. Just let me tell her we're okay. If we are—"

He stopped to look at Andersen's face. His stubble of red beard was still the same. He still looked tired, with dark half-moons under his eyes. But there was a difference, as if his eyes were on something far away.

"Are we?" he asked. "Are we okay?"

"We're doing what we must." Andersen looked hard at him, shaking his head. "Except maybe for you. We hadn't planned for you to come. I'm sorry you're here, and sorry for your mother." His voice seemed strange, not quite his own. "A misfortune, but I see no remedy. We can't take you back—"

Day had made a strangled squeal and then a string of grunts and whistles like something out of another language. Andersen tipped his head to listen as if he understood and answered with the same odd sounds. They weren't Spanish, or the French he had spoken with Cruzet.

His hand shaking, Kip pulled at Andersen's sleeve. He paid no attention. Bent over the wheel, he was steering around a patch of uneven ice. Beyond it, the spider moved suddenly faster, rocking and swaying. He searched Day's face again, and Andersen's, and saw no amphibian beads.

"Andy?" He tugged once more. "Andy, can't you hear me?"

Andersen didn't answer or seem to feel the pull.

"How long—" he tried to ask. "How long will we be gone?"

Standing with his eyes fixed on that cluster of yellow stars, Andersen ignored him. Day sat on the monitor, her glazed and sleepy eyes fixed on Andersen. Kip was still watching when she turned her head to make a weird whistling chirp, and he saw the bright black bead hidden in the hair behind her ear. Andersen answered with an odd quick grunt, and he saw another bead stuck close behind his ear.

Trembling, he caught his breath, but he felt afraid to speak again. He could only stand silently watching as Andersen drove them on toward that golden arrowhead above the starlit frost in the south. Day never moved, except now and then to make sounds that should have come from animals, maybe birds. Afraid even to move, he stood there till he felt stiff and cold. He got sleepy, because he had woken up too early. With breakfast time long past, his stomach was an aching hollow.

"Andy?" At last he had to speak again. "Dr. Andersen? What has happened to you?"

Day squeaked to Andersen. He answered with a queer little click, but they still ignored him. He felt weak, with a sour ache in his stomach. Finally he left them and climbed down into the cramped engine bay. The floor had the curve of the hull, with the fusion engine humming very softly at one end and the fans of the air cycler whirring at the other. Cruzet knelt at the control console beside the fusion engine, which fused helium 3 and deuterium to make steam for the turbine.

"Tony?" Kip spoke softly, hesitant to bother him. "Tony?"

He didn't answer, didn't move. Fixed on the dials, his eyes looked as glassy as Day's. Leaning closer, Kip found the black gleam behind his right ear.

"Dr. Cruzet?" He raised his voice. "Are you okay?"

Cruzet stayed as rigid as a frozen man.

Frightened again, he climbed back into the main cabin. Needing to pee, he found a tiny toilet room at the end of the curtained berth at the rear of the cabin. On his first ride in the spider, Andersen had showed him the pantry locker. The door made a little table when he pulled it down, a water spigot and a little sink beside it. He found plastic cups and soyasweet wafers on the shelves, and a real red apple from Earth.

He drank a cup of water and ate the hard dry wafers with the apple. The soya stuff was almost good, and he liked the apple's juicy sweetness. Feeling a little better, he looked into the engine bay again. Cruzet still knelt, as motionless as marble, rigid fingers stretched across the console.

In the pilot bay, Andersen stood where he had been, steering toward that cluster of bright yellow stars. Day sat watching from the monitor. She wore a strange little smile, and she sat as still as a blue-eyed doll. He shouted at them, but they seemed not to know he was there. Climbing back into the bubble, he found a dim red glow on the frost around them. The heat lamp had come on. They must have come too far from the ship for anybody to see them.

Beyond that feeble glow there was nothing else to see, even with the binoculars he found on the navigation desk. Though they seemed forever rolling fast toward that golden arrowhead, they got nowhere. The starlit ice lay smooth and flat and dimly white, just the same in every direction all the way to the star horizon. Nothing ever changed in the dead black sky.

The black sun never rose or set. When he focused the binoculars on it, it looked like a cracked black plate, or maybe an ugly face. Thin yellow lines like frowning wrinkles ran across it. Cracks, Andersen said, where volcanic lavas shone through the hardened crust. One angry red spot looked like an eye, glaring at him.

He didn't like the frown, or the furious eye. He put the binoculars back on the desk. The arrowhead of stars had moved to the right when he looked again, but it crept slowly back till again it hung straight ahead. Andersen must have steered around some obstacle too far off to see.

Nothing else happened. He got sleepy, but he felt afraid to sleep. Something worse might happen. With nothing else to do, he longed for his Game Box. Captain Cometeer and his crew had thrilling adventures on strange new planets, but nothing this bad had ever happened to them. He was nodding, fighting to stay awake, when he heard Day making those shrill whistles again. Andersen squealed like some hurt animal, but then Kip heard words from Day that he could understand.

"Turn right. Eighteen degrees."

The golden arrowhead crept slowly to the left, till she spoke again.

"There! Hold us there."

Andersen made a squeak and click that must have been a question.

"Twenty-one kilometers," Day told him. "We reach the archipelago at the prehistoric crossing. Then due west five thousand six hundred kilometers to the continental ice."

How did she know words like archipelago and continental? How did she know the distance to the ice? He felt afraid to wonder. The watch clock chimed, and later chimed again, but nobody paid any attention. He thought it must be night again, ship time. Hungry and thirsty again, he felt sorry for Day. With no breakfast and no lunch, she had even missed her afternoon nap. He thought she should be starving, but when he heard her whistle at Andersen again, she sounded more like some strange bird than anything human.

The spider still rolled on, the golden arrowhead to the left of them now. Stiff from sitting at the navigator's shelflike table, he stood up to watch. At last something loomed out of the dark, something that grew into a great square shadow on the stars.

Andersen drove them toward it, up a wide frosty pavement that looked dimly red under the lamp. They came so close he saw that it was a great square building of some dark stone. The spider's lights showed huge monsters carved into the walls that Dr. Singh and the engineers had died trying to climb.

The spider slowed. He heard a tiny cheep from Day, and a hoarse croak from Andersen. He wondered if the madness of the beads was going to kill him and Cruzet the same way. Maybe even his little sister? His fists clenched, but he had no weapon, no way to fight for her.

Feeling a cold sickness in his middle, he had time to wonder about himself. Would he be safe, since he wore no bead?

Would they leave him alone in the spider? Could he drive it himself, to take the news back to his mother? It would be a long way. The dangers frightened him, but at least he could try. . . .

Day made a little yelp like a hungry puppy. Andersen grunted and drove them around the building. The spider slowed again. Kip searched the foot of the high black wall, looking for the frozen bodies of Singh and the engineers, wondering if he and Day and the men were going to freeze and die here, trying to climb the wall.

His breathing stopped. The wall was too long for the lights of the spider to reach the end of it, but he couldn't see the bodies. Looking again he found three blankets on the frost, farther from the wall. They lay very flat, with nothing under them.

"Andy?" He shuddered, shouting into the interphone. "Weren't the bodies here? Indra's? Nik's and Kobo's?"

He heard no reply. After a moment the turbine hummed louder and the spider rolled on across the platform toward another pavement that led down to another frozen ocean. He shivered again, wondering about the bodies. But the beads weren't killing them, at least not now.

"West." Day's voice had turned sleepy and slow, but she spoke human words. "Toward the Sky Fish."

Andersen's new voice asked a question he didn't quite hear.

"Eighteen degrees right," Day said. "Toward that con-stellation."

The spider turned till the nose faced a tiny cluster of blue-white stars shaped like a cowboy hat. It pitched and swayed a little on broken ice near the beach, but the frost lay smooth beyond. Andersen drove them faster again, toward the continental ice five thousand six hundred kilometers ahead.

Twenty-three

Rima held her breath till the knock came again, impatiently louder. Glancing around the room, she found no possible weapon, no way of escape.

"Who . . ." Her voice was a husky whisper. She tried to raise it. "Who's this?"

All she heard was another sharp knock. Uncertainty became unendurable. She opened the door.

"Dr. Virili?"

Carlos Mondragon stepped inside and quickly closed the door. One hand was dripping blood. The other gripped a heavy strip of steel. She saw black tape wrapped around the end he held. The other end was broken to leave a jagged point.

"Mondragon?" She shrank from the weapon. "What do you want?"

"I'm not here to frighten you." He turned to lay the bar

on Kip's empty berth. "Dr. Virili, we have trouble on the ship. I believe you're in danger. I want to help you if I can."

"Thank you." Breathing again, she motioned for him to sit. "I heard gunshots. A scream. What's the trouble?"

"Mutiny—if you ask Captain Stecker." With an uneasy glance at the door, he sat beside his weapon. "It began in the dining room. Roak and the captain were eating beefsteaks out of Jake Hinch's hoard. Men from the pit gang wanted the same. Roak called security. They refused to fire. Now . . ."

He spread his hands uncertainly and paused to wipe at a drop of blood that had fallen on the sheet.

"The shots I heard?" she asked.

"Who knows?" He shrugged. "Stecker's locked in his cabin with Roak. Threatening to explode their bomb and kill us all. Glengarth is barricaded in the control dome, holding off a mob."

"Somebody was fighting in the corridor."

"I saw blood on the deck." He spread his hands in helpless desperation. "Fighting everywhere."

"I thank you, Carlos." Suddenly weak in the knees, she sank down on her berth and frowned at his bleeding hand. "Let me see the wound."

"A scratch." He shrugged again. "A bullet grazed me."

A shot crashed in the corridor outside. Hard-heeled boots pounded by the door. Silence followed. She sat listening, fingers to her lips, till he spoke.

"This is an ugly time, Dr. Virili. I fear for you."

"I'm afraid for us all." She managed a bleak little smile. "What can we do?"

"Quién sabe?" Pausing a moment, he cocked his head to study her. "Perhaps," he said, "perhaps there is a chance. I believe the Beta spider is still in the hangar." He paused again, listening. "I doubt that it is guarded—security has other business. We might perhaps steal it—"

"And follow the Alpha?" She caught her breath. "Could we?"

"We can try." He shrugged. "If you wish . . ."

"Let me dress. I won't be long."

She drew the curtain around her berth. He sat waiting, frowning at the thickening blood on the back of his hand, till she pulled the curtain aside and stepped out in an orange-yellow jumpsuit, carrying a light bag.

"Nothing sure." His voice was hushed. "But we can try."

"First, let's see your hand."

"Nothing," he said. "Only a scratch."

But he let her see the bleeding hand.

"Not too deep." She nodded. "Let me dress it."

Opening the first-aid kit on the wall, she sprayed the wound, swabbed it clean, sealed a dressing over it.

"Gracias," he murmured. "Now . . ."

He put his ear to the door, drew it ajar enough to let him peer out, and pulled it wide. Rima, her heart pumping hard, followed him into the empty corridor. With a warning head-shake at the elevator, he led her toward the stair and down its endless spiral. She saw a pool of darkening blood and a long smear where a body had been dragged off a landing, but they heard no sound, met nobody until he stopped abruptly at the exit to the main deck.

"Washburn." She heard his dismay. "Still on duty."

With a warning nod, he shrank back from the doorway.

"I thought she'd be above," he whispered. "With Roak and the captain. She's no friend."

"But Kip and Day—" Her voice caught. "We can't give up."

"Quién sabe?" He shrugged. "We'll see."

●

She followed him across the brightly lit deck to the security station. Reba Washburn sat staring fixedly at nothing. Her left eye was dark-rimmed and swollen, with a reddening patch above it and a drying smear below.

"Lieutenant Washburn?"

She started at Mondragon's voice and spun her chair to face him. Her good eye narrowed.

"What do you want?"

He cringed from her stare. Suspecting that he brought the bomb aboard, she had urged Glengarth not to trust him.

"There's fighting above." Uncertain what to say, he watched her battered face. "Dr. Virili was afraid—"

"Reba, I'm desperate." Rima came up beside him. "My children are gone, I don't know where. And I'm afraid of Jonas Roak."

"You should be!" Her face twitched into a bitter grimace. "He's slime!"

"Roak?" Mondragon spoke in astonishment. "I thought—"

Still wary of her, he cut himself off.

"Pig!" Washburn snarled the word. "He got me into his cabin. Tried to get me into his bed. Threatened me with that bomb—" She broke off abruptly and searched Carlos with a one-eyed squint. "He runs the ship with threats of it. He tried to bribe me with it. Promised to make me his queen. Turned so nasty I slapped him. That's when he did this." She touched the red-stained patch on her temple. "Snatched a brass lamp off the captain's desk and smashed it across my face."

She grinned and flinched with pain.

"Knocked me flat, but I got up laughing at him. I told him his bomb was a dud. It is." She nodded soberly at Rima. "I sabotaged the ignition chip when the captain left it with me for inspection."

"The bomb?" Mondragon stared at her. "Is it in fact still disabled?"

"Judging from Mr. Roak's fury, I'd say it is. But he says he has a demolition engineer in his camp. Says they found the damage and replaced the chip with a spare he says he brought with him. Likely one more lie, but I guess we'll never know. Not unless he and Stecker do try to blow us up.

That's their bluster now. Shut up in their cabin, daring any-body to call their hand."

"Would they?"

"Quick and probably painless." Washburn shrugged. "If they've got the guts."

Dismally, Rima's shoulders hunched.

"If we can't help the kids, I don't think I care."

"But if we can . . ." Mondragon frowned uncertainly at Washburn and back at her. "We must."

Rima straightened, searching Washburn's battered face.

"Reba, here's what we want." Voice quivering, she spread her hands. "Carlos says the Beta's standing in the work bal-loon. We want to take it out. To look for my kids. If you'll let us through the lock—"

"Why not?" Washburn brightened, with a painful little grin. "Mr. Roak and the captain have been plotting an escape of their own, if the ship gets too hot for them. Loading the spider with their private supplies." She smirked with satis-faction. "One up for me."

●

The deck shuddered and they heard a rumbling boom some-where above. Rima held her breath till silence came, smiling uneasily at Mondragon.

"Why not?" Washburn muttered again, fumbling at her belt. "One down for Jonas Roak!"

She turned a key in the console behind her. The ship's lock slid open. Rima waved at her and hurried after Mondragon into icy darkness. Blind for a moment, she heard the hiss and thud of the valves sealing behind them. Light came on. Shiv-ering in the chill, she stared up at the spider. Crouching over her on its ungainly metal legs as if about to spring, it looked huge and strange, alien as the planet itself. Stark terror brushed her, terror of the unknown masters of the dark and the ice.

"Rima? Dr. Virili?"

Mondragon's call broke that spell. He was already climbing the ramp. She caught her breath and followed him up into the monster's belly. Behind him at the controls, she watched him close the lock, listened to the muffled roar of the salvage pumps that let the balloon's deflated fabric collapse upon the frame overhead, watched its own wide portal open to the stars.

"So far, 'sta bien."

Seated at the wheel, he turned for a moment to grin at her. She heard the turbine hum. Her shoulders were hunched against the cold and the dread that haunted her, but he seemed deft and sure, driving them down across the ancient beach. Watching him, she found a sense of comfort she had not felt for many days.

She stood for a long time close behind him, reluctant to leave him, but at last she climbed into the bubble, where she could see the waste of starlit frost and the blaze of the arching constellations. The ship was already far behind, a thin sliver of polished metal gleaming dimly against the dark ridge behind it. The pale gray ice ahead looked bewilderingly flat and featureless, but he steered across it as if he knew where to go.

"Beta! Stecker to Beta!" The sudden yelp from the radio took her breath. "Mondragon! Virili! You are guilty of mutiny. Theft! Treason! Get the Beta back here at once, under penalty of death—"

Stecker was cut off. A moment of silence, then Jim Cheng's voice, hoarse with tension.

"Rima! Carlos! Listen please. A message from the captain. He's still holding off the mutineers, but we're desperate. You're in no danger—at least not from us. But you've left us in a hopeless mess. Trapped aboard. Both spiders gone. We can't get out to do anything. And you're throwing your own lives away. Bring the Beta back, and we can promise you a pardon—

"Oh God!"

A startled gasp. Rima heard a crash like a gunshot, cursing voices, Cheng again.

"Glengarth's on the phone." He sounded frantic. "The mutineers are storming Stecker's cabin. He's triggering the bomb—"

A brittle snap, and all she heard was the interstellar static.

●

Climbing into the bubble with her, Mondragon pointed back the way they had come. Looking, she saw the frost gone blindingly bright, the ice-crowned cliffs etched against the dark. A ball of fire swelled from where the ship had stood, reddened swiftly, and faded into the eternal night.

She rubbed her eyes and blinked at Mondragon.

"Thanks to los santos!" He crossed himself, hoarsely whispering. "We got away in time."

"But Mr. Glengarth." Knees gone weak, she sat down at the navigation table. "Jim Cheng. Reba. Everybody." She caught a long breath. "Carlos, we're all alone."

"Except for the Alpha." He shrugged. "Los niños. We can still follow them." He studied her sharply. "There's Stecker's whisky, if you need it."

"Coffee." She nodded, grateful for his calm. "Coffee will do."

She followed him down into the cabin and sat on the berth, watching him brew a pot of Stecker's Kona coffee. She sipped it slowly, while that balloon of fire burned and vanished again and again in her mind.

"It's done." He stood up when his cup was empty. "The saints have saved us from the bomb." He crossed himself again. "Let them guide us on."

He returned to the controls. The turbine hummed again, and the spider glided on. She sat for a time at the table with another cup of coffee. Wishing she had Mondragon's faith, she began to feel some spark of it. The new launch facility had always been a hopeless dream. The bomb, after all, had really changed nothing. Not for them. Resolved to face what she must, she put the cups in the cleanser and climbed to the bubble.

She was swept for a moment into homesick longing for Earth, but soon she found the sun's dead blot and a few stars she had begun to know. She watched them swing right, swing left and right again, as Mondragon followed the Alpha's track. At last the sun hung still on the left and she saw that Mondragon was driving them toward the arrow-shaped cluster of yellow giants low in the south. She climbed down again to watch his lean brown hands steady on the wheel, his head often bent to follow traces too faint for her to see.

"You found the trail?" she asked him. "Tell me how."

"I used to track my father's goats."

Leaning to peer over his shoulder, she found nothing but the limitless frozen flatness.

"Look close in," he said. "For the tire marks in the frost. It's the last wisp of atmosphere, frozen into a crystal fluff. The tires crush it, leaving a pattern you can see when they come under the lamp."

She frowned again through the thick quartz plate and shook her head.

"You can learn," he promised her.

"I'll try." She tried for a time, found marks too faint to follow, and asked him at last, "Aren't you hungry?"

"I could eat. You'll find supplies in the pantry locker."

She found the locker, deep and generously filled. Soya stuff enough, but more from the captain's private stock. Irradiated ham and bacon, steaks and chops. Fresh fruit, eggs, mushrooms, crisp asparagus, all in stasis wraps. Stecker had meant to live well. No bread; tofusoya toast would have to do. She made ham and eggs, then set the tiny table the locker door made when it was folded down.

"Carlos," she called. "Stop the spider and come down to eat."

"I smell the coffee," he answered. "Bring me a cup and a sandwich, and I'll drive on."

Walking forward, she found him still leaning over the wheel.

"I am desperate to save the kids," she told him. "But it may take all our lives, even if we can. We must save ourselves. Right now, you need a break."

●

He stopped the spider and came back to join her. In spite of all the strain and dread, she felt a wave of relief as he sat across the little table. A stubble of beard shadowed his blood-freckled face, yet he was good to look at, smiling as he watched her pour the Kona coffee.

"Rima—" He spoke on impulse. "If I may call you Rima."

"Of course." Her tired face lit. "Please!"

They were alone together, comfortable together, sharing a common goal. He liked the deft grace of her fingers, spreading the captain's real dairy butter on her tofusoya toast. Passing it to him, she paused for a moment, eyes on his face.

"Carlos," she said, "I don't know how to thank you. It's a terrible time, but now I feel very lucky. I thought my world had ended. You've brought me back to life. I'm grateful to you."

"I'm the lucky one."

He had to gulp and blink back sudden tears. For all his daring dreams, he had never expected such a moment. He sipped the coffee to cover his emotion.

"Carlos—" Something caught her voice and made her shake her head. Silent a moment before she went on, she seemed more relaxed than she felt. "You know, we're almost strangers. Tell me something about yourself."

"If you—if you ask."

Confusion had taken his voice. He gulped the hot coffee.

"Or do you mind?" Her fine eyes had a look of keen appraisal. "If you do—"

"No! If you care." His voice came back, and the English was easier now. "I grew up in a dead mining town called Cuerno del Oro. We never had much money for anything, but I did learn what I could. I heard about the starships. I dreamed of going out to the stars—though never to this one."

Ruefully, he nodded at the black sun in the holomonitor beside the locker.

"I cared for my mother through her last year or so. Came north and got across the border when she died. I saw you at the launch site. . . ."

Remembering the moment, he laid his fork down and forgot to go on. Even now, hollow-eyed with worry, her tawny hair in disarray, she had a beauty that ached in his heart. A wave of emotion carried him on.

"I was waiting with the pickets at the gate because I had no pass to get inside. I saw you in the taxi, smiling when you spoke to the children. You were beautiful. I knew you were kind. I knew I loved you—"

Her startled look checked him. She was staring past him.

"My Kona coffee." It was the voice of Jonas Roak. "Pour me a cup."

He turned to see Roak climbing the steps out of the engine compartment, a smug grin on his narrow face, a blue steel gun in his hand.

Twenty-four

"Where's this?"

Kip was standing at the little table under the pantry locker, spreading tofujam on a hard slab of soyamax toast. In spite of the ripe red strawberry on the label, the jam had a bitter aftertaste he thought he would never learn to like. But he was hungry.

"Where's Mom?"

Looking up, he found Day slipping into the cabin from the pilot bay. Her pale hair fell in an uncombed tangle across her face. Dark shadows ringed her eyes, but they had lost the glassy stare that frightened him.

"We're in the spider," he told her, "out on the ice."

"To look for Me Me." She nodded. "But I'm awful hungry." Her eyes were on his toast. "Can I have some?"

"Sure." Looking for the black bead, he saw it still stuck behind her ear. It unnerved him for a moment, but she was once more his little sister. "The locker's full of stuff."

"Thanks to the captain and Mr. Roak."

He saw Dr. Cruzet coming down the narrow steel steps from the bubble. The bead still shone behind his ear, yet he was smiling at Day, asking if she wanted fruit with her cereal. Whistling softly as he did when he was busy, he made scrambled eggs out of a yellow powder and cooked slices of the captain's ham in the microwave. When he had them ready, Andersen stopped the spider and came to eat.

Cruzet had made soya milk for Day and a mock orange drink for him. That was no better than the tofujam, but Cruzet let him have real coffee when he asked. All of them were so hungry, they ate without talking. Cruzet was standing, draining his cup and yawning sleepily, until Day yelped at him. A sharp animal sound, like the yip of a startled pup.

"Okay." Suddenly very serious, he nodded at her. "I'll drive us on."

Frowning in a strange way, she watched him go back into the nose. The turbine hummed, and the spider lurched into motion.

"We have to hurry," she told Andersen. "Me Me needs us."

"I know," he said. "We're pushing on as fast as we can now."

"Me Me says . . ." She was rubbing her eyes, and her voice was fading. "Me Me . . ."

She was suddenly asleep, her head on the table. Andersen carried her to the curtained berth at the rear of the cabin. He came back to clear the table and put the dishes away.

"Andy—," Kip began. A shiver stopped him. Andersen had turned to frown inquiringly, but he saw the bead's black glint, and it was a moment before he could go on. "If you don't mind, there's a lot I don't understand."

"I suppose you don't." Frowning soberly, Andersen nodded. "I wish you hadn't come."

"But here I am!" his words burst out. "And Day's gone crazy! I know she does miss her panda doll. She cried back at

White Sands when they made her leave it, but that's where it is."

"Could be you're right." Andersen shrugged, nodding reasonably. "It doesn't matter. Tony and I want to push ahead toward the source of that signal."

"The city of giants?"

"Whatever it is." Andersen shrugged as if giants were common. "We had just a glimpse of it from far out in space, but it did look like a cluster of buildings—if you can imagine buildings the size of mountains."

"So we're really going there?" Blinking at Andersen's lean brown face, he saw a look that bothered him. Eager excitement, but also something cold and strange. It took him a moment to get his breath and go on. "Across all those thousands of kilometers? To the middle of the ice?"

"A hard trip." Andersen nodded calmly. "But your sister knows the way."

Did she? he wanted to ask. If she really did, how had she learned? Why did Andersen believe her? If she was actually their guide, how did they understand her queer chirps and yelps and grunts? What had the black beads done to her? To all three of them? He didn't ask, because he was afraid he wouldn't like the answers.

"My mother," he said. "She'll be terribly worried. Can I call her on the radio?"

"We've come too far." Andersen frowned and shook his head. "We're now below the line of sight, with the peninsula ridge in the way."

"Mr. Glengarth said signals reflect from space."

"Sometimes." Andersen nodded. "From orbital dust. But most of the time the clouds are too thin and patchy. Even if you happened to get through, Stecker wouldn't let anybody follow us. He needs the other spider at the pit."

"Can I try to call?"

"Why not?" Andersen shrugged. "Use the radio up in the bubble."

He stretched and yawned and lay down on the berth. Climbing the narrow stairway, Kip heard him already snoring.

●

In the bubble, Kip felt lost in a still, cold hell. The stars burned hard and bright in the dead black sky, never dimming, never twinkling, as they had burned forever. The turbine's muffled hum was hard to hear. He felt no motion. Beyond their own tiny island of dim red light, the pale frost reached out to the straight black horizon, the same everywhere, with no landmark to show direction.

Stark terror chilled him for a moment, till he found the sun's round black shadow on the sky behind, and the tight little cluster of stars that made a high-crowned cowboy hat, still straight ahead. Peering down, he made out their wheel prints in the frost, unreeling steadily behind.

He turned on the radio.

"Beta to ship." He called and listened and tried again. "Beta spider calling the ship."

Silence. He turned up the volume till he heard a crackling whine. Interference, maybe, from the fusion engine or the motors that drove the wheels. He backed off the volume and called again. Again and again, till he felt dead for sleep. Maybe the people on the ship were all busy, rushing the pit project. He never got an answer, and he had no way to know about his mother. At last he crept back down the narrow steel stairway. The cabin was empty. He used the tiny toilet and dropped onto the berth.

●

The next he knew Day was jogging his arm.

"Wake up, lazy-head. Dr. Cruzet is making dinner."

He smelled something better than tofusoya and saw Cruzet busy at the little counter under the locker, whistling to himself.

"Hello, Kipper." Cruzet liked to call him that. "Nearly five hundred kilometers made, and we're all okay."

Andersen had stopped the spider.

"On smooth ice." He was coming back from the pilot bay in the nose. "Except for a couple of seismic faults too small to cause a problem."

Kip rubbed his eyes and peered at them. All three looked like their normal selves, but they still wore the bright black beads in the hair behind their ears. And normally, he thought, they would never have seemed quite so carefree about the long trek ahead, or so little bothered by what might be happening back on the ship.

He caught the rich aroma of broiling steak.

"One of the captain's precious sirloins," Cruzet said. "Shared four ways, because the stuff in the locker won't last us forever."

The steak was rare, the way he liked it. The first good meat he'd had since they left Earth. He could have eaten more, but the mashed potatoes made from powder were nearly as good as his mother's. Cruzet had made lemonade for him and Day. Dessert was a vanilla milk shake that had the taste of actual milk.

"Capital!" Mopping his plate with a soya crust, Andersen grinned at Cruzet. "Tony, you missed your calling."

A shrill little squeal from Day froze his grin. Andersen got up quickly, and she followed him back toward the nose.

"Daby," Kip called after her, "don't you care how much Mom misses us?"

"I care." She turned back, and the voice was her own again. He saw tears rolling down her smooth baby cheeks. "I do. But Me Me needs us more."

She trotted on in a moment to catch up with Andersen. Cruzet was still sitting across the little table, sipping a second cup of coffee.

"I'm sorry for you, Kipper." Sympathetically, he shook his head. "I know it's hard, but none of this is quite what we expected. You've got to remember where we're going."

He seemed so human and friendly that Kip dared to ask, "What will the ice cap be like when we get there?"

"Rough." Soberly, he shrugged. "Looking down from orbit, we saw mountain ranges that rimmed a high plateau on the only continent. The major area of mountain building on the planet, Andy says. We'll have big problems. Thousands of kilometers of ice. Cliffs to climb. Glaciers and crevasses to cross. Unknown hazards."

Yet he was whistling cheerfully as he showed Kip how to work the microwave and load the dishes into the cleanser. Suddenly, however, the whistling stopped. Silent again, he hurried down into the engine bay.

Feeling very much alone, Kip looked into the nose. Andersen sat rigidly straight at the controls. Day had perched again on the monitor beside him. Her blue eyes were wide, fixed on the high-crowned hat blazing in the blackness just above the west horizon. Her lips were slightly parted in an empty smile that gave her the look of a glass-eyed doll. He shivered when he found the bead behind her ear, shining in the dimness with an eerie blue glow. Afraid to speak to them, he climbed back to the bubble.

He sat there a long time, watching the wheel tracks unrolling in the frost behind him. Perhaps the stars that made the hat had climbed a little higher; maybe the black sun blot behind had sunk a little lower, but nothing else showed any motion. No glow of dawn would ever break here. The bitter night would never end. He looked away from the hat, wishing for his Game Box.

●

Cruzet and Andersen took turns tending the controls and the fusion engine. Wearing the beads, they seemed to need little sleep. Day slept more, but she still spent most of her time sitting on the monitor, searching out the way ahead. They never stopped the spider except for hurried meals. The watch clock chimed and chimed again, but nobody seemed to care. Their meals came a long time apart.

Andersen and Cruzet were nearly human when they did stop the spider, laughing and joking, talking about how many kilometers they had made, as if the trip really was a great adventure. But those breaks never lasted long. Pushing on again, they had no time for him.

He ate when there was food, and cleaned the dishes afterward. Sometimes he stood watching Cruzet or Andersen at the wheel, and Day perched beside them, but they never spoke to him. Once he followed Cruzet down into the engine room. Without a word for him, Cruzet pointed at a red-glowing sign that read, Warning! High Voltage! Keep Clear!

Keeping clear, he spent most of his time alone in the bubble, watching the wheel tracks behind and the guiding stars ahead. Worried about his mother, he sometimes tried to call the ship, but all he ever heard was the meaningless murmur of the cosmos. Sometimes he wondered if anybody had tried to follow in the Alpha. No matter if they had. The Beta was moving too fast to be overtaken.

●

Day's sharp squeak came over the interphone, and then her human voice, just as urgent.

"Dr. Andersen, no! Don't drive around it. We're stopping there for something Me Me needs."

The high-crowned hat had crawled a little to the left. He watched it creep back again till it was almost straight ahead.

"There!" Day squealed. "Hold us there."

"Okay," Andersen said. "I'll hold us there."

He watched the hat till a ragged black shadow crept up from the flat horizon. The shadow of a tall mountain peak. The ice grew rough. The spider lurched and swayed, lumbering over hummocks of broken ice and then across a boulder-cluttered beach. It stopped close to the base of a high black cliff.

He heard Day's shrill squeak again, and Andersen's almost human voice.

"I don't think so. It looks impossible."

She answered him, speaking in her uncanny language of grunts and trills and clicks.

"For Me Me," she finished. "It's something she must have."

"It's a difficult climb," he muttered, "but I guess we must try."

Kip heard the thunk of the closing air lock and the muffled hiss and drum of the pumps. Andersen came out, looking lean and tall in the yellow airskin, a lamp burning on the crown of his helmet. He walked back and forth, searching for a way up the cliff, and finally began to climb.

The interphone brought a sharp yip from Day.

"I'm suiting up," Cruzet told her. "I'm going outside."

She shrilled something that sounded like a question.

"We've been pushing the machine pretty hard," he said, "with a lot of rough country ahead. I want to inspect the drive motors and the wheels."

A long half minute of silence.

"A prudent precaution," she agreed at last, in a half-human voice. "Me Me says you may go."

The air lock hissed and the pump drummed again.

Andersen went up the sheer black cliff, clinging with fingers and toes to narrow cracks and ledges Kip could hardly see. Once he slipped, but he caught himself and inched down again as slowly as he had climbed. Back on the ground, he searched the foot of the cliff again, and climbed once more. High up, he disappeared.

Waiting for his light, Kip heard the lock cycle again. The interphone brought a murmur from Cruzet. Day grunted something he didn't understand.

"It's been too long." He heard Cruzet's lifted voice. "Andy's in trouble. I've got to follow."

"No!" It was Day's voice, still strangely hard. "Me Me says he is okay. Just very busy, doing exactly what she told him."

●

"There!" Kip had been nodding, dreaming he was on an expedition with Captain Cometeer to the far Crimson Cluster. Cruzet's eager voice brought him wide awake. "Andy Andersen, the human fly!"

He looked up and found the lean yellow figure climbing down again, a bulging plastic bag slung from his belt. An awkward burden. Again and again he seemed to slip or paused to rest, but at last he was back on the ground, limping toward the spider. Kip heard the air lock, and crept down to the cabin.

"Bones!"

Andersen tossed a yellow plastic bag on the cabin floor.

"Bones of predators. Bones of prey. Big bones and baby bones. Fish bones and worm bones. Round amphibian skulls and dagger-jawed monster skulls. The flying predators nested in the cave; nothing else could reach it. The history of the planet is written in the bones, if we knew how to read it."

Kip saw no bones, however, when he upended the sack. What rolled out was something dark and shapeless, glinting like a huge black crystal.

"Beads?" Cruzet squinted at it. "Amphibian beads?"

The honeycomb was a black-glinting mass of the tiny prisms stuck together, side by side and end to end. He pulled one of them off, polished it on the leg of his yellow jumpsuit, peered at it through a pocket magnifier, and frowned inquiringly at Andersen.

"What else?" Andersen grinned. "I found one with every amphibian skull. Not that I've got a clue what they are. Harder than diamonds and adhering like magnets, with no magnetism in them. Unchanged, I think, by all the ages since the planet froze."

Day snatched one of them, with an eager little squeal.

"No!" She scowled in disappointment. "No good."

She tossed it back to try another and still another, till at last she tilted her head as if to listen.

"Me Me's voice!" She smiled triumphantly at Andersen. "Really clear, like she was right here with us. She knows the way and she needs us to hurry."

Cruzet and then Andersen himself bent eagerly over the honeycomb, trying replacements for the beads they had worn. They stood up at last, smiling in satisfaction.

"Me Me needs us," Day urged them again. "She needs us terribly."

"Not quite yet." Wearily, Andersen shook his head. "I'm used up. I want a shot of Stecker's bourbon and a good long nap."

"And something to eat?" Kip urged them. "I'm famished."

They turned to Day. She looked far off, listening again, and finally nodded.

"She says we have a long way to come. We can eat when we have to, but we can't waste time."

Andersen mixed himself a bourbon and water from a bottle in the locker. He sat on the berth, sipping it sleepily, while Cruzet broiled another of Stecker's stasis-wrapped steaks. After they had eaten, Andersen stretched and yawned and started toward the curtained berth.

Day stopped him with a sharp little bark.

"Me Me called," she told him. "We must move. If you really require it, you can sleep while Dr. Cruzet drives the spider."

"Tell her we're on our way," Cruzet said.

Andersen picked up the bag of crystals and carried them into the curtained berth. Day followed Cruzet back to the wheel. Left alone in the cabin, Kip stacked pans and dishes in the cleaner. Suddenly heavy with sleep, he had started for the berth when he saw a black crystal lying where Day must have tossed it.

"Tony!" Shrinking from it, he shouted into the nose. "Day! You left a bead on the floor."

He heard no answer. Walking to the door of the pilot bay, he found Cruzet at the wheel, backing the spider away from the cliff. Day sat watching, her eyes gone glassy again. He shouted once more, close to their ears. They weren't listening, not to him.

Feeling very lonely, he climbed the steel stairs into the bubble. The heat lamp, high on its mast, was a dim red sun among the stars overhead. Beyond its feeble glow, the starlit frost reached ahead to the midnight sky, unbroken by anything.

He sat down at the narrow navigation table, listening to the turbine's steady hum, watching the faint tracks the tires left behind, wondering about the bones. Were the amphibians still alive? Guarding the planet and flashing keep-off warnings? More likely, he thought, those giant flying predators had killed them all before the planet froze.

Cruzet and Andersen wanted answers. Or they said they did when Day was asleep and they were almost themselves. What she wanted, or what the beads wanted, he had no way to know. He had no way to guess what would happen next. His head ached from wondering.

He wanted his Game Box and Captain Cometeer. His adventures were never quite so strange as this drive to the ice cap, but they were always thrilling enough, and when he wanted to quit he could always hit the exit key. The box was back on the ship, and he had no key to cancel the terrible power of the beads.

The spider rolled on. The turbine hummed. All he could see anywhere was the empty ice ahead, the faint tire tracks behind the strange stars above. Half-asleep, he stumbled out of the navigator's chair when Cruzet came up the steps. Without a word, not even seeming to see him, Cruzet sat at the desk and picked up the binoculars to sweep the ice horizon.

Feeling uneasy there, Kip went back down the stairs and looked into the pilot bay. Andersen was back at the wheel, standing stiffly straight, watching the dials and gauges. Day sat on the monitor beside him, as motionless as an actual doll, her glassy eyes fixed on the black horizon.

"Andy, I'm hungry." Andersen didn't answer, and he raised his voice. "Can't we stop to eat?"

"Broken ice ahead." It was Day who spoke, the cold and toneless voice not at all her own. "Steer twenty-two degrees right for the next two hundred kilometers to get around it."

His little sister. How did she know there was broken ice two hundred kilometers ahead? Of course she didn't. The bead behind her ear was talking. Shivering, he went back to the cabin. There was nothing he could do about her or the beads, but he still felt hungry. Looking in the locker, he found a box of soyamax crackers and a can of mock orange powder. He mixed a cup of juice and ate the dry crackers with it. They were almost good.

Suddenly he had to sleep. Keeping as far as he could from the black bead under the curtain, he crawled onto the narrow cabin berth and lay there with his back to the bead. He tried to forget it, but he had no way to send it away. He lay a long time wondering what was waiting for them on the ice ahead, till at last he slept.

Twenty-five

"Sit where you are!" Rasping hoarsely at them, Roak waved the gun. "Obey my orders, and nobody gets a bullet."

Mondragon clutched at the knife he had used to cut the ham. He dropped it when the pistol swung toward him. Rima sat frozen.

"Surprised?" Roak squinted at her with one blood-rimmed eye. He looked desperate, his long hair matted and tangled, but he was grinning through the stiffened mask of black stubble and drying blood that covered half his face. "Well, so am I. Happy to find you got us away from those maniacs on the ship." He waved the gun at Mondragon and leered at Rima. "Happier to find you here, my dear. Where did you think you were going?"

"To find my children," she whispered.

"You never will." He laughed at her, harshly. "Because I'm not as crazy as Cruzet and Andersen. We're not chasing them across the ice cap. Or returning to the lunatics in the ship. I like it right where we are."

Unsteady on his feet, he swayed to the middle of the cabin where his gun could cover them both.

"Stecker's precious Kona coffee." Glancing at the table, he scowled imperatively at Mondragon. "Boy, I'll have a cup."

"I'm not a boy...." Mondragon began, and stopped when the gun swung toward him. "Okay," he muttered, and filled a coffee mug. Sipping it, Roak made a sour face and turned to Rima.

"Sweetheart, I'm sorry you dislike me—"

"I despise you!" Her voice rose raggedly. "I'd kill you if I could."

"I don't think you can." He gave her a sardonic smirk. "Because now I've got the upper hand, with no more guff from Stecker." He nodded at Mondragon, who stood beside her. "If you want to keep your pet Mex alive, tell him to relax and sit down."

Mondragon shrugged uncomfortably and sat back at the table.

"Here we are." Roak waved the gun at the cabin around them. "Our own little world for the rest of our lives. My own little world." Warningly, he shook his head at Mondragon. "I don't want anybody hurt, so don't get rash."

He sipped again, made another bitter face.

"I'm lucky, in fact, to have you here, because I was in an ugly fix." He shrugged and flinched as if the movement hurt. "It all began when our good captain's interphone went dead. He sent me out with orders for Washburn. That black bitch!"

Scowling at the coffee, he set it back on the counter.

"She shot me. Sent her hoodlums after me. I was lucky to get away alive. Luckier when you two got aboard, because I can't run this damn contraption." He frowned bleakly at Mondragon. "How far have we come from the ship?"

"Forty kilometers."

Calculating, he frowned through the blood.

"Far enough," he decided. "Far enough so the bastards can't sneak out in their airskins to end our honeymoon."

He grinned at Rima's shudder.

"A lovely honeymoon, my dear." His thick voice taunted her. "With all the goodies Stecker had me load for his own getaway. And your boyfriend here for a servant."

Squinting warily at Mondragon, he paused to listen.

"Stop the engine," he snapped. "I don't want anybody calling the ship. Or them trying to trace us."

"Better let me keep the turbine turning," Mondragon told him. "At least on standby, to run the generator. We'd freeze without the heat lamp. The cycler needs power, if you want to keep breathing."

Roak hesitated, scowling suspiciously.

"Okay," he grunted. "But no tricks. For the lady's sake."

"No tricks," Mondragon agreed. "Just let me get us out of drive mode. That can build up a dangerous back pressure if we aren't moving."

Which wasn't quite true, but Roak was no fusion engineer.

●

Roak let the pistol trail him into the pilot bay and turned to grin at Rima.

"Just us three, my dear." She cringed from his mockery. "You may not like it, but you'll learn to get along."

Out of the corner of her eye, she saw Mondragon coming silently back from the control bay, clutching his iron strip.

"Jonas Roak, you were born a fool." She raised her voice to hold him. "You'll die a fool. Touch me, and I'll kill you—"

Close behind him, Mondragon raised the club. Roak must have seen the fleeting movement of her eye. He spun. The club came down. Her ears rang from the crash of the shot, but the gun went spinning across the floor. Roak moaned and toppled toward her. Mondragon dashed to recover the gun and stood staring at a wide red blot across the back of Roak's yellow jumpsuit.

"Don't!" Roak raised his head, whimpering like a hurt child. "Don't kill me, for God's sake!"

"Por qué no?" Mondragon stood over him, breathing hard. "Un cabrón!"

"Reba! The sneaky bitch!" Roak tried to rise and sagged back to the floor. "Hurt me. Hurt me bad. Shot me in the gut." He twisted his head to look up at Rima. "Help—you've got to help me."

Mondragon stepped warily back, holding the gun on him.

"Rima, please!" he begged. "Don't let me die."

Weak in the knees, she swayed farther away.

"What do you say?" Mondragon looked at her. "What do we owe him?"

"He's a contemptible beast!" she whispered bitterly. "We ought to throw him out. But we're human. Even here, we've got to stay human."

Mondragon slowly nodded. Roak moaned again and let his head drop back to the floor. Together, they lifted him into the curtained berth.

"I'm no doctor." She frowned at Mondragon. "But we've got to do what we can."

Roak seemed unconscious. Mondragon helped her strip the blood-sodden jumpsuit off his torso and she examined the wound.

"The bullet hit his left side," she said. "Just below the heart. There's no exit wound; it's still in him. There would be damage to the lung. Probably a lot of internal bleeding."

He found a first-aid kit.

"Sedative and antibiotic Syrettes." Opening it, she shook her head. "Antiseptic foam and a handful of healer patches. Enough to help ease his pain, but not much else."

Leaving Roak unconscious, his breath now a slow and

bubbling rasp, Rima drew the curtain. Mondragon had made hot coffee, and she sat with him at the little table.

"Not much I could do." Her hands still shaking, she lifted her cup. "We're not equipped for surgery."

"Must we watch him?"

"He's dying," she said. "No threat now."

●

They sipped the coffee, recovering.

"A nasty jolt when he came out." With a wry shrug, she looked across at the door to the engine bay, where Roak had hidden himself. "He's still a burden to us."

"Perhaps we can't toss him out," Mondragon muttered. "But we can't forget the children."

"We'll drive on," she said. "When we can."

Without much appetite, they finished breakfast. Mondragon drove them on. Rima opened the curtain to feel for Roak's failing pulse, and went forward for a driving lesson.

"Easy enough," Mondragon said, trying to cheer her, "if you learn to see the wheel prints when the red light picks them out. On level ice, they run straight toward those yellow stars that make a crooked arrow, just over the horizon."

He let her take the wheel. She could see the tracks when he pointed them out in the bottom window, faint parallel lines in the frost below the spider, blurred by their movement and lost in the starlight ahead.

"No problem," he told her cheerfully. "Not after you've trained your eye. Just keep those yellow stars straight ahead."

At last she thought she could follow that shadowy trace of darker darkness that narrowed and vanished ahead. Leaving her alone at the wheel, he turned to listen for Roak's labored wheeze.

"Not a sound," he said. "I'll take a look."

He was gone a long time. She called to him and turned her head to listen. When she looked back, the trail was gone.

They were lost. All around, the pale gray frost lay flat and featureless forever. She found the black sun still low on her left, the broken arrow still low ahead, the shadow track of their own wheels still stretching back behind, but no mark she could see ahead. Chilled with panic, she stopped the engine and sat shivering, listening till she heard his call.

"Rima? Anything wrong?"

"I've lost the trail."

She left the wheel and met him in the passage.

"Take a look at Roak," he said. "No sign of life I can see."

"I've lost us."

"No le hace." He shrugged. "I can find it."

"I don't know how." She shook her hand. "Here in the dark on a million miles of ice, with never a sign—"

"No hay problema." His grin cheered her. "My father's goats never had a star to follow, or left a track so straight. They're driving straight down the peninsula, toward the old temple."

"The amphibian temple?" She trembled, staring at him. "Where Singh and her crew were killed! What will happen to my children?"

"We can hope for the grace of the saints. Shouldn't you look at Roak?"

Leaning to look, she had to turn her face away from his odor.

"No breath I can hear." She felt the lax wrist. "But there's still a pulse. Very faint, but he's alive. I must change the dressing."

"If you must." He bent to look and recoiled. "I'll drive us on."

The turbine hummed again, and the spider glided on. She found a basin in the bottom of the locker, brought warm water to scrub Roak's hairy body, replaced the dressing.

"Las huellas!" Mondragon called from the controls. "I'm back on the trail. You must sleep."

She did. The need was suddenly overwhelming. She closed the curtain on Roak and fell across the berth in the cabin. She was suddenly dreaming, an evil dream that she was frantically chasing Day, who was lost on the ice, hugging the panda doll and running nowhere faster than she could follow. A jolt of the spider roused her. She felt it slow and tilt and move again. The turbine hum decreased, and she heard Mondragon's call.

"Dr. Virili, climb to the bubble. We're on the isthmus. You'll see the old temple."

Suddenly wide awake, she ran up the steel steps. The spider had stopped on the wide platform where Singh and her crew had died. Mondragon was sweeping his searchlight across the mosaic wall ahead, tracing the gem-bright inlays that pictured the amphibians waddling out of the water, falling prostrate as if in worship, bursting from their outgrown shapes, finally spreading rose-hued wings to climb into a sky still blue.

"The Alpha?" Disappointment stabbed her. "Have you found it?"

"Not yet."

The turbine purred. He drove them on around the corner and stopped again. His light brushed a dark and doorless wall, a high balcony, the oval openings above. He pulled them around another corner and stopped again. His light swept a billion years of frost on the empty platform, another wide ramp, empty ice beyond.

"Nada," Mondragon murmured. "They drove on."

"Where?"

She knew the answer, yet she waited desperately for his voice on the intercom.

"The ice cap," he called. "Andersen always wanted to know what made the flash we saw from space. Stecker never let him go. I think he's finally on his way."

"With Kip? With little Day?" A cry of agony and terror. "Why?"

Only silence, until he asked, "Shall we go on?"

"What else? We couldn't go back, even if we wanted."

"But think about it, Rima." His tone had a warning ring. "If they're really headed for the cap, I doubt they'll ever get there. I'm afraid we never could. Across several thousand kilometers of this frozen sea, till we reach the continent. Then another five thousand kilometers of ice and mountain ranges. With no map to show the way."

"I know," she said. "We'll go on."

"Está bien." He paused and added, "Por los niños."

"Gracias." She liked the music of his Spanish.

He drove them on, turning back toward the temple. The search beam swept another towering wall, pausing on the yellow gleam of monstrous crystal eyes inlaid in ink black stone, shifting to trace the deep-cut outlines of gigantic flying things that dived with wicked crimson talons spread to snatch the amphibians out of the sea.

"I wonder—" She couldn't help the sudden dread that closed her throat. "If there are survivors, could they be descendants of those predators?"

"Quién sabe." She felt grateful for his unbroken calm. "We've found riddles enough, and few signs of friendship. I hope we live to learn the answer."

His light swept on to the end of the wall and came back again.

"The bodies." His whisper was hushed and hoarse. "The bodies of Dr. Singh and the fusion engineers." He narrowed the focus of the light to pick up three blue Mission blankets on the frost. "That's where we left them. They're gone."

"Andersen? Did Andersen and Cruzet pick them up?"

His light searched the frost.

"Creo que no. Their spider came no closer than we are. I see no new footprints."

"So what moved them?"

Mondragon didn't answer. The spider sat there a long time. At last the turbine purred again, and he drove them slowly down the ramp, into another endless desert of eternal ice.

●

The Alpha's track took them straight west, the black sun now low behind and another star cluster ahead, a tiny group of bright blue giants that made an inverted teacup or perhaps a high-crowned hat. Rima asked for another lesson, and learned at last to follow the tracks.

"Suddenly, somehow, they seemed to come into focus," she told him. "The marks of all eight wheels. I don't know how I learned to see them."

"The grace of the saints, my mother would have told you."

"You must sleep." She gestured him away from the wheel. "I'll drive us on."

"If you're ready—"

"I am."

He went down to sleep, and she drove them on. The tracks ran straight toward the hat-shaped cluster ahead, the black sun sinking very slowly behind. He stopped her when he woke, and made coffee while she opened the curtain to look at Roak.

"I've done all I could," she said. "He's bleeding internally."

"You've done enough. Perhaps he's human, but not very human."

He set the little table and poured the coffee while she microwaved a small block of tufatuna roast.

"There's still a long road ahead. We'd better ration the captain's steaks and hams."

●

Roak lived three more days. When the feeble pulse had ceased, Mondragon put on his airskin to cycle through the lock with the body. He spread the soiled bedsheet and blanket over it, murmured the words he recalled from his mother's funeral, and left an empty helium cylinder standing at the head as a marker.

"A kind of immortality," he muttered wryly, back in the spider. "That cylinder might last a million times longer than the sphinx or the pyramids."

A little happier, they followed the track. At the wheel the next day, she heard a sudden crash of static and then Kip's anxious voice.

"Alpha to ship. Alpha calling ship."

"Kip?" She stopped the turbine. "Kip, where are you?"

"Mom? Mom, is it you?"

"Are you all right?"

"Okay, so far."

"Day? My baby girl?"

Static rattled for an endless moment.

"I—I don't know. She looks okay, but the black beads have got her."

"Where are you?"

"Stopped under a tall black cliff. Under a cave high up, where I guess the flying things went. Dr. Andersen climbed up to it, and brought back a big mass of the beads. I don't like them, Mom. I don't like what they do.

"And I'm afraid—"

A crash of static cut him off, and the radio was dead.

Twenty-six

Kip woke with a jolt.

Something had happened to him.

Somehow, the cabin was gone. He lay out in the open, with no airskin, yet he was still breathing. His whole body felt strange, so stiff he could hardly lift his head. Stars shone in the west but the sky was dark purple overhead and brighter toward the east, blood-red around the sun.

And the sun—

No longer black, it glowed like red-hot iron. Swollen to three times its size, it was mottled with ragged dark splotches like black continents. The largest splotch was pocked and scratched with fiery red that made an ugly face. He lay shivering under its heatless glow.

Too cold and clumsy to stand, he got his arms beneath him and raised his head to see where he was. He lay sprawled facedown on something flat and hard. Metal, maybe, though the color was an odd yellow-green. It floated in a pool of dark water rimmed with a jagged wall of ice that glittered dimly under the crimson in the east.

Pushing higher to look beyond the wall, he saw a flat field of ice that reached as far as he could see. Turning stiffly toward the west, he found a square black shape far off across the frost—

Skygate!

The place of the changers.

He had been confused for a moment, feeling lost and not himself, but the sight of Skygate cleared his head. Certainly he was growing old and stiff and clumsy, but at least he knew where he was. He had always known Skygate. The holiest place. It stood empty and abandoned now, since ice had closed the ramp, but ten thousand generations had come here to change in the times before the ice. He had never been closer, but his father had stopped to see it after he changed, and come back amazed with its wonders.

The vast ramp where so many millions had come out of the water to shed their sea skins. The tall mosaic walls set with gemstone pictures of the metamorphosis. The balconies where the skylers could perch and the high windows where they could enter the temple. The black stone blocks of the rear wall, deeply carved with images of skylers trying their new wings, and the monstrous blackwings diving to kill them.

The skylers had brought the raft when the ocean froze. The raft's heat was dying, but it was still warm enough to thaw the ice around it. A sloping ramp on one end helped the changers climb out of the water, and a high perch at the other end let them spread and preen their wings before they tried to fly.

His name had been Sky Seeker once, but he was only Watcher now. Good for nothing else. He had lain here too long, watching for blackwings—monstrous predators, starved and desperate since the long freeze closed their fishing grounds. He had dived again and again to warn his mate when they were diving at the raft. She was Wave Rider; her name had come down from long ago, when waves still ran on a liquid sea.

He watched too, more hopefully, for a skyler returning. Born in the sea, his people lived there till the change gave them wings to reach Shadowland. The new skylers always promised to return with lifestones for those they left behind, but nobody had ever come with one for him. Now that his own time for change had passed, his desperate hopes were for Wave Rider and their son, Far Diver.

He was desperate, because they had grown desperate. She was diving for fish, but the long freeze had killed most of the fish. The air-gaspers had disappeared with the open water. The deep-swimming silverfins had grown rare and wary. Far Diver had always gone deep to dig in the sea mud, searching for the bones of some unlucky skyler who had drowned with a lifestone on him.

"Watcher! A gift from the Eternals!"

He found Wave Rider's head breaking out of the water. Scrambling to help her up the ramp, he ached with pity for her. Exhaustion had dimmed the glow of her crest, but beauty still shone in the fine bones of her face and her un-shielded eyes. Her velvet fur was still dark and sleek, but he felt her bare ribs when she nestled against him. The best fisher of the three, she had shared too much of her catches with their son.

"Silverfins!" Elation lifted her voice. "I thought the last of them were gone, but I caught these inside the reef. One sonic shot got them all." Anxiously, she peered around the raft. "Far Diver? Isn't he back?"

"Not yet. He goes too deep and stays too long."

He drew her closer, listening to the slow rush-and-sigh, rush-and-sigh of the air the dive had starved her for. Proudly, when she had recovered enough, she spilled three small fish from her pouch.

"Honor the Eternals!" Her head fin bent in reverence. "They saw our need, and found a fish for each of us."

She laid the largest fish under the perch to keep it cold for Far Diver.

"Our splendid son." She gave Watcher the middle fish, and kept the smallest for herself. "The most precious gift of the Eternals, yet he has always hurt my heart. Too proud of his endurance when he was young, too daring out under the ice, always probing for some forgotten wreck sunk too deep for salvage. So unhappy now, because he has never found a mate."

"Yet always hopeful," he tried to cheer her.

"He never will," she muttered bitterly. "Because none is left for him to find."

"Nobody, perhaps, here in the sea. What he wants is a lifestone, and his chance to reach Shadowland."

"I remember . . ." Her eye shields closed, she relaxed against him, speaking slowly as she found her breath. "I remember when he saw your father's lifestone. He was still a tadpole then, no longer than my flipper, but the stone fascinated him. He had to touch it, and he asked what it was.

"It was a second brain, your father told him, that would wake his body for life in the air. Your father told how he had found it in the wreck of a skyler ship that went down when skylers still sailed the seas. He wanted to know how the skylers made the stones. They grew them, your father thought. Grew them out of their crests in the third stage of their lives.

"He listened to all that with his eye shields wide. Wider when he watched your father struggle out of his sea skin. He made me hold him high to let him watch your father fly away across the ice toward Skygate and Shadowland.

" 'I'll learn to dive the way he did,' he told me. 'I'll swim out under the ice till I can find my own lifestone and follow him to Shadowland.' "

Watcher held her close, reliving those lost moments with her.

"So long ago." A wistful sadness edged her voice. "Just a

tadpole then, but he never forgot. He was always diving deeper than anybody else. Digging up the sea mud as soon as he could reach it. Searching the rotten hulks of buried ships for lifestones he has never found—and never will."

Lying huddled against him, shivering a little from the frigid air she had been gasping, she raised her shields again to sweep the sky from the blood-stained east to the stars over Skygate in the western dusk.

"Never will," she murmured again. "Because our world is dying. I think we three are the last still in the sea. As for the skylers—" Her head fin quivered with doubt. "I've watched friends change since I was a child, and listened to their promises. Nobody ever came back. Not even your father."

"Now is a hard time." He tipped his crest toward the heatless sun. "A cold time. A hungry time. But Far Diver has the heart we've lost. The long freeze may never end, but he'll keep on pushing farther, staying longer, searching deeper, till he finds his lifestone."

"I hope." She sighed. "I try to hope."

●

"I have it!" That triumphant shout rang from the water. "A perfect lifestone!"

Far Diver plunged out of the water. Rider moved to help, but he needed no help. Climbing the ramp before she could reach him, he held up his crest fin. Brightly glowing, it was flexed around the bright black prism.

He sank flat on the raft, drawing long gasps of air and shivering from its bitter chill.

"You distressed us;" she told him when he had revived enough to lift his head. "You were down so long."

"The wreck I found," he said between the gasps, "was a long way out. Too far for me to get there again. Sunk very long ago. Nothing remains of the craft itself, but I found the cargo. Glass, porcelain, gold that never decayed."

He dropped flat again, and she waited for him to catch his breath.

"Tell us," she urged when his shields came open, "about the stone."

"Those relics first." With an affectionate flicker of his crest fin, he reached to touch her heart. "Wonderful porcelains. Paintings on them showed people without wings, living on land that had no ice. Land scattered with queer green towers splashed with colors. Trees and blooms, they were called. The sun was larger then, brighter. Sometimes low, sometimes high, sometimes gone. I think because the world still turned."

"The lifestone?" she asked again.

"I dug there in the mud. Searched and dug again till my crest began to dim. No bones, no stone. Not even an anchor rock. I dug till I was dead for air. Swimming back, I came on something I never expected there above the mud. Bones scattered over a high coral knob. Bones of a blackwing, the skull and the claws and a dagger-fanged jaw. And a skyler's skeleton."

"The stone?"

He pulled it out of his pouch and offered it to Watcher.

"Father, for you."

Watcher's shields quivered and closed with emotion. He blinked till he could see again, but a proud admiration dazzled him again when he looked at his son. Handsome as always, Far Diver was drawn lean from hard toil and long hunger, but still muscular and fit, strong enough to dive again.

Still young and fit enough to change.

"A noble offering." Crest fin bent deep, he waved the stone away. "A gift to earn you the light of the Eternals. It would prove devotion to your secret name, if it needed proof, but I have lived long beyond the stage for change. Give the stone to your mother."

Far Diver offered it to her.

"For you, my loving mother, if my father wishes."

With no move to take it, she wrapped them both in her swimming fins.

"My good . . . good son." She was shaken with emotion, her voice a broken wheeze. "You offer more than I can take. The stone is your own life. Your chance for Shadowland and skylerhood. I love you for the offering, more than I ever have. But I can't leave your father here to die alone. The stone is yours, to use while you have the strength to change."

●

Far Diver refused at first to leave them.

"You go for us," his mother said, "as much as for yourself. Your life in Shadowland will be your greatest gift to us. And your sacred duty to the Eternals."

"I will return if I can, with all I can bring for you."

He ate the fish they had saved for him. Restoring himself, he lay a long time asleep in the sun's red glow. Once his swim fins flapped, and he gasped for breath as if he had dived again. Then, having relaxed again for a time, he cried out as if in sudden pain.

"He was dreaming," Rider said. "Waking now."

He lay quietly again, however, and dreamed again before he raised his head.

"Strange dreams," he said, "of my own transformation. I thought the time was long ago, long before the ice closed the way to Skygate. When my change time had come, I had friends who made a feast for me. I left them at sunset and swam to Skygate. Free of my sea skin, I learned to use my wings and flew west toward Shadowland.

"The sun was larger then, hotter, but almost still in the sky. It climbed as I flew, and stood at noon before I reached the continent. The long night had buried it with snow, but except on the high mountains most of the snow was gone. Green forests covered most of the great central valley.

"I was tired by then, and famished. I found farmlands

below me, surrounding high-walled towns. Skylers welcomed me when I came down in the middle of a town, begging for news of their seaside families and friends. I stayed there a long time, learning the ways of the greenside, working to pay for my keep.

"The skylers seemed prosperous and happy, but they had good reason for the walls. Their enemies were the flying monsters we call blackwings. The adult creatures are no great danger, because they seek their prey from the sea. But they are form-changers, as we are, with two stages of life. The young are voracious wingless wormlike things with savage jaws. They hatch at night. When day comes, they swarm over the land, devouring everything.

"The skylers were already saving their crops. They had need for haste, because the larval killer-crawlers came swarming in soon after I arrived. They ate the stubble in the fields to bare clay, ate the leaves off the trees, killed and ate every animal they could surround, finally attacked one another.

"They terrified me, but the towns are well defended. The cold nights kill any crawlers that fail to grow their wings and fly back to the sea before darkness falls. I volunteered to join the soldiers on the walls. They told me I was needed more at Skyhold.

"That's their great fortress city. It stands on a high table-land at the center of the continent. High mountains and higher walls defend it. Many of its levels are carved deep into the granite below, and its towers are so tall that the ice can never cover them. The crawlers are no threat to it; they don't climb so high or get so far from the sea. Skyhold was planned to stand against greater dangers, designed to keep the race alive forever, even after the sun is dead.

"A hundred generations of workers have been toiling to complete it. Joining them, I worked in a quarry—an enormous pit where granite mountains had stood. I ran a machine that controlled gravity. Using it, I could lift enormous masses of stone to the carrier.

"Later they sent me on to Skyhold itself. There I moved those masses off the carrier. They were not ready for the wall. Common granite was too fragile for that. It had to be powdered, mixed with other stuff, molded finally into gigantic blocks of something harder than diamond and tougher than steel.

"Working there all the rest of the day, I learned to enjoy the skyler's life. I made good friends. Though skylers bear no children, our native emotions are never lost. The stone, in fact, widened the scope of my mind in ways I can't describe. My wits and senses were sharpened, my memories and skills enlarged by all that earlier wearers of the stone had known.

"I met a beautiful woman who had come through Skygate before I was born—the skylers' lives are long. Her name was Lifestar. We expected our love to endure forever; we hoped in fact that skyler science could give us actual immortality, perhaps elsewhere in the universe. Our dying sun has no other planets, but the skylers were hoping to reach some kinder world. They had built an interstellar ship, using their gravity technology.

"Lifestar volunteered with me for its first flight. Accepted, we finished our training, passed all the tests, went aboard together. The ship lifted. The planet fell away and vanished. We were safely out in space, with stars blazing all around us, when I woke. My heart still aches from the pain of that bitter instant when I knew that my beloved Lifestar had been only a dream, now lost forever."

Far Diver stopped with a dismal sigh, his crest gone black.

●

"A prophetic dream, I think," Watcher said. "There is an old tradition of very vivid dreams that came from lifestones and foretold the future."

"It was vivid enough." Diver nodded forlornly, turning to his mother. "Lifestar was as real and dear as you are."

"We heard you cry out," she told him. "A cry of pain."

"Pain sharp enough, when I knew she was gone." His eye shields closed for a moment, and his swim fins shivered. "But there was a second dream that hit me just as hard."

He lay silent, remembering.

"It began right here, when I dived off the raft this last time. I thought I'd found that ancient wreck again. Gold and glass and porcelain buried in the mud. Out of breath and rising, I found the skeletons on that coral knob. The skyler's and the blackwing's—but this time I found an anklet I knew around the skyler's shinbone. A guardian at Skygate had given it to me. I thought the skeleton had been my own."

"A dreadful dream." Rider's fin caressed him. "We should have waked you."

●

"I slept on through another dream. Was it prophetic?" His eye shields blinked at Watcher. "I hope I never know. Again it was a long-past time. The planet still turned, but even more slowly. Those ragged black scabs had covered most of the sun. The seas were already freezing, but the skylers had not yet brought this floating lifegate. The few of us still here had to spend the endless nights breaking the ice from the holes where we came up to breathe.

"We were always hungry, with most of the fish already gone. I was diving with three friends, dreaming of the greenside of the old epics and seeking the lifestones that might let us escape into the sky. When we found a stone, I won the game we played for it. The losers lifted me to an ice floe for the transformation, and wished me the light of the Eternals.

"High overhead when I left, the black-scabbed sun sank lower as I went west, till I was flying into freezing twilight. The long day had thawed much of the sea ice, but the world seemed empty. No blackwings rose to attack me; perhaps they were gone, with no prey left.

"No longer the greenside, the great continent was buried under glaciers that spread from the mountain ranges. No skylers rose to welcome me. The valley cities had vanished, and the killer-crawlers that once had swarmed against them. The cold grew ever more savage as I pushed on into the frozen highlands. At last, flying under brilliant stars, I came to Skyhold.

"It was clearly the work of giants, if the skylers were ever giants. Its walls have no gates. They rise out of the glaciers, so tall the air was too thin for my wings. I had to perch and rest before I saw the towers inside. They are dead black stone, higher than the wall, with steep-pitched roofs to shed the snows. Sealed against time and change, they have no doors, no windows. I saw no lights, no motion, never a hint of anything alive.

"I flew on beyond Skyhold, around the night side, back into the sunlit side. I found no skylers anywhere, nothing alive, till I was back above this half-thawed sea and saw a blackwing diving after me. Drawn with famine, it flew so clumsily that I might have escaped if I hadn't been so tired and cold. It caught me, but lacked the strength to carry me. We went down together."

●

Far Diver had lain flat on the raft as he spoke, eye shields almost closed. Moving now, he raised his head to stare silently out across the empty ice field under the dim crimson sun.

"Such frightening dreams." His mother's crest flickered dimly. "I don't understand them."

"Memories?" Watcher asked. "Memories of skylers who had worn the stone before you found it?"

"Perhaps." He bent his crest in agreement. "Perhaps that's why they seemed so real."

"Do they trouble you?" Rider asked him. "Make you fear to change?"

He turned to gaze at the square black block of Skygate and the faint stars above it.

"They awe me, but no matter." His lean shoulders lifted.

"We've no future here. Nor anywhere, unless I find our people still alive in Skyhold. It hurts to leave you, but I must go."

He embraced them both, and pushed the lifestone into the hollow tip of his crest. It burned suddenly bright. He fell flat on the float, moaning and writhing in the agony of change. They crept back to watch him burst free of his sea skin. Climbing to the perch, he looked down on them with the blood red fire of his new life blazing in the lifestone. His eyes held no recognition.

"A stranger," Watcher whispered. "He has forgotten us."

"He is our son," Rider said. "He will remember."

The gauze of his spreading wings dried swiftly in the bitter air, and she shuddered when the sun touched them with the color of blood. Wavering a little at first, he circled close above them, calling a promise to return, and flew off to vanish among the faint stars in the dusk-dark west.

"A good son," she murmured. "He will be back."

"I hope," Watcher said. "With a lifestone, I hope, for you."

With nothing else to hope for, they waited for him. Though Watcher denied that he was hungry, Rider dived again for silverfins. She came back with none, so weak with long starvation that he had to help her back to the ramp.

"My last dive," she whispered when she could. "No matter. The silverfins are gone."

She saw him moving toward the ramp.

"Don't go down!" she told him. "You've no more strength than I do."

"Just for mudworms," he told her. "They're full of grit, and they taste like mud, but they can give us strength."

He dived to search the mud banks toward the coast and found none of the tiny pits that marked mudworm siphons. Like the air-gaspers and the silverfins, they were gone. He made it back to the raft, but his leap for the ramp fell short.

"Diver!" Rider called when she saw him, vibrant with joy. "He's back! I see him over Skygate."

She helped him to the ramp, and he saw their son returning, flying low above the far black block of Skygate, his wings a fleck of scarlet in the sunlight.

"Our magnificent son!" Rider's crest was radiant. "Perhaps with good news for us."

Or perhaps himself in trouble, Watcher thought. He flew too low and too slow, laboring hard to stay aloft. He said nothing to dim her delight, but her sudden sobbing cry was crueler than the cold.

"No! No! Pray the Eternals to save him."

The blackwing dived from high behind him, a thin black arrow in the somber dusk. Too late, too feebly, he swerved to evade it. It talons caught his right wing. They struggled, tumbling in the air.

"A clumsy strike," he whispered. "The creature must be weak with hunger. I think he has a chance."

The bodies separated, but Diver's wing was mangled. Side by side, they fell to the ice.

"That dream." He shivered. "His dream of the skeletons on the coral knob. It was prophetic. The stone was warning him."

"My precious son." She moved toward the ramp. "I must go to him."

"You can't!" He caught her fin. "It's too far. You aren't able—"

She broke away from him and dived off the ramp. Her first leap carried her only halfway up the slippery rim of the pool. She splashed back, dived, leaped higher. Struggling over the edge, she got her breath and swayed to her feet.

He was moving toward the ramp.

"Don't!" She flashed her crest to halt him. "You've no strength for it."

That was true. He sank back to the deck, eye shields clenched in shame for his weakness and his age. She was still there when he could see again, waving a silent farewell. She turned when she saw his answer, and set out across the ice.

Helpless, he could only watch. Far Diver had fallen far-off across the ice, and it took her a long time to reach him. Starved too long, and her sea shape was never made for walking, she fell and rose, fell and rested and rose again, till at last she dropped beside the crumpled body and did not move again.

Watcher lay alone and blind on the raft, his eye shields closed, till he ceased to feel cold or hunger, grief or pain, till he had no will to move again, till memory and emotion darkened and he knew his world was dead.

●

He sat up and rubbed his eyes, blinked and rubbed his eyes again. The raft and the ice and that dull red sun had vanished. Half of him was still Watcher, filled with a terrible sadness for Rider and Diver and the dying world, but he began to recognize the spider's cabin, not quite real until he saw the bright black gleam of the amphibian bead still lying under the hem of the curtain.

A lifestone. He shrank from it, shivering. Perhaps it had lain a billion years, or ten billion, in that cave with the bones of the skylers, but something in it was still alive. He shuddered from the unknown power that had drawn Indra Singh and the engineers to die at Skygate, and captured the minds of Dr. Andersen and Dr. Cruzet, and possessed his little sister.

"Kipper? Having fun?"

Andersen came out of the pilot bay. Day hung limply in his arms, fast asleep. He stopped for a moment before he walked on across the cabin to open the curtain and lay her on the berth behind it. He seemed relaxed and cheerful, that glazed intentness gone from his eyes.

"Fun?" Kip pointed at the bead on the floor. "Not with that thing here."

"If it bothers you . . ."

He picked it up, frowned at it for a moment, and stowed

it in the locker under the berth with the others he had brought back from the cave. Glad to have it out of sight, glad to be almost himself again, Kip felt Watcher's sadness lifting from him. The turbine's hum had stopped. The only sound he heard came from Cruzet at the kitchen counter, humming tunelessly as he made breakfast.

"Okay, Kipper?" Andersen asked him. "You look a little woozy."

"I'm okay," he said, but his voice was slow and hoarse. Like Watcher's. "I think."

"I know bad things have happened." Andersen grinned with a warm concern for him. "Things you never expected. But we're on our way to the great ice continent! Mountains and glaciers to climb! And the mystery of the spectral signal!

"What do you think we'll find?"

Skyhold? The fortress of the skylers that he had seen in the dream? Built to stand forever, was it still standing? Was something there still alive, using the power of the lifestones to defend the frozen planet?

"Exciting, don't you think," Andersen urged him again. "Better than your games with Captain Cometeer?"

"Maybe," Kip said. "Maybe."

This was no game. He had no exit key to hit if he wanted it to end. He was still a prisoner in the spider. The bright black gleam still shone behind Andersen's ear. His little sister would soon be awake to take command again, to take them on toward the ice cap.

He decided to say nothing of the dream.

But he was alive and warm again, no longer Watcher. Andersen and Cruzet seemed almost human. His mouth was watering to the scent of the frying ham. They were on their way to Skyhold. This really was a great adventure.

Twenty-seven

The rock rose out of the frost ahead, a jagged shadow against the stars. Sharp peaks of naked stone climbed out of starlit ice. Sheer black cliffs below them walled an ancient beach. Mondragon stopped half a kilometer out and they climbed into the bubble.

"The cave." Rima scanned the cliffs and gave him the binoculars. "See it? That darker spot high up the cliff. Kip said Andersen was trying to get there."

"A hard climb." He searched the beach. "I see a lot of footprints made when he looked for a place to climb. Maybe he found none."

"Or maybe he did. We need to know why they stopped. Let's look."

"Can we take the time, when they're still so far ahead—" He saw her frown. "I'll try it if you think we must."

She took the binoculars to look again.

"Difficult." She nodded. "But my father used to climb on

his vacations. I went with him to the Alps and the Andes. I think I can do it."

"Pero yo—"

"Drive us closer." Her urgent voice stopped his protest. "I'm going out."

He stopped them close beneath the cave and watched from the bubble. Slim and quick in the yellow airskin, graceful as a deer, she came out of the lock, stood for a moment inspecting the cliff, chose a narrow chimney, and began to climb. A dozen times her bravery took his breath, but at last she vanished into the cave.

Waiting forever, all he could see was starlit stone, weathered and cracked and eroded in the ages when the planet still had weather and erosion. Back in sight at last, she dropped a thin yellow rope to aid her descent, cycled through the lock, and climbed into the cabin.

"Nothing!" She made a face and spread her empty hands. "The cave's a boneyard. A den of those wide-winged vultures. It's filled with bones of everything they caught. A lot of unlucky amphibians. Andersen dug through their skeletons. Looking I guess for their beads. He took any he found."

"Por qué?" He stared at her. "Why?"

"We can ask him for answers, if we ever overtake the Alpha."

The rock had been the peak of a drowned seamount. They pushed on beyond it, toward that crooked cowboy hat. In the bubble again, she called the Alpha and listened forever to the meaningless murmur of the stars. She made a frugal meal and called him to share it.

The hat climbed slowly as they crept around the planet. A bright red star appeared beneath it. The eye of a bucking mustang, he said, with the unfortunate vaquero sprawled across the sky above it. And perhaps a cactus beneath it, spreading thorns to catch the vaquero if he fell.

"You're dreaming," she told him. "Worn out from pushing too hard. Let me drive."

She was at the wheel when the Alpha's track turned sharply north. She stopped and woke him.

"Why? Why would they turn?"

"Quién sabe?" He rubbed his hollowed eyes and climbed into the bubble to search the way ahead. "The ice looks flat as far as I can see. The trail runs straight." He shrugged. "Yo no sé."

Turn by turn, they pushed the spider on till the track bent sharply south. He searched again, and still found no reason for the turn.

"Unless they know Kip was calling." He frowned uneasily. "Unless they want to shake us off."

●

In a dream of her own she was naked, running barefoot across the ice with Roak wheezing close behind her, his hot breath foul with death. She screamed when his cold hand clutched her shoulder.

"Qué es?"

The hand was Mondragon's. She sat up, sobbing with relief. The turbine had stopped.

"I was dreaming." She shivered and asked him, "Trouble?"

"A problem."

He beckoned, and she followed him up the narrow stairwell to the bubble. Silently, he pointed to a dark boulder, half buried in a crater of broken ice.

"Ejecta, Dr. Andersen calls it," he said. "Thrown from an impact crater. They must have been steering around it. The boulder's stone instead of ice. Thrown from land. We must be near the continent."

"And overtaking them?"

He shook his head.

"But look. Farther out."

She peered at the shattered ice around the boulder and turned blankly back to him. He pointed. Beyond the rubble, beyond the land's pale glow, the ice lay black and slick and bare.

"No frost," he said. "Hot gases from the impact burnt off the frost. There is no trail." He spread empty hands. "We've lost them."

"So what can we do?"

A helpless shrug. "Yo no sé."

"Let's drive on," she said. "Toward the continent. Maybe we can pick it up."

She drove them on. He stayed in the bubble, calling directions to guide her through blocks of broken rock and fields of shattered ice. Again and again they had to retreat and search for another way.

"Stop the turbine," he called at last. "Something new ahead." She climbed into the bubble. "We've come past the impact area." He gestured. "There's the continent."

●

All across the west a wide white stripe had risen between the ice and the stars. It hid the crooked hat and most of the bucking mustang. When her eyes adjusted to the starlight, she saw that the white stripe was ice, a vertical and endless wall that looked a full kilometer high.

"A glacier," she said. "With icebergs all along the foot, where the lip of it was crumbling into the sea. I saw something like it once, when I flew with my father along the edge of Antarctica."

"Magnificent." An ironic shrug. "But it looks like the end of our road. Also, I think, for our friends in the Alpha. It looks impossible to climb."

She peered into his dismal face. "Where could they have gone?"

"Not up that wall." Lean shoulders sagging, he shook his head at it. "They'd never even have got to it, through all the ice falls."

"Can you find the trail again?"

He only shrugged.

"So it's checkmate?" Her voice had risen sharply. She stood a long time shuddering, staring at the glacier. "The amphibian beads have won their game."

●

She bent suddenly over the navigation desk and huddled there, laughing wildly, till he caught her arm. She stopped herself then and sat up weakly.

"I'm sorry, Carlos." She gasped for breath and wiped at her tear-smeared face with the sleeve of her jumpsuit. "The joke just hit me. The jokers are the little black beads. And the joke's on us."

"Qué lástima," he told her. "A terrible joke."

"Not funny." She made a bitter face. "Not funny at all."

Trying to rise, she swayed for her balance. He helped her down to the cabin. She sat on the edge of the berth, staring at him so stonily that he wondered if the beads had seized her. He found Captain Stecker's bourbon, mixed two highballs, and sat down with her.

"We've lost the trail." She shivered so violently that the drink splashed out of her glass. She sat frozen for a moment, and gasped for her breath. "It's too much! Too much to take. The ship blown up. My kids gone. We're all alone on this damned snowball."

"But the game's not over. Not so long as we're alive." He reached to touch her arm, but hesitation stopped him. He was still the Mexican mojado, she the gringo queen and a haunted stranger now.

"Not so long as we're alive."

Repeating the phrase, she sipped what was left of her drink and tried to smile.

"Gracias," she whispered. "I lost my nerve. You helped me get it back. I thank you, Carlos, for all you've done." Her face quivered. "For me and my children."

"I love them. May the saints defend them."

"And we must find them if we can."

●

He unfolded the little table and went down to check the engine and the cycler while she rummaged in the locker. The table was set when he came back, the room redolent with the fragrance of a stew she had made from Stecker's irradiated beef, served with soyamax crackers.

"Enough?" she asked, when their bowls were empty.

"Bastante." He nodded. "I might have eaten more, but the captain's private hoard can't last forever."

They cleaned the dishes and tried to sleep, she behind the curtain, he on the berth outside. When no sleep came, he climbed into the bubble and picked up the binoculars to search the frozen sea behind and the glacier wall ahead. Finding no hint of the Alpha, he laid the binoculars back on the desk. He stood lost in what he saw: the blazing constellations of a galaxy no human beings had seen before; the ice wall ahead, defending the secrets of a world where time had stopped, where life and hope could not exist. A fresh terror of it froze him.

"Carlos?"

Rima's voice startled him. She had started up the stairs with two fragrant mugs of Stecker's Kona coffee, but stopped to gaze around her at the starlit frost and the glacier wall.

"A strange place—" He saw her shudder. "A strange place to die."

"But we aren't dead." He tried to grin. "Not yet."

She stared blankly past him for a moment before she seemed to see him.

"I couldn't sleep." The forgotten coffee mugs were shaking in her hand. He took them and set them on the navigation desk. "Not here. Not now."

Wrenched with emotion for her, he took her in his arms.

Stiff for a moment, she made a kind of sob and pulled him hard against her.

"Rima! Rima!"

He gasped her name and felt her body quiver. She was firm and warm in the thin jumpsuit, her quick breath sweet in his face. Trembling, he found her warm lips, the taste of her mouth. His eager hands caressed her till her body stiffened and he felt a shock of fear.

In Chihuahua he had gone with a classmate to visit una casa de putas, but he had been afraid of women and all he didn't know. He made excuses and sat with a beer till his friend returned. He stood frozen now, afraid of offending Rima.

"No! Not here!" She suddenly pushed him away. "Not now!"

He cringed from her, shaken with waves of bitterness and longing and shame.

"Carlos, please!" Her voice was half a sob. "I don't want to hurt you. It's not because of who you used to be. It's where we are. It's my children."

"I love you," he whispered. "That's all I know."

"That's enough." She caught her breath and made a broken laugh. "Let's drink the coffee while it's hot."

●

He took the mug from her unsteady hand. They sipped the coffee, standing a little apart, until their breathing had quieted.

"Carlos, you remind me—" She paused, looking into his face. "It's twenty years since I last saw my father, but I adored him. I barely remember my mother, a blond beauty in a picture he had. She left us before I was five. He brought me up. He was the only family I had—till finally he left me to go out on a StarSeed ship."

Her face quivered, and she wiped at a tear.

"He was as tall and lean as you are, with dark eyes and

hair. He was an engineer. He used to take me with him to jobs all over the world. Latin America, mostly. That's where I learned my Spanish. He loved the people and their culture. That's half the reason he went out. That ship's company were mostly Latinos. He hoped to help them find a better future.

"I still miss him."

She paused again, unspoken emotions flowing over her face.

"I begged to go out with him. It nearly killed me when he left without me, but he said I had a life of my own to live. He waited till I was sixteen and enrolled in college, with a trust fund set up to see me through.

"But that world's gone." Her voice rose raggedly. "No use remembering."

"I—I remember." His voice broke, and he had to brush the wetness from his own eyes. "I was standing with the Fairshare pickets outside the launch site when your taxi passed." He shook his head at her, a little painfully. "It's worth remembering, if that's all we have."

Shivering, he turned to look out at the barrier of ice, the empty frost, the far-off stars.

"It is a dreadful place." His own calm surprised him. "We may die here. Yet still it has a splendor. Look at the sky." He gestured. "Stars brighter than they ever were at home. Look at the glacier. A great waterfall frozen as it poured off the continent. And look—

"There!" He pointed at the top of the glacier. "Did you see it?"

She blinked at him dazedly.

"It's gone." His voice fell. "But there it was! Far to the south, high on the rim of the ice. A dim red spark that flickered and vanished."

"The Alpha?"

"Their heat lamp! They've found a way to climb the ice. They must have left a trail we can find."

Twenty-eight

Kip could feel almost happy when Day was asleep. Andersen and Cruzet were nearly themselves, making little jokes, excited with the planet and all the riddles they hoped to solve, checking the engine and the cycler. They fixed food, took showers, took little naps when she gave them time. They were tired and grubby, their eyes hollow for want of real sleep, yet they seemed to be having great fun.

Yet, even when she slept, they never removed the black amphibian beads stuck behind their ears. Sometimes Andersen would brush at his with his hand, as if it were a bothersome fly. Sometimes it would slip out of place, back into his curly red hair or down to his neck, as if he didn't know he wore it. He always turned very serious when she woke, sliding it back to his ear and waiting for her commands.

Those were bad times for Kip. Nobody talked to him, or even seemed to hear anything he said. Nobody cooked anything, not till Day slept again. Without the Game Box, he had nothing to do. Most of the time he stood or sat in the bubble, watching the black horizon ahead for anything new. Sometimes he tried to sleep.

Sometimes he stood at the door to the pilot bay, watching Day where she sat on the holomonitor, telling the driver which way to go. The beads had done something terrible to her, something he didn't understand. It made him want to cry, till he thought of Captain Cometeer and the Legion of the Lost; they always had terrible problems, but they never gave up.

He always felt better when Day slept again. Andersen and Cruzet were getting pale and thin, but they seemed as eager to explore the planet as Captain Cometeer had ever been when he landed on some strange world. Andersen had known the geology of Earth. He was anxious to see the ice cap, and he knew a lot about it.

"It's not far ahead," he said once, when Day was asleep and Kip could ask about it. "Half the planet's water must be piled up there. The sun evaporated water, so long as it shone at all. Warm winds carried it to the cold night side, where it fell as snow. The snow froze into glaciers that flowed back to the sea till they got too cold to flow."

"The ice cap?" Kip felt nervous. Perhaps this expedition would have made a great game for Captain Cometeer and the Legion of the Lost, but it was too real and strange for fun. "We're really headed there?"

"To that high plateau in the middle of the continent." Andersen nodded, grinning with his eagerness to see it. "To whatever it is that flashed that signal when we came down."

"It's so far," Kip said. "Can we get there?"

"With your sister for a guide, we can." He stopped to listen for her. She was still asleep behind the curtain. He looked back at Kip, his blue eyes shining. "There's so much to discover! The ice cap's half a world. Just ahead, all unknown, ours to explore!"

"So much to learn!" Cruzet had always been calm and quiet, ready to take things as they came, but now he seemed as anxious as Andersen to rush ahead. "I want to see those gigantic structures—whatever they are—where we saw the flash. And meet whatever built them."

"The amphibians?"

Kip couldn't help shrinking from the bright black beads behind their ears. Now he knew they were the lifestones of his dream, but he was still afraid to speak of them. He didn't want them to take him the way they had taken Day.

Andersen shrugged and pushed absently at his bead.

"What about them?" he asked cautiously. "Do you think they came out of the sea to build some kind of fort on the ice? Do you think they're still there?"

"They had big brains." Andersen rubbed his red-stubbled jaw, considering that. "We know they were engineers. They dug the canal across the peninsula. Built the temple on the isthmus, and that tower on the island. But still—"

He frowned and shook his head, squinting off at nothing.

"Whatever they are, those mountain-sized objects we saw on the cap, they looked pretty big to be artificial. Yet they certainly don't look natural. I can't imagine . . ."

He shrugged again.

"If the amphibians knew their world was freezing . . ." Kip hesitated, careful not to speak of the dream. "Wouldn't they want a secure place where they might live forever?"

"Could be." Andersen seemed serious. "But I doubt they did, considering what feeble little things they must have been. Maybe in danger of extermination by those flying predators. That's the sort of question we hope to answer."

"Do you think—"

Day woke, calling out to Me Me that they were on their way to save her, and Kip never heard what else Andersen thought.

●

She emerged from the berth behind the curtain, face flushed and puffy, the black beads stuck tight in the pale tangled hair

behind her ears. Andersen begged her to wash her face and
eat her tofusoya cereal and soya milk, but her eyes had glazed
again and her voice grew sharp and cold.

"Me Me needs us now," she said. "She says we have to
hurry."

"I'm starving," Kip said. "Can't we take time to eat?"

Nobody listened. Day caught Andersen's hand to urge
him back to the pilot bay. Cruzet went down to check the engine. The spider lumbered on. Kip ate the cereal Cruzet had
fixed for Day, drank the soya milk, and climbed back into the
bubble to watch the red-lit frost sliding under them the way
it always did. He dozed and woke with a cramp in his leg. He
ran up and down the stairs to work it out, and finally went to
sleep on the berth in the cabin.

Endless day after endless day was very much the same—
days measured only by his need to eat and sleep, because nobody seemed to hear the watch clock chiming. They came off
the open ice at last, into a region where great boulders had
rained out of the sky. From an asteroid that had struck the
land ahead, Andersen thought.

Day was always sitting by him on the monitor, her glassy
eyes staring into the starlight. Somehow she seemed to see
the boulders, and the broken ice around them, many kilometers before he could, even with the binoculars. Somehow
she knew the way around them.

●

At the controls of an antimatter hornet with a squad of Captain Cometeer's Green Star Rangers, Kip was diving to save
the crew and passengers of a disabled space liner. The Crimson Killer, the notorious space pirate, had wrecked it and left
them to be crushed in the gravity well of a great black hole.
Waiting near the wreck, the Crimson Killer fired a
megaquark space torpedo at the hornet. He swerved to avoid
it. Too late. He felt the hornet rock—

And found himself in the bubble of the spider, about to

slide out of the navigator's chair. It was all a dream, but better than his dream about Watcher, he thought, because the amphibian beads had nothing to do with it.

The spider rocked again and he heard the turbine slow.

"Nap time, Kipper?"

Cruzet and Andersen were coming up the stairwell from the cabin. They snatched the binoculars off the desk and passed them back and forth, peering out into the midnight.

"We're stuck right here." Cruzet frowned, handing the binoculars back to Andersen. "Unless the spider grows wings."

"No way to get any farther. None that I see." Andersen shrugged. "Unless Day can find it."

She was asleep again. Kip hoped they would take time to cook, but they were too anxious for that. They stayed in the bubble, staring through the binoculars and shaking their heads. He blinked and squinted into the starlight, but all he could see was scattered chunks of broken ice, far off in the haze.

"Here, Kipper. Take a look." Andersen gave him the binoculars. "We've come to the cap."

In the powerful lenses, the ice was near and bright, an endless line of great sharp-edged masses rising out of the frost. Icebergs, he thought, that had drifted here before the ocean froze. Higher ice mountains rose beyond them, great chunks of ice that had tumbled down from a long white wall that looked too high to climb.

"The ice continent." Andersen pointed. "And bergs that caved off the glaciers."

The skyler in Far Diver's dream had flown over this great wall of ice, and on across the wild tangle of bare mountain peaks and enormous glaciers beyond, all the way to the titanic towers of Skyhold, but the spider had no wings and still he felt afraid to talk about the dream.

●

Cruzet swung the binoculars back and forth, studying the glacier wall.

"It runs all along the horizon, as far as I can see." Discouraged, he laid them back on the desk. "I think we've come to the end of the line."

"Leave it to Day." Andersen grinned. "She'll find us a way."

"Maybe." Cruzet shrugged. "Let's look for chow."

Kip followed them down to the cabin. They scrounged in the locker and found chicken-algae powder and tofusoya noodles that made a stew so good they all scraped their bowls. Yawning before they finished, Andersen was soon snoring softly on the berth. Cruzet put on his airskin and went out to check the tires and drive motors.

When he had the dishes cleaned, Kip climbed back to the bubble. Searching the awesome barrier towering ahead, he remembered what the skyler had found beyond it. Mountain range beyond mountain range. Desert plains of cracked and hummocked ice. Deep canyons cut by mighty rivers when rivers still ran, filled now with glacial ice.

He wondered if he should try to warn them of all that lay ahead, but of course nobody would believe him. Nor would any warning stop them, even if they did believe. They'd only shrug and call the trip a wonderful adventure and keep on doing what Day told them.

With the binoculars, he searched that endless wall again. Searched the ice mountains that had crumbled from it into the frozen sea. Searched till his eyes ached, and still he saw no hint of any way to climb it. He went down to the cabin when he heard Cruzet cycle back through the lock, and found him asleep on the floor, with that plastic bag of amphibian beads for a pillow.

Tiptoeing away from that, he went back to the navigator's chair in the bubble and tried the binoculars again, expecting nothing new. Nothing had changed here in all the ages since the skyler in his dream had flown over the ice wilderness to the dead fortress city. Or was the planet just asleep? Had it begun to wake when the ship came down?

He sat there wondering what lay ahead, wondering where his mother was, till he ached from sitting still. Till he nodded and found himself on the space hornet again. He had been the pilot, but Day pushed him away from the controls. She was diving into the great black hole. Its terrible gravity was going to kill them, to tear their atoms apart. He begged her to turn and try to climb out.

"It's Me Me." Her wide doll-eyes seemed blind to him. "She needs us now."

●

The spider woke him, lurching into motion. He crept uneasily down the stairs to find Cruzet and the bag of lifestones gone from the cabin floor. Andersen was back at the wheel, Day on the monitor beside him, telling him where to steer. Looking in the locker, he found a can of apple-soya powder, mixed a glass of juice, and went back to the bubble.

Day had turned them away from the glacier. Threading back through the towering bergs to open ice, she took them south along the glacier front. It seemed to have no end. He watched its slow march across the west till his eyes were tired again. He walked down the stairway to stretch and came back to try the binoculars again. The glacier wall looked no lower. Suddenly famished, he went down to the cabin and found a can of tofunut butter in the back of the locker. He ate a few soyamax wafers smeared with that and lay down on the berth.

"Hola! Kipper."

Andersen stood grinning at him. The spider had stopped. Cruzet was busy at the kitchen counter and he smelled coffee brewing.

"Your sister's sleeping." Andersen jerked his thumb at the curtain. "She's found us a way up the glacier. A rocky ridge we can climb. It's the tail end of a mountain chain. No ice on it."

He sat up and rubbed his sticky eyes. For a second he hoped that Andersen's amphibian bead was gone, but he found the black glint of it, half buried in the red curls at the nape of his neck.

"No ice ahead?" Cruzet was pouring coffee. He turned to look at Andersen. "Why?"

"Wind," Andersen said. "Wind that blew when the sun still shone. Warm air flowed off the sea side of the planet. Cold air flowed back, dried and heated by compression when it came down off the high ice. Heated enough to keep the glaciers moving, and dried enough to take the snow off that ridge."

Day woke, went to the bathroom, and came out with her puffy face half washed and her tangled hair pushed back, the two black beads still in place. She ate a few bites of an omelet Cruzet had made with powdered eggs and algaham, drained a glass of soya milk, and said Me Me couldn't wait.

Andersen followed her to the pilot bay. The turbine purred louder. The spider rolled on. Kip climbed back to the bubble when he had the dishes done. Cruzet was ahead of him there, already searching the starlight. He handed Kip the binoculars without a word, and went below.

The lenses brought scattered icebergs out of the haze. He heard Day's strange voice on the interphone, guiding Andersen between the bergs and finally to a rocky slope that climbed steeply toward the midnight sky. Above a boulder-cluttered beach, she led them into a narrow canyon.

Frost crystals glittered under the heat lamp like scattered rubies, but the rocks here were clear of snow. Slowed to a crawl, the spider lurched and pitched, but they kept it climbing. The canyon swallowed them, towering walls shutting out the stars. It forked again and again, where the streams that cut it had come together.

The forks were puzzles to Kip and even to Andersen, but Day always knew which one to choose. Or was it the beads that knew? Tired of wondering, tired of watching, Kip went back down to the cabin. He finished Day's omelet, which he had saved in the cold locker, and lay down again on the berth.

●

"Top of the mountain, Kipper!"

Andersen stood with Cruzet at the little table under the locker. They both looked gaunt and drawn. Cruzet had managed to shave, but Andersen's face bristled with a curly stubble. Cruzet was filling mugs with Stecker's precious Kona coffee.

"We're on the cap." Andersen lifted his mug to Kip, grinning jovially. "Your sister got us here before she had to sleep. A great view ahead, if you want to look."

He followed them up to the bubble. The spider had stopped on a high ridge. Craggy slopes fell into the narrow canyon behind. Mountain ranges rose ahead, range beyond range, higher and higher till they reached the black sky and the stars, jagged peaks sharp as sawteeth and white with ice and frost.

"Magnificent!" Andersen swept his arm across those barriers of ancient ice and naked granite. "Just imagine! Half an unknown world still ahead!"

Kip shrank back, remembering the endless maze of glaciered summits the skyler had flown over in his dream. Nothing he wanted to hope for.

"We're going on?"

"To the middle of the cap." Andersen lifted his coffee mug as if it were wine. "To find whatever flashed that signal."

"We'll never get there—" Andersen's sharp look stopped him. He wanted to explain why he thought so, but nobody would believe a dream. "I just think it's too far," he muttered. "Too far for the spider."

"Just trust your sister," Andersen said. "She knows the way."

"She calls it the sky road." Cruzet gave him the binoculars. "Take a look."

"She says we follow this valley, right under our feet." He fumbled to focus the glasses, and Andersen was pointing. "It's U-shaped, because it was scraped out by glacier ice. Rivers cut V-shaped canyons, like the one we climbed."

"What became of the glacier?"

"Warm winds thawed it. The snows ahead fell after it had grown colder."

The view took his breath away when he got the lenses into focus. Everything was suddenly bright and close and huge. Clean white snow lay banked deep just ahead, where the last blizzards had carried it over a ridge at the summit crest. Below the snowbank there was nothing—nothing but a vast pit walled with ice-carved cliffs.

"It's too steep." He shook his head at Andersen. "There's no way down."

"Your sister knows a way to take us down." Andersen reached for the binoculars. "If we're careful not to start an avalanche."

●

Day woke. Cruzet made a bowl of tofusoya cereal for her, but she came out of the bathroom with no time for it. Back on the holomonitor, she called her orders to Andersen. Very slowly, he eased the spider down the steep slopes of snow. The bare rock below looked even steeper, but she guided them to a narrow ledge that ran across the cliffs, far around the canyon and finally down to the level floor.

"Another riddle, Kipper," Andersen told him when Day let the spider stop. "That's no natural geologic fault. It's an artificial road. The question is who made it. And why."

The skyler farmers, Kip thought, when they lived in the valley and wanted a way to the sea. But the amphibian bead still gleamed through the copper red curls of Andersen's hair, and he was afraid to speak of skylers.

"On beyond?" he asked uneasily. "Will the road be open through the mountains? Or has the ice buried it?"

"Don't fret." Andersen shrugged. "Just trust your sister."

Cruzet was making sandwiches with slices of algabeef loaf between slabs of toasted tofumax. Day ate part of hers before her head dropped to the table. Andersen carried her back to sleep. Yawning, he collapsed on the berth in the cabin. Cruzet put on his airskin and went out to inspect the wheels.

With nobody to talk to, Kip climbed to the bubble and picked up the binoculars to scan that path the skylers had cut when the planet was alive. Remembering his dream of Watcher, he wondered how such small creatures had built the island tower, the temple on the isthmus, the fortress city ahead.

They had been master builders. Clever engineers. Brave enough in their long war with the blackwings. But clever enough to defeat ice and time? Still alive in Skyhold? Able to detect the approaching wavecraft still far out in space and flash that signal to it? To kill Jake Hinch and Indra Singh?

Andersen and Cruzet were driving hard for answers. Kip wasn't sure he wanted to know.

●

The radio crackled.

"Alpha?" His mother's voice! It startled him. "Beta calling Alpha. Do you read me?"

"Mom?" He found the red spark not far behind them, creeping along the line between the starlit snow and the dead black sky. "I see your lamp."

"Kip?" He heard her catch her breath. "Are you okay? Is Day all right?"

"She's here," he said. Maybe okay. How could anybody know? "And you?"

"Fine, since we've found you. Just wait for us."

He saw the red spark moving faster.

"Careful!" he shouted. "Careful on the snow! There could be an aval—"

He heard her scream.

Twenty-nine

Mondragon felt a sudden tremor. The spider swayed. "Earthquake!"

Above him in the bubble, Rima screamed the word. But that couldn't be. This wasn't Earth; this dead planet shouldn't be quaking. Yet rocks were toppling off the cliffs above them.

"Kip was on the radio!" he heard her whisper. "He tried to warn—"

The spider pitched again, and he felt snow moving. A wide sheet of crusted snow was sliding under them, crumbling over the lip of the glacial col. A jutting granite knob split the flow ahead. He spun the wheel, steering for it. The spider skidded. The tires slipped, caught, and brought them to the knob, a tiny island in the avalanche. He stopped the spider on it and joined Rima in the bubble.

"My children!" Her cry was almost a moan. "Did we start the slide—"

Her voice was gone. They watched the broken snow

sweep past them, faster, faster. All around the col, masses of age-old ice were tumbling into the chasm. He found the red spark of the Alpha's heat lamp, far away and far below.

"They're running." He whispered. "Maybe—"

His breath stopped. Rima clung to him, trembling. The far red point was crawling too slowly ahead of the ice. Far and faint in the dimness of the pit, the front of it was near and bright and dreadful in the binoculars, a rolling flood of broken ice that overtook the Alpha, drowned it, spread far beyond where it had been.

"They're dead!" She clung to his arm. "Did we—did we kill them?"

"I don't think so." He stared at her, shuddering. "I felt the tremor before the avalanche began. I think it was los demonios. The demons of the ice. Stopping us the way they stopped Jake Hinch."

"Why?" she whispered. "Why? We haven't dynamited anything."

"Yo no sé. We don't know the powers of the planet. I think we never will."

●

"The Alpha?" Her voice quivering, she stood peering into the col. "Could we get down there to look for them?"

He reached for the binoculars and stood a long time searching the naked slopes where the snow had lain and the vertical walls of the glacial trough, cliffs polished smooth by stones the ice had carried.

"It looks so steep," she whispered. "I see no way."

"They got down." He shook his head and gave the binoculars to her. "I don't see how."

"Nor I." She searched and gave them back. "We'd only roll down the way the boulders did."

"I was following their wheel tracks." He spoke almost to himself. "They were turning to the left . . ."

He was scanning the canyon walls again.

"There!" His voice sharpened. "That looks like a road, if you can believe it."

"A road?" She frowned at him. "Not here."

He gave her the instrument and she found a thin scar in the rock that began on the high slopes near them, where the snow had lain. It ran far around the canyon, sloping toward the floor.

"If we can reach it . . ."

●

The sliding snow had left bare and steep stone that shone darkly beneath their lamp. Back at the wheel, he pulled the spider gently off their granite island. Another skid took his breath, but he got them to the path, a narrow shelf cut into the ice-polished cliffs. Too narrow, really, for the spider's big-tired wheels on their sprawling legs, but he found a control on the console that pulled them closer in. Top-heavy on the narrowed wheels, they started down the cliff. Two kilometers down, the shelf widened into a deeper cut. He stopped the spider and climbed into the bubble.

"Trouble?" Rima asked.

"A tunnel." When he pointed into the cut, she made out a narrow archway. "I'm going to look inside."

"Have we time to spare? My kids buried—"

"I'm going out." Bluntly, he cut her off. "I want to know."

She wanted to protest again, but something in his manner almost frightened her. He went below. She heard the lock hiss and clang and saw him come out in his yellow airskin. Helmet light burning, he walked into the tunnel, moving as briskly as if he knew his way. Framed by rough dark walls, his light receded and vanished.

Impatiently waiting, she tried the radio, tried it again, searched the valley floor once more. The sliding ice had spread a broad white fan where the Alpha had been. Its pale red spark was gone.

Mondragon came back at last, striding down the tunnel. The lock hissed and wheezed and clanged. He hung up his helmet and came out to meet her in the cabin, still in his airskin.

"A copper mine." He was crisply matter-of-fact. "The reason for the road. I found an amphibian's skeleton a few hundred meters back. Killed by a rockfall. Nuggets of green malachite scattered around him. Beautiful specimens, but I got something better."

He unzipped his breast pocket and showed her a black amphibian bead.

"Perfect."

He studied it briefly, nodded approval, and put it to his forehead. It stuck there. She saw his body stiffen. His face went blank for a moment, and firmed with purpose.

"The other spider vehicle has severe trouble."

His voice was suddenly cold and flat.

"Carlos—" She shrank back from him, trembling. "Are you all right?"

"We must get on at once," he said. "We must render assistance."

"If we can!" She caught her breath. "If we can help—"

"You will go up to lookout bay." He gestured stiffly at the stair to the bubble. "Use binoculars. Locate spider vehicle."

●

He drove them on.

"Spider vehicle?" he called on the intercom, and called again. "Do you discover spider vehicle?"

"I don't. Not yet."

"Continue." A sharp command. "Imperative!"

He pushed on. Twice they came to ancient rock slides where he had to ease the spider over fallen stones, tilting it till she held her breath. The road widened as they reached gentler slopes, until they lost it beneath the avalanche. Shattered and crumbled ice lay spread to the farther cliffs.

"Spider vehicle?" he barked again. "Do you discover vehicle?"

"Not yet. I'm looking."

They jolted out across the ice.

"Stop!" she gasped at last. "I've found it!"

They had gone past the mast, sticking at an angle out of broken ice. The heat lamp was dead. He came up to the bubble and took the binoculars to study it.

"Mast protruding." His voice was an emotionless staccato. "Inclined at sixty degrees. Hull covered by three meters of ice."

"Three meters!" She stared at the leaning mast. "Can we dig—"

Her voice caught, and she cringed again from his hard, unfeeling face.

"The being called Day," he said. "She is needed."

"Both! Both children!" She searched his face for the human he had been. "They must be frantic. With the lamp dead, the power must be out. The cycler, too. They're likely hurt. Suffocating in the dark." She shivered. "Can we dig three meters—"

"Rescue effort essential," he barked. "We proceed."

●

He drove them toward the buried spider. Anxious to do whatever she could, she went down to get into her own airskin and climbed back to the bubble. She saw their two front wheels moving, thrusting ahead on their shining legs. She heard the lock and saw him emerge with a box of tools. Wondering, she watched him remove the wheels and bolt the ends of the legs together.

"What are you doing?" she called on the interphone when he came back aboard. "If I can help—"

Ignoring her, he backed the spider away from the mast. Dropping the bolted legs to the ice, he used them to plow a long furrow beside the slanted mast. He backed and plowed again, bulldozing ice away from the buried machine. The black curve of a tire came into view, finally the bright curve of the hull.

"Body of vehicle exposed." His voice on the interphone might have been a robot's. "Condition of occupants unknown. You will attempt sonic contact."

Grateful for anything to do, she found a hammer in his tool box and cycled through the lock. The bright side of the tipped spider was almost bare, though shattered ice still covered most of the lock. She tapped on the hull, stooped to put her helmet against it, and tapped again. Faintly, through the insulated wall, she heard answering taps, then the whine of the salvage pumps.

"They're alive," she told him when she got back inside. "They're trying to get out, but there's ice over the lock. I don't think it can open."

"Ice will be removed."

He plowed more ice away. She saw the exterior valve slide open. Andersen climbed out. He stood there half a minute, shading his eyes even from the starlight, peering around him at the field of broken ice and the towering canyon walls, before he staggered toward their lock. She heard it cycling and came down to help him unseal his helmet.

"Rima?" He shook his head in a dazed way, his sunken eyes widened as if in dazed astonishment. "Where are we?"

Staring at him, as baffled as he was, she found no answer.

"Sorry." He peered around the cabin. "I'm just—just out. Can't remember anything."

He stood there blinking at her, rubbing at a swelling bruise on his forehead. His beard had grown into tawny stubble, and drying blood from a gash on his temple streaked the side of his face.

"Kip? Little Day?" She found her voice. "Are they alive?"

"Alive," he mumbled dully. "Alive."

"Are you sure?"

"I think." He shook his head. "Don't know anything."

●

Mondragon came back from the wheel, brushing by Andersen as if he were a stranger.

"Air lock open," he said. "I will go into Alpha vehicle."

He seemed clumsy with his helmet. She helped him seal it and reached for her own. Before she could follow, however, he was cycling through the lock. She had to wait with Andersen.

"Trying to remember." His haggard head shook with frustration. "Something—something like a dream. We were climbing the cap in the Alpha. Your little daughter was our guide." He spread his hands in bewilderment. "A small child from Earth! How could she show the way across this dead planet? Where no human being had ever been?"

Trembling and terrified, she didn't try to answer.

"The dream—" He stared around the cabin. "I thought you were following in the Beta. This is the Beta?"

"The Beta," she whispered. "But this is no dream. It's a nightmare."

Muttering under his breath, he stumbled back to the little closet inside the lock, peeled his airskin off, and came out in his blue jumpsuit. He sat down on the edge of the berth and squinted sharply at her.

"It's true? We're actually on the cap?"

"It's true."

He sat there, looking groggy and lost in himself, muttering under his breath. She climbed back to the bubble. The Alpha's lock was opening again. Mondragon came out carrying an inflated airskin that looked empty. Cruzet followed. She ran down to meet them in the cabin.

"The infant."

Mondragon gave her the inflated suit. She unsealed the empty helmet and heard a whimper. Trembling, she unzipped the suit.

"Mommy?" Day reached out. "Mommy, is it you?"

"Darling!" She gathered her into her arms. "My poor little darling!"

"Mom, hi." Kip came out of the lock in his own neat yellow airskin, his helmet under one arm and his other arm lifted to wave his greeting. "You got here just in time."

A very casual greeting, but she felt the sobs that shook him when he dropped the helmet to throw his arms around her.

●

Cruzet fumbled his helmet off and gazed around him, as dazed as Andersen had been.

"Dr. Virili?" He took a moment to recognize her. "I don't know how you got here, but you've bailed us out of hell."

"There's coffee," she told him. "If you want it."

"I'm dying for it."

"Task incomplete." Mondragon stood squinting out of his helmet as if they were strangers, the amphibian bead shining strangely on his vacant face. "Urgent necessity to salvage supplies and equipment from spider vehicle Alpha."

Rima was sitting on the edge of the berth, Day sobbing in her arms.

"I'll help." She moved to rise.

"Mommy, no!" Desperately, Day clung to her. "Stay here with me. I need you bad."

"You better stay." Grinning at her, Kip picked his helmet off the floor. "I'll go."

She sat crooning to Day while he followed the others into the lock. Day was asleep before they began bringing back cartons and crates and bags of food, boxes of tools, replacement cartridges for the cycler. There was even a case of Stecker's Kentucky bourbon.

"That does it."

Andersen was moving to unseal his helmet. Mondragon raised a hand to stop him, and stooped to inspect the stacks as if making a mental inventory.

"Item missing." His radio voice rang hard. "Urgently required."

He cycled back through the lock and returned with a yellow plastic bag.

Thirty

Day wriggled suddenly out of Rima's arms and ran to snatch the yellow plastic bag from Mondragon. She up-ended it to dump the contents. Kip expected the honeycomb-shaped mass of black amphibian beads. What he saw instead was a shower of small gray stones that rattled across the floor.

Day picked one of them up and scowled in disgust.

"Dead." She tossed it back. "Killed."

"Darling—" Staring at her, Rima started to rise and sank weakly back. "What has got into you?"

"That stone—" Day pointed at the bead on Mondragon's forehead. "Give it to me."

He pulled it off and she stuck it behind her ear. Her body stiffened. Her small arm lifted in a gesture of command.

"Hear this." She turned back to her mother with an empty doll-smile. Her eyes had widened strangely, no recognition in them. "Me Me requires us urgently." Her loud flat voice was not her own. "We will move forward without additional delay. Virili and Mondragon will resume operation of spider vehicle."

"My child!" Stunned, Rima shook her head. "My baby— baby girl."

Kip put his arm around her.

"She's like this," he said. "She has been ever since we left the ship. Just look at her now."

Walking with a stiffly awkward gait—like a mechanical doll, he thought—Day had started toward the control bay. She turned back to Cruzet and Andersen.

"You will eat and sleep. Prepare yourselves for further service to Me Me."

"Okay." Andersen nodded, with a nervous shrug. "Okay."

"Señor Mondragon." She beckoned. "You will operate spider vehicle."

●

Huddled miserably on the edge of the berth, Rima stared blankly after them. The turbine whined louder. The spider lurched forward.

"Accelerate." Day's sharp voice came back from the control bay. "Steer left twenty degrees."

"My poor baby!" Blinking at her tears, Rima turned imploringly to Andersen. "What has happened to her?"

"That amphibian stone," he said. "It controls her. The rest of us, too, whenever it likes. If you want to know why—" His lips twisted wryly. "It's all because Me Me needs us."

"Me Me?" She shook her head in disbelief. "You say we've really come halfway around the planet to look for the doll she had to leave on Earth?"

"She thinks it's here, lost and in trouble."

"And you believe her?"

"Not exactly." Andersen shrugged. "But we do obey when the beads take control."

"Andy?" Her gaze sharpened. "Are you insane?"

"Could be. Nothing I can explain." Silent for a moment, he spoke again. "We do obey. Not that I fret. In fact I'm glad to have her help."

"Help?" She shuddered. "You are insane!"

"We're marooned here, remember."

"Marooned?" Bitterly, she mocked him. "The word is condemned. Condemned to die here!"

"Could be." He waved his hand in protest. "But there's a brighter side—"

"What's bright?" Her face twisted. "Here in this damned dark?"

"Rima, just remember how we got here," he urged her. "StarSeed never promised we'd land in any kind of paradise. We came to make the best of what we found. This planet is a pretty stiff challenge. A million exciting questions to answer. Never mind what your little girl thinks about her doll—" He shrugged. "Tony and I are happy enough to be pushing on."

"Happy? When you look at Day and those damned beads?"

"They did frighten me at first." He shook his head at her concern. "But they're pretty wonderful, whatever they are. Or were."

He bent to gather a few of the small gray stones off the floor. He stirred them on his palm, tried to fit them together, peered at them through a pocket magnifier, scratched one with a penknife.

"Look at these."

He held them toward her.

"A fascinating riddle?" He ignored her horrified recoil. "We've no notion what they were to the amphibians. Or how they've endured since the planet died. They seemed indestructible when I studied them, but these have gone soft. Lost their shine. Your daughter says they're dead."

"What does she know?"

"More than I do."

"The damned things have taken your own mind," she told him hotly, "like they did Day's."

"So what?" His shoulders tossed. "So long as we're moving on." He scowled at the beads in his hand. "I want to know what destroyed them. How? Why?"

Listening, Kip remembered his dream of Watcher. The beads had been the precious lifestones that stored amphibian memories and let them leave the sea. He wanted to tell what he knew, but he felt chilled again with Watcher's terror and despair. He knew no way to explain the power of the stones, no good answers to the questions they would ask.

He leaned to look at those in Andersen's hand. Their black shine was gone, with the force that had stuck them together. And the memories, he thought, of beings dead almost forever. He felt sad for Watcher, for all of them, and felt a tingle of dread at the nape of his neck.

●

Cruzet had been storing the tools and cycler cartridges they brought off the Alpha. Back in the cabin, he sank wearily down on the end of the berth and grinned at Rima.

"Day promised us food," he reminded her. "We need it."

"You've earned it." She gave him a smile of tired gratitude. "Since I have my children back."

She filled coffee mugs for him and Andersen.

Kip asked, "And we can eat?"

When she nodded, he opened the locker and found a can of Stecker's hoarded Vermont maple syrup. She made pancakes out of soyamax flour and alga-egg powder, and served them with strips of betabacon. When it was ready, she wanted Mondragon to stop the spider so that he and Day could join them.

"Day won't let him stop," Kip told her. He was right.

Grateful for his mother's cooking, Kip ate his fill. Andersen and Cruzet were soon snoring gently behind the curtain. With no appetite, Rima went to the pilot bay doorway and stood watching Day in sad silence as she sat on the monitor, her hard inhuman voice telling Mondragon where to drive.

"Mom, you look awful tired." Kip caught her hand to pull her away. "You ought to sleep."

"I can't." Her face was pinched and bitter. "Not with little Day like that."

She came with him up to the bubble, and slumped down at the desk, looking at nothing. He pointed at a long, boulder-strewn ridge that lay across the canyon floor.

"A funny-looking hill."

With a wan little smile, she roused herself to answer. "Dr. Andersen would call it a glacial moraine."

"What's a moraine?"

"The ridge of rocks and gravel that a glacier leaves when it retreats."

She sank back into herself and he stood looking ahead. Climbing the moraine, the spider came back to the ancient road. It twisted so far along the foot of the canyon wall that he reached for the binoculars. The lenses made it near and bright, exciting with the promise of surprises to come.

"Mom, look!" Trying to lift her spirits, he offered her the binoculars. "Look where we're headed! Through the narrow space between those two high cliffs. They look like a gate. Don't you want to see what we'll find beyond?"

"I don't care." Her voice was tired and dull. She didn't take the binoculars. "Why should I care?"

"Please, Mom!" He caught her lifeless arm. "You can't say that."

She frowned so sharply at him that he thought she wondered if the beads had seized him.

"Just look where we are!" he begged her. "Exploring a strange new world."

He heard her breath catch.

"I know where we are." Her face worked, and he thought

she was going to cry. "All alone and waiting to die here on the ice, since the ship's gone—"

"The ship?" He blinked at her.

"I didn't mean to tell you, but Stecker blew it up."

The frost came into the bubble. Shivering, he felt so weak and sick that he caught the edge of the deck. His throat hurt when he thought of Jim Cheng, who had made his airskin, and Roy Eisen, who had taught him how the spiders worked. Even his Game Box was gone, Captain Cometeer and all his friends in the Legion.

●

When he looked at Rima again, she was asleep with her head on the desk. He jogged her arm till she was half awake and made her come down to sleep on the berth in the cabin. She almost stumbled on the steps, and he felt a shock at the thinness of her arm when he tried to steady her. Lying on the berth, breathing softly, she looked so small and weak that a surge of pity filled him.

She had endured too many hard knocks. When his father left them. When the trust fund ran out and they lost the house. When she got the notice that her Mission job was terminated. So much more now, since the black sun stopped the ship. He stood with a lump in his throat, wishing he had done more to help her, till he felt the spider lurch and jolt.

They were still pushing on. Even if the ship and so many friends were gone. She would surely feel better when she rested. He was tired himself, with a bruise on his shoulder from his tumble when the avalanche hit the Alpha, but he remembered Andersen, so eager to see more of the great ice continent. Thinking of that, he climbed back to the bubble and watched the road again.

Clinging to the cliffs, the road brought them into a deeper canyon that sloped east toward the frozen sea. The glaciers that cut it were gone, their moraine ridges left across the

U-shaped floor. The road turned west, into the continent. Toward the high ice. Toward the towers of Skyhold.

And toward what else?

Wondering, trying not to ache for Jim Cheng and Roy Eisen and all the others, he rubbed his aching eyes and kept the binoculars on the pavement. The canyon walls grew higher, blocking out the starlight till he was blind without the binoculars. The drone of the turbine rose and fell as they climbed one slope and ran down the next. Stiff from sitting, he stood up till he got tired of standing and finally sat again. Yawning, he wished sadly for his lost Game Box. With Captain Cometeer, things had always happened faster.

●

"Okay, Kipper?" Andersen's hearty hail woke him. "Look where we are!"

Stiff and cold from sleeping with his head on the desk, he pushed himself up and found Cruzet and Andersen coming up from the cabin. He looked out of the bubble. What he saw took his breath. The spider had come out of the canyon into a pit that might have been a grave dug for something really gigantic. The walls were cleanly cut, rectangular and straight, climbing sheer to the white ice of the cap.

They had stopped down in the end of the pit, on a floor that seemed oddly level. He found their wheel tracks, and the road that had brought them through a narrow gap in the black cliffs behind.

"Strange!" Andersen took the binoculars and stood a long time scanning the cliffs, craning his neck to look up at the ice that capped them. He shook his head, passing the glasses to Cruzet. "Nature never made this pit, no nature I know. Yet I can't imagine anything able to dig it."

Kip remembered the skyler working at the quarry in his dream, lifting great chunks of granite to be made into building blocks for Skyhold. Would they laugh if he tried to tell about the dream, or understand and thank him? He had caught his breath to take the risk when Cruzet gestured with the binoculars.

"Andy, what do you make of that?"

Andersen took the glasses. Peering without them through the starlight, Kip found a long boulder ridge a kilometer or so ahead. Another moraine, perhaps? But that odd hill?

"Ruins!" Andersen's voice was hushed with awe. "The ruin of something monumental!"

He looked again, and finally offered the glasses to Kip.

"Here, Kipper. Want a look?"

Eagerly, he seized them.

"The beings that built the road," Cruzet was saying. "They had a city here."

The tumbled boulders on the ridge were huge granite blocks, many of then smoothly squared or rounded. Here was the corner of a massive wall, there the stump of a great column rising out of the wreckage.

"What was that?" Cruzet pointed at something a kilometer farther ahead. "It must have been as tall as a skyscraper."

It had been cone-shaped; the top of it was now shattered into piles of rubble around it. He saw oval openings high up. Doorways, he thought, for flying things. Andersen took the binoculars and turned to look behind. Even without the glasses, Kip could see rows of dark holes high in the cliffs.

"Nesting places?" Cruzet stared up at them and turned to gesture at the ruins ahead. "For our amphibians? If they actually sprouted wings and migrated here. If they dug that mine. Made the road. Built this city—if it was a city."

He made a baffled shrug.

They had been the workers in the quarry, Kip thought. Digging granite to build Skyhold. Had the beads made Day imagine that Me Me was a prisoner in Skyhold? That seemed so unlikely that he said nothing.

Cruzet gestured toward the end of that enormous pit, lost in the starlight many kilometers away.

"Day said we were going that way, but how do we climb a six-kilometer wall?"

"Day got us here." Andersen shrugged. "She'll take us on."

Kip followed them down to the cabin. His mother and Mondragon sat together at the little table, eating soyamax pancakes with Stecker's Vermont maple syrup. Day had drained a glass of alga-orange juice and scraped her cereal bowl. She lay in her mother's lap, sleeping quietly. Mondragon picked up the small gray prism that lay on the table beside his plate and handed it to Andersen.

"The last bead," he said. "It fell off her head when it changed. I found it on the floor."

Andersen frowned at it through his pocket magnifier and scraped it with his knife.

"Destroyed," he muttered. "Like the others. How come?"

Thirty-one

Rima carried Day to the berth behind the curtain and went to sleep with her. Groggy for want of sleep, Mondragon asked Andersen's permission and lay down on the berth in the cabin. Cruzet drove the spider on to the cone-shaped ruin ahead. When Kip saw him and Andersen getting into their airskins, he begged to go with them.

"Why not, Kipper?" Andersen grinned. "The next best thing to landing on a new world with your Captain Cometeer."

They helped him seal his helmet, and he went out with them to walk around the great piles of shattered granite blocks that had been the top of the cone.

"What wrecked it?" he asked Andersen, his voice a hollow boom in the helmet.

"Seismic shocks, as the planet cooled?" On the radio speaker, Andersen's answer seemed strange and far away. "Or who knows? A lot can happen in a billion years."

"Look at that." Cruzet stood peering at a toppled stone twice his height, roughly fractured on one side, cut to a smooth curve on the other. "It must weigh a hundred tons. The amphibians were smaller than we are. How did they move it?"

"Small men moved big rocks back at home." Andersen shrugged. "Remember Stonehenge."

"These are bigger than anything at Stonehenge."

"Do you think—" Kip decided to risk the question. "Do you think maybe they could control gravity?"

"Not likely." Cruzet spoke shortly, as if it had been a stupid question. "That's a nut we've failed to crack, even with quantum science."

"They didn't fly the blocks," Andersen added. "They built the road." He gestured toward the pavement, which ran on beyond the ruins. "I want to know where it goes."

●

Kip climbed back to watch from the bubble when they drove on, Andersen at the wheel. The pit had the shape of a gigantic room, he thought, with dark rock walls and a black strip of sky for a ceiling. The ruins lay on a shelf here at the end. A sloping ramp led down to the floor, which was a dim expanse of starlit frost that lay perfectly flat as far as he could see.

"A lake." Cruzet came up to the bubble. "A frozen lake. That's why it's so level."

Meltwater had flooded the quarry after Skyhold was finished, Kip thought. The road makers must have come here after it froze. He remembered the skyler who had awakened from the dream of flying into space with his beloved Lifestar. Had the amphibians moved off the planet? Were the owners of it now some remote descendants of the black-winged predators? He felt half afraid to know.

"Your sister—" Cruzet shrugged and focused the binoculars. "She said we would follow the road, but she's no help now."

He tilted the binoculars to study the ice-capped walls that towered to the stars ahead. He looked a long time and finally laid them down with a shrug of frustration.

"She didn't say we'd have to sprout amphibian wings."

Andersen called him down to check the turbine. Trying the binoculars himself, Kip wished the spider had wings. The walls of the pit rose as straight as if a great knife had cut them, slicing cleanly through a layer cake of rock. Smooth black granite climbed kilometers high, with light-colored limestone and sandstone above, and on top of that the white cap of ice.

He saw no way out.

The spider rolled on with never a lurch or jolt. The turbine droned like a faraway bee. He sat at the desk, wistfully trying to imagine how his friends in the Legion would have escaped a fix like this. Captain Cometeer had never let them give up, no matter how hopeless they were.

"Wits can be sharper than swords," he always said, but Kip saw no way for wits to help them here. Or swords either, for that matter. He was nodding sleepily when a new star blazed out, rising on the ice horizon high ahead.

●

Or could it be a star? Stars here neither rose nor set, because the planet no longer spun. This was a hot point of violet light, right at the rim of the pit. Its color changed as he looked, to indigo, to blue. Hands shaking with excitement, he got the binoculars on it and saw that it shone in the ice that rimmed the pit.

"Andy!" he shouted into the interphone. "There's a light shining ahead!"

The spider stopped. Andersen ran up the steps with Cruzet close behind. He seized the binoculars to study the light. It was yellow, just changing to green.

"Spectral colors!" he whispered. "The colors of the flash we saw from space . . ."

His breath caught.

"It's forming a target pattern now, like the one we saw in the ocean ice. And on the tower wall . . ."

Cruzet was reaching, but Andersen clung to the binoculars.

"Another minute, Tony. The bull's-eye is turning red. And stabilizing." He gave up the glasses. "The changes have stopped."

To Kip's unaided eyes, it was only a dim fleck of light in the edge of the ice.

"The same pattern," Cruzet said. "Red at the center, ringed with concentric circles. The colors all in spectral order, out to violet at the edge. Certainly a signal."

"Of what?"

"There's the road!" Cruzet swept the glasses back and forth across the end of the pit. "It zigzags up the cliffs to a dark spot just beneath the light. Maybe the mouth of a tunnel."

Andersen reached for the glasses.

"Do you think it—" Cruzet stared at him, eyes wide with a sudden unease. "Do you think they're showing us the way?"

"Could be." Andersen shrugged and raised the glasses. "Could be."

"Why?" Cruzet had seldom shown emotion, but his voice had fallen to a husky half-whisper now. "What could they want with us?"

"We're on our way to know."

●

They went below. The turbine sang. The spider rolled on. With the binoculars, Kip found the road for himself, a thin black line across light-colored strata. It was lost in the darker layers, but he traced it up to the rim of the pit, where the rock gave way to ice.

It ended at a dark gap just below the shining circles. A tunnel, really, that might take them somewhere under the ice?

Wondering, he felt again that they were on a great adventure, exciting enough for Captain Cometeer. He kept the binoculars on the road and the circles till Andersen came up to study the tunnel mouth again.

"It's right at the bottom of the ice," he said. "Could be it was once a surface road. Roofed when the snows began to accumulate. But that shining spot?" He shook his head. "I'd like to know . . ."

He shrugged and grinned.

"There's a lot I'd like to know."

Kip stood wondering if he could tell about his dream.

"Comments, Kipper?"

Andersen must have seen the expression on his face, but Kip was still afraid to tell about the dream.

"I just wonder." He shook his head. "It really is exciting."

●

Andersen went down to take another turn at the wheel. The spider ran fast, but they took most of an hour to reach the bottom of the wall. There the road became a sloping ledge cut into the rock. It looked so narrow that Cruzet and Andersen went out to measure it.

"We can do it," Andersen decided. "With all the wheels pulled under us. If we're careful enough. If we don't run into rockfalls. I think."

They pulled the wheels together and climbed the wall, easing the spider very gingerly around sharp hairpin turns at the corners of the pit. They found no fallen rocks, and they came over the top at last, into the tunnel. Andersen let Kip come with them when they went out to inspect it.

"Huge!" Cruzet peered up at the pointed archway overhead. "A good fifty meters wide and twice the height of our mast. Why would the amphibians need anything so big?"

Andersen flashed his helmet lamp down the tunnel and

found only blackness. Frowning, he turned to look back down at the frozen lake half a dozen kilometers below.

"Do you want a crazy guess?"

"A crazy place." Cruzet nodded, with a wry little twist of his mouth. "A crazy world."

Andersen stood a moment longer, gazing back into the pit.

"There's a lot of granite gone," he said at last. "Several hundred cubic kilometers. I'd guess it went down the tunnel. This could have been a quarry, but I wonder what they were building."

Skyhold, Kip thought.

"The spider!" he heard Cruzet shout. "It's running away from us!"

●

They had left it in the tunnel mouth. It was gliding away. The pavement under it, dead black when they stopped, was softly glowing now. They ran to overtake it. Kip and Cruzet tumbled into the lock. Andersen waited outside, kneeling at the edge of the pavement, reaching down to feel it with his glove.

"Andy!" Cruzet shouted from the open lock. "Come on. Now!"

Looking up, Andersen discovered that he had fallen behind again. He sprinted to overtake them, and Cruzet pulled him into the lock.

"Thanks! I wasn't looking."

"A crazy road!" Cruzet muttered when they were back in the cabin and out of their helmets. "It was moving faster in the middle, like a faster current in the middle of a river."

"High-tech." Andersen nodded. "Very high-tech. But there's no motion in the pavement itself. It's a surface vector effect that carries us along. Actuated, I imagine, by the burden on it. The spider was gaining on me because it's heavier." Puzzlement narrowed his eyes. "A man named Clarke once suggested something like it. I'd like to know the physics and the math."

Kip followed them into the pilot bay. Andersen at the wheel, Cruzet behind him, they stood looking through the windows. Dimly lit by their own lights, the tunnel walls were some smooth blue-gray stuff, broken with dark vertical seams. Spaced many meters apart, the seams marched very deliberately past them.

They stood a long time looking in silence.

"Tony." Andersen turned at last to Cruzet. "What do you say?"

"I was thinking." Cruzet frowned. "Watching the stripes on the wall, I'd guess we're making six or eight miles an hour. At that rate, we'd be a long time on the way to the source of that flash. If that's our destination."

"I guess the old architects had time enough." Andersen squinted at the slowly marching seams. "No rush to move stone from the quarry. We can drive ahead a lot faster. Let's do it."

●

Cruzet went down to tend the engine and Andersen drove them on, keeping to the center of the tunnel. Kip stayed in the bubble. They were rushing into darkness, the seams in the wall racing past them now. The pavement shone dimly under them, a pale gray glow running a few dozen meters ahead and fading out behind. The quiet hum of the turbine neither rose nor fell. Nothing ever changed the dull gray blur of the wall. He watched till he got tired of watching, and went back down to the cabin. Mondragon was sitting up on the side of the berth, blinking at him sleepily.

"Adonde? Where are we?"

"Out of the pit," Kip told him. "In a tunnel under the ice."

On their way to Skyhold, he thought, though he didn't say so. He was at the kitchen shelf, mixing mock orange powder into a glass of water, when his mother and Day came out from behind the curtain.

"Me Me?" Day rubbed her eyes and looked anxiously around the cabin. "Where's Me Me?"

"I don't know," Rima said. "But please, dear, you mustn't worry. I'm sure Me Me's all right, wherever she is."

"I do worry." Day was very positive. "She is not all right. She's still running from the black things and crying because she can't get away."

"We'll help her when we can, but let's get some breakfast now. Eggs and toast, with orange juice?"

"I've got to listen." Day shook her head. "Me Me needs me bad."

Rima made breakfast of powdered eggs and soyamax toast. Mondragon took the wheel while Cruzet and Andersen came to the table, but Day didn't eat. Her face pinched with distress, she stood silently listening.

●

They drove forever down the tunnel. The men took turns at the wheel. Rima spent her time with Day, who hardly ate, hardly slept, and seldom even spoke. Kip slept on a foam pad in the bubble, and sat for long hours staring down the tunnel, never seeing more than that pale glow that moved down the pavement with them.

Grieving for his old brave companions in the Legion of the Lost, he tried to remember his best adventures with them. Sometimes he tried to invent new worlds to explore with Captain Cometeer, but he could never imagine another planet as strange as this one, or any enemies as terrible as the blackwings in his dream.

When Mondragon was off duty, they sometimes sat together in the bubble, remembering Earth. Mondragon always asked to hear more about his mother and their home in Las Cruces. Kip liked to hear about Cuerno del Oro and the fiestas in the plaza and Don Ignacio's tales of the great birds of space.

"Carlos, aren't you ever sorry?" he asked. "Sorry you left your home to stow away with us?"

"Nunca!" His voice was loud and clear. "I'm happy to be here with your mother and you and la pobrecita Day. No matter about la mala suerte, I'll never have regret."

●

Once, when Cruzet was at the wheel and Andersen asleep behind the curtain, Mondragon found Rima sitting forlornly on the berth in the cabin. Day was in her lap, hollowed eyes wide, head alertly tipped, silently listening.

"You look so tired," he told her. "May I hold the child?"

"Thank you!" She looked up at him, her lips suddenly trembling. "I'm dead. Dead for sleep. Dead from this everlasting strain. From trying to cope with all this—all this madness I'll never understand."

He sat down with them and held out his arms to Day.

"Querida . . ."

She turned away from him, clinging to her mother.

Rima shrugged and sighed, looking so worn and hopeless that his arm was suddenly around her. She felt lifeless, neither yielding nor pulling away. He had to gulp at a lump in his throat before he could speak.

"I—I love you, Rima. Always." He felt her tremble, and let his voice run on. "Ever since the poor mojado came out of Chihuahua and saw you smiling at the children with you in the taxi." He gulped again. "Please, Rima! Please let me love you."

She caught a long breath, and he saw her dry lips quivering.

"I'm sorry for you, Carlos." She looked at him sadly, her voice tired and dull. "I'm sorry for Day. I'm sorry for all of us, caught in this awful trap. It's all too much for me. I just can't—can't think of love."

He sat there beside her for a long time, and finally got up to make coffee for them, using the last of Stecker's precious Kona blend.

●

Kip was sitting in the bubble, dreaming that he had found his Game Box safe and opened it to rejoin Captain Cometeer, who was holding off the nanoforms besieging the outpost on the Pygmy Planet. A sharp cry from Day brought him wide awake.

"Me Me!" Her sharp voice came up from the cabin. "Me Me, we're almost there!"

He blinked and looked and found a faint gray glint far ahead of the pavement's racing glow.

"Starlight!" he shouted into the interphone. "Starlight ahead."

Mondragon was at the wheel. Cruzet and Andersen came rushing up to study that dim gleam, impatiently passing the binoculars back and forth. Cruzet clung to the glasses when Andersen wanted them again, and muttered something under his breath. Kip saw Andersen shake his head, saw a scowl tighten his face. The light ahead grew brighter, till at last they came out of the tunnel into a titanic ruin.

"My God!" Cruzet whispered. "My God!"

They were in another pit. Mountains of ice behind them towered to the stars. Mountains of shattered masonry rose all around them. A solitary summit of fused and crumpled metal blocked the road a few kilometers ahead.

"Something happened here," Andersen muttered. "The planet was killed by something more than cold and darkness."

Thirty-two

Cruzet and Andersen passed the binoculars back and forth, scanning the monumental ruin around them and the ice behind, sheer white cliffs that climbed to higher whiter cliffs and finally to the blazing blackness of the sky.

"Actually a city?" Staring at Andersen, Cruzet laid the glasses down. "It must have been magnificent!"

It had been Skyhold, Kip thought. The mighty fortress of the skylers, designed to survive the death of the planet. He felt a shiver of dread at the piles and ridges of toppled and shattered masonry, the tangles of twisted metal, the mountain of wreckage that blocked the road ahead.

"What hit it?" Cruzet was reaching for the glasses. "An asteroid?"

"I see no impact crater." Andersen shook his head. "There was something hot."

"Very hot." Cruzet nodded. "It melted a hole in the ice cap."

"Or vaporized it." Andersen nodded. "Water wouldn't stay liquid here."

"Metal fused and stone gone to lava." Cruzet gestured at the nearer rubble piles. "But not from fire. You get no fire without air."

A heat ray? Kip remembered the Legion of the Lost's raid to rescue the trapped galactic ambassador from the Hidden Planet. Captain Cometeer's space mirror had reflected Killer Kong's flame ray to crisp the pirate with his own secret weapon.

"Was it war?" This was no time to speak of his dream, not after he had waited so long, but he thought the question was safe enough. "The amphibians under attack from space?"

"Could be, Kipper." Andersen grinned at his excitement. "You want a look?"

The rubble filled the lenses, so near it seemed to topple over him. He found a towering wall beyond the mountain of ruin on the road. Built of dark enormous blocks, it covered the stars halfway to the zenith. He saw no damage to it, and felt relieved that Skyhold was not entirely gone.

"I'd like to know—"

Cruzet had taken the glasses to sweep the wreckage again. Twisted beams and shapeless metal fragments jutted like broken bones from mountains of broken stone.

"Factories, perhaps? Walls tumbled down on wrecked machinery?"

"And something else." Andersen pointed at clustered towers of rough dark rock around the tunnel mouth behind them. "Blocks of raw stone piled where they came from the quarry."

The skyler in the dream had worked here, Kip remembered, lifting quarried stone off the transporter, turning it to powder, shaping it into something harder than stone, perhaps to build that sky-high wall ahead.

"What was that?" Andersen studied the enormous pile of ruined metal that blocked the road ahead, and passed the glasses to Cruzet. "It looks as if it fell there."

"Out of space?" Cruzet gave the glasses back with a frown of frustration. "I can't imagine."

"I can," Kip said. "I think it was a battleship."

They stared at him.

"It looks like the wreck of the Iron Giant's *Battle Moon* after Captain Cometeer's stasis ray knocked it down on the Phantom Planet. I saw it on my Game Box screen."

It must have been as round as an orange, but the fall had flattened and split it, spilling its mangled metal guts far around it. Ugly snouts like the muzzles of enormous guns jutted out of its fused and twisted armor.

"A spacecraft?" Cruzet frowned at Andersen.

"Could be." Andersen shrugged. "The place does look like a battlefield." He took the glasses to study it again. "Whatever it is, the impact dug quite a crater." He grinned at Kip. "If you're right, you've earned a medal from your Captain Cometeer."

●

The pavement here no longer shone or moved them, but Andersen had Mondragon drive them on toward the wreck till its black shadow hid most of the towering wall beyond. The spider wallowed over shattered rock and broken metal till a house-sized boulder stopped them. Andersen laid the binoculars back on the desk, and Kip followed them down to the cabin.

Mondragon came out of the pilot bay.

"Too much rock and wreckage ahead," he told them. "I think we've come as far as we can."

"Me Me?" Rima had emerged from the rear compartment. Day clung to her hand, peering anxiously up at Mondragon. "Have we found her?"

"Not yet."

"I know she's close." Hopefully, Day turned to Andersen. "Can't we look?"

"We're looking," he told her. "As hard as we can."

"Hurry!" Her voice was her own again, and quivering with anxiety. "Me Me needs us really bad."

"Andy?" Rima turned to him, frowning. "We were asleep. What has stopped us?"

"Hard to say." He shrugged uncomfortably. "The road's blocked. Ruins all around us. Piles of it too high to climb."

"Trapped!" Cruzet muttered. "No way to get much farther."

"Please, Dr. Andersen." Day was shrill with emotion. "We've got to go on."

"Maybe we can." Andersen grinned to cheer her. "Not with the spider, but I think we can climb over the wreckage. The road may go on beyond it." He turned to Cruzet. "Game for that, Tony?"

"Game enough." Cruzet nodded grimly. "What else?"

"Don't ask." Wry-faced, he turned to Mondragon. "Carlos, you wait for us here with Rima and the kids. Keep in touch with the radio. We'll try to see where the road went."

●

Mondragon found coils of rope and light hand axes for them to carry. Kip watched them check their breather units, get into their airskins, shut themselves into the lock. He climbed with Mondragon into the bubble, and watched their helmet lights zigzag into the maze of ruin ahead.

The going got harder when they came to the rim of the crater the falling thing had dug. They roped themselves together. Andersen climbed ahead. Twice he hauled Cruzet back to his feet when he slipped and fell. They stood at last on top of the ridge, looking beyond it.

Day came up the steps from the cabin.

"Ask them, Carlos," she begged. "Have they found Me Me?"

"Andy?" Carlos called. "What do you see?"

"The road goes on." Andersen was breathing hard from the climb. "The pavement looks clear enough out past the crater. It runs straight into that great wall. You'd expect to find some kind of door or gate, but it seems to stop dead against solid rock. Makes you wonder."

"Too much wonder!" Cruzet's bitter mutter. "Ever since we landed."

They turned to look ahead.

Andersen spoke again. "We're pushing on for a closer look at the wall."

"To meet the amphibians?" Cruzet mocked him. "Or your ice gods?"

"I want to know what they were." Turning back toward the spider, he raised his voice. "The wall ahead looks two or three kilometers high. Built of some blue-black stuff; blocks the size of four-story houses. No sign of any gate or door, not from here."

"Pushing on." Cruzet jeered him. "Till we kill ourselves—"

He clutched abruptly at Andersen's arm. They stood motionless, silently staring.

"Qué es?" Mondragon whispered. "Qué es?"

"A light!" Andersen caught his breath and seemed to collect himself. "A bright spot on the wall, down at the end of the pavement. The same expanding circles we've seen before."

"An invitation?" Cruzet muttered. "To freeze our bodies on the wall, like Singh and the others . . ."

"Or maybe something better." Andersen's voice rose decisively. "Carlos, hold the fort for us. I don't know what this means, but we'll try to get back before our breather units die."

The starlight washed all color out, but Kip found their yellow airskins when Mondragon gave him the binoculars. They clambered along the ridge toward that enormous wreck, stopped to scan it again, and finally disappeared down the crater's farther rim, still roped together, Andersen ahead.

Waiting in the bubble, Kip and Mondragon watched the ridge and the wall beyond, a black shadow on the sky. Stars shone through gaps along the top. A fortress wall, Kip wondered, with gaps where weapons were placed? Captain Cometeer would look for weapons.

Time passed. Mondragon looked at his watch, looked again, went down to the cabin and came back with a mug of syncafe. He set it on the desk and forgot to drink it.

"Call them, Carlos," Kip urged impatiently.

Mondragon called. They heard no answer.

"I think we're cut off," Mondragon said. "The metal in the wreckage would be a radio shield."

●

Mondragon said waiting made him nervous. He went down to check the engine and the cycler. Alone in the bubble, Kip watched the ruins and imagined he was here on the dead planet as a secret agent for Captain Cometeer. His mission was to recover the ultratech weapon that could save the universe from the Mind Wipers.

He imagined the amphibians were dead, wiped out by the surprise attack, but they had struck back before they died. Their ultraweapon had brought down the Wiper raider that lay wrecked on the pavement. His orders were to search the ruins for the weapon, but he couldn't imagine what it would look like, and he didn't want to think of what it might do to Day.

He decided to forget the whole idea. Feeling thirsty, he went down to the cabin. His mother was sitting in the rear compartment with Day in her arms, trying to rock her to sleep. Careful not to bother them, he got a drink of water and climbed back to the bubble.

He was waiting in the navigator's seat when Mondragon came back from the engine bay. He got up to offer the chair, but Mondragon shook his head and sat staring at the rubble and the wall. Bored with waiting, Kip asked him to tell about the bruja his father had hired in a dry time to make rain and pasture for the goats.

The rains had never come, and Mondragon seemed too anxious for talk. Wishing for the Game Box, Kip started to tell him how the Legion had hunted the Iron Giant. He stopped when he saw that Mondragon was looking at his watch, not listening.

"How long?" Kip asked.

"Only nine hours," he said. "It just seems longer."

Rima called them down at last for a bowl of tofabeef stew. After they had eaten, Mondragon offered to sit with Day if she wanted to rest.

"I can't sleep," she said. "Not at a time like this. But Day should. If you can get her to relax."

Rima went up to the bubble to watch for Cruzet and Andersen, and Mondragon tried to make friends with Day. She was willing to sit on his knee while he told her how he used to herd his father's goats, and how he shivered when the coyotes howled at night. She smiled at first, but soon slipped off his knee to stand listening for Me Me.

"It's the black things," she said. "They won't let her call."

●

Mondragon kept frowning at his watch.

"Their breather cartridges?" Kip asked. "How long do they last?"

"Rated for twelve hours. They've been gone almost eleven. They should have been back . . ." His voice trailed uneasily off.

"They still have an hour." Rima was doggedly hopeful. "And don't the units have a safety margin?"

"Maybe—" His voice abruptly lifted. "Trust the saints, my mother would say, but also trust yourself. I think they're in trouble. I'm going after them."

"Carlos—" Rima spoke his name, and paused uncertainly. "If they need help, do anything you can. But don't—" Her voice trembled. "Don't go too far. I couldn't bear to be here alone."

He checked his own breather cartridge and got into his airskin. Kip climbed to the bubble with Rima and Day. They shared the binoculars, following him up the rubble ridge. He stood there a long time, gazing all around him, before his voice crackled from the speaker.

"I'm looking down the crater rim. A steep slope of broken rock and scraps of broken metal. The ground is clear beyond it, a kilometer out. The pavement runs straight on to a dead end at the wall."

"Andy?" Rima asked. "And Tony?"

"Nada. No sign of them. Or anything alive."

"The signal light?"

"Nada," he said. "Except the light from the stars. I'm going closer."

"Why?" Her voice rose sharply. "You don't know what the danger is."

"The slope below me looks like hard going. I'm afraid they had trouble on it."

"If they need help—" Her voice caught. "But careful, Carlos! Come back to us."

Rima had the binoculars, but Kip saw his helmet light flicker and vanish. They waited in the bubble. Day climbed into her lap to look out into the starlight.

"That's where Me Me is." She pointed over the wreck at the top of the wall, where its crenelations cut notches in the sky. "The black things have her locked up there. She needs us to save her."

"Darling, you know we would. If we could."

They waited till Kip got tired of waiting. He tried to get Mondragon on the radio. He tried to tell Day how Captain Cometeer had followed the secret tunnel into the Iron Giant's citadel to recover the stolen codes. She told him to hush. Slipping off Rima's lap, she stood staring up at the wall, listening silently, till the radio was suddenly alive with Mondragon's fast breath.

"A hard climb down." Kip saw the helmet light. "But they made it safe. I found their tracks, walking straight on toward the wall."

"Toward the signal light?"

"Nada." He spread his arms. "There's no light. No sign of them."

"Where did they go?"

"Yo no sé. They're just gone."

Kip watched his helmet light bobble slowly down the ridge. The air lock thumped and wheezed. Back in the cabin, he shrugged unhappily at Rima.

"Me Me?" Day went anxiously to meet him, tears in her hollowed eyes. "Did you find her?"

"Not yet. We'll keep trying."

"Me Me's gone." She stumbled blindly back to her mother. "I can't hear her voice. I'm afraid we'll never find her."

Kip saw Mondragon look at his watch.

"Andy?" He felt afraid to know, but the words came out. "Tony and Andy? Are they dead?"

Looking gravely at him and then at Rima, Mondragon took a long time to answer.

"Maybe not," he said at last. "We just don't know."

"We can hope," Rima said. "We have to hope."

She made syncafe, but Mondragon took only a sip of it. He frowned at his watch, told them to call him if anything happened, and limped wearily into the rear compartment. Rima finished her syncafe and sat down on the berth. Day crawled into her arms and sobbed herself to sleep.

Back in the bubble, Kip watched the ridge. Watched the ruined spacecraft and the ruins around it. Watched till the binoculars were too heavy to hold. Then watched without them. Finally, too sleepy to watch any longer, he lay down on his foam pad.

●

The hiss and clunk of the air lock woke him. Had Andy and Tony come back? He scrambled to his feet. Glancing out as he started for the stairs, he saw a light moving up the ridge. A helmet light? Groggily, he turned back and fumbled to focus the binoculars.

It was Day!

Or another nightmare? Dazed with dread, he remembered Dr. Singh and her companions, their naked bodies frozen to the wall of Skygate. He got his breath and tried the binoculars again. It really was Day, out alone in the terrible night, going up the ridge as nimbly as one of Mondragon's goats. She wore no airskin, only the thin red jumpsuit. Only now it didn't look red. Her body shone strangely white, lighting the boulders and metal scraps as she climbed them.

"Mom!" Feeling sick, frozen with shock, he had to gasp for his breath. "Mom—"

He heard no answer, but in a moment he saw her. In her own yellow airskin, she was already outside, running desperately after Day.

"Mom, wait!" he shouted into the radio. "I'll get Carlos. We'll come with you."

"No!" She looked back. "Wait for Andy and Tony. Maybe they can help."

She ran on.

Mondragon came rushing out of the rear compartment, searching frantically for Rima.

"They're gone!" Kip was breathless with shock. "Mom and Day. Day's out with no airskin."

"Qué?" Mondragon stood blinking dazedly. "Qué dice?"

"My sister!" he gasped. "She's shining all over. Like a lamp."

"Outside?"

"She's climbing the ridge, the way Andy and Tony went."

Mondragon ran up the steps to the bubble and groped for the binoculars. Kip followed. Peering through the starlight, he saw a tiny fleck of white light dancing along the crest of the ridge. Day, still shining, still moving. In a moment she was gone. He found his mother's light, already far toward the ridge.

"Rima, I'm coming!" Mondragon shouted into the microphone. "As fast as I can."

"No, Carlos! No!" Rima stopped for an instant, gasping for breath. "Don't leave Kip."

She ran on.

"Los santos sagrados!" Mondragon looked hard at Kip. "Are you afraid to stay alone?"

"I'm coming with you," Kip said. "But we must leave a note for Andy and Tony."

"They won't get back." He glanced at his watch. "It's been too long."

But he scrawled a note and left it on the desk.

●

"Cabrón!" Mondragon pulled his suit off the hanger and stopped to squint at the air pack. "My breather unit. It must be replaced."

"Hurry!" Kip urged him. "They'll be gone."

At last, the unit replaced and their helmets sealed, they ran down the ramp. Kip felt lost in the dark. As his eyes adjusted, he made out the towering wreck ahead. The high shadow of the wall beyond. When he found Rima's helmet light, she was already at the top of the ridge. The light flickered and vanished.

"Vamanos!"

Mondragon was already tramping ahead. Kip scrambled to keep up. Mondragon paused to give him a hand when he needed it. Together on the crater rim, they stood breathing hard, looking down the slope beyond. Kip found the pavement, a pale straight streak across the frost. No helmet light moved on it. No signal light shone on the wall where it ended.

"They're gone." Mondragon stared from his helmet, hoarsely whispering. "Something took them."

The never-ending night seemed suddenly darker.

"Perhaps—" Mondragon hesitated. "Perhaps we should go back. Your mother was concerned for you."

"I'm concerned for her."

"Yo también," Mondragon breathed. "Let's go on."

Down beyond the rubble, Mondragon found footprints on the pavement.

"Your mother's." Mondragon pointed. "Dr. Cruzet's. Dr. Andersen's. Your sister's."

Most of them were faint, hard to see. Day's tiny prints were darker than the others. He wondered if whatever made her body shine had also thawed the frost. The prints led straight to the wall, ending against a huge blue-black block.

"No sign—"

Mondragon's voice broke off. A point of bright violet light had appeared at the center of the block, a few meters above them. It swelled into a violet disk, with a bright blue point at its center. The blue grew into an inner disk, a sharp green point at the center. Green disk, yellow disk, orange and red, the whole pattern spread down to the pavement level. Rainbow colors fringed their shadows on the frost.

Trembling, Kip reached out to touch the glowing stone.

"Don't!" Mondragon gasped. "Remember Indra Singh—"

His hand met no stone. It went through the violet glow.

Thirty-three

Off balance when his reaching hand found nothing solid, Kip stumbled forward into darkness. He felt Mondragon clutch his arm. The stars were gone. They stood in darkness, groping blindly to turn up their helmet lights, until he saw the pavement shining softly beneath their feet. The glow spread ahead of them, faintly lighting the walls of a high-arched passageway, wider than the tunnel from the quarry.

He felt the pavement moving them.

"Madre de Dios!" Mondragon crossed himself. "Are you okay?"

"Copasetic!" Kip whispered. That was a word of Captain Cometeer's. "This is a better adventure than I ever had in my Game Box!"

Slowly at first, then faster, faster, the pavement swept them on till they came out into a space so vast that it took his breath. A full kilometer wide, it looked three times that high.

The floor swept them along it, toward no end that he could see.

"Too fast!" Mondragon muttered. "Let's try the edge."

The motion slowed as they walked toward the wall. Tiny points of light shone over it, rising row on row until Kip lost them in the twilight overhead. Each light burned above a small black spot. As they came closer, he saw that the spots were pits in the wall. The motion of the floor stopped before they reached it, but Mondragon walked ahead to look into pits.

"Huesos! Amphibian bones."

Kip came closer. The pits were triangular, a meter wide at the bottom, tapering to a point at the top. His light found yellow-white sticks lying in the dust inside them. The light above one was a tiny six-sided prism that shone dimly red. The next was faintly green, another pale blue. Many were gray and dead.

Lifestones, he thought, like the skylers had worn.

Mondragon reached to pick up the yellow sticks. A thin-walled tube with something like a knuckle at the end. A curved shard of something like plastic, longer than his arm. Something round and ridged across the top, with great hollow sockets where eyes had been.

"Tumbas. Graves." He stepped back to look up at the endless rows of them, climbing till they blurred into dusky gloom. "Millions of graves. The amphibians came here to die."

Kip stood remembering his dream. The lifestones had been strange magic. They seemed stranger now.

"My mother saw fantasmas." He felt Mondragon grip his arm. "She said my father came to visit her after Don Ignacio heard he was dead."

●··

Kip shivered, backing farther from the rows of dusty vaults. They rose too high, reached too far along the endless wall.

Too many amphibians had left something that still flickered in the stones they had worn.

"Fantasmas—" Mondragon stared up at the wall, and something caught his voice. "They've haunted us. They've possessed your sister. They killed Indra Singh and her crew." He turned abruptly. "Let's get on."

The floor shone again as they drew farther from the wall, and it swept them on. Forever, it seemed to Kip, until at last it brought them out into an even vaster space. A circular room, kilometers wide, kilometers high. Towering archways were spaced all around it, opening into cavernous dim-lit halls like the one they had followed.

"They were smaller than we are." Kip shook his head, gazing up into that dim, enormous cavern. "Why did they build so big?"

"They could use the space," Mondragon said. "They were fliers."

The far-off roof was a swarm of brilliant stars.

"Strange constellations." Mondragon craned to search them. "Not the ones we have seen."

"Brighter. I wonder—"

Shivering, Kip found stars he knew. They were the constellations Watcher had known in the western twilight. The floor carried them on. Awed into silence, he stared into the dark archways around them, stared up into the starry dome, stared at Mondragon.

"Alli!" Mondragon pointed, and Kip saw a cluster of tiny figures far off in the dimness. "There!"

The glow beneath them slowly faded, and their motion stopped.

●

"Vamanos." Mondragon gestured. "Come on."

Tramping on, they found the floor brighter again, shining dully red. A wide red strip faded into orange as they crossed it, into yellow, into green. The strips made circles, he saw, circles inside of circles.

"Andy!" Mondragon's shout crashed in his helmet. "Dr. Andersen."

Andersen had left the group ahead, walking to meet them, His head was bare. Stopping near them, he gestured for them to unseal their helmets.

"—safe enough." Kip caught the words when Mondragon helped him lift his helmet. "They breathe oxygen."

Who are they? Kip wanted to ask, but Andersen was leading them on toward Cruzet and his mother. They were perched a little awkwardly on tall T-shaped stools around a big round table at the center of a wide violet spot beneath the center of the dome. Their helmets lay beside them. Day sat on the edge of the table in front of her mother.

"Hi, Kipler Nipler." Day knew he hated the name, but she waved and smiled as if only trying to tease him. "Welcome to Me Me's place."

She wore a bright ruby lifestone behind one ear, a bright green one behind the other. She looked happy, with no harm he could see from being outside without her airskin. He looked for the panda doll and couldn't find it. His mother slid off the odd T-bar to hug him and help him climb to the perch beside her.

Perches made to fit amphibian feet, not human bottoms.

"Glad you made it," Cruzet greeted them. "Saved us a trip outside to bring you in."

"Hungry?" Andersen asked. "Tony says they're going to feed us."

"I don't know." Rima frowned uncertainly. "Their biochemistry must be different. Their foods may not be safe."

"Ask Tony."

Andersen nodded at Cruzet, perched across the table. Kip saw a pale blue bead stuck high on his forehead, almost where the skylers in his dream had worn the lifestones in their crests.

"They've studied several of us," Cruzet said. "Jake Hinch first. Then the bodies of Singh and her crew. Now Roak's. They've found our DNA compatible and identified foods of their own that won't kill us."

Why do they study us? Kip asked himself. *What do they want to do with us?*

He felt too uneasy to ask questions, but Mondragon was pointing at the pale blue jewel on Cruzet's forehead.

"The beads? Can you tell us what they are?"

"Relics, apparently, of dead amphibians." Andersen nodded at Cruzet. "Tony, can you tell us anything?

Cruzet narrowed his eyes, moving the bead as if to adjust it, and shook his head. Kip nodded to himself. The skylers in his dream had seemed to use the lifestones almost like telephones, but also for a lot more. They had turned swimming youngsters into flying skylers. They had held the memories of drowned skylers buried for ages in sea mud.

"Andy—"

Now at last, he thought, Andersen might believe him if he told about the dream. He had caught his breath to speak, but they had all looked away, at the table top. It shone for a moment with that familiar pattern of swelling circles. The rainbow colors vanished. A dark point spread from the center. It became a round opening, with a crystal dish lifting into sight.

"Yes, Kipper?"

Andersen had turned inquiringly back to him, but he had forgotten the dream.

"A magical banquet!" he shouted. "Like the feast of death in the Castle of Skulls, where the Lethal Lady served poisoned wine to the Purple Emperor."

Nobody heard him. Their eyes were on the little nut-brown wafers stacked in a neat pyramid, and the shining bubbles arranged around them.

"Thank you, Me Me." Hands together, Day gazed up at

the star-dusted vault. "Thank you very much." She turned to smile at her mother. "Me Me made these just for us."

The dish was too far for her to reach. She scrambled to her feet and ran across the table to pick up the wafers and hand them around. Rima accepted one, frowning at it doubt-fully.

"Taste it, Mom! Just taste it. A lot better than all that soya stuff."

Rima took a tentative bite and smiled. Kip tried the cake she gave him. Crunching crisply in his mouth, it tasted a lit-tle like wheat toast and more like the beef jerky he used to buy after school at the corner grocery in Las Cruces.

"It's good." He grinned at Day. "Even if a doll did cook it."

"These are water." She was passing out the bubbles. "The skylers need water like we do. This is how they fix it."

Kip sucked at it. Cold water came into his mouth.

"Mom! Mom!" Suddenly excited, Day was pointing up into the dome. "It's Me Me!"

●

Straining to see, Kip found a tiny black shadow drifting across the dim-lit vault. It grew, descending in a slow spiral.

"It's really Me Me!" Day watched with shining eyes. "The black things can't get her now."

It glided down on long transparent wings that glistened in the violet glow of the floor, and perched on a T-bar across the table. A bright golden bead shone from the crest of its strange head. Its eyes were huge and round. Fixed on Day, they shimmered with swelling rainbow circles.

"Me Me! Me Me!" Day turned to her mother, sobbing with joy. "Here she is!"

Rima shrank from the creature, voiceless with horror.

"Speak to her, Mom!" Day started across the table toward it. "She's so terribly glad we found her."

With a gasping scream, Rima grabbed to stop her. Twisting away, she ran on, arms lifted high. A thin pink snake ran out of its snout, coiled around her, lifted her.

"Stop it!" Rima slid off her perch and dashed around the table. "Help me, Carlos! Help my baby! Andy, Tony—"

"Mon, don't fret," Day was calling. "I'm okay."

The creature had cuddled her against the sleek brown fur on its breast. Rima stopped, trembling, staring blankly.

"She understands if you don't know her." Day smiled fondly up into the rainbow shimmer of it eyes. "She's grown up now, but she still loves me."

It hugged her to its heart again, and set her back on the table. The snake slid back into its snout. The wide wings folded. Its body was shaped like Wave Rider's, Kip thought, sleekly tapered, evolved for life in the sea. Shifting for its balance on the perch, it flashed its huge eyes at Rima and made a strange, hollow bellow.

"She says hello," Day said. "She wants to make us happy."

●

Shivering, Rima came weakly back on the awkward perch.

"What's that—thing?" Cringing from it, she appealed desperately to Andersen. "What does it want with my baby?"

Andersen shrugged and nodded at Cruzet.

"They did need her." Cruzet pushed at the shining bead on his forehead, as if adjusting it. "They've wanted to talk ever since they felt us coming. Your daughter seems to have been their most useful link, maybe because she's so young."

"What—" Day was still standing in front of the creature, stroking its velvet breast. Rima stared at them, shaking her head. "What is it?"

"A female amphibian." Cruzet seemed unsurprised by anything, his voice precise and dry. "We may as well call her Me Me, since of course she has no English name. She is one of the fortunate few who survived the attack."

"Attack?" Andersen echoed.

"The wreck we saw was one of the attackers," Cruzet said. "They failed, but it was a very close call. Only a few amphibians escaped. They've been frozen, with only their mental net awake. Me Me was revived when the net detected us."

"Slow down," Andersen told him. "What's the net?"

Cruzet frowned, pausing for words.

"Let's begin with the objects we've been calling beads. They are special organs of extended memory and long-range communication. In contact, they formed a network that held the mind of the race. They've always survived the death of the individuals who grew and wore them."

Lifestones. Kip nodded to himself.

"Day! Baby Day!" Hoarse with emotion, Rima held out her arms. "Come back to me."

"Please, Mom." Day shook her head. "Just a minute." She turned back to the creature. "Me Me? Are you hungry?"

The creature bellowed again, a muffled rumble like distant thunder. Day offered it an orange-colored cake off the table. The pink snake came out again to take it from her fingers and lift it to a full mouth of fine white teeth. The snake stabbed back to kiss her cheek. She smiled happily, and Rima shuddered.

"The attackers?" Andersen asked. "Who were they?"

"The history isn't clear." Cruzet frowned and shook his head. "Many of the mindstone records were damaged or destroyed, but here's the picture as I get it." He paused to shift the blue bead again. "They knew their sun was dying. This fortress was part of a grand plan to keep them alive forever, even on a frozen world. The attack's a tragic irony—"

He paused, looking up into the creature's shimmering rainbow eyes, and abruptly went on.

"Their grand plan defeated itself. Not content with the stronghold here, they tried to colonize the nearest stars. They never discovered quantum-wave propulsion, but they did develop gravity-propelled spacecraft. Those were slower. Interstellar flights took thousands of years, with the passengers in stasis sleep. The attackers were descendants—"

He stopped himself, pushing at the bead. The amphibian's eyes were fixed on him. Smiling into them, he was silent so long that Andersen prompted him.

"Tony? Can you go on?"

"Sure." He blinked in a startled way. "I've got it now. A dozen ships went out, carrying colonists. They were in mindstone contact for—I'd guess the term means something like a light-year—but they all went on beyond contact range. The attack came ages later, after they had been almost forgotten."

He stopped again, with a puzzled frown.

"From them?" Andersen asked. "Why?"

He touched the bead and tipped his head as if listening to the amphibian. Its eyes flickered, and he turned abruptly back to Andersen.

"We never knew." His voice was suddenly sharper and quicker. Kip thought the amphibian was speaking through him. "Perhaps the colonists had lost their own mindstones. Perhaps distorted recollections had made them paranoid, afraid we might threaten them. Whatever the reason, they certainly came to exterminate us. They attacked without warning, and they were well prepared. You saw the harm they did outside the walls, with heat weapons and nuclear missiles.

"Our best defense was a weapon of theirs—" Cruzet looked inquiringly at the amphibian. "A weapon given to us by an agent they had sent to spy on us. Knowing us, he had come to see their tragic folly.

"I inquired about the weapon." Touching the bead, he spoke more naturally to Andersen. "The word for it seems to suggest something like mental illness or contagion. It damaged the mindstones. Often killed them. More or less, I suppose, in the same way that a virus disables computers."

His voice changed again, no longer quite his own.

"It stopped the attackers, but our defenses were destroyed. Many thousand sleepers died in their cells. Millions of our most precious mindstones were killed. Expecting another attack, we believed we were beaten. We went to sleep, the few of us still alive, with no hope of ever waking."

"Mom, don't you see?" Day called across the table. "We woke them."

She was standing with the pink snake wrapped around her. Rima gasped when it held her up to the enormous eyes. Day gazed into their dance of color, squealing with delight. After a moment, it set her back on the table and cuddled her against its breast. It rumbled gently, and she turned her head to beam at Rima.

"Me Me thanks us, Mom. She she's so very happy that we woke her. She might have slept forever."

●

Cooing softly at Day, reaching out the thin pink snake to stroke her hair, the amphibian seemed so friendly that Kip caught his breath and dared to speak.

"If you don't mind, I'd like to ask a question."

She boomed gently at him, the wheels of color spinning in her eyes, speaking a language he hadn't learned to understand. He turned to Andersen.

"Captain Cometeer had to fight the Quake Master on the Trembling World. Did the amphibians cause the quake that made the avalanche?"

"Did they, Tony?" He spoke to Cruzet. "I was wondering."

"Matter of fact, I think they did." Cruzet waited for the play of light in the amphibian's eyes. Nodding at her, he swung deliberately back to Andersen. "When the sun died, they went underground to tap the planet's heat. They learned to stop quakes, or make small quakes to prevent greater ones."

The amphibian was sharing one of the wafers with Day, its nimble tongue putting a bit to her lips and the next to its own. Rima sat staring, frozen in shock. Cruzet moved the blue gem on his forehead and spoke again, his voice almost natural.

"We tripped the old perimeter defense system deployed around the tunnel mouth. That's what erased the mindstones we found in the blackwing nest and set off the quake. A larger quake would have closed the tunnel if Day hadn't got back in contact."

Day and the amphibian had finished the wafer. Smiling raptly up into the luminous eyes, she sang something that was eerily musical and strange. It answered with the same eerie syllables in a voice that was almost Day's. The pink tongue kissed her lips and slid back into its snout.

"Tell me!" Rima was suddenly on her feet, shouting hysterically at Cruzet and Andersen. "What do they plan for us?"

"Nothing." Cruzet shrugged. "Wakened so recently, Me Me's nearly as bewildered as we are. She has been asleep in an underground refuge. The world around us now must be as strange to her as it is to us. She's still searching for her own memories, and trying to recover what she can from the net."

●

"My children?" Shivering, Rima looked imploringly at Andersen. "What will happen to them?"

"Hard to say."

"My God! Don't you care?"

"We just don't know." Soberly, he shook his head. "We're in a critical spot. Alone here, with everything we ever knew lost in time and space behind us. Maybe alone in this galaxy. Alone in the universe, for all we know."

"So what can we do?"

"Wait," he said. "Hope. Try to cope."

"How?" She shuddered, huddled miserably on the T-bar. "How?"

"We'll look for ways," he said. "Even back at home, we never really know the future. Bad things happen, but good things, too. We take what we must and do what we can. That's life."

Mondragon had come around the table to stand beside her.

"We're alive," he whispered. "We're together."

She gave him a wan smile and caught his hand. Kip had come up beside them.

"Mom," he told her, "I think we'll be okay."

She didn't seem to hear, but Andersen grinned at him.

"All copasetic, Kipper?"

"I think." He looked up into the amphibian's rainbow eyes and off at the towering archways that led off the enormous floor. There was still a lot to see. A lot of exciting things to learn. "I think it will be."

The amphibian was booming again, her eyes shining at Cruzet. He nodded, touching the bright blue stone, and cleared his throat.

"The amphibians are pleased to greet us." He spoke in a precise and careful way, as if reading a formal document. "They are grateful that we wakened them. They are anxious to plan for our future together."

He turned to Andersen, waiting expectantly.

"Thank them," Andersen said. "We can learn from them. They can learn from us. Our future is beyond my imagination, but together we can live forever."

"I hope," Cruzet said. "We can hope."

"Me Me wants to live," Day called across the table. "She wants to learn. She wants to help us. Now she wants to show me where we are."

The pink snake lifted her again. The amphibian lurched off the perch and carried her away. Mondragon heard Rima's anxious gasp and felt her arm tighten around him. He drew her closer. Silently, they watched the creature take Day on a circuit of the enormous archways.

Andersen stood craning to study the architecture of the great dome overhead. Cruzet gathered the discarded helmets off the floor and laid them in a neat row on the edge of the table. Kip climbed on a T-bar and leaned to take another cake off the dish. Gliding back at last, the amphibian perched beside them and put Day in Rima's arms.

"Thank you, Me Me!" Day called as she soared away. "Don't leave us long."

They watched silently as she climbed and vanished among the ancient constellations.

Thirty-four

They lived there a week, eating the odd foods that came up through the middle of the great table and sleeping on the floor when they slept at all. They all wore the bright black beads they were calling mindstones now, even Kip and his mother. The little stones turned them into strangers and kept them busy with things Carlos seldom understood.

Day commonly sat cross-legged near the middle of the great table, with the others perched on the T-bars around her. The top of the table was sometimes like a blackboard; they could write or draw on it with pens or even their fingers. Sometimes it was like a TV monitor that could turn their drawings into pictures, or show them new pictures.

Sometimes they used words that sounded hardly human, sometimes English that was just as confusing. Nobody paid much attention to Kip. He used a little toilet, like the one in the spider, that had come up through the floor, and wandered around that enormous room and always came back to the pictures and the maps on top of the table. Out toward the glacier wall, there was a vast separate building. Pictures showed the roof of it lifting open and a cluster of huge silver balls rising out, climbing into the sky.

"A gravity ship," Day said in that odd quick voice that wasn't her own. "Meant to carry another colony out to the stars."

"They've all been born in the sea," Andersen added. "A dying race, since that froze. They hoped to find and colonize a living world, but their luck had run out when the colonists came back to kill them."

"The ship had no damage in the war," Day said. "It's still ready."

Ready for what? Kip felt sad for the amphibians. They had tried so long and hard to stay alive, tried until only their ghosts were left. The gravity ship looked wonderful, though maybe not so wonderful as their own quantum ship had been.

Thoughts of that made him even sadder. He grieved again for all his friends lost with it. For Jim Cheng, who had fitted his airskin and always smiled and tried to turn their troubles into jokes. For Reba Washburn, who had seemed cold and hard until he got to know her. Really, when she joined Mr. Sternberg in the fight against Captain Stecker and Jonas Roak, she had saved their lives. He grieved for Mrs. Sternberg and her kids, and all the others who had been Day's friends till the stones began to make her so strange they were afraid of her.

That sadness made him think of Chichen Itza. That was the Mayan city he had seen when his mother took him and Day on a vacation trip to the Yucatan, the summer before they left Earth. She wanted them to remember the world they were leaving, but the ruins had made him glad to be getting away. A dead city of queer temples and pyramids built of great stone blocks, carved and painted with mysterious hieroglyphs, its ruins had lain buried under the jungle for five hundred years.

He'd felt a pang of sadness for the civilization that had died there. Maybe not so strange as this one, because the old Mayans had been human. Their descendants still live around the ruins, peddling postcards and trinkets to the tourists. It struck him now that even those peddlers were gone long ago. Dead with the Earth and all its life in the millions or billions of years while the quantum ship was in flight.

A shadow of sorrow fell over him, for his mother and Day, Carlos and Andy and Tony—they and he were surely the last humans alive anywhere in all the universe. They would die here, he thought, leaving their bones to last forever here on the ice with the dust of the dead amphibians. He shivered at the thought, and tried to get it out of his mind.

●

His spirits lifted a little after that first week, when Me Me let them move into new apartments somehow fixed up for them, in a space larger than any room he remembered from Earth. Its vast walls glowed softly blue when they were moving about and faded to a gray dusk when they were not. Dark oval openings pierced them, rising in row upon endless row until they blurred in the dim blue dusk.

"Nests, I guess you would call them," Andersen said. "Empty homes that were ready for changing sea folk that never got here."

Doors along the bottom of one endless wall opened into their apartments, small rooms with berths and bathrooms like those in their rooms on the ship, and tiny kitchens that looked like copies from the spider. The men went back to the spider to bring human-type food. He was glad for that, and for the comforts of a bed and a shower, but Day was soon rushing them back to that great central chamber.

"My Me Me!" Her voice was soft and glad, the way it had

been when she used to hug her panda doll. "I always knew she was in bad trouble here on the ice. I'm happy the black things never got her. She says they're all dead now."

"What were they, dear?" Rima whispered. "I was terribly worried when they frightened you so."

"Things that hunted us." She shivered. "Things with terrible claws and great black wings. They hunted us everywhere, but they're all gone now."

"I think they were a racial memory that Day picked up," Cruzet said. "A memory of the black-winged predators. A sort of racial nightmare, I think, that had come to haunt all the mindstones."

"Me Me says they'll never come back." Day was nodding happily. "And she's so glad we came to wake her up. So glad to have us here, because she needs us as much as we needed her."

"How?" Kip asked. "How could she ever need us?"

"She's coming down to see us again," Day said. "Maybe she will say."

They waited around the table, staring up at the strange constellations that shone in the gloom of that enormous dome, until the amphibian came gliding down again on her softly shining wings. Perching beside them, she picked Day up with that quick pink tongue and cuddled her against her velvet fur, caressing her with sounds like the cooing of the doves Kip remembered hearing back at White Sands before they climbed aboard the quantum ship.

At last she set Day back on the table. Kip tried to listen, waiting to learn why she needed human beings here, but he never heard her say. His mother and the men asked questions that she seemed to be translating. They seemed to understand Me Me's answers, and asked more questions about things he never understood.

He was tired and bored before he saw Me Me's tongue reaching into the kangaroo pouch on her glossy belly. She gave Day a little cluster of the black stones and picked her up to hug her again before she spread her bright wings and soared away. Day stood waving until she was lost among the strange stars overhead.

"Mindstones for us." Happily, she handed the stones around to the men and her mother. "These come from different people, with different skills. An engineer, a teacher, a mathematician, a poet. Me Me says we can learn from them."

She offered one to Kip.

"From Me Me, a gift for your birthday," she said.

"I don't want it." He shrank away. "And I can't have birthdays here, because there aren't any days."

"I'm Day." She grinned at him. "And Me Me says no le hace." She had learned a little Spanish from her baby-sitter back on Earth. "Me Me thought you'd like it because it comes from somebody you know. The Watcher, don't you remember? He was the last of the sea folk."

"Keep it away." He shook his head. "It gave me nightmares."

"Kipper?" They were all staring at him, and Andersen was asking, "What's this about?"

"The stones." He pointed at them. "Cosas del diablo, Carlos used to call them. You left one on the floor when you brought them back from the cave. Somehow it got to me, while I was trying to sleep. I never touched it, but it gave me a terrible dream. I was this Watcher, old and dying on a raft at the edge of the freezing sea."

"Kip!" His mother was almost scolding. "You never told us."

"I was afraid. I didn't know how to explain."

"You saw the planet dying!" Cruzet was excited. "That's history! The history we're trying to learn! But how did the stone get to that cave?"

"Me Me says the Watcher died on the float," Day said. "A predator found him and carried the body there."

"The mindstones are nothing devilish," Andersen said. "They formed in the brains of the amphibians after their metamorphosis. Organs of memory a little like computer chips, though we still have the science of them to learn. They're all in contact; I don't know how."

"We'll find out!" Cruzet was silent for a moment, peering at the one Day had given him. "One more riddle left to crack. It's a long-range effect; they detected us far out in space. In contact, they formed a kind of racial mind. Most of it was lost of course, with so many mindstones dead or damaged."

●

"Try the mindstone." Day offered it again. "It won't bite."

Uneasily, he put it against the scalp behind his ear. Something stuck it firmly. They all watched him, waiting.

"Nothing." He shook his head, feeling relieved. "I don't feel a thing. Or maybe—" He stared at Day. "It does bring back the dream when I was the Watcher. I remember how he loved his mate and their son. How sad he was he had no strength left to dive for fish or help when they were starving."

He reached to push it closer to his ear.

"It really doesn't bite." He grinned at Day. "It lets me remember a lot, but I'm still me."

"Bueno!" Andersen clapped his shoulder. " 'Sta bien. We'll be asking you for more about this Watcher and all about what you remember of the way the planet died."

Still perched around the table, they did keep asking questions, but most of them were for Day, about what Me Me had told her. Most of them he didn't understand. He really didn't want to remember the Watcher or the bones in the cave, or think about how all their bones would finally be left here, frozen forever and ever. He wanted his lost Game Box.

He waited unhappily until they finally broke for a rest. His mother and Carlos sat smiling at each other, holding hands. Cruzet and Andersen slid off the T-bars, reaching across the table for bubbles of water and juice and the funny-tasting cakes that were really better than soya-tufa cookies.

"Mopy-Dopy!" Day came across the table, shaking her finger at him. "Aren't you happy here with Me Me?"

"Not very," he said. "Not really."

"She wants us to be. She's doing everything to help us."

"It's all too strange."

"At first it was." His mother nodded. "But don't you see how lucky we are? I thought we were going to die on the ice. Me Me is doing her best to help us."

"A chance for us," Andersen added. "And a new chance for the amphibians." He turned to the others. "We've begun to get their story. The mindstones are almost eternal. With their planet freezing, they looked for ways to keep their common mind and their culture alive. Built this fortress on the ice. Looked for a younger planet.

"The war—the attack from the colonists—nearly wiped them out. The survivors went into stasis sleep, to be awakened if they were ever discovered. Our approach woke them. Me Me sees a chance that we can save each other, surviving in a sort of symbiosis."

He frowned doubtfully at Rima.

"If we can—"

"We can try." Rima nodded thoughtfully, smiling at Day. "They'd lost their will to live, with the sea frozen and no more sea folk born. We can bring them new hope, new life."

"If God wills." Solemnly, Carlos bent his head.

"With luck enough. With Day and Kipper growing up." Andersen grinned at him. "An exciting prospect, don't you think?"

"Not really, sir." Andersen looked so serious that Kip hesitated. "I—I'm sorry, sir, but I can't help what I feel. Everything here—everything is dead. Like all our friends we left on the ship. All we've ever found is bones. The amphibians have been dying since the oceans froze—"

He pulled the mindstone off his scalp.

"This thing turned me into the Watcher. I was dying the

way he died, there in the freezing sea a billion years ago." He
held it back toward Day. "Nothing I want to remember. I
don't want it haunting me."

"Kip, dear!" His mother looked hurt. "Don't say that! I
think the amphibians can be revived. They'd never invented
genetic engineering. With what we know and what we can
learn from them, I think a new generation might be born."

"Where? With the seas all frozen solid—"

"It can be done." Cruzet nodded to Day, as if she had spoken. "They are pumping heat from deep in the planet.
There's a big reservoir. Frozen now, but it can be roofed and
thawed. The new sea folk can grow up there."

"We can't give up," his mother said. "No reason to,
though we do have a long way to go. A lot to learn, but we
can all learn from Me Me. She says she can wake more teachers when we're ready. Please, Kip. Please!"

She turned to Carlos, who sat smiling at her, holding her
hand.

"Forget the fantasmas," Carlos told him. "Los santos are
with us now. You're alive. Your sister's alive. You can help us
all stay alive."

"Kipper, just imagine!" Andersen reached to prod his
ribs. "Imagine you were landing here with your Captain
Cometeer. Another world to save! A great new adventure!
Maybe a hard job to do. A new language to learn. A new science. A new culture. So much you never knew before. That's
the thrill of it!"

"Maybe." Kip nodded doubtfully. "Maybe."

He didn't want to be a coward, but a job like that looked
too big, even for the Legion of the Lost.

"A job cut out for you and Day." Andersen was looking
solemn. "We've been working hard, and Me Me does all she
can, but I've begun to wonder if Tony and I aren't too old for
it." He turned to include the others. "We humans are born
programmed to absorb language and culture and general

competence while we're very young. The aptitudes fade as we get into our teens. But look at your sister."

He nodded at Day, who was searching the big dish at the middle of the table for something she wanted.

"She became half-amphibian with no effort at all. It isn't going to be so easy for the rest of us." Sighing, he turned back to Rima. "Maybe not really easy for Kip. If more of us were children—"

"Don't fret, no sweat." Day looked up, sucking at a little globe of some golden juice. "There will be more children."

Kip frowned at his mother and Carlos, wondering.

"Don't forget all the kids on the ship." Day sucked happily at the ball of juice. "Mrs. Sternberg's kids. Chris Zane. Kelly Kovik. And remember all the other women, like Reba Washburn—"

"Crazy-Daisy!" Kip scowled at her. "You know the ship blew up. They're dead. All dead."

"But they aren't." Day drained the globe and dropped it back on the dish. She stood up, pushing the new stone higher behind her ear. "I just heard about the ship."

"What's that?" Cruzet whispered. "What about the ship?"

"The bomb did go off," she said. "Captain Stecker and Mr. Kelleck had taken it to the control dome. They were about to blow up the ship unless everybody did what he said, but Mr. Sternberg and Dr. Cheng never surrendered. They sealed the safety doors and opened the escape hatch to let the air out of the dome in case Captain Stecker triggered the bomb. He set it off. It killed him and Mr. Kelleck, and wrecked the top of the ship, but the safety doors saved everybody else."

They all slid off the T-bars, blinking at her.

"Really, Day?" her mother asked. "How do you know?"

"The new mindstone Me Me just brought down for me. It can talk to the one Dr. Cheng uncovered in the bottom of the new launch pit."

"Seguro?" Carlos slid his arm around Rima to pull her close, and they both stared at Day. "Seguro que sí?"

"Seguro. Dr. Cheng has the mindstone now. He's driving the spider, coming after us across the ice."

"What spider?" Kip demanded. "They don't have a spider."

"Mr. Smarty, wrong again." Day grinned at him. "They've got a spider now. Mr. Sternberg found spare parts and Dr. Cheng made new parts to build another spider."

●

Me Me came down again with an airskin for Day. They were all waiting by the pavement when the spider rolled out of the tunnel. The airlock opened. Jim Cheng came down the ramp, Reba Washburn behind him. Then the Sternbergs and their children.

"Hi, Mr. Kip," Cheng greeted him. "Here's a little gift we've brought for you, from halfway around the planet."

The gift was the Game Box he had left on the ship.

"Thank you, Jim." He hugged it to his chest. "I've been missing Captain Cometeer and all my friends in the Legion of the Lost. I'm happy to have them back, but I don't need them like I did."

He stopped to look at the Sternberg children in the airskins Cheng had made for them. A little awkward in helmets too large for them, they were laughing and hugging Day.

"I thought we were done for," he said. "But I guess we're all copasetic now, since you got here."